MARGUERITE ALEXANDER

Grievance

FOURTH ESTATE · *London*

First published in Great Britain in 2006 by
Fourth Estate
An imprint of HarperCollins*Publishers*
77–85 Fulham Palace Road
London W6 8JB
www.4thestate.co.uk

Copyright © Marguerite Alexander 2006

1

The right of Marguerite Alexander to be identified as the author of
this work has been asserted by her in accordance with the
Copyright, Designs and Patents Act 1988

A catalogue record for this book is
available from the British Library

ISBN-13 978-0-00-721356-6
ISBN-10 0-00-721356-5

Typeset in Sabon by Palimpsest Book Production Limited,
Polmont, Stirlingshire

Printed in Great Britain by Clays Ltd, St Ives plc

For Rachel, Chloë, Hannah and Tom

PART ONE

Animals

London

It is, Steve supposes, the particular quality of the September afternoon that makes the group so picturesque. The air is so still that the few leaves that are ready to fall drift to the ground with a kind of languor, their colours, in their slow descent, caught in the slanting rays of the sun. It was to enjoy the effect that Steve had lingered; otherwise he might not have noticed the young people at all. There are about half a dozen, mostly seated, one or two of the young men lying, under the handsome chestnut tree in the college quadrangle.

A picnic seems to be in progress. A woollen rug is spread on the grass, dotted with plates of food and large jugs of Pimm's, its colour harmonising with the autumnal tones of the setting. It must be somebody's birthday, or perhaps a celebration of reunion at the beginning of the new academic year. Their clothes are unusually bright for undergraduates and one of the girls, who is wearing a floral printed summer dress, has some kind of wreath on her long, crinkly red hair. As Steve watches, she picks up the jug and fills the glasses that stretched arms hold out to her. None of the group is familiar to him, but he's just returned after a year's sabbatical and is unlikely to recognise students he doesn't teach.

He is just about to move on when one of the reclining young men suddenly sits bolt upright and, as he speaks, waves his long, gangly arms in the air. Steve is too far away to catch what he has said, but the gales of laughter that greet the young man's performance drift across the quad towards him. He smiles to himself, shut off from the joke but pleased by the scene.

He is just about to move on to his office when another group of young people, equally striking but quite different from the first, claims his attention. With an immediate feeling of revulsion, quickly followed by shame, Steve realizes that a number of this second group have a severe mental handicap. They roll their heads and mutter to themselves, apparently indifferent to their surroundings. It seems that, left to themselves, they would shuffle aimlessly along, but the expedition is given an air of purpose by the others, young helpers who are all linked by the arm to their special charges, whom they are guiding across the quad. There is a young woman with Down's syndrome, whose shoulder-length silky light-brown hair briefly reminds him of his daughter, Emily, but this one point of resemblance heightens the cruelty of the contrast between them. He takes in her face, its tiny features puckered with anxiety; her hands, clutching the arm of the athletic young woman who is leading her; the large thighs and buttocks in the shapeless tracksuit bottoms. Then he turns away, finding his own curiosity inappropriate.

He can't think what they might be doing here. He wonders whether, in his absence, his colleagues have initiated some outreach programme, possibly attracting government money. It's the kind of well-meaning, but ultimately pointless, scheme that a junior minister might consider worthy of funding. Unless it's an initiative by one of the student Christian groups. His interest withers, as it always does, at the thought of active religious commitment (but only in this context: religion as an expression of nationalism or oppression or political discontent is another matter entirely).

Because he doesn't want to cut across the slow, straggling line, he switches direction and makes a loop that brings him closer to the party of picnickers and, for the first time, notices a girl who, from his earlier position, had been partly obscured. She is more simply and austerely dressed than the others, in white T-shirt and black jeans, small, slender, finely moulded and delicately featured, with the kind of colouring – black hair, blue eyes and pale, almost white skin – that immediately makes his heart leap.

He is particularly struck by her attitude. She is kneeling, body upright from the knees, looking intently away from her friends. Steve slows down and sees that she is following the progress of the last pair in the group crossing the quad.

At first he thinks that her interest is in the young guide, so unlikely does it seem that an educated girl of her generation would stare so blatantly at someone with an obvious mental handicap. The young man is tall, fair-haired, tanned and would, Steve imagines, gaze deep into the eyes of anyone prepared to listen and tell them how much God loves them. He feels a vague resentment that such a remarkable girl should squander her attention on such an unworthy object.

Almost immediately, however, he decides he's mistaken. To his practised eye, her manner does not suggest sexual interest. He looks as closely as he can at the muscular Christian's partner, who is on the far side and can only be seen in profile. He, too, is tall and fair-haired, but his features, like those of the girl who reminded him of Emily, are marked by Down's syndrome. Their arms are linked, but the arrangement seems purely mechanical, the one showing no awareness of the other's presence.

Steve's attitude to the guide changes to respect, particularly for his attempts to interest his charge in their surroundings. His free arm is busy indicating points of interest in the quad and he keeps up a steady flow of conversation, but the other boy's head remains averted, whether or not as a deliberate snub, it's impossible to say. Then as the pair, who have been drifting away from the rest of the group, turn to catch up, Steve sees that the boy with Down's syndrome is holding a long chiffon scarf in a brilliant pink. Never taking his eyes off the scarf, and with remarkably deft and practised movements, he waves it in an elaborate series of loops to produce an effect of some beauty.

Steve supposes it was the scarf that caught the girl's eye, and then she became mesmerised by the performance. Still a puzzle remains, that she should find the boy so compelling that she forgets her friends and the party taking place around her. He is struck by the irony: he has been transfixed by the girl, who shows no awareness of his presence, while the boy, who has eyes only for his scarf, absorbs her.

Then suddenly this long, suspended moment, to which the still September air and slanting rays of golden sunshine have contributed, is broken. The young man and the boy with the scarf are gone, along with the rest of their group. And the young woman has dropped back on her heels and turned to her friends, who now seem to Steve noisy, even raucous, after the intense quiet of the boy and the girl who was watching him. He turns away in the direction of his office.

As the afternoon slides into memory, Steve comes to

see it as marking the end of his sabbatical, gaining importance with the new turn of events. But memory can be treacherous. What stays in the mind is the girl, for whom everything else becomes merely setting – not just the chestnut tree and the early-autumn sunshine, but her friends too. In the manner of sheep and goats, they serve to emphasise her difference: her apartness, her seriousness and her intensity.

Her beauty is striking enough against her own immediate background, but when the other young people, so cruelly served by nature, are brought into play, it acquires iconic value. What he forgets, as the days pass, is her mysterious absorption in the boy with the pink chiffon scarf. It may be that it's beyond his scope to see someone so signally lacking in beauty and intelligence as capable of meaning.

In responding as he does, reordering and refiguring the world according to unexamined prejudices, he makes a fatal error, one that he is always careful to warn his students against. He ignores the context in which he first saw the girl, all those other elements in the scene that are crucial to understanding. And context, as he has spent so much of his professional life arguing, is different from background, which gives the central object transcendent status, encouraging the interpreter to impose his own meaning.

Meanwhile Steve picks up the threads of his professional life and falls back into patterns and routines. There is his new undergraduate course on Irish literature to think about. He has his first sessions with two new doctorate students, both too awed by his reputation to do more than mouth the platitudes into which his own once groundbreaking work has fossilised. There are emails and letters to answer and papers to read, but while he dispatches everything with his usual efficiency, he feels himself to be only half there, semi-detached from his professional self. This isn't just because he's been away from it all. The truth is that, although nobody but his wife Martha yet knows of his plans, he is already planning at least a partial escape, in search of another outlet for his talents, and hopes to make an even bigger impact than, as a young scholar, he made on the academic world.

He's pulled back sharply into the here and now when Charles Rowe pays his welcome-back call. Just for that moment Steve wishes, as must his colleague, that they were still in the time of Rowe's beloved Jane Austen when a card left on a platter might do the trick.

Steve knows that it's Rowe even before he's in the room. There is a shuffling sound outside the door, the unmistakable signal of Rowe's approach, then a light, tentative knock, followed by a much louder one, in case the first wasn't heard, both indications of his unease at the prospect of seeing Steve.

'Yes, come in.' Steve turns from his desk as Rowe's overlarge head twists round the door. He wonders whether, as a boy, his colleague was encouraged to see it as stuffed with brains to compensate for the embarrassment it must have caused.

'Ah, Steven. Good. You're here. Excellent.' The words are carefully articulated, suggesting a stutter, once painfully overcome, which always seems on the verge of returning in Steve's presence: although they've rubbed along well enough together for some time now, it's clear that Rowe has never recovered from the shock he received when Steve was first appointed to the English department and set about overturning the cherished assumptions of his older colleagues.

This was in the early eighties, the beginning of the Thatcher era, when young men (and a few young women) like Steve brazenly presented themselves as a counter-cultural revolutionary force. Ignoring much of the traditional canon, Steve required his students to read French critics and philosophers like Foucault and Barthes. Rowe, ever eager to learn, dipped into them himself, and finding the prose impenetrable – an unhappy afternoon spent struggling with one paragraph of Derrida has left painful scars on his memory – dismissed them as rubbish, then found to his dismay that the students lapped them up. When they started quoting what he came to think of as the 'Gallic wreckers' in essays he had set, he was at a loss how to grade them.

For Rowe and others of his generation, there was a seismic shift. Literature as a repository of eternal values was dismissed in favour of the idea that it was all culturally determined. Even worse was the thought that some of the most valued works in English were hoodwinking their readers into accepting bourgeois values. Jane Austen came under scrutiny and Rowe had to swallow the bitter pill that *Mansfield Park*, his own favourite, was not after all about personal morality and religious vocation but slavery. It seemed that the only 'correct' way to read a text was to concentrate on those who were 'marginalised' (another new concept) by it: colonial subjects, women, homosexuals. And slaves. The forces of righteousness had arrived.

Traditionalists like Rowe, who in the beginning found comfort in dismissing the new critical theories as absurd – 'the emperor's new clothes' was the phrase he used with like-minded colleagues – were soon silenced by Steve. His face had a way of setting in contempt at opinions different from his own, and this induced an acute sense of humiliation in those who had been foolhardy enough to voice them. For one so young, Steve was remarkably confident – a confidence that was rapidly justified by events. His first book sold in numbers previously undreamed-of in academic circles and made him something of a celebrity. Overnight it seemed that the ideas he and others of his generation pioneered had become the new orthodoxy, leaving Rowe and his bewildered colleagues with no choice but to conform.

Once the battle was won, harmony of a sort was restored; since Steve's early appointment to a professorship, which made him, in hierarchical terms, Rowe's equal, he has behaved with impeccable courtesy towards him, as he does now, getting to his feet in deference to the older man and ushering him to a chair.

'Well, just for a few minutes, perhaps,' Rowe says. 'Far be it from me to disturb you when you're h-hard at it.'

Steve tries not to look while Rowe, clutching a stack of papers as justification for his visit, makes his ungainly way to the chair, then sinks into it. His condition seems to have deteriorated rapidly over the past year, since Steve last saw him, if indeed there is a condition, other than the process of ageing. He can't be more than sixty-three or -four, Steve thinks. Only fifteen years older than I am. Christ.

'You're looking very well,' Rowe says. 'Restored, if I might say so.'

Steve, who is leaning back against his bookshelves, arms folded and ankles crossed, raises an eyebrow in reply. He's not sure that he likes the idea of being in need of restoration, of being on the downward side of a curve where his inevitable decline may, from time to time, be halted, but never reversed; where a renewal of youthful vigour, after much-needed restoration, will inevitably be short-lived.

'Not that you ever . . .' says Rowe, hastily. 'Oh dear, you work so admirably hard that I imagined the break . . .' This sentence, too, fails and Rowe lowers his eyes in shame.

'It was, as you say, restorative,' says Steve, suddenly relenting. It seems churlish to take out his disaffection on Rowe.

His colleague rewards this small act of kindness with a relieved smile that briefly shows discoloured teeth. 'Not too much time in the library, I hope?'

'Some, but I also did the Joyce trail – Dublin, Paris, Trieste, Zürich.' Steve has always avoided studies of individual writers before, preferring theoretical exposition, accompanied by theatrical sleight-of-hand, to overturn the received meaning of canonical texts. Before his sabbatical, however, he announced his intention to write a book on James Joyce.

'Ah, I envy you.' Rowe is beginning to relax, to lose the persecuted expression that he wore on entering the room. 'Jane Austen doesn't provide her acolytes with quite the same opportunities for travel.'

'No, I suppose not. So, what can I do for you, Charles?' Steve nods in the direction of Rowe's bundle of papers.

'Ah, yes,' says Rowe, leafing through them. 'Here's something to get you back into the swing of things. I thought I'd bring you up to date with preparations for the Gender and Ethnicity Conference.'

His manner is shyly confident, that of a man offering

a particularly rare treat. His confidence is all the more poignant, or piquant, in view of the battering he has received over the years from the keepers of the new orthodoxies. If anybody is responsible for his present sorry state – his pathetic anxiety to please, his physical deterioration, the stutter that seems always on the verge of returning – then it's probably Steve himself, in creating a climate in which Rowe has been obliged to conform to ideas that he may not even understand, let alone endorse.

'That's very thoughtful of you, Charles,' Steve says. 'Leave it with me and I'll give you my comments as soon as I've had the chance to read all the material.'

Rowe fails to respond to Steve's dismissal. 'We've taken the liberty – or, rather, I've taken the liberty – I must take full responsibility here . . .' he pauses to send Steve a complicit smile, a sure sign, for all his disclaimers, that he has little doubt of pleasing '. . . to put your name forward for the main session of the conference. Something on Irish ethnicity, perhaps, since that seems to be the direction your interests are taking? I thought some advance publicity for the book – not, of course, that you ever need . . .'

No, I don't, thinks Steve, angry even while knowing that Rowe means no harm. His reputation alone is enough to guarantee all the publicity he needs. Besides, the department ought to be able to see that he's moved beyond giving a paper at any conference Rowe is capable of organising. Of course, his name is associated with these ideas – his book on critical theory, although published twenty years ago, is still included on reading lists, not just for literature but for history and anthropology students – but now it's for the foot soldiers to carry on a battle that's been largely won. It's true that he's about to teach a course on

Irish literature, but if he has to teach, he might as well amuse himself.

He's sufficiently in control of his own reactions, and aware of the danger of burning his boats, to say, 'Thank you, Charles. It's nice to know I wasn't forgotten in my absence. But may I think about it? I'd really rather not commit myself to anything until I see how much time I can squeeze out of all this.' He makes a sweeping movement with his arm that vaguely encompasses the full range of professional duties suggested by the crowded desk. 'More than anything, I'm anxious to get on with the book.'

Rowe is disappointed, but not crushed. He has suffered so many defeats in the course of his working life, even when, as on this occasion, he is sure that his actions will be welcomed. 'Of course, Steven. Whatever you think best. If you could let me know in time to find an alternative speaker – if that's what you decide, of course . . .'

He struggles to his feet, makes his ungainly way across the room, then pauses at the door and lifts his arm in farewell before leaving.

Steve sinks into his chair and sits for a while with his head in his hands, wondering how he's going to be able to put in his time until his means of escape materialises. He had embarked on his sabbatical, and his book on Joyce, with the idea of changing direction but without realising how far in a new direction he would be taken. He'd known for a while that the critical revolution he had helped bring about had peaked; that there was no longer any shock value in overturning expectations when, for new generations of students, deconstruction was already commonplace. He had become a victim of his own success. But the nature of that success was, he had come to feel, rather limited.

In the decade and a half since he made his name, public interest in the academy has shifted away from the post-structuralist approach to literature that once tore apart English departments (the new craze is for reading groups, where no expertise is needed to pitch in with an opinion) towards science and the grand narratives of the neo-Darwinians and astrophysicists. The change can be charted through radio talk-shows, where he is no longer a valued guest, in which the hosts, former devotees of the arts, struggle to ask scientists meaningful questions.

At the same time, those of his arts colleagues who have maintained or strengthened their public profiles – for Steve's weakness is that he craves public recognition, only feels fully alive when he is ahead of his peers – have moved into biography and cultural history (in at least one well-known case, the history of science), where they have found a way of overturning received ideas through a gossipy, personality-driven, accessible approach. If anything short of a miracle is capable of restoring a spring to Rowe's step, Steve thinks, it would be the knowledge that he, the once formidable champion of the obscure and arcane processes of critical theory, is now weighing the merits of accessibility.

What attracted him to Joyce was the opportunity he saw for a flashy *tour de force*, a critical and biographical work that mimicked Joyce's own writing. Through a combination of deep scholarship and a light, knowing manner, he would illuminate Joyce and find his own way back to the talk-show circuit. And there was an additional beauty in his original idea: that it needn't look like a desperate move to revive a flagging career since it could be presented as a development of his earlier interests. For was not Joyce himself, like many Irish writers, a kind of deconstructionist? And wasn't the shift in focus to an Irish writer entirely consistent with his own known interest in colonial writing?

It certainly wasn't a disadvantage, in his original calculations, that Ireland had become a fashionable topic, not just for former colonial oppressors but, it seemed, globally: Ireland was the only country in the European Union that all the others could agree to admire, a nation that had transformed itself economically without losing any of its lovableness. A new book on Joyce would be a reminder of a different moment in Irish history and of the persistent literary creativity of the Irish. And it would also launch Steve into a new phase in his career, as commentator on Ireland more generally, an informed outsider with the skills and knowledge to take on Ireland's new identity.

His motives, while self-interested, were never cynical. He was genuinely engaged by the subject, while the still unresolved situation in Ulster – where his allegiances were and are, of course, with the minority Catholic population – would offer him full scope for the committed political position (on the side of the oppressed, the marginalised, the silenced) with which his name is associated. Once that wider role, to which his book on Joyce would give him access, has been secured.

Then an extraordinary thing happened. During his sabbatical he visited Ireland – Dublin, Galway, Cork, places associated with Joyce and his wife Nora – and fell in love. Not with a person, but with the place and its people. It seemed that all the clichés currently employed for contemporary Ireland, about its dynamism, its vibrancy and vitality, about a young, highly educated population that was comfortable both with ideas and popular culture, about a nation that had thrown off the shackles of the past to forge a new identity, were true. And although he never visited the North, his experience of the Republic confirmed his political sympathy for the Northern Irish Catholics, who had only to free themselves of the last vestiges of colonialism to effect the same transformation.

He felt a euphoria of a kind that was new to him. He had gone to Ireland deeply committed to the theoretical position that had underpinned his work – that there is no such thing as a fixed national character that justifies hostile stereotypes, only a set of characteristics that are a response to historical circumstance – and had the satisfaction of seeing his theories triumphantly vindicated. The drab, pious, inward-looking Ireland that he had visited once as a student and found uncongenial, despite the magnificent literature and a history that could only enlist his sympathy, had disappeared as the people had responded to new opportunities. What had been for Steve an idea had become a romance.

Having always seen himself as the least sentimental, most rational of men, this new emotional attachment to his subject has taken Steve by surprise so, of course, he rationalises it. His enthusiasm, he argues, is for the pleasure of being right, of testing a theory and finding it true. And he has enough self-awareness to see that the revelation of Ireland came to him at a moment when the need for change in his own life had become a yearning. Ireland's transformation was an inspiration.

So why is he sitting in his office, with his head in his hands, the picture of misery? He's begun to wake up in the night with a feeling of dread because his book on Joyce has stalled and the bright new future he has envisaged for himself seems to depend on it. He urges himself to be patient, that it's only his eagerness to move his life into a new phase that has produced the deadlock. But this has no effect on the panic he feels whenever he tries to work. What if he never achieves anything again, comparable to that precocious leap to academic stardom? Sometimes he feels on the verge of a creative breakthrough, the realisation of which will confound the world and force the admission that, highly though he was estimated before, he was in fact underestimated. At such times, the germ of a startling idea hovers on the edge of his consciousness, but when he tries to pull it to the centre of his mind, where it can be examined and developed, it proves elusive, not only refusing to shift but disappearing altogether.

He gets up and wanders over to the window, hoping to see something that will distract him, like the scene under the chestnut tree, but there's nothing beyond the usual comings and goings. Maybe, he tells himself, this period of sterility is the prelude to a major breakthrough. If he can only be patient, not panic and be alert to possibilities, who knows?

There are more immediate claims on his attention, however, and soon the opening session of his course on Irish literature arrives.

'So, one of our objectives on this course is to restore to the Irish their literary heritage.'

The room is packed with second-year students who have come in expectation of a performance from Professor Steven Woolf. His reputation has preceded him and so far he's done nothing to disappoint them. He's seated on, rather than behind, the desk, his motorcycle helmet perched next to him, and his stance draws attention to his effortless command of the subject, for he is speaking without notes, enforcing their attention, demanding their complicity in the critical position he's outlining. He's dressed like them, in leather jacket and jeans, though his were almost certainly bought new rather than second-hand, which both erases and confirms the differences between them. He hasn't lost his youthful edge, the impression he gives of belonging to a generation in the vanguard of change, but he is also a legendary figure, occupying a position to which they might aspire but will almost certainly never reach. In asserting his intention to restore to the Irish what they have lost he speaks as their champion, as one who has the authority to make a grand gesture of restitution.

Except, of course, that such an act of restitution is now redundant. He is impressive, but the group is not without sceptics.

'I'd have thought they'd got the hang of claiming their own heritage by now,' says Nick Bailey, one of the stars of the year, to his friend Pete Taylor, who is sprawled across his chair as usual, as if he doesn't know where to put his unusually long arms and legs.

'World leaders, my son,' says Pete. 'But you can see his problem. What do you do when the disadvantaged refuse to stay shackled and destroy all your arguments?'

Steve stops abruptly and glances in their direction. As his eye comes to rest, first, on Pete, then on Nick, he is briefly puzzled, before the professional mask is resumed. 'This isn't a lecture,' he says. 'You're quite free to make your point to the room at large – if it's something you're prepared to share.'

The two young men exchange a look, and then Pete says, 'We were saying that the Irish seem to be pretty good at exploiting their own heritage these days. That's when they can spare the time from being a tiger economy and relaxing with sex, drugs and rock and roll. I just wondered whether our idea of the Irish wasn't a bit out of date.'

Steve is too practised to take offence, or at any rate to show that he has, especially since Pete's point has been made with a good-humoured lack of aggression. When he responds, his manner is smooth and impenetrable.

'You're quite right that the Irish are no slouches in manipulating popular history for tourism, but that isn't quite what I had in mind. I'm merely signalling my intention to look at texts not as timeless works of imperishable genius that are part of the English literary canon but in the context of Irish history, Irish society and Irish politics, and of the power relations that, however concealed, have shaped the writers' attitudes.' He pauses before landing his parting shot. 'And it's worth remembering, before we get too carried away, that there is one part of the island of Ireland where history isn't yet over, and where the inhabitants don't yet feel free to surrender themselves to the rock-and-roll culture. I don't intend putting this to the test, but I would hazard a guess that even here, in this very room, there are pockets of ignorance about the historical roots of the situation in Northern Ireland that you've all grown up with.'

There is no doubting Steve's political engagement and, duly chastened, Nick, Pete and the few others who are inclined to levity, settle down. However predictable Steve's views might be to those who have read his books, his own history commands respect. This generation of students hadn't yet started primary school when his book on critical theory was published, at the beginning of the Thatcherite revolution. The left, disabled by defeat, had embarked on a long and acrimonious quarrel with itself, but Steve's particular brand of Marxism – playful, subversive, disrespectful of authority – offered a new kind of Utopian vision. English lecturers were being hired and fired according to divisions Steve had helped to create. People subscribed to a belief in him as they might to a religion. His ideas, like the Falklands War, created opposing camps. And, of course, it went without saying that if you were in favour of Steve you were against British action in the Falklands.

His status, however, is not just a matter of the theories promoted in his published work. He marched with the miners and was kicked by a policeman. This is a matter of record, captured by a BBC cameraman. And when he appeared on late-night arts programmes – for this was the beginning of his career as a minor television personality – he extended the academic debate into the public issues of the day, claiming, as he is now, that there is no distinction between critical and political practice.

He is known to have turned down a chair at Oxford, where he started his career as an undergraduate, and although some of his colleagues have hinted – privately, to one or two favoured students – that Steve's preference is to be as close as possible to the television studios, that he may even, at this moment, be turning his attention to Irish literature because, in the current political climate when ideology is felt to be a handicap, Ireland is the flavour of the month and an issue on which righteous indignation might still be expressed, many here prefer to believe that he rejected Oxford on the grounds of élitism.

He is a star turn, and they are as mesmerised by his personal style as by what he has to say: the leather jacket, the desert boots, the motorcycle helmet on the desk, while the satchel that holds his papers is thrown casually onto the floor. And it isn't as though the style has been cultivated to compensate for deficiencies in appearance, as is all too evidently the case with one or two of the younger lecturers. His black hair, brushed back from his face, is thick and only slightly greying, his mouth is full, red and sensual, his eyes, behind the wire-framed glasses, large, dark and – well, yes, brooding, as one or two of the girls concede to each other, cliché though it is.

The mind of Phoebe Metcalfe is as likely as not to be preoccupied with such matters, so her friends are surprised when, instead of a note to that effect – enlivened, as her communications usually are, with a little drawing of a smiling face and other icons expressive of good cheer – she makes an intervention that shows she has been attending to the substance of Steve's argument. He has just delivered his thoughts on the question of national character.

'I must make clear, right at the outset,' he has said, 'that I don't want any of the texts that we'll be reading explained by a woolly reference to national character, as though that's a fixed and mysterious essence that we all more or less understand. The Irish have suffered more than most from the stereotypes that other people have imposed on them. Like all national stereotypes, they tell us more about the prejudices of those who use them than about the Irish themselves.'

He sounds genuinely indignant, and one or two remember that Steve is Jewish, which might account for his fellow feeling with another racially stereotyped group. He removes his glasses to massage the bridge of his nose and in that pause of temporary sightlessness he fails to see Phoebe, who is already bobbing excitedly up and down in her chair. His sight restored, Steve returns to his argument.

'We've already had a contribution to that effect, of

course. We used to see the Irish as commercially back-ward and God-fearing, one or both due to some flaw in the national character. Now, the Republic at any rate is an economic model for the rest of Europe and one of its coolest holiday destinations. Meanwhile, revelations of child abuse have undermined the hold of the Church in less than a generation. So, characteristics that once seemed fixed are vulnerable to changing circumstances.'

Phoebe finally explodes: 'Oh, but the Irish are special and, like, different?'

Steve has been intermittently aware of her throughout the session, although so far he has restrained himself from showing annoyance. There is a general air of noise and bustle about her that suggests, to his trained eye, someone with poor concentration. Her chair seems to scrape every time she moves, which is a good deal more often than others find necessary. She has spent most of the class so far trying, and rejecting, a series of pens that are kept in an enormous carpet bag; and each time one is replaced by another, the bag is dragged from floor to lap and back again. And in the gaps allowed by her fidgeting, she has made a series of attempts – all, so far, unsuccessful – to engage the girl next to her in whispered conversation. Now, however, all her efforts are concentrated on devel-oping her argument.

'I mean, we all, like, know that the Irish are spiritual and charming and fantastic story-tellers, which is why they're such brilliant writers? Why is that a stereotype? It's, like, common sense? And if we need a reason for it, surely it's because they're Celts? And the Celts are amaz-ingly imaginative and sensitive. And surely they have an oral tradition? You know what I mean?'

While she's speaking, the ripples of amusement

throughout the room suggest that her views are known and affectionately tolerated. Steve takes in her long, crinkly red hair, pale freckled face and light blue eyes. She could be Irish or, since her accent – English public school overlaid by London demotic – doesn't suggest that, of Irish descent. Whatever her racial identity, however, she favours a Camden Market ethnicity in dress. A sheepskin Afghan coat, which must take real dedication to wear on such a close, muggy day, is slung over the back of her chair, while a flowing Indian print dress, decorated with quantities of beads, scarves and silver bangles, covers her soft, full figure.

Steve's own particular brand of Irish romance (though it's a term he's reluctant to use), rooted as it is in historical reality, makes him particularly hostile to the one so aptly embodied in this flabby, messily eclectic girl.

'It's as well Phoebe doesn't realise she's just made his point for him,' Nick says to Pete. 'She's told him pretty much everything he needs to know about her.'

'He's wondering whether he's got an alien in the class,' Pete whispers back. 'Phoebe will challenge his rationalism, if anybody can.'

What's challenging Steve about Phoebe, however, is the niggling sense that he knows her from a different context. Then he remembers the scene under the chestnut tree and places her as the Dionysian figure in the summer dress, with the wreath of daisies in her hair, holding the jug of Pimm's. The picturesque stillness of that moment, snatched from time and larger circumstance, evaporates in the human reality of this girl, who is mouthing clichés as though nobody has thought of them before.

When he replies, he ignores Phoebe and addresses the group more generally. 'The Celtic origins of Ireland were so distorted and sentimentalised in the nineteenth century that they exist for us as myth rather than useful historical reality.'

While he is speaking, however, he thinks of the other girl, who claimed his attention for herself, not as an element in a larger picture, beautiful in any setting, her face enlivened more by thought than by the occasion. He glances quickly round the room, to see if she, too, is there, and as his eyes come to rest on her, the girl next to Phoebe, who has been keeping her head down, resisting her companion's attempts to distract her, looks up. She is unmistakably the girl in the black jeans and white T-shirt.

His eyes meet hers and, at this closer range, he sees their clear, dark blue, set in a small face of perfect symmetry. He notices, as he did before, a remarkable self-possession; that she is unusual in being able to look at another person without smiling. She seems to him complete and apart, isolated from the commonplace reality around her. The difference between her and Phoebe is so marked, the one so grossly material, the other light and ethereal, that they could belong to different species. Before she lowers her eyes he tries to read their expression but finds it unfathomable.

Steve's total disengagement is broken abruptly by another student, a fierce-looking girl with many-studded ears. 'Could I take us back to a point you made just a minute ago – about child abuse among priests weakening the power of the Catholic Church? I'd say that you were taking too rosy a view of modern Ireland in implying that all that – the power of the Church and of patriarchy generally – is now in the past when Irish women are still denied the right to abortion.' Emma Leigh is a notable feminist, women's officer in the union and scourge of any lecturer who fails to give due prominence to the female perspective.

Startled out of his reverie Steve, who prides himself on his sharpness and speed in argument, finds it difficult to adjust to the change in topic. When his brain clears, he is immediately irritated by the stridency of this young woman, so different from the stillness and quiet of the other, whom he has been contemplating with such pleasure. That doesn't stop her being right, of course. All his life he has been a champion of women's rights, but her intervention suddenly seems like a meaningless cliché when set against his own recent experience of Ireland.

Forcing himself to look at Emma, who is sitting back in her chair – smirking with satisfaction, it seems to him, at having landed a punch – he says, 'I don't think that's an issue that can be discussed without considering the full complexity of modern Ireland.'

His manner is dismissive, one that he perfected early in his career for crushing older colleagues, who were forced, often against their better judgement, to concede that he knew more than they did. Emma, although silenced for now, doesn't conceal her outrage, and may well prove a tougher opponent than the likes of Rowe. And although most of the group are relieved by this reprieve from Emma's agenda, which has been known to dominate entire sessions, some see that Steve has been wrong-footed, that in failing to give modest support to Emma's views, he has violated his own known principles. Are they to take it that he is always right, even when he is wrong?

Smiling now, as though aware that he has lost ground, Steve says, 'I suggest that we turn aside from these general observations, seductive though they are, and look at the first text on your syllabus, Swift's *Modest Proposal*, published in 1729 – or, to give it its full title, *A Modest Proposal for Preventing the Children of poor People in*

Ireland, from being a Burden to their Parents or Country; and for making them beneficial to the Public. All beginnings are arbitrary, of course, but for me Swift marks the start of an authentic tradition of Irish writing in English.'

On the subject of Swift, their first writer, and Swift's famous essay, their first text, Steve becomes particularly animated. When Pete asks whether Swift, a member of the Protestant Ascendancy, was 'really' Irish, Steve replies, 'It's difficult to say what he "really" was, just as it isn't always easy to decide what he "really" thought, because he occupied some kind of boundary between competing versions of reality. On the one hand he was an Anglican clergyman who tried to gain preference in London, to be close to the centre of power. On the other, his experience of Ireland made him an increasingly robust critic of English policy there. Like a number of Anglo-Irish writers – Beckett, Wilde, Yeats – he was a master of assumed identities and used them to destabilise the reader's sense of reality within the text.'

Some of these contradictions belong to Steve too: he craves to be at the centre, where the action is, yet has made his reputation by championing the marginal and silenced. Unlike Swift, who was born in Ireland, he has no claim to an Irish identity, yet speaks as though he alone can get beyond the disfiguring stereotypes to an understanding of the 'real' Ireland, even though he rejects the validity of such a concept on theoretical grounds.

There follows a brief discussion on whether Swift was mad – Phoebe remembers a television programme to that effect – and on his persistent use of irony, ably led by Nick Bailey, who shows welcome signs of intelligence. As Nick is speaking, Steve recognises him, and his friend Pete, as members of the group under the chestnut tree, and tries to resist the temptation to speculate on their relationship with 'his' girl, who still hasn't spoken, though she smiles when Pete takes over from Nick the lead in discussion.

'I really like the way he softens you up,' says Pete. 'The voice or speaker or whatever he is goes on about how sorry he is for the Irish and how they can't feed their children and there's no work for them, and he's come up with a solution for making the children useful.'

Steve nods. '"Sound and useful members of the Commonwealth" is the ideal proposed.'

'Right,' says Pete. 'And you think he's going to come up with some kind of light, clean industry – children did work at this time, didn't they? – maybe with some kind of government investment, and instead he suggests that as soon as they're a year old, and won't be, like, breast-fed any more, Irish babies should be eaten.'

'Why babies?' Steve asks.

'Well, I suppose you wouldn't fancy them when they're any older,' Pete replies. 'He says that fourteen-year-old boys would be a bit stringy.'

When the laughter has died down, a girl Steve hasn't noticed before – small, with dark, curly hair and, Steve thinks, what children's books used to describe as a 'merry' look, the kind of girl who is usually the heroine's confidante – takes the audacious step of topping Pete's remark: 'But at least they'd be organic.'

Instead of just laughing with the rest, Pete beams his appreciation at Annie Price, whose remark will be remembered as one of the highlights of the course. Their paths haven't crossed much before, but each recognises in the other a kindred spirit and their partnership will be one of the success stories of the year.

Then, just as Steve thinks that the class will be over

before 'his' girl has spoken, she intervenes in a way that alters the course of the discussion.

'Surely we're outraged because babies are so vulnerable,' she says, and as she speaks two little spots of colour rise to her cheeks. There is an awkward sincerity about her, as though it requires effort for her to speak so publicly, but she's been driven to it by her concern for babies. Steve notices none of this, however, or that the self-possession he's attributed to her isn't total. What is electrifying is her accent, which is immediately identifiable as Northern Irish; and Steve, who is the least superstitious of men, has the strange and elating sense that fate has intervened on his behalf.

What he'd really like to do is end the session now, take her off and find out everything about her, but instead he nods enthusiastically and says, 'It is outrageous, of course, you're right to remind us of that, and the more so because it's shockingly funny. I'm sorry, you didn't introduce yourself . . .'

'Nora. Nora Doyle,' the girl says, looking at him levelly without smiling.

There is a suspended moment of silence throughout the room as they observe Steve's reaction. It's known that Steve is writing a book about Joyce, and that Joyce's wife, Nora, was the model for Molly Bloom. And although barely a handful of them have read *Ulysses*, more have read Molly Bloom's notorious soliloquy, whose scatological preoccupations couldn't be further from what they know of the demure and reserved Nora Doyle.

Steve acknowledges the connection with a raised eyebrow and a smile. 'It's good to have an Irish member of the class. You must be sure to keep us all on our toes.'

At this point Emma weighs in with the claim that no woman would write about the eating of babies, even with satirical intent. And while Steve could point out that such unfounded assertions are inappropriate in academic discourse, he privately acknowledges that, outside this rarefied field, she's probably right, and lets it ride, hoping that indulging her in this instance will go some way to placating her.

'Killing babies is about the most transgressive of all human acts,' says Nick, 'but surely the whole point of this piece is that the Irish are described as though they're animals, of a different species, and it's a small step from that to see them as a saleable, and edible, commodity.'

'That's right,' says Steve, oblivious of his own recent, private relegation of Phoebe to a different species from Nora. 'What's interesting is that the speaker seems initially to be complicit in the way the English, or the Protestant Ascendancy, view the Irish, but then manages to turn the argument against them by taking their attitude to its logical conclusion. He's saying, in effect, that you might as well be eating them for all the effort you're making to keep them alive. And, of course, history tells us – I'm thinking here of the Holocaust or apartheid – that the persistent use of animal imagery creates a climate where those others can be treated in any way that the ruling hegemony sees fit.'

Then, just when he's on the point of dismissing them, Nora speaks again, but this time she is almost playful; he wonders whether she is teasing him. 'I hope we shan't be seeing the Irish as victims of the English all the time,' she says.

Steve is surprised, forced to confront the unwelcome possibility that, despite her name, she might be Protestant. 'Unfortunately that has been the history of the two countries.'

'Just as long as we acknowledge that the process we've just been discussing isn't all in one direction. It's true that the Irish haven't had the opportunity to oppress the English, but they might take a certain comfort in seeing them as animals.' Then before he has framed a reply, she says, 'I don't suppose that the IRA bomber sees – or saw, if the peace process holds – his victims as human beings with the same capacity for suffering as himself.'

Relieved, Steve says, 'None of us would argue with that, although we still have a responsibility to investigate the cause of the violence.'

As he finishes speaking, he gives a nod of dismissal, turns away from the class and walks over to the window. He is not quite as absorbed in his own thoughts as he seems: he is aware of his students packing up their bags, pulling on jackets and forming into groups as they drift out of the room. He turns to face Nora as she, too, makes her way between the seats.

'I just wanted to repeat what I said earlier,' he said, 'that it's good to have an authentically Irish member of the class. At least, I assume you're the only one, unless there are others who are keeping their heads down.'

'I wouldn't know,' she says, attentive but not smiling. Steve realises that, although he has seen her smile, she hasn't yet smiled at him, and wonders how long he'll have to wait for that. 'I've come into contact with most people in the group, but not everybody. And there are what you might call the London Irish, like Nick.'

'We don't get a large number of Irish students here, though there are a few. May I ask what brought you?'

'Oh, this and that. You know.'

'You thought you'd spread your wings?'

'Something like that.'

This is much harder work for Steve than the class he's just given, but he persists none the less. 'Well, we're honoured. These are exciting times in Northern Ireland. You must feel you're missing out.'

'You mean with the Assembly and all?'

'Well, yes. You are in favour of what's going on?'

Nora hesitates briefly and, when she speaks, chooses her words with care: 'My family's Catholic. On the whole, Catholics are more likely to support the Good Friday Agreement.'

Steve smiles his relief, although he is puzzled by the form her reply takes, as though she is at pains to give as little information as is consistent with candour. 'I thought as much. Your name, I suppose. It tends to be something of a giveaway in Ireland.'

'Well. Certainly according to Seamus Heaney it does, though I've never been stopped by an RUC man.'

'No, I suppose not. Young women aren't usually thought to pose the same kind of threat as young men.' Finding nothing else to say, and uncomfortable at her reluctance to volunteer any information about herself – a rare characteristic in his experience of young people – Steve releases her. 'Well, I'll see you next week.'

He watches her leave the room and notices that Phoebe Metcalfe is just outside the door, waiting for her. Not for the first time he wonders at the friendships formed by students and remembers some of the people he has had to avoid since Oxford. He gives them time to move on – he wouldn't put it past Phoebe to waylay him and offer him her views on the little people – before picking up his helmet and satchel and leaving.

Half an hour later, Phoebe, Nora and Nick are seated at a Formica table in Marco and Gianna's, the local Italian coffee bar. Usually Pete would be with them, but when last seen he had given them a distracted wave as he chatted up Annie Price. They are all drinking cappuccinos, and Phoebe, having declared herself to be 'sinking' with hunger, is eating a large cinnamon Danish that her friends have declined to share.

'So, what did he want?' Phoebe asks Nora, not for the first time, but now that they're seated Nora can hardly evade the question. Phoebe's learned from experience that Nora will give away as little as possible without appearing eccentric, and so attracting an even more unwelcome degree of attention; persistent questioning usually produces some result, however grudging.

Nora takes time to form her reply. Her manner, as so often, suggests someone much older. 'He wanted to make sure that I was a Catholic.'

Phoebe's round face, pink now from the coffee and the steaminess of the atmosphere, puckers in bewilderment. With Nick and Nora she often seems like a child, puzzling out the ways of the adult world. 'But why? He doesn't strike me as someone who cares about religion. Is he going to ask all of us? Is that allowed?'

'It's because he doesn't want the embarrassment, some way into the term, of finding out that he has a wicked Ulster Protestant in his midst,' explains Nick.

'But why does it matter?'

'Because it would be politically compromising for him to single out Nora as a favoured student, then find that she was on the wrong side.'

'But what does politics have to do with religion?' Phoebe asks, but before either of them can answer, says, 'On second thoughts, don't bother. I wish he'd stop banging on about it, whatever. I thought this was meant to be a literature course.'

'Everything is political for Steve, but when he comes to Ireland he happens to be right.'

Nick is watching Nora as he says this, but she is staring absently into the remains of her cappuccino. Like Steve, he has given some thought to the nature of Nora's friendship with Phoebe, and thinks he has arrived at a partial explanation. Phoebe, for all her questions, is fundamentally incurious. As on this occasion, she dismisses any information that is incompatible with her worldview. He judges that this suits Nora well. In the year he's known her she's been persistently evasive about her background – remarkably so, given that her accent immediately identifies her as coming from one of the few parts of the United Kingdom that impinges on everybody's consciousness.

She is sometimes eager, as she was in today's class, to express a view on Ireland, often with the implied suggestion that the English fail to understand it, then seems to regret drawing attention to herself. Always her opinions on Ireland are cast in strictly impersonal terms, as though she has arrived at an opinion through studying the subject rather than as a result of experience. As far as he can remember, she has never volunteered an anecdote about her childhood or parents, the kind of stuff that's common currency among students who, in the early days of friendship, like to define and establish who they are. When such occasions arise, and members of a group try to outdo each other with stories of an outrageous parent or eccentric upbringing (for everything is exaggerated in the interests of glamour), Nora falls silent, or turns the conversation, or makes an excuse to leave. It's as though she's afraid of being found out.

There is some discussion between them about whether Nora can't or won't talk about herself. Pete has always

Marguerite Alexander

subscribed to the view that Nora doesn't choose to talk, that she preserves her mystery so that they (the men particularly) can project their fantasies on to her. If she were known to have had a conventional middle-class background, albeit in a different place, she would be like the rest of them, apart from her extraordinary looks, of course.

Nick isn't so sure. Within the limits she has set herself, Nora is often touchingly eager to please, almost too compliant to other people's wishes – a characteristic that Phoebe has been quick to spot and ready to exploit. He thinks that Nora is genuinely inhibited, but by what he hasn't yet decided. Privately – because in a gossipy environment like a university where any hint of the glamorous, subversive or criminal is immediately seized upon and enlarged – he's speculated about an IRA connection. It's difficult to imagine Nora actively involved, but her conformity to the role of model citizen and outstanding student – like him, she gained a first in her first-year exams – would be the perfect cover.

On the other hand, the revulsion she sometimes expresses against terrorism could be genuine. Sometimes he thinks that her adaptability, her unwillingness to impose her will, might indicate that she's been a victim of aggression; that she's used to keeping her head down. Whatever the cause, it's thought that she never goes home and, as far as he knows, she spent the entire summer working in a hotel in Devon, presumably to help pay her way through college.

He wonders what it would be like to have a relationship with her. The idea certainly appeals, but she seems to be as inhibited about sex as about everything else, and Nick is so used to girls who leave no room to doubt their willingness that he's not sure how he would begin to break down her reserve.

Putting aside for the moment thoughts about that particular reserve, Nick decides to chance his luck with a direct question about Ireland. 'So tell me, Nora, how, in your opinion as an insider, did Steve tackle the Irish question?'

She turns her head judiciously to one side, exactly as she might, he thinks, if she were marshalling an argument for an essay or a class presentation. It occurs to him for the first time that, although she never draws attention to her successes, she is most at ease with academic discourse, as though she has developed that side of her character at the expense of the rest.

'He talks a lot about stereotypes, and how they tell us nothing about the country, only about the prejudices of those who subscribe to them, but he has all the prejudices about the Irish of the liberal London intelligentsia – how we're all victims and it's all the fault of empire, as though there's no such thing as personal responsibility and morality. Irish Catholics are all angels, and all the others are now animals. He's just turned the traditional model on its head.'

He wants to ask her, 'Then what, for Christ's sake, is the reality, or your reality?' but knowing that will get him nowhere, says, 'In his own way, Steve's an old romantic. He may subscribe to a cool, post-structuralist approach, but you could see that he fancies himself as a bit of a Swift – an outsider who uses his mordant wit and superior intelligence to see further and deeper than an insider.'

'I don't think he's at all romantic,' says Phoebe. 'I'd heard so much about him that I was expecting something more . . .' Unable to find the word she wants, she lifts her arms, then drops them to express her disappointment, only just missing, in their cramped surroundings, the empty cups and plate on the table. 'I thought he was a bit of a cold fish.'

'So what was he like – close up and personal, I mean?' asks Nick.

'He looked older,' Nora says. 'Tired, as though a couple of hours' work had exhausted him.'

'I suppose he's getting on a bit. It's hard for ageing rebels like him to know what to do with themselves, with younger generations yapping at their heels. Do they go back on everything they've believed in, like those Old Labour people trying to look comfortable in a New Labour government? Or do they find a new cause for themselves? I guess that's why he's taken on Ireland. At the moment it's sexier than Marxism, but I'd say he's a bit of a late-comer to the game. Wouldn't you, Nora?'

Nora merely shrugs, as though she's reached the limit with this particular conversation. What she doesn't say is that, throughout the session, Steve kept reminding her of her father. She doesn't say it because she hasn't yet found a way to talk about home, and to explain the resemblance she would have to tell her entire family history.

Ballypierce

Nora's earliest precise memory is of a day shortly before the birth of her brother. She remembers that the baby's imminence hung in the air that afternoon, charging the atmosphere and releasing in her father a restless energy. Always a boastful man, his pride in himself, and in her, seemed to know no bounds. And while she is sure, without having a clear memory of them, that there were other, similar occasions before that afternoon, she knows that there were none afterwards. This, she thinks, is why she remembers the afternoon so clearly, that it marked the end of an era: with Felix's birth, another, altogether different, phase in their lives began.

She remembers sitting on the counter in her father's shop, surrounded by a group of admiring men. The pretext for her being there was that her mother needed to rest. Her father had come home for lunch, as he was in the habit of doing when it was just the three of them, leaving in charge one of the succession of young women that he had working for him. His routine was sufficiently established for people to know not to take in their prescriptions over the dinner hour, when many of the other shops, which couldn't afford extra help, closed. Her mother had told him that the midwife had called, that her blood pressure was up again and she needed rest.

'Will I take the wee girl back with me, Bernie?' he had asked.

'Since when have you needed my permission?' her mother had replied.

It was acknowledged between the three of them that she and her father were a team, and while her mother boasted of this to her acquaintance – the degree of interest that Gerald took in his four-year-old daughter was sufficiently unusual to arouse the envy of other women – her resentment at being excluded sometimes surfaced at home. Nora was hoping that the baby would be a boy, not for herself or her father, who were perfectly content, but for her mother. She and the baby boy would then form another self-contained team and the family would be perfectly balanced.

So Gerald took her back with him and she spent the first hour or so sitting at a little desk that Gerald had rigged up for her in the corner, drawing and doing a few sums that he had set her. Really, this was only marking time until a sufficient crowd had gathered, mostly other shopkeepers who had left their wives, now released from kitchen duties, in charge while they slipped out for half an hour.

Without understanding at that point precisely why, she knew that it was a mark of her father's importance that his shop acted as a magnet for men with time on their hands during the slow, early-afternoon hours before the schools were out. Ballypierce was a largely nationalist town where incomes were low and trade rarely buoyant. But Gerald, who had grown up and gone to school with many of the other traders, was a great man among them, a pharmacist who had gone to Belfast to study. They could leave their shops, but he had to stay at his post to make up prescriptions, apart from the hour dedicated to lunch, when he insisted on a home-cooked meal. He was one of the few whose family didn't live above the shop, having chosen instead a new bungalow, built to architect's specifications on a hill at the edge of the town with a view over the valley. The flat above the shop was let so he was a landlord in addition to his professional status.

People might not have jobs but they still became ill and needed medicines that the Health Service funded so, whatever else was happening, the Doyles were always comfortable. And Gerald, instead of joining the Protestants at the golf course or sailing club, as he was entitled to, had stayed one of them, always ready for good craic, always pleased to see an old friend who dropped in. By comparison with others in the town, his shop was like a palace, with large plate-glass windows on both sides of the door, all the fittings built to the highest standards, always sweetly smelling from the soaps and perfumes and ladies' cosmetics, and gleamingly clean, because Gerald insisted on the highest standards of hygiene and had been known to sack a girl whose hair always looked unwashed. And when the party was under way, Gerald would send his assistant into the little kitchenette to make them all cups of tea.

That afternoon Nora was lifted on to the counter, the one with the little room behind it where Gerald made up his prescriptions. She was wearing a navy blue smocked Viyella dress with matching tights – Gerald had requested that Bernie change her before they left – and her hair was tied back into a tight ponytail. When Gerald had started this routine, as soon as she could walk and talk and had no need of nappies, she would recite a few nursery rhymes or count to a specified number, but since he had taught her to read she was always required to show off her current level of attainment. That afternoon she read from a simplified picture-book version of *The Lion, the Witch and the Wardrobe.*

'You're a great girl, so you are,' said Malachy McGready, the greengrocer. 'It's no wonder your daddy's so proud of you. But if he gives you books like this to read, you'll start to think you're a wee Brit. You won't find many Susans and Edmunds around here.'

Gerald gave a satisfied little smirk, having come prepared for just this rebuke. 'Don't you know who C. S. Lewis was?' he asked. 'Your man was born in Belfast and ended up a professor at Oxford.'

This was greeted with smiles all round, not so much that one of their own (they were by no means convinced that a man who wrote like this could be so described) had achieved so much in the wider world but because Gerald had outmanoeuvred them yet again. These afternoon gatherings, whether Nora was present or not, were not so much exchanges between equals, as enactments and affirmations of Gerald Doyle's superiority, and if he had ever been caught out or bettered, they would have felt keen disappointment. Malachy's scepticism was, none the less, a necessary component of the drama.

'Is that what you're after for the little lady here – for her to be a professor at Oxford? What's wrong with Queen's, or Trinity, if she must leave home?'

'I want the best for her, and she deserves it. And if when the time comes the best is still Oxford, then we'll have to make the sacrifice.' As he spoke, Gerald looked down fondly at Nora, who sat swinging her legs and munching a biscuit.

'But tell me, Gerald, your man, Lewis,' said Malachy, who had picked up the discarded book and was peering at it to make sure that he had the name right, 'would I be right in thinking he was a Protestant?'

'Well, you would, of course. How many Catholics do you suppose went from here to Oxford before the war?' There was that in Gerald's manner of a man who is playing a game so elaborate that his opponent, at the moment of thinking he has caught him out, finds himself the victim of superior strategy. Gerald's air of victory took no account of his having ignored the drift of Malachy's argument. Then, with a sudden shift of tactics, he addressed the point that Malachy had been labouring. 'You want to know why I give Nora stuff like this to read? Because it's what the children of the ruling classes read, and if you want them to get on in that world, you give them a head start. Rather than have her, at forty, feeling aggrieved at the way the world has treated her, I want her out there with the best of them, showing what can be done.'

A number of them felt mildly rebuked by this, but they would no more have thought of challenging him than they would a geometric theorem or a doctor's diagnosis. Gerald loved imparting information, surprising people, over-turning their expectations; and while he needed a patsy like Malachy in order to shine, none of them was prepared to risk losing his goodwill and, with it, the dim reflection of his glory that touched them as welcome members of his circle. They enjoyed the sense of inclusion that allowed them, later, to say to a wife or customer, 'Gerald Doyle was saying to me only the other day . . .' Besides, they believed, because he had told them, that his was the voice of science, reason and progress, and they were all reluctant to pit themselves against these mysterious forces. If he seemed more than usually pleased with himself that day, they put it down to the imminently expected baby, and were prepared to indulge him.

'The teachers will have their work cut out when she starts school,' said Liam Doherty, who owned the best of the nationalist bars. 'You haven't left them much to teach her.'

'It's a problem, right enough,' said Gerald. On this particular point, if on no other, he was prepared to acknowledge himself baffled. 'But there, I almost forgot. I've been looking into Shakespeare with her, and her memory's prodigious. Come on, darling,' he said to Nora, as he lifted her down from the counter and gestured to his companions to clear a space around her. 'Show us how you do Shylock.'

Nora composed herself briefly, then stretched our her arms and recited, '"I am a Jew. Hath not a Jew eyes? Hath not a Jew hands, organs, dimensions, senses, affections, passions? Fed with the same food, hurt with the same weapons, subject to the same diseases, healed by the same means, warmed and cooled by the same winter and summer, as a Christian is? If you prick us, do we not bleed? If you tickle us, do we not laugh? If you poison us, do we not die? And if you wrong us, shall we not revenge?"'

After the first two short, monosyllabic sentences, this was delivered in the chanting monotone of small children reciting prayers that are beyond their understanding – a style that she had learned not from Gerald or from her mother but at the little nursery she attended in the mornings, where prayers were part of the routine.

Then, after a look of encouragement from her father, she shifted her position, hunching her shoulders into a forward stoop and holding out her right hand in a grasping gesture. 'O my ducats, O my daughter, O my ducats, O my daughter,' she growled, with as much depth, intensity and malice as she could muster. When she had finished, she ran over to her father and clutched him round the knees.

Her audience was genuinely speechless, not sure what to make of her performance, for all its precociousness. As was customary, it was Malachy who found a way of expressing their doubts: 'This Shylock,' he said tentatively, 'wasn't he a fellow?'

Gerald nodded. 'The Jewish moneylender. The first Jew in literature, when writers weren't afraid to tell the truth.'

'She says it bravely,' said Malachy. 'I doubt there's another girl her age who could match her. But were there no girls' parts you could teach her?'

Gerald nodded slowly. 'I looked into it, of course, but most of the young girls in his plays are only interested in love and such like and I didn't want her head filled with that kind of nonsense. Now Portia's different, of course. I tried her out with the "quality of mercy" speech, but there were words that even she couldn't get her tongue round, and you have to be careful with a child like this not to tax the brain with more than it can handle.'

There were murmurs of approval for Gerald's commendable fatherly concern. These he stilled by raising a warning finger. 'But don't make any mistake about it,' he said, 'They can't learn soon enough how the world works.'

'You want her to know about the Jews?' asked Liam, doubtfully. This struck all of them as an entirely unnecessary lesson. As Irish Catholics, they had never questioned the received wisdom that Jews were treacherous, money-grubbing and only out for themselves. On the other hand, none of them had ever met a Jew, or was likely to do so.

'I want her to learn something much more useful than that,' said Gerald, who was, as usual, a step ahead of them. 'I want her to realise that, not just in this instance but in almost everything you could name, people's instincts are being suppressed by those who think they know better. Now, take the Jews.'

'I'd rather not, thank you,' said Tom O'Neill, the butcher, raising the biggest laugh of the afternoon.

'Very well, then. Take Shakespeare and the Jews. Now, the English are only too ready to accept what he has to say about England – all that jingoistic nonsense about sceptred isles and brave English soldiers throwing themselves into the breach, without knowing that he was more or less forced to write it, but they don't want to hear what he says about Jews. And yet the man was ahead of his time. He said – you heard the girl – that they're not animals, they're human beings, like the rest of us. They bleed, they laugh and all the rest of it. I'll go along with that. But – and it's an important "but" – revenge matters as much to them as food and drink, and they don't have the same feelings for their flesh and blood as we do. His daughter runs away, and all he can think about are his ducats. But you're not allowed to say that any more, not in England or the States. No, I just want her to learn to respect the evidence and to be fearless in saying what she knows to be right. That's all. The Jews are incidental, they're just an example.'

Signalling that the session was over for the afternoon, he lifted Nora up and held her, legs dangling, face on a level with his, as if he were displaying her. 'And I want her to know that she's more precious to her Daddy than anything else in the world, even ducats. Especially ducats.'

There was no doubt that they made an appealing picture – Gerald fresh-faced, well-tended (it was rumoured that he took home some of the lotions and creams from the shop for his own skin, and that he needed a wife at home all the time to iron the shirts that he insisted on wearing, clean, every day), dressed in the finest tweed, linen and leather, a man in the prime of life, and Nora as dainty and delicate as a little fairy.

'And what if the next one's a boy?'

'It'll make no difference. There isn't a boy who can match her.'

Nora's companion memory to what was to be the last occasion when her father took her to the shop with him to demonstrate her cleverness fell within days of the first. The two stand side by side, an end followed by a beginning. Everything about that second day was different, from the moment she woke up and sensed an alteration in the sounds of the house. Still in her pyjamas, she wandered through into the kitchen where her mother would be preparing the breakfast – hers to be eaten at the kitchen table, her father's to be placed on a tray and carried through to him in the bedroom. Instead of her mother, however, there was Mrs Daly from next door, a woman of late middle age, whose children had grown and left home, moving about and, as she described it, making herself useful.

'Now, pet, you mustn't fret,' she said. 'Your daddy's taken your mummy into the hospital, and when she comes home, please, God, she'll have a new wee brother or sister for you. Now, what would you like for your breakfast? Will I cook you an egg or fry you a rasher?'

Nora sat and spooned cereal into her mouth while Mrs Daly pushed a cloth over the work surfaces in a show of activity. She wondered how her mother felt about having another woman in her kitchen. She knew her to be ill at ease with her neighbours in this most select area of the town and that she suspected Mrs Daly, who had time on her hands and an imagination actively engaged in the lives of others, of a tendency to snoop.

Bernie often said that her neighbours regarded her as fortunate, not just because they lived so well but also because, as an exceptionally pretty young woman, she had caught Gerald's eye when she had come to work as an assistant at the pharmacy. And she suspected that 'fortunate' carried connotations of something in excess of what she deserved. Convinced that everybody around her was looking for evidence against her, she was an anxious, if unenthusiastic housekeeper, and kept her family, modest country people of whom she was now ashamed, at a distance.

There was to be no nursery this morning, and Mrs Daly was clearly relieved when, after breakfast, Nora demonstrated that she was quite capable of amusing herself. Although she wasn't very good at playing with toys, she had other resources, and after she had spent some time drawing and looking through books, she put on her rubber boots and jacket and wandered round the garden while Mrs Daly sat with yesterday's newspaper at the picture window in the lounge, keeping an eye on her.

At this time Gerald took considerable pride in his garden, which deteriorated sadly in the years that followed, and Nora, in her progress, named the shrubs and bulbs that were in flower, as her father had taught her: magnolia, viburnum, the quince-bearing japonica and daffodils. The daffodils were a concession to popular taste, as represented by Bernie: for himself, Gerald favoured those plants that his neighbours couldn't identify when they passed the time of day with him while he was working in the garden. Nora talked to herself as she padded through the damp grass, conducting an endless conversation in her head – a habit that persisted with her into young adulthood.

She was growing hungry and thinking it must nearly be lunchtime when she noticed that Mrs Daly was no longer at her post by the window. Assuming that the old woman must be preparing something for her to eat, she went back into the house, took off her boots as she had been trained and, without putting her indoor shoes back on, passed through the central corridor in the bungalow to the kitchen, which was at the front of the house facing the street. The architect whom they had consulted after buying their plot of land had convinced Bernie that, with his design, she would have a livelier time while she was working, but she had always felt exposed in there and had come to resent his advice.

Just before she reached the kitchen, Nora heard voices, those of Mrs Daly and another woman, who seemed to be telling her something. They were speaking softly, but there was an undertow of excitement; suspecting that they would stop if she joined them, Nora hovered outside the door, which was ajar, as though someone had gone to close it without checking that it had held.

'Lord love us,' she heard Mrs Daly say. 'Who would have expected such a thing?'

'It can happen to anybody,' the other woman replied.

'But the Doyles, of all people,' said Mrs Daly. Then she

used a word that sounded to Nora like 'gerbil'. They didn't have pets, but Nora had once seen a gerbil when she had gone to play with Katy, a girl who lived in one of the neighbouring houses. It was a little rat-like creature in a cage, and when Katy had lifted it out, petted and kissed it, the sight had sickened her and she had refused all subsequent invitations to play. Why would Mrs Daly bring gerbils into a conversation about her family? But then, as the women continued, it seemed that they were talking about her mother's new baby. Trembling, she crept away down the corridor and, not knowing what else to do, put her boots and coat back on and went out again into the garden. She didn't feel hungry any more so she sat huddled on the bench wondering what to do.

She felt numb with cold and misery but never considered approaching Mrs Daly for comfort or enlightenment. She had already absorbed some of her parents' pride and touchy reserve about anything that might reflect less than well on them, so she had no intention of letting the two women, whose presence in her house she now deeply resented, see her fear, shame and bewilderment. She didn't want them to know that she had overheard their conversation, so she sat there and hugged to herself the horrific possibilities that the word 'gerbil' had unleashed.

Nora stayed in the garden until Mrs Daly, with a great show of bustle and concern, came out to get her.

'Whatever can you be thinking of, pet, to stay out here for so long, catching your death?'

Nora knew that, in the grand scheme of things, it was Mrs Daly's task to call her in, and that she had suddenly woken up to the time she had allowed to pass while she was gossiping in the kitchen with a woman who had no business being there anyway.

'Now, you come inside and warm yourself up while I make you a bit of dinner. I've had a wee look and there's sausages, ham, fish fingers, soup. You just tell me what you'd like.'

She allowed herself to be led into the house, but eluded all Mrs Daly's attempts to take her by the hand. When they reached the kitchen the other woman had already left, as Nora had suspected would be the case. She sat, composed and docile, at the kitchen table, while Mrs Daly heated some soup and toasted bread for them both, and although her appetite had not returned, she forced herself to eat a few mouthfuls. More than anything, she didn't want Mrs Daly to know that she had heard the word 'gerbil', as though the word itself had a special power and the mere act of saying it might bring into being what she most feared. She felt sure that, if the subject were raised, Mrs Daly would smother her with a pity she didn't really feel, for what she had picked up from the overheard conversation wasn't concern but relish in other people's misfortune.

Besides, she was trying to convince herself that what she had heard was a mistake. Nothing was real unless her father told her it was so, and she remembered now her father's poor opinion of women like Mrs Daly, whom he described as ignorant and superstitious, and on one occasion had had to explain to her what he meant by 'forces of darkness' when something that had upset her mother was being discussed. When her father came back from the hospital Mrs Daly, who seemed to Nora to be swelling with importance, would wither and disappear back into her house.

In the middle of the afternoon, while Nora was doing her best to occupy herself in her bedroom, the telephone rang. She heard the kitchen door close before Mrs Daly answered it. Then, shortly afterwards, it rang again, and after that it seemed that it never stopped.

Finally Mrs Daly appeared at her bedroom door and said, 'That was your father, pet. They're waiting for an ambulance to bring them back from the hospital. Then they'll all be home.'

Nora nodded. It seemed that the baby had indeed been born, but Mrs Daly was volunteering no information about it.

'Will you come and sit with me?'

'I'm fine, thank you.'

When, shortly afterwards, she heard the bustle of arrival at the front door, Nora went and sat on the floor, her back to the wall, waiting to be called. There were sounds of movement, and strangers' voices, and then she heard Mrs Daly say, 'The Lord love him, the poor wee boy. But they do say they bring luck to a house.'

'They do, do they? Well, I suppose "they" would know, whoever they happen to be,' said her father. 'And who told you anyway? Did I say anything to you about this baby?'

'Well, Mary Donovan popped in. She has a friend, a nurse at the hospital who—'

'So, the bush telegraph has been functioning as well as ever, I see. I wondered why it was taking me so long to get through on the telephone in my own house.'

'It wasn't like that. Don't make it so hard for yourself, Gerald. I know it must be a terrible shock, and my heart bleeds for you, but everybody wishes you well.'

'Do they? Do they indeed? Just as they say this will bring me luck? Well I'm sure that will be a great comfort to me.'

Rigid with fear, Nora lay on her bed. Normally, she was his first thought when her father entered the house, but muted sounds of conversation, and the louder noises of people moving about, continued outside, and nobody came to get her. Straining her ears, she thought once or twice that she was picking up new and unfamiliar sounds, of a tiny living creature hovering somewhere between human and animal, but she couldn't be sure. Then the doorbell rang, and shortly afterwards rang again, and she heard the clear, measured voices of men other than her father.

Suddenly she could bear the suspense no longer. She went out into the empty hall and tracked the new voices to her parents' bedroom, but the door was closed. She wandered into the kitchen and there was her father, standing at the kitchen counter staring at the teapot and waiting for the kettle to boil. He turned when he heard her and looked at her, not as if he had never seen her before but as if he now saw her differently and was having to make up his mind about something.

'The house is full of priests and doctors and it's all cups of tea and little snacks, though if I know Father McCaffrey there'll be no leaving this house until he's seen the whiskey bottle.'

'I've a baby brother, then,' said Nora.

'That's right,' said Gerald. 'And I have a son. What every man's supposed to want. Am I not right? They do say, be careful of making a wish, it might come true. You know what's going through my mind?'

Nora shook her head.

'There's this book, *Nineteen Eighty-four*, written by this Englishman, years ago, before anybody knew what 1984 would be like, but he made it sound like the end of the world, the people not really human – not what you could call human – any more. Well, this is 1984, so we must give him the credit for getting something right.'

He loaded the tray with tea and fruit cake, cups and saucers, milk jug and sugar bowl, and Nora realised she had never seen him perform even the smallest household task before. All that had been left to her mother. In its way, the sight of her father fussing over cups and saucers was as frightening as anything else that had happened that day, and she wondered whether that was the way it was going to be from now on.

Lifting the tray, he said, 'I'll take this through to the vultures who've come to prey on our misery.'

When he had left the room, Nora sat at the kitchen table, eating the cake crumbs and bits of dried fruit left in the tin. Her father hadn't asked her if she had eaten, what kind of day she had had, how Mrs Daly had been towards her. He hadn't said when he would be back to attend to her, whether her mother had been asking for her, or given any clue as to how life would proceed. All these concerns had to a degree displaced her fears about the baby, but she was also doing her best not to dwell on her new brother. In particular she avoided visualising him. She sat there while the telephone rang intermittently and was answered elsewhere in the house, staring at the empty blackness of the window, where nobody had thought to draw her mother's flower-patterned curtains.

After what seemed a very long time, she heard her parents' bedroom door open, and then her father was with her again.

'You'd better come in,' he said. 'Father McCaffrey and Dr Murphy want a word with you.'

He didn't take her hand but led the way to the bedroom,

where he waited at the door while she went inside. He didn't go in himself, but closed the door behind her from outside. Opposite, her mother was sitting up in bed, with the cradle she had prepared for the baby beside her. She gave Nora a wan smile, as if everything was out of her hands. This in itself was not unusual since, within the family, she had always seemed the least powerful of the three, taking directions from her husband on most household matters, and resentfully acknowledging that she came after Nora in his affections.

What was more startling was that, while she was recognisable of course, she seemed completely different, as though she had been rearranged. She looked as though something had happened to her face, though it was impossible to say what. Nora carried around with her the memory of her mother's face that day and, years later, when she heard a woman describe herself as 'shattered', by what seemed to Nora a rather trivial event – she came to judge much of the substance of other people's lives as trivial – she thought, 'Yes, that's it. She had been shattered, broken up and hastily put together again, but none of the pieces fitted in quite the way they had before, not any more.'

At the foot of the bed were Father McCaffrey and Dr Murphy, one on each side, like guardians. Nora saw a look pass between them and, after a nod from the priest, the doctor cleared his throat.

'Well now, Nora,' he said. Nora had often been taken to visit him, or had received visits from him at home, and he was always brisk and reassuring. Now he was frowning with concentration, as if struggling to find a manner appropriate to the occasion. 'We thought you should be told – it's always best to be clear about these things from the beginning. Your little brother has what's known as Down's syndrome. At one time he would have been called a "mongol", a term you might still hear people use, but now we prefer Down's syndrome, after the man who discovered it.'

Before he could go on with his explanation, Father McCaffrey, who appeared to think that the doctor had struck the wrong note, interrupted: 'These are very special children, Nora. Special to God, who wants us to cherish them, so he only sends them to those families he knows will give them the love and care they need.'

Nora said nothing, as she tried to assimilate the implications of 'special'. She had always been led to understand that she was special, but there was evidently more than one kind of special.

As if sensing her confusion, Dr Murphy said, 'He won't develop in quite the way you have, he won't learn so quickly. But you'll find yourself surprised at some of the things he can do and he will be a very loving brother to you.'

'Exactly,' said Father McCaffrey. 'They're generally very loving, and you shouldn't bother your head too much with what he can and can't do. Too much is made of all that in the world today. He'll be special to God because of his innocence, and that's a very precious gift indeed.'

Nora nodded, feeling that something was required of her, but really her mind was elsewhere. The doctor had said 'mongol'. That was what the word had been, not 'gerbil'.

'Now, I know we don't need to tell you to be a really good girl, and to help your mother and your wee brother as much as you can,' said Father McCaffrey.

Nora glanced across at her mother. She certainly looked in need of help.

'Now, why don't we leave you here, to start getting to know your brother and to have some time with your mummy?' the priest concluded. The doctor said something to her mother about visits and midwives, then they both turned to go. On their way to the door, however, the doctor paused briefly to catch Nora's eye and give her a sad smile.

Everything about that day had been strange – not just Mrs Daly and the strange woman who had come and sat in the kitchen as though it were completely natural, and her father's changed manner towards her, and the doctor and the priest referring to her brother all the time as "they", as though he weren't a single baby but one of a group, all identical: the presence in their house of a priest who behaved as though he were entitled to exercise some authority was also a novelty. Her father was not a practising Catholic, and while he didn't actively discourage priests from visiting, he liked them to know that their presence was on his terms. If they were going to drink his whiskey, he would say, then he had every right to give them his opinion of the papacy, or of the role they had played in keeping people poor and ignorant.

Now, just as strange as anything else was the sudden silence in the room and Nora feeling instantly at a loss. Something seemed to be required of her and she didn't know what. It didn't seem that her mother was in a position to offer her a direction on how to behave in these changed circumstances. Tentatively, she walked along the side of the bed towards her mother and the baby. She wondered whether she ought to kiss her mother, but felt estranged and awkward. Instead she said, 'Will I look at the baby?'

'If you want,' said her mother indifferently.

Nora peered into the cradle and all her anxieties suddenly evaporated. He was, after all, just a baby, not unlike any other that she had seen. No, that wasn't quite true since he had long, fair hair – hair the same colour as her mother's, just as she had her father's black hair – and all the other babies she had seen had been bald. She bent over and touched his hair and was surprised to find it silky, not unlike her own when it had been washed. As she touched him, he stirred and opened his eyes. She saw that they slanted up at the corners, but they were large and a deep, deep navy blue, unlike any other eye colour in the world.

She looked up and said, 'He's really pretty,' but her mother's face was blank and she turned her head as soon as their eyes met and sank back into the pillows.

There followed another of the periods of blank time that had punctuated the day – a day that had alternated strangely between boredom and fear. Normally there was a routine, and wherever she was in the day, Nora knew what would happen next. But now, although it was long dark, she hadn't had her bath, or tea, or a story, and as far as she could tell, her parents had forgotten that she had come to depend on this clear sequence of events. She kept her position by the baby, who was silent in a way that, from her limited experience of babies, she hadn't expected. Once or twice there was a slight stirring and he seemed on the point of crying. His mouth opened, but no sound came out, as though it were too much effort for him. She wondered whether he needed to be fed. She crept round to get a better view of her mother, who she assumed was sleeping, but she found her as before, staring blankly at the wall ahead. If she was aware of Nora, she gave no sign.

It was some time after the doctor and priest had left before her father came to the bedroom door, where he stood, as if reluctant to enter. 'Will you have something to eat, Bernie?'

'I couldn't swallow a thing.'

'A cup of tea?'

'I've drunk so much tea today that I don't think I'll be able to get the taste out of my mouth again.'

'Right you are, then,' he said, clutching the door handle as if to retreat.

'Gerald, will you wait a minute? There's something I want to talk to you about.'

'Can't it wait?'

'Please.'

Gerald stepped into the room, closed the door behind him and leaned against it.

'Won't you sit down?'

'I'm right enough like this.'

Bernie shifted herself into a sitting position, wincing slightly from the stitches. 'We should decide what we'll call him.'

'Not now, Bernie. I can't believe there's any urgency. There are families of ten in this very town where the last ones had to wait weeks for a name, until their parents could summon up the energy.'

'There may not be any urgency for you but they've been at me all the time – the nurses, the doctors, Father McCaffrey, and it will be the same with the midwives tomorrow. I'd just like them to leave me be, with all their talk about bonding and giving him a name so that he's part of the family.'

Gerald sighed deeply. 'Well, if you've got any ideas, you just go ahead. It's all the same to me.'

'Father McCaffrey wondered about Felix.'

'Isn't that the name of the cat in the cartoon? I didn't realise that the old boy had a sense of humour. Well, I'll just take a wee look and see whether I think it suits him.' He walked over to the cradle and peered inside without touching the baby. 'What do you think, Nora? Do you think your brother looks like a Felix?'

'I don't know what a Felix looks like.'

'That's very good,' said Gerald, laughing grimly. 'I would say that makes it an appropriate name.'

'Father McCaffrey says it means "happy",' said Bernie wearily. 'He says it will help us if we think of him in that way.'

'Does he now? Well, at least he's consistent. Priests are experts at convincing themselves that what they want to believe is actually there, only they call it God. Maybe he'd like to take him off our hands and try it out for himself, since he's had so much practice.'

'We have to live here, Gerald. We have to do what's expected of us.'

'Go ahead, then, name him Felix,' said Gerald, on his way to the door.

'He says it's Greek,' said Bernie, delaying her husband's departure. 'He said it might appeal to you, as a man of learning. I said that we'd thought of giving him an Irish name and we'd talked about Sean and Liam if it was a boy.' Her voice caught on the memory of that distant, hopeful time before she had given birth, since when the world had changed for ever. Two fat tears made their way slowly down her cheeks, but she continued speaking, although her voice was thicker: 'He said it was only a suggestion, and that an Irish name might be even better. He said it would make him part of the community.'

'No, we'll call him Felix,' said Gerald. 'He doesn't look like an Irishman to me.'

With that he was gone. Apart from asking Nora's opinion of the name, he had scarcely looked at her. After he'd gone, her mother lapsed back into her torpor. Nora could scarcely stay in her parents' room all night, so she got up and crept to the door. Before she left the room she glanced back and saw that, although her mother was motionless, she was still crying. She had never seen her like that before. Usually she cried because she was angry, or feeling neglected, and the crying was accompanied by raised voices, but this time it was silent and she let her tears flow without drying them. It was almost as though she didn't know what was happening.

It didn't seem right to disturb her, so Nora slipped out of the room and into the lounge, where her father was sitting in his special armchair with a glass of whiskey in his hand, watching the television. It seemed to be the news. As she stood there, the face of Mrs Thatcher flashed on to the screen. As the Prime Minister started to speak, Gerald said, with unusual vehemence, 'The woman's a bloody animal.' Immediately Nora remembered that for a few hours that morning she had thought her new brother was a gerbil, and she felt again the terrible dread that had lasted until she saw him. Then, in her mother's bedroom, her father had made a joke about Felix the cat, which she didn't understand. She looked again at Mrs Thatcher and wondered what her father saw in this middle-aged English woman that she couldn't see. The idea that a person could be an animal was so shocking to Nora that her mind recoiled from it. Nora knew that her father didn't like Mrs Thatcher, and that she shouldn't like her either because of what she had done to the Irish, but she had never heard him call her an animal before. She placed herself in his line of vision and said, 'Will I go to bed now?'

Barely glancing at her he said, 'Does your mother need you any more?'

'I don't think so.'

'Then you might as well go to bed.'

PART TWO

Servants

London

It's late October and the remaining leaves are turning colour and falling across the squares of Bloomsbury. In one of those squares, Pete Taylor, Annie Price and Phoebe Metcalfe are sitting huddled on a bench, eating sandwiches. Pete and Annie ran into Phoebe earlier in the morning when they had just come out from a lecture that Phoebe should have attended but had somehow managed to miss. She was wandering aimlessly around the building looking, as Annie said later to Pete, for someone to play with. It was Phoebe who suggested the *al fresco* lunch – a rather lavish affair, for the circumstances, which she's assembled herself since the arrangement was made, incurring expenses that she's refused to pass on to them, insisting that it's her treat – and they, taking pity on her, agreed.

There has, since the beginning of term, been realignment in their group. Annie wasn't even thought of last year, and although she has taken care to recognise the claims of Pete's longer-standing friends, they sense that Pete is now semi-detached, the radiant good humour that once encircled them now more often, and with a particular fondness, bestowed on Annie alone. Meanwhile Nick and Nora, whose friendship until now has been defined by belonging to the same group, have become closer. It isn't clear what's brought about the change, beyond a growing confidence in Nora, who is regularly singled out by Steve for special attention. And since Steve is the star of the English department, some of that stardust has fallen on her. Nora and Nick are, at this very minute, to the certain knowledge of their friends, sitting side by side in the library, preparing to dazzle the rest of them in the afternoon's Irish-literature class.

'You must admit, they make a lovely couple,' Annie says. 'Like the hero and heroine of a novel who are destined to come together at the end because no one else will quite do.'

'When you see them together, she kind of brings out the Irish in him,' Pete says. 'I've never noticed before, but there's something about him of the young Yeats, when he was a mere broth of a boy. A touch of the aesthete.'

'Surely Nick isn't Irish too,' says Phoebe. Although she started off at the picnic in high spirits, she's grown sullen as the conversation has turned to their absent friends. Now she sounds despondent, as though yet another way of excluding her has been devised.

'Some generations back,' says Pete. 'I'm glad to say he has the grace not to brag about it. As far as I know, he's never even been there.'

'So what's the current state of affairs?' asks Annie. 'Have they – like – got it together yet?' She asks the question because it's likely to engage Phoebe.

'Not under my roof,' says Pete, who shares with Nick, although Annie spends much of her time at their flat, retreating every so often in simulated outrage at the smell of dirty socks and takeaway curry and the evenings given over to football on the television.

'Nor mine,' says Phoebe, who lives with Nora. Although she's been dying for the information that Pete has just given her, pride – or the unwillingness to admit that she feels excluded from Nick and Nora's confidence – has stopped her asking. Her face lightens as she bites into a large slice of cheesecake.

'It's as I thought, then,' says Pete. 'A meeting of minds. When they're both distinguished scholars, they'll make little jokes in the footnotes of their learned volumes that nobody else will understand.'

'That's how I imagine Steve's married life to be, assuming he has one,' says Annie. 'No small-talk, with bouts of intellectual sparring for relaxation. You just can't see him watching television, or going down to Homebase, like my Dad, for a few planks of wood and some screws.'

'I can't see him living in the kind of house that needs DIY,' says Pete, 'no disrespect to your Dad. I see him in a loft or warehouse conversion, with an amazing view over London. Very minimalist, but with loads of books and periodicals, a state-of-the-art espresso machine to keep him fuelled while he's burning the midnight oil and just one marvellous picture – Matisse, or one of those guys.'

'He's a university professor, not a corporate lawyer,' says Annie. 'You're confusing him with your own fantasies, although you don't seem to be doing much to bring them about. You could make a start with your laundry.'

Pete and Annie's amiable domestic bickering, which suggests already established routines and the continuing conversation of a shared life, excludes Phoebe more effectively than public displays of affection. When her anger finally explodes, however, it's directed against Steve.

'What is it with everyone and Steve? You'd think, to hear everyone talk, that he was, like, a god, but I totally fail to see it. I can't see the point of one single thing that he's made us read this term, and if you want my opinion, he's just showing off because he knows all about these books that nobody else has even heard of.'

Pete keeps his face averted while Phoebe's speaking so that she doesn't see the here-we-go-again look that he can't suppress, but Annie, who watches her with motherly attention, sees the crumbs of cheesecake in her hair and the way the tip of her nose has reddened in the cold and feels sorry for her.

'It is a bit of a slog,' Annie says. She's actually enjoying the course, but understands Phoebe's need to be soothed and stroked and to have her feelings acknowledged. 'It will get better later, once he's established the historical context.'

Phoebe is not soothed. The very word 'history' suggests to her a tyranny of fact over imagination, and as for 'context', she wouldn't care if she never heard the word again. But since she doesn't know how to get these points across, is beginning to lose the confidence in her own opinions that she has always taken for granted, she directs her rage instead at their book of the week, Maria Edgeworth's *Castle Rackrent*.

'As far as I'm concerned, I've spent the best part of a day reading the ramblings of someone I'd run a mile to avoid in real life – some old servant guy who tells stories about his masters getting drunk and falling over as though we're meant to find them hysterically funny but leave me cold.'

'A very neat summary of the plot, if I might say so, Phoebe,' says Pete. 'I'd be surprised if anybody can better that.'

'Oh, Nora will, you wait and see. She'll know exactly why it's important and how it fits into the "historical context". And you know something? She behaves as though she doesn't have one at all. Don't you think that's a bit hypocritical?'

'It's frustrating,' Annie says, diplomatically deterring to Phoebe's point of view before weighing it against alternatives. 'You do feel you can only get so far with her before you meet a barrier. But I don't think she's secretive by nature, so she must have her reasons.'

'I'm with Phoebe on this one,' Pete says. 'I think we've all been a bit too soft on young Nora. She looks so fragile that you're afraid to press her too hard in case a crack opens up down the middle, but it can't be good for her to keep everything bottled up. My mum wouldn't approve. "Better out than in" has always been her policy.'

'And you're a living monument to it,' says Annie.

Phoebe's mood is immediately transformed. Noisily she sucks smears of cheesecake off her fingers, lets the remains of the picnic slip from her lap on to the ground, stands up and runs to the nearest pile of fallen leaves. Scooping up an armful, she says, 'Let's have a leaf fight.'

More than half-way through the class, Steve finds that most of the group are still preoccupied with Thady, the old servant who provoked such outrage in Phoebe. Usually so insistent on structured argument, he is for once allowing the class free rein. Like Phoebe, who is no more likely to regard him as a kindred spirit than he would her, he is feeling aggrieved and rejected, outside a charmed circle to which he had assumed he had free access. This morning he suffered a bitter disappointment, which he finds difficult to assimilate, let alone accept. Raw and wounded, he has had to rely on ingrained professionalism to get him through the day; and now, noticing the time, he rouses himself to explain the concept of the unreliable narrator and its relevance to the text.

'He's a servant commenting on the behaviour of his

masters. Now this in itself, I should have thought, indicates some kind of political dimension to the story, but we can take that further and observe that some of the Rackrents in this family saga spend as much time in Bath, a fashionable watering-place dedicated to pleasure, as they do in Ireland, where they pay little attention to their duties as landlords and let their estate go to rack and ruin. Yet they are central to the story, while Thady, the native Irish steward, is a bystander. That, it seems to me, is emblematic of the condition of the Irish throughout the colonial period.'

In addition to his other worries, he's been brooding on changes in the seating arrangements. Students generally are remarkably territorial, sticking rigidly throughout the course to the places taken in the first session. But this afternoon, for the first time, Phoebe is no longer with Nora, by the window, but seated between Pete and Annie, in a quasi-family group, with Phoebe, the child, flanked by her parents. Since she appears to have a light dusting of leaves on her hair and at the cuffs of her sweater, as though she's been rolling on the grass, the analogy isn't that far-fetched. What a handful for her adoptive parents. Nora, meanwhile, is in her usual place, but with Nick beside her. Although they haven't, as far as he has observed, exchanged a word since the class has been in progress, he senses, from the way their chairs are positioned, and their apparent physical ease in relation to each other, some kind of understanding between them. He should be glad for Nora that the balance of friendship appears to have shifted away from Phoebe towards Nick, who is more her intellectual equal, but he cannot find in himself sufficient reserves of generosity.

They certainly make an attractive couple. Nora's beauty

seems, if anything, enhanced since he first saw her. She isn't quite so pale, and although she hasn't lost her elusiveness, the sense she gives of not quite inhabiting her surroundings, she is more animated. As for Nick, Steve is noticing for the first time his rather elfin look – the full but upward-slanting brown eyes, the high cheekbones, hair curling round slightly pointed ears – and tries to resist the thought, worthier of Phoebe than of himself, of legendary Celtic heroes. Only a man as young as Nick, he's forced to acknowledge, can turn that degree of dishevelment – fraying pullover, trailing shoelaces, battered jeans – to advantage. He is himself reaching the age when, if he were to attempt such a look, he'd risk being mistaken for a tramp.

'What I want to know,' says Annie, 'is how we should "read" Thady. He calls himself "honest" Thady all the time, but isn't it a bit like "honest" Iago? He turns a blind eye, after all, when his son grows up and systematically rips the family off. He strikes me as a cunning old sod, if you'll pardon the expression.'

'As far as I'm concerned,' says Nick, who, when he speaks, doesn't look at Steve, but keeps his eyes lowered, as though the open book in his lap has more claim on his attention, 'when you read *Castle Rackrent* what you mostly experience is irony, just as when you read Swift. As Annie said, you don't know how to "read" Thady, but that applies to almost everything in the book. I suppose you could say that that's the literary expression of a kind of ambivalence in the Irish situation.'

He's certainly good, Steve thinks, noticing that Nora has kept her eyes attentively on Nick while he's been speaking. He wonders whether, like the conscientious students they are, they've been discussing the novel in advance of the class. Which would make him an indirect facilitator of their relationship.

'That's right,' says Steve, aware that he's withholding from Nick the praise he's earned. 'But how in particular is Thady an expression of that ambivalence?'

In the silence that follows, Nick catches Nora's eye and nods, as though encouraging her to take up the challenge.

'Thady is a dependant in the Rackrent household,' she says, 'so it's important to him to maintain the goodwill of his masters. One of the things they require is admiration. Perhaps we're meant to think that he really does admire them on some level. They're presented as generous, and that always goes down well. But the position of dependency often involves some kind of underhand activity to secure its own interests. If we were to go for a psychological interpretation, we might say that he presents to the reader his love for them but represses his resentment.'

Steve is struck, as he often is, by the impersonality of her tone. He would be the first to insist that a scholarly debate isn't the occasion for personal anecdote and reminiscence, which tend to mark the contributions of weaker students like Phoebe. He senses in Nora, however, an imperative that has little to do with observing convention. It's as though she's at pains always to establish an objective truth in which she has nothing invested.

Perversely, this thought brings him back to Thady, whose narrative is so slippery and open to interpretation because, as a servant, everything he says is subject to constraint. It seems to Steve that, while the effect is so different, Nora, like Thady, has no authentic voice. Is this because, in London, she feels obliged to conform to an idiom that is alien to her, or is there another reason that might, in time, reveal itself?

For all that, she shows a growing confidence in her chosen idiom and he speculates on whether any of the others is nursing a grievance towards her. The likeliest candidates would seem to be Phoebe or Emma or one of what he characterises as the huddled masses, who sit there taking notes but rarely speak, whose names he's been careful to memorise but, beyond that, is content to leave be. So it's a surprise when Pete, whose presence in the group is unfailingly benevolent, responds in a way that might be interpreted as hostile.

'Is that how you feel about us, Nora?'

Steve wonders whether to intervene but, because he, too, is curious, holds back for the time being, keeping in reserve the right to slap Pete down if necessary.

Nora turns round sharply and says, 'I can't see the point you're making.'

'It just occurred to me that, as an Irish person inhabiting an English reality, you might feel that kind of ambivalence towards us. I'm sorry, I'm probably completely out of order, but I'm just testing the assumptions we're making about the novel against life.'

There is, as far as Steve can tell, no malice in his tone. On the other hand, he is clearly seizing the opportunity to break Nora's guard.

Again, Nora chooses her words carefully, so that Steve considers at what cost to herself spontaneity is so routinely denied. 'I don't think my situation is directly comparable to that of a fictional character in a Protestant Ascendancy household in a novel written two hundred years ago. As far as more recent history's concerned, I don't believe in bearing grudges towards individuals who aren't directly responsible.' As she finishes, she gives a tight little smile, which Pete returns more broadly.

'Just checking,' he says.

In order to bring closure, Steve says, 'I think we should avoid personalising this. As far as your more general point is concerned, Pete, it's a valid one. Thady presents an unstable self, an unstable perspective on the world he inhabits because the terms of that world are largely dictated by other people.'

That, Steve hopes, will deal not just with this matter but with *Castle Rackrent* more generally. He's had enough. He doesn't want to look, or avoid looking, at Nick and Nora sitting side by side, and speculate, or avoid speculating, about their relationship outside this room – whether they'll go back somewhere together, eat together, laugh together, sleep together. Except that, Steve's instinct tells him, there's still something untouched about Nora. But for how long? Like Pete, he's finding that the pressure of lived experience is displacing the theoretical speculation that he once found so seductive. He wants desperately to be on his own and to think about all of this, and to go home and lick his wounds after the blow he received this morning . . .

'I don't think we should ignore the gender perspective on all of this.'

'Go ahead,' Steve says. It was too much to hope that they might get through an entire class without Emma Leigh putting her oar in.

'Wouldn't you say that, as a woman, Maria Edgeworth brought a particular perspective to Thady's position? That as a woman in a male-dominated society she, too, was living in a world whose terms had been dictated by other people? And that this helped her develop an empathy towards servants and other dispossessed people?'

If only it were that simple, Steve thinks. Even as a man who prefers the company of women, he's not sure that he's willing to cede to them all claims to virtue on quite these grounds.

Before he has to answer, Pete says, 'Hang on a minute. Are you saying that being a woman cancels out every other advantage? That every woman, however fortunate, is on a level with the lowest in society? She was the daughter of a rich, enlightened landowner, and was educated and treated as an equal by her father, unless the bloke who wrote the introduction I read got it all wrong.'

'Right,' says Emma. 'But what she suffered from having such a prominent father was that nobody believed she wrote the books herself. Everybody thought they were really her father's work.'

'Then she's had the last laugh,' says Pete. 'The old man's only remembered now as Maria Edgeworth's dad, so justice has been done.'

'And Dombey and Son was a daughter after all,' says Steve, as he gathers up his belongings. Since Emma ducked answering a serious point that deserved addressing, allowing instead her self-righteousness to get the better of her, her argument doesn't deserve serious attention. As he leaves the room, he hears her voice, raised to a level to be heard above a class breaking up, saying, 'What is it about men that they always have to have the last word? Don't they know it's a sign of weakness?' *Tant pis*, he thinks. At least the worst of this wretched day's now over.

Less than an hour later, Steve is sitting in his basement kitchen with his wife and daughters, drinking tea. The setting would confound Pete, whose ideas of minimalist splendour in a riverside or Clerkenwell warehouse, the architectural equivalent of Steve's monochrome clothes, leather jacket and motorbike, are rooted in magazines rather than experience. The tall, early-Victorian house is in Primrose Hill, an area of London that acquired a fashionable status among intellectuals at a period beyond the reach of his students' memories. It was bought with a mixture of family money (an aspect of his background on which Steve has kept so uniformly silent that he has almost forgotten it) and the earnings from his groundbreaking book on critical theory. And far from being minimalist, the kitchen is cluttered with the residue of family life – schoolbags dropped on to the floor; a cork board covered with notices of school events, parties, dental appointments and photographs of Steve's daughters, Jessica and Emily, making funny faces for the camera; and a cat sleeping in front of a stove in which a real fire – albeit the smokeless-fuel variety that is permitted in London – is burning.

All the internal walls of the basement have been removed. At the front of the house, facing the street, there is a refectory table, currently strewn with interrupted homework. The working kitchen area is in the middle and a family sitting room, with the stove and a french window leading into the garden, at the back. Jessica and Emily have rooms fully equipped with desks and computers, but often prefer to do those parts of their homework that require less concentration within reach of their mother. In the Woolf household, work, conversation and the rituals of family life are part of a continuous, seamless process.

Steve is stretched out in front of the stove that his wife, Martha, has lit for the first time this year, at one end of a once elegant, now sagging, sofa, with a mug of tea in one hand and his free arm round the shoulders of his younger daughter, Emily. At fifteen, Emily is a reluctant teenager who has yet to engage her parents in the turbulent pitched battles of adolescence, preferring instead to prolong her enjoyment of the physical and emotional warmth of child-hood. Martha is standing at one of the kitchen counters, preparing vegetables for the sauce they will eat, with pasta and a salad, for dinner but, thanks to the kitchen design on which she herself insisted, she is still enough part of the group to be involved in what is happening.

Jessica is sitting cross-legged on the rug next to the cat, reading an essay on the Reformation that she finished half an hour ago. She is quicker, livelier, more ambitious than her sister, and hopes to read history at Balliol; and although Steve is opposed on principle to all forms of élitism, he thinks none the less that it would be a waste of his daughter's considerable talents if she were to entrust them to a lesser institution, where the best possible teaching in her subject is not available.

It's difficult for Steve to remember now (although Martha occasionally teases him about it) how reluctant he was to have children. The life of the mind has always played a crucial role in his own personal mythology – not just the level of his intelligence but his insistence on living according to reason – and it seemed to him that the desire for children was pure biological determinism. Not only would his own life be more satisfactory without them, in terms of personal freedom, but he'd seen the deplorable effects of parenthood on his contemporaries. Their brains turned to mush, they had no shame in drooling over the most routine achievements of their offspring, recounting every early utterance as though it embodied the wisdom of the ages, but most shocking of all, they lost the ability to make principled and objective decisions. Self-interest, disguised as laudable concern for their children, ruled.

In the event Martha went ahead in the teeth of his oppo-sition, saying that, if it came to it, she would bring up a

baby on her own. As she had known all along, there was
no need for such desperate measures. He was overwhelmed
by his own feelings, falling in love, first with Jessica, and
then, despite his fears that an experience of such magni-
tude and importance couldn't be repeated, with Emily. They
forced him to acknowledge the blind spots in his own
reason. Now, despite the preoccupations he brought home
with him, and his urgent need for Martha's good sense and
counsel, he is in a kind of heaven, with Emily nestling
comfortably against him and Jessica, who has inherited his
looks, intellectual ambition and restlessness, filling him with
pride for her powers of argument and elegant prose style.

She ends with a flourish and a graceful tribute to his
tuition. In a clear, ringing voice, she quotes from Donne's
third *Satire* –

> '"On a huge hill,
> Cragged, and steep, Truth stands, and he that will
> Reach her, about must, and about must go . . ."'

In the course of an earlier consultation on the essay, Steve
supplied the quotation, to illustrate the tireless questioning
of the English Protestant at the time of the Reformation.

'Well, what do you think?' Jessica asks, when she has
allowed a short pause for her achievement to be assessed.

'I'm speechless with admiration,' Steve says.

'That isn't good enough,' says Jessica. 'Nothing's perfect,
you must have some criticism. You can't put your critical
faculties aside just because I'm your daughter. Unless the
fire and the prospect of dinner are making you lazy.'

'You've silenced and stunned my critical faculties,' Steve
says. 'By showing them perfection, you've rendered them
redundant.'

'What would your students say if they could hear you now?' asks Martha, who has finished her preparations for dinner, and is now sitting in an armchair facing the sofa. 'They'd think you'd gone soft in the head.'

'They would be just as impressed as I am. Only the chronically resentful fail to recognise true excellence when they're presented with it.'

'So, how many of your students are as good as I am?' Jessica asks.

'Oh, pipe down,' says Emily. 'I bet none of his students are as vain as you are.'

'I wouldn't bet on that,' says Steve. He looks at Jessica steadily, consideringly. 'No, none of my students is as good as you.'

'In that case, I have a request.'

'There are almost certainly none as crafty as you,' says Martha.

Steve's deep sigh expresses the dilemma of the doting father, who finds himself unable to refuse his daughter something she really wants but fears that what she wants may not be good for her. 'Go on, Jessica, I'm listening,' he says, in a deliberate parody of the Victorian paterfamilias.

'I want to go clubbing in Leicester Square on Saturday night with a crowd from school, and I want not to have to leave at a set time, and not to have to ring you in the course of the evening, and then I want to go back and sleep at Louisa's house. I intend to turn up here at around lunchtime on Sunday, a touch jaded, perhaps, in the short term, but reinvigorated by a much-needed shot of youth culture. That'll leave me with plenty of time to do any outstanding homework, although as it happens I'm well ahead of the game. Please, please, please.'

Jessica still has the manner of the precocious child. Her

mastery of the situation, of the language and argument required to present her case, is charmingly at odds with her childlike demeanour. And Emily, who feels that, however hard she tries, she will never be able to achieve her sister's dazzling blend of naïveté and sophistication, leaves the shelter of her father's arm and slumps at the other end of the sofa. In many ways she would prefer not to be a witness to the scene that is being enacted, but she is fascinated by Jessica's performance none the less.

Steve gives another deep sigh and, released by Emily, adjusts himself into a more purposeful sitting position. His opinion of Louisa is well known within the family. He first made her acquaintance when he bumped into her on the landing one night, not knowing that she was in the house, on his way to bed after arriving home late. A mask-like face, of a kind that could only be achieved with the application of several layers of makeup, had loomed out of the darkness, and further inspection had revealed the shortest skirt and tightest top he had ever seen – or so he claimed later in his exaggerated account of the episode. Then this strange young woman had greeted him with perfect confidence, as though he were already well known to her, as presumably he was by repute. Later, reeling from the shock of the encounter, he woke Martha as he got into bed and learned that she was a friend of Jessica's and they had been out together for the evening. He still claims not to have slept a wink that night, after making such an unsettling discovery.

Steve rarely mentions his Jewish background, which Martha does not share, and never allows it to colour his position on any issue: he persistently takes a pro-Palestinian stance on the situation in the Middle East. Yet he is aware of traces in himself, which he does his best to conceal, of the more traditional outlook associated with Judaism. Obscured for years, these ancestral leanings have surfaced in a protective attitude towards his daughters, which Jessica in particular claims to place her at a disadvantage in relation to her friends. Confident though he is in most aspects of his life, he sometimes feels disabled in his dealings with her by an unresolved conflict between reason and a powerful paternal instinct.

'What do you think, Martha?' he asks.

The two girls smile and exchange a look at this evidence of their father's growing reliance on their mother. Martha is soothing (a quality he has come to need more with the passage of time), has great reserves of common sense (denigrated by Steve in the classroom and lecture hall, it has its use in solving family disputes) and, perhaps most valuable of all, a quality of attentiveness that gives her judgements particular weight. Whatever problems are brought to her, at home, at work or within her own large circle of friends, she is apparently able to put herself on one side, so that even when her advice is not to the liking of those who have sought it, they feel she has offered it in their best interests.

'I think we should be preparing Jessica for university,' she says, 'not academically – that's taken care of – but in how she handles the social life. Once she's away, we won't know where she is or whom she's with at any given time. We should trust in her good sense, but we'll make sure she has a mobile, in case there are problems she can't deal with. And meanwhile, Jess, I'll ring Louisa's mother –'

'Oh, Mum, do you have to?'

'– and make sure that she'll be there and expecting you. We'll also insist on knowing how you intend to get back to Louisa's.'

Shortly afterwards, once Jessica and Emily have gone off

to their rooms, Steve and Martha settle down to enjoy a glass of wine before they summon their daughters for dinner.

'So,' Steve asks, 'how was life among the stacks today?'

Martha works at the British Library, which has been beset by difficulties since its recent move to Euston Road. Steve is often amused by her stories of life at the library where, despite the reputation enjoyed by librarians for having quiet, retiring natures, there seem to be as many prima donnas as there are in the academic world.

'Don't even ask. This is a day when I'd prefer to forget all about it.'

Steve watches as Martha performs her own exhaustion. She lets her head flop to one side, her arms go limp, while her legs, which are already stretched out in front of her, relax apart. Her eyes are closed, so she doesn't notice that he takes in the details of her appearance – her long legs, still shapely, clad in black tights as they were when he had first met her, her body still pretty much what it was then, slim and agile, in a black skirt ending just above the knee and a soft blue polo-neck sweater. Her face is more lined but, he is pleased to note, not sagging, and while she doesn't inspire in him the kind of pride of possession that he feels for his daughters, he has for her a growing tenderness. The adjective that is most likely to hover in his mind in connection with her is 'steadfast': as their time together lengthens, it becomes increasingly appropriate.

Having made her point, she recovers her original position and says, 'In fact, I'm feeling so feeble this evening that I'm going to curl up after dinner with a Joanna Trollope that I bought on my way home.'

Steve throws up his arms in mock-despair and says, affectionately, 'What are we going to do with you?' This is one of their recurring routines, provoked not just by Martha's

occasional taste for light fiction but by the chocolate wrappers that sometimes emerge from the debris of her handbag,
the furtive cigarettes that, once or twice a week, he finds
her smoking in the garden or in an empty room with the
window open, and by the long, involved, often raucous telephone conversations she has with her friends. In truth,
however, he admires her capacity to find pleasure in small,
harmless acts of self-indulgence, while he can never enjoy
more than fleeting moments of contentment. He is always
measuring himself, not by what he has already achieved but
by those goals, not yet reached, that he is currently pursuing,
and is too easily cast down by setbacks.

'So, what about you?' she asks. 'Any news yet?'

This is the moment Steve has been dreading, as much
as he's been longing for it, throughout the day. He needs
to unburden himself, but an admission of failure is painful,
even to an audience as loyal as Martha.

'I didn't get it,' he says, staring into his glass; and as
his smile fades, she sees the look of utter desolation.

'Oh, Steve, I am sorry.'

He was being considered as the front man for a series
of projected programmes on Ireland, covering history and
broader cultural issues. When he was asked to apply he
had embraced the opportunity as the ideal platform for his
talents, the escape route that had become necessary since
his return from Ireland. He has discussed the project
endlessly with Martha, and although she has done her best
to share his enthusiasm, his craving for celebrity – however
it is dressed up and disguised, that's what it comes down
to – has saddened her. She respects his ambition, but can't
help feeling that he's elevated something essentially tawdry
above the valuable work to which he's dedicated his life.
At the same time, the deep shame she reads into his averted

gaze, as though he can hardly bear to look at her, arouses in her an instinct to protect and comfort.

'It's probably a political appointment, rather than one based on merit,' she says, hoping that if it isn't it can be interpreted in Steve's favour. 'Did they tell you who is doing it?'

'Oh, some Irishman,' he says, then laughs at his dismissive tone.

'Well, then, at least it isn't personal.'

'I know, I know, and of course, objectively, I can see that it's the right thing. If I'd been making the appointment, it's probably what I would have done. But it makes me wonder whether I'm doing the right thing in changing direction, whether I'll ever be taken seriously. There are those already who see me as something of an opportunist, which is allowable as long as one is successful in seizing opportunities. But a failed opportunist becomes a laughing-stock.'

Martha takes a deep breath while she considers which, among the options available to her, is most likely to lift Steve out of his gloom. Nobody else, not even his daughters, suspects Steve's talent for despair, the way that after every setback, even the most trifling he can reduce everything he's achieved to nothing. She thinks that this was why he married her. There were a number of available candidates, women with flashier intellects or more obvious glamour, but he found in her the one person to whom he could expose his weakness and find solace. She felt then and still feels that if her one advantage over the rest of the field is that she can perform this particular service for him she might as well make the most of it.

'You do have your book on Joyce, and it sounds wonderful. That will be a far more solid achievement than hosting a few television programmes that everybody will have forgotten within a month or two.'

'It sounds more wonderful than it is,' Steve says. 'I imagined something really creative, but realisation's dawning that, whatever my talents may be, they don't lie in that direction. Joyce's wife said that Joyce envied Shakespeare, and I'm starting to think that maybe I envy Joyce.'

'I'm sure that's not true. Not about envying Joyce. Who wouldn't? I mean about the quality of your own book. I'm sure that it's only been going badly because you've been distracted by this other thing, but once you give it your full attention you'll find it's everything you hoped for.'

Steve is still slumped, still resistant to Martha's determined optimism, so she shifts to what they both know is unarguable. 'You're still the most popular lecturer they have. I know and you know and most of the English department knows that you're single-handedly responsible for attracting some of the best students away from Oxford and Cambridge.'

'I've been regretting all afternoon that I didn't take that chair at Oxford when it was offered. No, more than that, I've been regretting ever becoming an academic. It seemed then that it was where all the best people went, but it's become more and more marginal. A place for nerds, clever enough, but people who can't hack it in the outside world, like convents and monasteries.'

'I'll ignore most of that. What do you know about convents and monasteries anyway? As far as Oxford's concerned, I'm glad you didn't take it. I wouldn't have been able to move, and a divided life is never satisfactory. Besides, how would Jessica feel, when the time comes, to have you crowding her space and keeping a paternal eye on her?'

In spite of himself Steve smiles. He knows she's doing her best to distract him, but allows it to happen.

'What about this new Irish-literature class?' Martha asks. 'You haven't said much about it. Do you find it enjoyable?'

'Yes, I suppose. They're quite a lively bunch.'

'Now that Jessica's not here, you can tell me. Any particularly bright students?'

Martha knows that, unlike many academics who see teaching as a distraction from their own research, Steve takes his responsibilities as a lecturer seriously and is careful to nurture real talent when he finds it.

'Two, as it happens,' Steve says, and gets up to pour more wine. 'And a couple of class jokers who, as long as they don't get out of hand, can be an asset.' Seated again, he says, eyes averted, 'Actually, there's a girl.'

A pause, like a missed heartbeat, follows. Martha allows it to lengthen. While she is alert to the implications of what Steve has said, she sees no reason why she should make it easy for him. The truth is that, from the beginning, there have always been girls, or women, and it was clear to her that, if she wasn't prepared to tolerate them, there would be no marriage, despite Steve's total reliance on her. Some ambitious men, she knows, are able to confine the drive to succeed to their careers, their public lives, but Steve isn't one of them. Particularly at the times of disappointment that are inevitable in any life, Steve needs a sexual conquest to boost his morale.

Martha married Steve out of deep love, but without illusions, and this readiness to face reality has been a source of pride and strength, sustaining her in circumstances that might otherwise have undermined her. She's never seen it as a strategy, but so far it's worked. None of the women –

academics, like himself, producers of programmes in which he has featured, publishers – has threatened her marriage, because what Steve wanted from them was soon over and forgotten. She has never known whether to be grateful or disillusioned by his capacity for sex without emotion, but she's never colluded in it or pampered his weakness. And within her own moral frame of reference, to pretend not to know, while less painful, would be a kind of collusion. The imperative of openness has never been breached, allowing Steve a continuing belief in his own integrity and Martha the right to make him feel uncomfortable.

Jessica and Emily, on the other hand, have been spared all knowledge of their father's extra-marital activities. In this household, where hypocrisy on the part of the older generation is regarded as a cardinal sin, there has been this one secret. And the secrecy, as well as protecting them, has come to seem justified by events. Martha approached Steve's sabbatical with some anxiety, anticipating, in his long periods away from home, the deadly combination of loneliness and opportunity; but he returned home with nothing to report, touchingly relieved to have his family around him again. She had assumed that this must signal the end of that particular craving.

At last, since he has shown no sign of clarifying his meaning but continues to stare into his wine glass, Martha's patience snaps and she asks, 'Do you mean 'There's a girl' in the sense I think you mean it? Or that there's a girl who stands out from the other clever, amusing students by virtue of her cleverness or amusing-ness?' This is the tone – brittle and detached – that Martha usually adopts when she is required by the rule of honesty to acknowledge the presence of another woman on the scene. Her manner suggests that, while she accepts his behaviour, she has never stopped deploring it.

'Well, both, as it happens,' Steve says. 'I don't know about amusing. Probably not. If anything, she's rather on the serious side, but she is an exceptional student. And yes, I do—'

'Fancy her?'

'If you want to put it like that.' Steve is clearly uncomfortable, and since he announced the existence of 'the girl' has not looked Martha in the eye.

'You've always steered well clear of students.'

Steve shrugs, as if the situation were outside his control.

'Isn't it rather dangerous, in the current climate? Didn't you tell me that Professor Rowe was cautioned for squeezing a student's shoulder when he handed back a bad essay?'

'Old Rowe lives in another world,' Steve says. 'I don't suppose he can interpret the signals.'

'Oh, I see, so you've been getting signals from this girl.'

'Well, no, since you ask. As it happens, she's extremely reserved.'

Martha nods slowly as she takes in all the implications of what Steve is saying. 'Is that the attraction – that, unlike most of your female students, she seems indifferent?' She pauses for an answer, and when none is forthcoming, says, 'Isn't it possible that you're not thinking straight after the disappointment over the television contract? That you might be looking for another challenge – one you're sure of succeeding in?'

Finally Steve looks her in the eye. 'I've been through all this myself and, yes, if it's any comfort, I am fully aware of the risks and of those aspects of my present situation that make me more – susceptible, shall we say? And I promise I'll do nothing to endanger us or my career.'

'But how can you be sure? I suppose you can feel reasonably certain of me, given our history, but I can't guarantee how I would feel if you formed a strong emotional attachment. I've never been faced with that, after all. And as far as your career's concerned, this girl's an unknown quantity. Do you know anything about her? If she's as reserved as you say she is, presumably she's something of a mystery.'

'Only that she's Northern Irish, from a Catholic background.'

'Oh, I see,' says Martha, undecided as to whether this makes her – the as yet unnamed girl from Northern Ireland – more or less dangerous. Throughout this conversation she has been feeling more than usually threatened, has begun to wonder whether Steve's uncharacteristically incautious behaviour indicates not just his craving, after a professional disappointment, for success elsewhere but something special about this particular girl; that after years of relatively harmless dalliance, he might finally have met someone with the power to disturb his emotional equilibrium and their carefully preserved marriage. It now seems likely, however, that it isn't the girl herself, however pretty and clever she might be, but the mere fact that she's Irish.

On the other hand, this could make her appearance on the scene even more alarming. Since he took up Joyce, Steve has made something of a fetish of Ireland, though he would strenuously deny this interpretation of his behaviour. It is, she thinks, the kind of folly to which intellectuals like Steve are especially prone. Suspicious as he is generally of judgements based on instinct or emotion, he has an accumulated store of sentimentality that he allows himself to direct at liberal causes. In Martha's view, this one passed its sell-by date with the Good Friday Agreement. None the less, he might well be at his most susceptible to a girl clothed in all the glamour of colonial oppression.

Steve, who has been deep in his own thoughts, says, 'I was wondering about inviting her here.'

'Here?' Martha asks. This is another possibly significant variation to an established pattern. 'But you never bring your students home.'

Indeed, Steve is not one of those academics who fraternise with students, preferring instead to keep his personal and professional lives entirely separate. Martha has sometimes regretted this, feeling that an important part of his life is closed to her, but she recognises in him a deep fear of exposure. To be seen as a husband, a father, a householder, a cat-fancier might compromise the mystique he enjoys in lecture and seminar rooms.

'Well, I thought I might this time.'

'Is that to reassure her or me?'

Steve smiles tenderly. 'Martha, you shouldn't need reassurance. You know that there is nothing I would do knowingly to hurt you. Look, if it's any comfort, I know what the risks are, and I've pretty much made up my mind not to take this any further – not in that direction, at any rate. Why not befriend her? She may well be lonely. And to have her here would erect a barrier as far as I'm concerned. Once she's met you and the girls, it becomes unthinkable that I should – well, you know what I'm trying to say.'

'You want to be saved from yourself. Well, invite her round, then.'

While Steve is in Primrose Hill, drinking tea with his family, Nora returns alone to the flat in Crouch End that she shares with Phoebe, having made her excuses to the others – Phoebe, Nick, Pete and Annie – not to join them for the post-class cappuccino.

Although the flat is empty, so for a while she doesn't have to respect Phoebe's prior right, as owner, to occupy the public space, Nora isn't tempted by the empty sitting room and the television set that she could, on this occasion, turn to a channel of her own choosing. Instead, she makes straight for her bedroom, where she drops her bag and jacket before curling up on the bed. This was her habit at home. Over the years she developed a sense of the rest of the house, apart from whatever spot was occupied by Felix, as hostile territory where at any moment she might stumble unwittingly on the landmine of her parents' many sensitivities. And her need for a refuge has continued.

Viewed objectively, her life holds more promise at the moment than at any time she can remember. It seems likely that she will achieve all the academic goals she's set herself, and a bright, if still undefined future should be assured. Nick's interest in her is clear, a source of secret pleasure when she allows herself the indulgence of daydreaming. She knows that this current state of suspense cannot continue indefinitely, that he's going to expect more from her than she's currently able to give, but any other girl would regard this as a blessed state. She's living in circumstances more comfortable than she thought possible when she first came to London, thanks to an act of generosity she could never have imagined. These are the facts of her immediate situation and, as she lies curled on her bed, she marshals them in her mind to dispel her anxiety.

The ability to think rationally has always been important to her and, since she was old enough to formulate such an idea, has defined who she is. Powerless as she was at home, the force of reason was her only defence.

And while she couldn't say that it was effective against her parents, who regarded it more as an incitement than as a challenge that they might meet by behaving rationally, it comforted her in the inner recesses of her being. When she planned her escape, the world she envisaged for herself was peopled by paragons who shared her commitment to objective truth.

If this was the premise by which she decided to live, she has only herself to blame for the anxiety that sent her fleeing from the company of her friends. If she really values the truth, she should have been more open about herself from the beginning. The longer she's left it, the harder it's become, and if she were to tell her story now, she would have to explain the reasons for her reticence as well.

She came to London in the naïve belief that she could reinvent herself. The anguish that drove her from home was in part because the daughter her parents saw bore no relation to the person she knew herself to be. She felt distorted and deformed by them. In London she would take control of her life and of the self she presented to the world.

She wasn't so much determinedly suppressing the past, as refusing to be defined by what she had left behind. The mere telling of her story would skew people's reactions to her. And as she listened to other people talk about their families, her own came to seem grotesque, to the point at which she wondered if she would even be believed. When she rehearsed her story in her own mind, it seemed – to a judgement as fastidious as hers, as alert to genre – like the worst kind of sensationalist fiction. And the longer she left the telling, the more likely it was that her motives, when she finally came to unburden herself, would be misinterpreted. She was so sick of the relish in unearned victimhood she'd seen at home that she shrank from exposing herself to the charge of courting pathos.

What she hadn't calculated on was that, if she neglected to construct a narrative of her own life, other people would project stories on to her. And when Nora first got to know Phoebe, it was her poverty – not a condition from which she'd suffered in Ireland – that had first impressed her new friend.

Phoebe's own family circumstances were affluent beyond anything in Nora's previous experience. Her parents, in the version of their history that Phoebe told her friends, had travelled to India and Nepal as young, idealistic hippies in search of enlightenment, and discovered in themselves an unsuspected talent for commerce. This they turned to good account, building up a thriving business importing eastern bric-à-brac and antique furniture. For Phoebe, Nora's penury – minimally relieved by student grants and loans and what she earned during the holidays – was more exotic than anything she had encountered on the streets of Bombay or Kathmandu when travelling with her family. It was quite beyond her that another girl, in broadly the same circumstances as herself – studying at the same university, and exhibiting none of the usual marks if deprivation – should routinely exclude herself from shopping trips, cinema visits, college balls, drinking sessions in the union bar, from anything, in fact, that involved unnecessary spending. So she concocted a little romance around Nora which, at least in the beginning, Nora found mildly amusing.

As a Celt (a rather ill-defined group, held in special veneration by New Agers like the Metcalfes), Nora was infused with those spiritual values that Phoebe's own parents had travelled to Nepal to find.

'But, Phoebe,' Nora used to protest, 'that's like me thinking of you as an Anglo-Saxon.'

Phoebe looked blank, possibly because she had only the haziest notions of who the Anglo-Saxons were. Anyway, her family's preferred genealogy concentrates on more peripheral ancestral lines that link them to Italy, Wales and South America.

Nora's denial of her own Celtic heritage was, Phoebe was convinced, one of the pernicious effects of Catholicism. Phoebe's veneration of the spiritual life does not extend to organised religion, which is an instrument of repression, while her opinion of Catholicism in particular is supported by a film she saw about an Irish convent, and by another that showed priests in the olden days crushing nobly savage Incas in Peru. This, and what she knows about present-day Northern Ireland – a dark, dismal place, where men of outstanding ugliness and with a taste for horrible woolly hats shoot and kneecap each other – are more than enough to account for the peculiarities in Nora's behaviour. At the same time, a free spirit beats within her: why else has she appeared in London, her circumstances mysterious, her lips sealed about the horrors she has witnessed?

This has been Phoebe's version of Nora's story, in which she's cast herself as the agent of deliverance, the true friend who will release Nora's pent-up emotions, even if Nora has so far refused to jump into bed with any of the young men whom Phoebe assured her were 'up for it'. Meanwhile Phoebe's parents, in a fashion that is both careless and magnificent, have befriended Nora. For them she is a trophy, one of their many acquisitions. And just as every picture and cabinet in their house in Chelsea has a story that they delight in telling – about the special qualities, particular to the culture of the man or woman who sold it to them – so Nora has no difficulty in imagining the terms in which they describe her to their friends, dwelling on her Irishness, her poverty and likely status as a runaway, and Phoebe's great intuitive gifts in recognising her as someone worth cultivating.

If she's guessed right, their patronising is a small price to pay for their genuine patronage. For the refuge that she's currently enjoying – the very room to which she's been able to retreat – is hers for nothing: nothing financial, that is. As Phoebe's mother, Janie, said to her, 'Usually the friend pays the mortgage, but since Phoebe doesn't have a mortgage, we wouldn't feel right in asking you to pay rent.'

The Metcalfes' generosity has been astonishing, and there are times, when her mind dwells morbidly on arguments with her father, that she wants to say, 'They're not as you thought, the English. I know more about them now than you do and you were wrong.' At the same time, she's starting to resent the false picture that the Metcalfes have of her, which is as disfiguring in its own way as her parents' distorted view. 'I'm not really poor,' she wants to scream. 'I wasn't brought up poor, at any rate. My father is one of the most respected men in Ballypierce.'

She's forfeited the right to say that, however, just as she's been lumbered, by her own silence, with Phoebe's romance about her tortured Celtic soul. What's even more shaming is her anxiety that this romance, which for all its silliness is harmless enough, is cracking. Phoebe is no longer satisfied by telling Nora who she is, requiring only that Nora remain silent and allow her to babble on. Instead there have been more questions, and these, like her comments, have become pointed and barbed. Nora is in little doubt about what's behind the change: Steve's perceived 'favouritism' and, even more, Nick's growing interest in her (for Nick is not one of the young men with whom Phoebe would like to pair her off) have soured Phoebe's feelings towards her. What's more, she seems to have enlisted Pete as an ally.

If she were to tell Phoebe now that her father's a prosperous pharmacist, living in his own architect-designed bungalow, then Phoebe, in her current state of resentment, might well accuse her of exploiting her own parents' generosity under false pretences. And in the eyes of the world, she would probably be right. But what would happen to her now if she were dismissed from the flat and replaced by somebody else who'd caught Phoebe's fancy?

None of this brings any comfort to Nora, but she tells herself that she has already survived worse. She doesn't know what to do about Nick, other than hoping that one day instinct will take over and she will be able to surrender to her emotions. Phoebe, however, requires more immediate attention, because whatever precarious stability Nora has achieved in London depends on her. All she can do is try to placate her, try to make her forget her resentment by showing how indispensable she is to her comfort. She takes off her good clothes and hangs them up, then puts on the jeans and old sweater that she wears for housework. Although there was never a formal agreement with the Metcalfes that she should keep the flat clean in lieu of rent, she guesses, from the stress they place on how 'sensible' she is by comparison with their 'scatterbrained' daughter, that they rely on her upkeep of the flat to protect their investment.

So it's part of her daily routine to keep Phoebe's mess – the result, according to her father, of her 'indifference to the material world' – at a manageable level. This evening, however, her labours will be such that, even if Phoebe doesn't notice, she will be softened at some subliminal level. She starts with the kitchen. Covering every available surface is the detritus of the many snacks that Phoebe has enjoyed, or left half finished, since she arrived home late last night, after Nora had gone to bed, and until she left for college this morning. Every stage in their preparation can be reconstructed. Cupboard doors have been left open; coffee, cocoa and jam jars are missing their lids, cheese and melting butter left next to the toasted-sandwich-maker that, on this occasion, Phoebe has remembered to turn off; a saucepan has been abandoned with its mess of burned scrambled eggs.

She moves round the kitchen with swift, practised movements, then tackles the thick layer of videos, magazines, dirty mugs and glasses, discarded paper, clothes and magazines and the used ash-trays that are always strategically placed where they are most likely to be kicked over.

The only expression of resentment that she allows herself is a vicious swipe with a duster at the fat, complacent Buddha installed on what Phoebe likes to call a 'shrine', which now holds as much debris as the rest of the room. For reasons that she's never bothered completely to investigate, she associates the Metcalfes' extreme indulgence of their daughter, both materially and in always interpreting her behaviour in the most flattering way, with their commitment to a religion that appears to make no demands on any of them.

The cleaning, as well as being part of a strategy, has a calming effect on Nora, and by the time Phoebe returns at nine, Nora has eaten her eggs and toast and is sitting at the desk in her own room, writing her essay for Professor Rowe. Phoebe at once makes for Nora's room and, weighed down as she is by a miscellaneous collection of bags, slumps on the bed. Once she has Nora's full attention, she holds out her hands to display the red weals left by the bags' handles, stigmata from the shopping spree she went on after coffee with the others. Nora responds with a little show of sympathy, relieved to find, as Phoebe displays her purchases and gives a running commentary on where each was bought and what she intends to do with it, that spending large sums of money has had its usual therapeutic effect; that the aggrieved bad temper of the last few days appears to have lifted. Nora realises that her recent labours were unnecessary and that, given Phoebe's more immediate concerns, are unlikely to be noticed.

'I thought I'd give this to Mum for Christmas,' Phoebe says, as she tears at a slender square of pink tissue paper and pulls out a long, red and purple silk scarf.

'That's really lovely,' says Nora. She has put down her pen and pulled her chair round to face Phoebe. She wants to finish her essay tonight, but it's also important to take advantage of Phoebe's altered mood and restore harmony. Fortunately, Phoebe has a short attention span and will move on in due course to the television or her evening round of telephone calls. 'You're certainly well ahead of yourself with Christmas preparations.'

'You can't begin too early.' Phoebe's tone is severe, suggesting that, although others may be lax, this is a rule she observes with particular dedication.

'Well, I'm sure your mum will be thrilled. You couldn't have done better.'

There follows a series of garments – underwear, tops, a woolly scarf – which, to Nora's eyes, are indistinguishable from others already in Phoebe's drawers or scattered about the flat. Nora lets this display of excess pass without comment, nodding from time to time with approval, until Phoebe pulls out her *pièce de résistance* – a short, straight, black leather skirt.

'But, Phoebe, you've got one just like it. Surely you don't need two.'

It seems that Phoebe has anticipated the implied criticism and prepared her answer: 'That's too small. To be honest, it always was, but they didn't have the right size at the time. I thought you could have it.'

Because Nora benefits so hugely from Phoebe's largesse – the mortifications of her first year when, because she had had to pay for her accommodation, her poverty was constantly on display, are still a painful memory – she tries not to take advantage of her generosity in smaller matters.

'That's very kind of you, but really, I couldn't.'

'Suit yourself,' says Phoebe, shrugging, confident that Nora will eventually take the skirt. Nora's resolve often falters eventually, and some of Phoebe's discarded clothes have ended up in her possession.

'I'm sorry, I didn't mean to be ungracious,' says Nora. It isn't always easy to judge what will provoke Phoebe. Nora's refusal of the skirt might well have passed without consequence, but her subsequent apology is taken as an admission of guilt.

Phoebe gathers up her goods and leaves the room in a huff, after pausing at the door to remark, 'If the cap fits.'

Phoebe's response, churlish and unmerited though it is, lands like a heavy blow. It seems to Nora that she has moved into a phase in her dealings with Phoebe that replicates the position in which she found herself at home, where her efforts to please are ignored and the worst possible interpretation placed on words that, for her, are innocent in intent. Now, as then, her instinct is to confront her tormentor and guide her back through their conversation until that moment of illumination when Nora is vindicated.

She knows from experience, however, that she would meet nothing but blankness, so she paces the room until she's brought her anger under control. Then she picks up Phoebe's discarded bags, smoothes out the creases, folds and slides them into the largest bag, which held the skirt. Phoebe is given to occasional, impassioned outbursts about the degradation of the environment, but it's left to Nora to recycle her rubbish.

If confrontation is pointless, however, there is something to be said for biding her time. Because Phoebe's mind never dwells too long on anything, her sulks tend to be short-lived, and when Nora judges that this one is likely to have passed, she follows her into the sitting room. Only when her sense of security is restored will she be able to continue work on her essay.

She finds Phoebe curled up on the sofa, watching television. Nora sits down in an armchair and makes a neutral comment about the programme she is watching. Phoebe doesn't answer, but after a short silence opens the conversation on another topic: 'We were talking about you after you left.'

Nora takes a deep breath. 'Oh? Nothing too slanderous, I hope?'

'Would I be telling you if we were slagging you off?' She continues to watch television as she speaks. Of all Nora's oddities, Phoebe finds her self-possession the most irritating, and her intention now is to provoke her friend into a proper and natural state of curiosity. Nora, however, feels that she's humiliated herself enough already, to little effect, and refuses to play this particular game. Instead she stands up, as if she's about to leave the room.

Unable to contain herself any longer, Phoebe says, 'We all think Steve's going to make a move on you.'

Grievance

'What?' Nora stops short at the door. If Phoebe were not still clinging to the remnants of her assumed indifference by continuing to stare at the television, she would see that Nora has turned scarlet.

'You can't pretend you haven't noticed.'

'There's nothing to notice.' She can't say what she longs to say, that Phoebe is too apt to find a sexual undertow in any relationship, refusing to allow differences in age, sameness of sex or social taboo to limit her speculations. Nor can she say that if 'everybody' does indeed share Phoebe's suspicions, she is in all likelihood their source, her rancour fed by the contempt for her work that Steve can scarcely bother to disguise. On her own initiative, she recently wrote an essay for him that she was stubbornly convinced would win him round to her way of thinking on the links between Buddhism and Celtic spirituality. For the first time ever, she didn't seek Nora's help, nor did she do any reading, preferring instead to rely on her own original insights. This essay rendered Steve speechless, as if it belonged to an order of discourse he found unrecognisable. He refused to grade it, leaving instead a little note on the cover sheet to the effect that, when the time for assessment came, Phoebe would be glad to have it forgotten.

'He hangs on your every word and you're the only person he ever smiles at. You have to admit he treats you differently from everybody else.'

Nora says, 'Maybe . . .'

'He admires your brain?'

'I wasn't going to say that. It's just possible he notices that I work hard. It's what he's there for.'

Phoebe snorts dismissively. 'Emma says that if he does make a move, it's your duty to report him.'

'Was Emma there too?'

'She was kind of hanging about and I asked her if she'd like to come with us. I think everybody's a bit unfair on her.'

Nora feels an immediate stab of alarm. She's noticed Phoebe talking to Emma once or twice recently, and although friendship between them seems unlikely – Phoebe has always dismissed feminism as a denial of the essential female spirit, while Emma appears to think about little else – it's no more unlikely than her own friendship with Phoebe. She feels excluded and vulnerable. What if Phoebe decides to replace her in the flat next year with Emma?

'I'm sure the occasion to report him will never arise,' she says, unable to think of a mollifying answer that might remove the threat suddenly posed by Emma, and returns to the safety of her own room. When Phoebe calls her about an hour later, she's curled up under the duvet, crying soundlessly.

'Just a minute.' She wipes her face, runs her fingers through her hair and goes off in search of Phoebe, who is seated in front of the computer in her bedroom.

'There's something wrong with this, I can't seem to get into my emails.'

Phoebe's computer is new and she needs constant assistance from Nora to use it. Because she continues to stare at the screen while Nora presses the appropriate buttons, she fails to notice signs of recent distress.

'Do you want to see if there's anything for you?' she asks, by way of recompense. Nora doesn't have a computer of her own, relying instead on Phoebe's, when it's available, and the college's IT room.

Not expecting anything, Nora goes through the motions anyway to express her gratitude to Phoebe, and there, on the screen, is a message from Steve, inviting her to dinner with his family next Friday. Phoebe gives her a triumphant smile, but Nora, too, is smiling.

'With his family, Phoebe. He'd hardly do that if he were – you know. Surely that explains his behaviour, assuming there's anything in what you say. He probably thinks I'm away from home and in need of encouragement.'

This is one of the rare occasions when Nora has referred to 'home' with any emotion, but Phoebe is too enthralled by the words on the screen to notice and take advantage of the lapse. She's not convinced by Nora's explanation, but admits that the invitation is puzzling. More surprisingly, it doesn't provoke in her a relapse into resentment. Nora's unlikely to boast about the turn of events, so Phoebe will have the thrill of a fresh piece of gossip in her possession.

'I know,' says Phoebe. 'Let's go and look at the tarot cards to see if they give us a clue to what he's up to.'

Ballypierce

Nora arrived home from school to find her mother sitting in the kitchen with a woman she had never seen before. She had been brought home from school by Katy's mother, Mrs Hogan, who had assumed responsibility for fetching Nora to and from school when she started, two years before. This was one of the services now performed for the Doyles by neighbours, and while Bernie was civil to their faces, she disliked her dependence on women who were driven not by charity but by the desire to discover and expose her weaknesses. Bernie's world had changed, however, and this had been the only way she could manage her life since Felix's birth. With Nora and, on the rare occasions when he was trapped into listening, Gerald, she was eloquent on the subject of Felix's stubbornness, which made it impossible to predict how long it might take to get him ready to leave the house. He hated being dressed and undressed, refused on all occasions to wear a coat, so that they were confined to the house when it was cold or raining, and had resisted all attempts to toilet-train him. The whole process took so long that she was exhausted before she started.

Nora knew there was some truth in all of this. She, too, had experienced the strange sensation of Felix turning his shoulders inside out – double-jointedness was, it seemed, associated with his condition – as she tried to pull on his coat. She, too, responded with disgust and frustration when, immediately a nappy had been put on after a fruit-less session on the toilet, Felix disappeared, only to re-appear with it so full that it drooped down towards his knees. If her father happened to be there, he withdrew immediately, leaving Bernie to clean the brown, smelly mess that lodged in the folds of his thighs, while Felix laughed and twisted his body and kicked. But Nora had also seen her mother stooped over the kitchen table, sobbing into her cradled arms, or screaming hysterically at Felix before he had even had the chance to frustrate her because she found the mere prospect of handling him so appalling. On such occasions, when she turned to Felix and demanded his compliance, he was ready for battle.

And there was another version of why Bernie never took Nora to school that Nora had pieced together, although she was never directly addressed on these matters. Instead she heard snatches of conversation, conducted in undertones when she was supposed to be occupied or out of earshot by women at the school gates catching up on news and gossip before they bundled their children into their cars or began the walk home. They said that Bernie didn't want to be seen with Felix in public, that the touchy pride that had kept her separate all these years hadn't diminished now that she relied on the good-will of her neighbours; rather, much as it might choke her, this was the only way she could avoid being seen with the baby who shamed her.

'You'd think she'd be used to it by now,' one would say.

'Maybe it's something you never get used to.'

'That's not true. Now my cousin . . .' or neighbour, or

sister's friend. It seemed that everybody in this predomin-
antly Catholic community knew somebody with a child like
Felix and found that child loving, a blessing, a joy, a little
rascal, a real laugh. And these mythical figures, the mothers
– and sometimes the fathers – of children like Felix were
extolled as capable of amazing feats of good humour,
self-sacrifice and relentlessly hard work, encouraging their
children to levels of attainment undreamed-of in the past.
Reading, cooking, swimming, even driving seemed possible
for the children of mothers prepared to devote themselves
single-mindedly to the pursuit of such goals.

To Nora directly, the women at the gates behaved with
a careful show of ordinary civility, asking after Felix and
her mother and passing on little messages and offers of help
(all of which were received, when passed on, with angry
scorn). None the less Nora was left with the clear impression that, in the eyes of their neighbours, not only Felix,
who looked set to grow into a little savage, but her mother
– her mother who, until Felix's birth, had always seen herself
as the object of carping envy – fell well short of an attain-
able ideal. These two accounts – her mother's of herself as
victim and beyond reproach, and the judgement passed on
her by neighbours – were impossible to reconcile. For the
moment, family loyalty prevailed in Nora, but she was eager
and praying for the day when her mother might rise to the
heroic heights that she had heard described, just as she
hoped that her father would miraculously return to what
he had once been – that he would again seek out her
company and show the pride and pleasure in her achievements at school that she deserved.

Mrs Hogan had dropped Nora outside the bungalow
as usual, and Nora spotted the woman, sitting at the table
with her mother, as she walked past the kitchen window

on her way to the side door. Apart from the woman herself, the scene that greeted her in the kitchen was much as usual. The table and most of the kitchen surfaces were littered with the remnants of Felix's meals – a bowl from breakfast in which the remains of the instant porridge he favoured had caked and dried, a plate with half a fish finger and a pool of tomato ketchup from lunch, unwashed feeding bottles, each with a few inches of Ribena or milk remaining – while a quick glance at the floor revealed two or three sodden nappies, a little heap of crumbs where a biscuit had been trodden in, half a banana turning brown from exposure, as well as the less shaming evidence (toy cars, buses and trains) of attempts to interest Felix in play.

Felix hadn't been dressed for the day, although Nora thought – hoped – it was possible that their visitor might mistake the navy blue pyjama top that he was wearing with his nappy for a sweatshirt.

It was clear that, whoever the visitor was, she had not been expected. However, Bernie had tried to salvage the situation by bringing out her best bone-china tea set, with milk jug, sugar bowl and a plate of shortbread biscuits – relics from a former life when she had been careful to maintain standards.

After pausing for a while at the open kitchen door, absorbing both the strange and the all too familiar, Nora took a few steps into the room then paused again to wonder what response the situation demanded from her. Simultaneously both Felix and the woman turned in greeting. Felix was sitting on the floor, thumb in mouth, eyes glazed, apparently indifferent to the litter of toys around him, but when he saw his sister he stood up and staggered towards her, saying, ''Ora, 'Ora, 'Ora,' over and over. His eyes, no longer glazed, took on the luminous quality they reserved for her. She put down her bag, stooped over and hugged him. They stayed locked together, with Felix's hands gripped tightly behind her neck, until Nora released herself. For Felix never tired of Nora, and when he had achieved a moment of happiness, did every-thing he could to prolong it. As Nora detached herself from him, reaching at the same time for a tissue to wipe his nose, her eyes met those of the woman.

'Well, how's that for a greeting?' she said. 'There are no prizes for guessing who Felix's favourite person is – apart from his mummy and daddy, of course.' She smiled at Bernie as she acknowledged her prior claim on her son's affections, but Nora could see that her mother had already taken offence. Her pale skin had mottled with anger and her lips were pinched with the effort of controlling her feelings.

The woman, too, appeared to have recognised her mistake, and did her best to repair it. 'You must have worked hard to encourage the relationship, Mrs Doyle. You obviously know how important siblings are to the development of a child like Felix.'

'I've always tried to do my best by him,' said Bernie, only partly mollified, and Nora knew that this stranger's chance remark, almost certainly well intentioned, would be endlessly replayed until its underlying malevolence was established.

'No one could possibly doubt that. I'm Theresa Kennedy, by the way,' she said, to Nora. 'I suppose you would describe me as a cross between a social worker and a physiotherapist, but I expect that information leaves you none the wiser. Dr Murphy asked me to call in to see if I had any suggestions on what you might be doing with Felix to make life a bit easier for you all.'

Nora remembered the name as someone who had

telephoned a few times to try to make an appointment to visit but had been put off by her mother. She stood there, unsure whether to go or stay. So far Bernie had said nothing to her directly, leaving that to Theresa Kennedy, who glanced from mother to daughter and, after a brief hesitation, stepped into the gap. 'Please, Nora, don't let me stop you having your tea. I'm sure you must be hungry after a day at school.'

Without answering her, Nora poured herself some orange squash and took her place at the table with the two women. Her mother's antagonism had become more evident since Theresa Kennedy had declared the purpose of her visit. It settled over the room like a dead weight that none of them could shift, inhibiting further conversation. The angry outburst would come later, once Theresa Kennedy had gone, but meanwhile Bernie sat rigid and mute, fearful that, if she expressed her feelings before this woman, she would expose herself as common. Lacking the other woman's education and background – for it was clear that she hadn't grown up in a council house in the country, with a labourer for a father – she felt herself at a painful disadvantage. For a few short years she had enjoyed a precarious invulnerability, sustained by Gerald's income and status and the immaculate bungalow, but Felix's birth, and its aftermath, had eaten away at the foundations of her life.

For all that, the two women were not unalike. Or rather, it seemed to Nora, as she nibbled at her shortbread and stole little glances at Theresa, while Felix stood beside her own chair, back straight and hand on her knee, as though he were guarding her, that the social worker/physiotherapist resembled what her mother had once been. Bernie, for all her insecurities, had an instinct for dress, as an indicator of class, and Theresa Kennedy's straight black skirt, pale blue sweater, silk scarf, pearl ear-rings and court shoes represented a style Bernie had once favoured, until Felix had forced her into the machine-washable battle gear of tracksuits and leggings.

Their visitor made one or two attempts to engage Bernie in conversation but, finding her monosyllabic and un-responsive, though attentive with the teapot and plate of shortbread, turned her attention to Nora. 'So, how do you like school, Nora? You would be, what, now – seven?'

'Yes,' said Nora. 'I'm in Miss Heaney's class and it's very nice.' She couldn't think how else to describe it, but Miss Heaney's class was nice, with its bright colours and air of purposeful activity, the reassuring sense of everything happening at its appointed time and all the equipment having its appointed place so that you knew always where everything was and what had to be done. And what was nicest of all was that Miss Heaney really liked her. She was pleasant and patient with all the children, except for a few troublemakers, but she always treated Nora as though she were special, praising every aspect of her work as though it gave her real pleasure to read it and calling Nora her helper because she always knew what they were meant to be doing and would help the slower ones with their work when she finished early. Nora would have welcomed the opportunity to talk about all of this, since she was never questioned about school at home, except occasionally by her mother, who wanted to know whether the other mothers talked about her, but she sensed that Bernie would inter-pret it as a betrayal if she confided in this strange woman.

'I'm sure that you're a great success at school. Now, tell me, Nora, what do your friends think of Felix? I know what wee girls are like – they love playing with babies and small children, and I wondered whether you ever let them play with Felix?' As she spoke, Theresa Kennedy gazed earnestly into Nora's eyes, as though her answer really mattered.

Nora was startled by the question, and her first thought was to look down at Felix. He had relaxed his serious, upright, on-guard position, and was now nuzzled against her, his head resting against her leg, waiting for the caress that came his way whenever she remembered. He particularly liked having his hair stroked. It was long – too long for a boy, her father said, on the rare occasions when he commented on Felix, before he shrugged and said, what did it matter anyway? – silky and lovely to touch, and Nora, in the right mood, was as soothed by the activity as Felix. Now his face split open in a wide smile. Often he looked vacant – the lights were on but nobody was there, was one of her father's sayings for him – but not when he smiled. His position seemed awkward, but he could, if necessary, hold it for hours, indifferent to discomfort if his need for contact was satisfied.

Is this what was meant by playing with babies? She thought not, from what she had seen of her classmates when they joined their younger brothers and sisters after school. She suspected that none of them would be able to play – if playing it was – with Felix as she did; nor would she ever attempt to explain to a contemporary what it felt like to be with Felix. She knitted her brows in concentration as she tried to muster an answer, but her mother relieved her of the burden.

'We've enough to do in this house without extra children running about. Felix keeps me on the go all day.' Bernie sounded defiant, as she always did when asserting herself. She was quite clear in her own mind that Felix was an intolerable burden, and that already more was required of her than should ever be asked of any human being. At the same time, she had spent her life measuring herself against other people's expectations of her, and in her dealings with those professionally interested in Felix was always reacting against real or implied criticism.

'It must be very tiring for you.' Theresa Kennedy's tone was studiedly sympathetic. 'In fact, I'm probably keeping you now from things you have to do. I'll leave these with you.' As she spoke, she patted a set of ring-bound Xeroxed papers. 'Don't, for heaven's sake, see it as another obligation, but as a way of having some fun with Felix if you've five minutes to spare. You might find that it's time well spent. Once the exercises start to work, Felix should get easier. He'll certainly benefit from the stimulation, and some mothers report fewer bronchial infections. You were saying he's very troubled by those over the winter.'

Bernie nodded slowly as she stared at the programme of exercises. 'It will give us something to do, won't it, Felix?' she said brightly, having made a sudden decision to repair the afternoon by acting out the part she assumed had been assigned to her.

After Theresa Kennedy left there was an ominous silence. Nora had taken it for granted that there would be an outburst from Bernie once she felt free to express her feelings, and could pretty much predict the substance of that outburst: that nobody understood what she was going through, the intolerable strain that she alone was experiencing; that it didn't matter how often she said this because nobody ever listened; that it was like being in prison, serving a life sentence for a crime she hadn't committed. Because, when it came down to it, what had she done to deserve this particular fate? Though there were those, she was sure, who rejoiced in her misfortune but were two-faced and couldn't come out and say what they really felt, so would insinuate that this was a judgement on her, and would ask each other what she might have done that God in his wisdom and justice had seen fit to punish her in this way. And what had she done? Nothing, except always to do her duty as she saw it, but because she'd been lucky in the past nobody would give her the credit for it. Her own sisters, she was sure, were rejoicing, which was why she'd refused their offers to help. They didn't want to help but to gloat.

These were familiar refrains, likely on this occasion to be sharpened by Bernie's vituperative contempt for every-body in authority. For the awe that appeared to silence her in the presence of doctors, social workers and priests was, as she liked to explain after encounters like the one that had just ended, really contempt. If she told them what she really thought they wouldn't be able to take it, they would say she was mad and would probably get away with it because people like that were always believed over somebody like her.

When it came to it, however, none of this was forth-coming. Instead of resuming her seat after showing Theresa Kennedy the door and venting her feelings on Nora, she busied herself about the kitchen, clearing the tea-things and the accumulated debris of the day and peeling the potatoes for Gerald's dinner. Nora entertained a faint hope that maybe, even though her mother was angry now, some of what Theresa Kennedy had said might have struck home. Undoubtedly Bernie would have felt shame at the state of the house, would have wished to present herself to greater advantage. And maybe it was beginning to occur to her that it might be possible, with a little effort, to make things better.

Nora had a stubborn but unspoken belief that Felix was

capable of more than her parents thought possible. Because she found everything so easy, she hadn't yet understood the depth and scale of Felix's disabilities, and every landmark that he managed to pass fuelled her hope. He had, after all, learned to walk. He could say a few words, if not very clearly. He liked to curl up with her on the sofa while she read him some of her old baby books and would point to the picture while she said the word. Once she had found him with a book open on the floor at the picture of a little pink pig. To her amazement, he was trying to cover the pig with his own bare foot, almost to see whether it fitted. She sat with him and pondered over his actions, until enlightenment came. She sometimes played 'This little piggy' with his toes. When she thought about it, his fat little pink foot did bear a curious resemblance to the pig in the picture, which was curled up and sleeping. There must be something going on in his head for him to have made that connection. She had told Felix what a clever boy he was, and his face had lit up with pleasure.

She was eager to see what was in the funny, homemade book that Theresa Kennedy had brought, but something in her mother's manner warned her that this would be a bad move. Bernie was usually indifferent to Nora's efforts with Felix, but it was unsettling that she hadn't said a word since the woman had left, when she might have been expected to ask for her help in getting the kitchen straight. More worrying still, she had kept her back to her daughter, as if she, too, merited her anger. It was best, under the circumstances, to keep out of her way. She thought of going off with Felix to watch television, then had a better idea. She would bath him, and her mother's relief at having one task performed – albeit one that Bernie often skipped – would allay whatever misdemeanour she was suspected of.

112

After his bath, she took Felix into the lounge to watch the television. She was hungry, having missed out on her real tea – fish fingers, maybe, or sausages – because of Theresa Kennedy's visit. If she waited until her father came home, her mother might be minded to feed her and Felix.

Before Felix was born, Gerald had insisted, as far as possible, on family meals, having weaned his wife from her own family's practice of feeding the man, the breadwinner, as soon as he walked through the door, while the rest of the family ate whatever was available when it suited. Since Felix's birth, however, Bernie had reverted to that older tradition, but perhaps for different reasons. She had fallen into the habit of snacking all day, scarcely knowing any more what was and wasn't a meal, feeding Felix with Nora when she came home from school and Gerald later, as he arrived home. This created the impression of a household under siege, with Bernie chained to a succession of chores that never came to an end. And Gerald had offered no protest. He avoided his son whenever possible, and was relieved to be able to eat his dinner without having to look at him.

Hearing the door as her father came home, Nora waited a few minutes before she crept along to the kitchen, leaving Felix sucking his thumb in front of the television. Gerald was seated at the table reading a newspaper while he waited for Bernie to dish up his dinner. In the past he had read newspapers like the *Irish Times*, the London *Times* or the *Guardian*, but for a few years now he had been taking the tabloids, the *Daily Mail* in particular. His excuse was pressure of time. Although he took no part in the care of Felix, he, like Bernie, though with less justification, had the manner of someone with more to do than could possibly be accomplished. His frequent air of preoccupation hinted at claims on his mind and time that were beyond the understanding of his family so not worth the effort of explaining.

The likelier explanation for his choice of newspaper, however, was that he found the *Mail* more emotionally satisfying. On a number of issues – the threat posed by immigration or crime, for example – he was in agreement with the editorial line. Nor did he allow the irrelevance to his own life – immigration into Ulster and crimes other than the terrorist variety were inconsiderable – to prevent him feeling personally threatened. In other moods, when he was prepared to acknowledge the difference, it served to reinforce his sense of the moral degeneracy of the English, which had become one of his favourite topics. And where he disagreed with the *Mail*, as he did in its support for the Thatcher government and the continued colonial oppression of Ulster Catholics by that government, he enjoyed the greater satisfaction of venting his anger against the newspaper itself.

Catching sight of his daughter, he raised an eyebrow at her and said, 'Well?'

'Good evening, Daddy.'

'Good evening, Nora,' he said, before returning to the solace of the inflammatory printed word. In recent years, he had become punctilious about minor points of civility. Unlike Bernie, he was not allowing his standards to slip, however great the temptation to fall into the abyss. He would at least ensure that his daughter had good manners.

In that brief interlude from the newspaper, however, he had spotted something else – a half-full bottle of antibiotics, its cap unscrewed but resting at an angle on the neck of the bottle, which had been prescribed for Felix and was now sitting on the kitchen counter. Since birth Felix had suffered from almost continuous chest infections over the damp winter months, so that Gerald, in his more darkly humorous moods, could claim that his son was his best customer.

'How often do I have to tell you, Bernie, that this stuff has to be refrigerated?' Very deliberately, he laid his newspaper to one side, secured the cap tightly on the bottle and placed it in the door of the fridge, then resumed his place. The fact that he had had to do it himself was serious and sufficient rebuke. His lips were sealed, but his thick eyebrows were knitted with indignation.

This gave Bernie the opening for which she had been waiting. 'That's all I need,' she said, 'for my own family to turn against me. I should expect it by now from the social services, but you and that wee girl there should know better.'

Reluctantly, Gerald put aside his newspaper. 'What in heaven's name are you talking about?'

'I've had a woman here this afternoon, sent by Dr Murphy, if you please. He should be ashamed of himself, with the number of times I've had to take the boy to him these last few months.'

'What did she say?' Gerald, though less affected, was no more eager than his wife to be visited by the social services. In a small town gossip travels fast.

'Oh, well, you know the type, smiling sweetly while she put the boot in. She thinks – let me see, how did she put it? – that Felix would "benefit from a programme of exercises".'

Since this wasn't as bad as he had feared, Gerald allowed a small smile to play about his lips. 'You mean a bit of square-bashing? She wants to see the boy in vest and shorts doing press-ups and touching his toes? Well, that would be a sight for all of us, right enough. Maybe we could charge people to look in here for the floorshow. There's precious little other entertainment to be had from him.'

Gerald's refusal to take her distress seriously made her even angrier, but she was habitually more inhibited in using him as a target for her feelings than she was Nora. 'Oh, I haven't told you the worst. She starts sucking up to Nora, asking her about school and that, and Nora, of course, thinks nothing of showing me up.' For the first time since Theresa Kennedy had left the house, Bernie confronted her daughter, her face ablaze with indignation.

'Is this true, Nora?' asked Gerald, his tone severe. Deliberately, he folded his newspaper and put it aside to indicate the seriousness of the accusation.

Nora had picked up an atmosphere in Bernie's manner towards her, and sudden shifts in mood from sulkiness to outright hostility were not uncommon, usually provoked by minor domestic issues that featured in Bernie's recurrent litany of complaint. But she had been so careful to exercise restraint in the presence of Theresa Kennedy, and to ignore as far as possible her friendly overtures, that she was stunned by her mother's malice towards her. She went very still, and could only shake her head while her eyes filled with tears.

'Oh, she's a sly one,' said Bernie, elaborating on her theme. 'She was all over the boy, quite the little mother, so that this woman ends up thinking that Nora there is the one bringing him up. "We can see who his favourite person is," she says, as though I'm no more than a speck of dirt, of no account in this house whatsoever.'

Gerald, who was well aware of Felix's obsessive affection for his sister, which he couldn't have borne himself, saw no point in outraging Bernie further. He neglected his wife, but only challenged the distorted perceptions to which misery made her susceptible when they directly affected him. In this way he preserved his sense of himself as a long-suffering husband. 'You indulge the boy too much, Nora,' he said. 'It makes it impossible for your mother to control him.'

This wasn't enough for Bernie who, after her treatment by Theresa Kennedy, could only be mollified by statements of unswerving loyalty and assertions of her unparalleled level of suffering. 'Oh, but you haven't heard the worst of it yet. Your woman was petting her, and there was Nora, lapping it up, all smiles and sweetness, when I can never get a word out of her. Quite the little martyr, she was.' And then, turning to Nora, she said, 'Do you want to tell your Daddy what you said to her?'

Nora felt cold with fear. She couldn't remember saying anything to Theresa Kennedy, except that school was 'nice', and it seemed unlikely that even her mother could hold that against her. If her mother was going to make things up, so that her only defence was to accuse her of lying, her situation was truly desperate.

'You don't want him to know, do you?' Bernie was now in full flow, her cheeks burning, her breath coming fast, entirely absorbed in the expression of her own indignation. 'It doesn't matter what you do to me, but you want to keep your father's good opinion.' She paused for a moment, as if trying to remember Nora's incriminating words with absolute precision. 'She said that she wasn't allowed to bring friends home to play because of the boy.'

It was as though the ground had opened under Nora's feet and she were falling very fast into a deep, deep, bottomless hole. She felt sick and wasn't sure that she would be able to contain it.

'Is this true, Nora?' When Gerald had asked this question in response to Bernie's first accusation, he had had the air of a man going through the motions to placate a troublesome wife, but now he was in earnest. It was true that Nora had been discouraged by both her parents from bringing friends to the house, but this was never openly acknowledged to be the case. That this might have been exposed before strangers was a powerful threat to Gerald's carefully maintained public persona.

'I didn't,' said Nora. 'I didn't say that.'

'As good as,' said Bernie. 'You know very well what you were playing at.'

There was no need for her to say more for Gerald was now fully engaged. His face was flushed with anger and his voice harsh, and as he spoke, each syllable sounded like a hammer blow. 'Has anybody in this house ever, ever said such a thing to you?' Repeated stabs with his right index finger accompanied his words.

'No, but—'

'Don't "but" me, madam. I never want to hear anything of this sort again. Now, away to bed with you.'

Nora lay trembling on her bed for what seemed like hours, unable to separate physical sensations of hunger, nausea and shock from the sheer misery inflicted by her parents. She heard the sounds of Felix being put to bed, followed by her mother banging around in the kitchen and, from the lounge, the sound of the nine o'clock news. Then her mother appeared in the doorway. 'You'd better come and have something to eat, otherwise you'll be telling all who listen that I don't feed you.'

She followed Bernie into the kitchen, where her favourite meal was waiting for her – a couple of slices of nice thick ham, a sliced tomato and a piece of buttered soda bread. She judged from this that she was forgiven or, alternatively, that this was the closest her mother would come to an expression of remorse. Certainly, Bernie's anger had subsided, and while her daughter ate, she sat with her at the table, turning over the pages of the newspaper that Gerald had been reading earlier.

They were still there, both relieved that some kind of truce had been established, in a silence that passed for companionable, when Gerald burst into the room. He looked hectic, a reliable sign for his family that he was moved and excited by the only thing that could still engage his emotions.

'Do you know what those bastards have done now?' After a short pause when, as might have been predicted, neither his wife nor his daughter was able to answer his question, he said, 'They've imposed a broadcasting ban on Sinn Féin.'

'What does that mean, exactly?' asked Bernie. She wasn't much interested, but politics – or Gerald's need for an audience on political issues – guaranteed, if not his attention, then something approaching an extended conversation.

'Good point. What does it mean? It means they'll be able to make a fool of Gerry Adams, and the whole nationalist cause, by having him mouthing away silently on television while some actor speaks his words. An actor, if you please. They'll probably find some English boyo with a fake Irish accent, rather than give the job to an Irishman.' In the pause he required to draw breath, he paced up and down, looking, to Nora's eyes, particularly massive and looming in the small space available to him. 'That's what we've always been for the English – clowns and court jesters. Every Irishman a stage Irishman.'

His enjoyment of his own anger was clear. At one time he had prided himself on his scientific objectivity, on the education and intelligence that enabled him to grasp the complexities of the Irish situation, and established his superiority to his more simple-minded nationalist customers and fellow traders. Since Felix's birth, however, he had increasingly sought refuge in the victim status enjoyed by Northern Irish Catholics. He had taken care to create as much distance from Felix as possible within the family, and to avoid all mention of him to outsiders, but his sense of outrage remained. Having no one else to blame, he had fallen back on tribal loyalties and traditional enemies.

'I hope you're marking this, Nora,' he said. 'It's a lesson you can't learn too early in life.'

Nora had little idea of what he was talking about, but welcomed his abrupt change in manner towards her. She was always hoping that there might be a return to the kind of relationship she had had with her father before Felix's birth. Since then, as helper, as occasional confidante, as sharer of Gerald's neglect, she had been thrown more and more on the company of her mother, but the events of that evening had left a residue of mistrust, despite Bernie's clumsy efforts to make amends. Her mother had not only told a bare-faced lie but one that had made her, Nora, guilty of something she had not done. There seemed little point in trying to please her when, with no warning, she could find herself blamed for something of which she was innocent. Nora had been more frightened by her father's anger than by her mother's, but he had had the excuse of being misled.

It seemed to her that if Felix could be improved, could be brought to resemble a normal boy, then her father might revert to what he had been before his son's birth. And if she were the one responsible for the transformation of

Felix, then her father's former pride in her might return. After waiting for an opportunity, and taking care to do it unobserved, she rescued the book of exercises that had been left by Theresa Kennedy from the corner of the kitchen where it had been abandoned to gather food stains, and took it off to her bedroom to study its contents. It was mostly a series of line drawings of a mother and baby, both apparently laughing with joy and intensely focused on each other. The source of the delirium, it seemed, apart from the manifestly powerful bond between them, was the pleasure derived from the exercises shown in the draw-ings. In some, the baby, holding both of his mother's hands, was being pulled from a reclining into sitting or standing positions, while others showed more detailed work on arms and legs of a bending and stretching nature.

There was no problem for Nora in experimenting on Felix without her mother's knowledge. Bernie was only too happy for Nora to take him off to play in her room; and once she had memorised the sequences, Nora was able to run him through the programme without the book. What for Nora was a serious project could easily be passed off as horseplay if her mother should chance to come in, especially since the exercises and her lie to Gerald had passed for Bernie into oblivion. Only a general sense of grievance remained from the afternoon when Theresa Kennedy had paid a visit, which had merged effortlessly with the other grievances she nurtured.

More difficult initially were the exercises. Felix was now considerably larger than the baby in the drawings, and Nora much smaller than the mother. None the less, with practice and ingenuity, she was soon able to achieve with Felix something approximating to the images in the book.

And there was, if not a transformation, then a

perceptible improvement in Felix. Since he was older than
the exemplary baby, and already walking, it was difficult
for Nora to measure physical development, although she
noticed that his grip became stronger and his movements
more purposeful. There were subtler changes, however.
Where he had laughed helplessly at the beginning of every
session, in time he caught some of Nora's concentration
and determination. He would frown with effort as they
went through the process, reserving his laughter for the
end, when Nora heaped him with praise and clapped with
approval. He enjoyed himself so much that, when they
reached the end, he wanted to begin all over again, until
Nora added a little routine of her own. With her encouragement Felix, on the completion of his exercises, stood
up straight, like a soldier, then marched round the room,
with his head and chin held high and arms swinging at
his sides. She realised that, although these movements had
no meaning for him – she had shown him, to no effect,
pictures of soldiers in children's books – he was quick to
imitate her. Always eager for her attention, he was encouraged by her to feel a sense of pride in his own achievements, and she began to wonder whether there was
something else they might move on to.

It was at this point that she decided to involve her father.
He couldn't fail to be impressed by Felix, and grateful to
her, and while she knew that he was unlikely to involve
himself in a programme to encourage Felix's development,
he might take a benign interest. As the moment
approached, she became excited by the prospect, once
again, of showing herself capable of something that would
amaze and delight her father. Then she would occupy the
place in his life that she had before Felix's birth. And if
he could be brought to see that Felix might eventually,

with effort on their part, catch up with other boys, he might return to something resembling his old self.

It was a while before the right opportunity presented itself, since it was almost unknown for her father to be at home with Felix while her mother was out. In the event, opportunity came as an indirect consequence of Theresa Kennedy's visit. Bernie had resented the air of distinction and superiority conferred on her by faultless grooming. For the first time since Felix's birth, Bernie became aware that her teeth and hair were untended, that she no longer had any usable makeup and that she would need new shoes before she could even present herself to a dentist or hairdresser. Feeling both pitiable and neglected, she had shamed Gerald into staying at home with Felix one Saturday while she went to Belfast to repair some of the damage. His consent was conditional on Nora being around to keep her brother out of his way.

Nora approached him in the lounge as soon as her mother had left and before the rugby started.

'What is it?' he asked, turning back to the television as soon as he had registered her presence.

'I want to show you something.'

'Well, here I am, show me.'

'Not here, in my bedroom.'

'Can't it wait?'

'Please, Daddy, it won't take long.'

Gerald sighed heavily as he got to his feet. When he reached her room, he was immediately faced by Felix, dressed in the T-shirt and shorts she had found for him, standing straight-backed and frowning at the foot of Nora's bed.

'What is this?' Appalled, as usual, to be reminded of Felix's existence, he turned to go, but Nora pleaded with him.

'Please, Daddy, wait till we show you.'

He stood impassively by the door while they went through their routine, with Felix first on the floor, being pulled and manipulated by Nora, then marching round the room. When Felix was finished, Gerald seemed at a loss for words.

'Whose idea was this?'

'Mine,' said Nora, proudly.

'All yours? Where did you get the idea from?'

'The book that the social worker brought. The exercises.'

'You're wasting your time.'

'But—'

'Did you hear what I said? You're wasting your time. If you want to do something useful, then find a way of helping your mother.'

At the mention of her mother, Nora suddenly became frightened, remembering the day when Theresa Kennedy had brought the book into the house. 'You won't tell her, what I've been doing?'

'I'd rather forget it myself, to tell you the truth. I've never seen such an exhibition. I won't tell her if you promise to put an end to it.'

Nora nodded and, when he left, threw herself onto the bed. Felix soon joined her, hoping they might begin again. 'More, more, 'Ora,' he said, as he tugged at her hand.

'Not now,' she said, and rolled away from him, into her pillow.

PART THREE

Rituals and Meaning

London

As the autumn advances, Steve continues to brood on failure. Although he's had the odd setback in his career before, his frustrated bid for television stardom has assumed the status of the first real assault on his ambition, the first time when something he fervently desired has not been granted him. His fear is that it marks the beginning of a slow decline, when he will have ceased expecting anything for himself, and will begin to live through the achievements of Jessica and Emily. Proud though he is of them, he has a horror of droning on about them at dinner parties because he has nothing else to talk about.

He is in that state of mind where everything reminds him of his loss, even the season. After decades of conditioning, in which autumn, as the beginning of the academic year, had brought with it a sense of challenge and personal renewal, this year for the first time he finds in the falling leaves and dark evenings intimations of his own slide into anonymity and, sooner or later, death.

This particular evening, like an old man with nothing much to look forward to, he is allowing the weather to get him down and encourage a sense of physical discomfort. Rain is falling steadily, dulling the light from the street-lamps, turning the fallen leaves into a soggy, slippery mess, insinuating itself into his boots and into the gap between his collar and neck. He's feeling uncharacteristically sorry for himself, a condition he's always despised in others as a sign of weakness and failure.

Surrender to natural process is certainly tempting, but must be strenuously resisted. He woke to rain and, feeling bored already by the prospect of the day ahead, treated himself to a taxi, rather than struggling with the weather on his bike. He regretted the indulgence as soon as he had given in to it, and as he peered gloomily through the window at young joggers leaving the park, seemingly indifferent to the rain, he decided that he would impose on himself the discipline of walking home. After his shower this morning he had noticed an incipient paunch, and since he is no less complacent about seeing his body degenerate into middle age than to have his career stall or find that the brightest of his Ph.D. students now have sharper minds than his, the decision allowed him to feel he had the problem in hand.

His working day, however, was a reminder of everything he is trying to escape. The meeting that swallowed up most of the afternoon was dire. The triviality and over-familiarity of the agenda, the self-satisfied preening of his colleagues, the jockeying for position and petty intrigues, all combined to trouble him with a sense of utter pointlessness. For he is not, in the management jargon that is currently fashionable in universities, a natural team player. As a schoolboy, it was the one persistent criticism ever made of his conduct and behaviour, and he gloried in it. He has always been a star turn, a performer, the subversive who is so brilliant that he has to be accommodated within the system. But if his star quality begins to wane, the system will be all that's left. He's not sure that he will be able to bear it.

Trudging through a warren of streets north of the Marylebone Road, he thinks of his namesake, Stephen Dedalus, one of Joyce's *alter ego*s. He has always been secretly pleased to share his name and, although such a posture violates the principles of his teaching and writing, has identified with him – with his solitude, his questioning mind, his intolerance of authority. And, it has to be said, with his youth, his belief in his own genius and the brilliant future career that is implicit in the novel. It's as though he's never acknowledged that he's grown up and become Bloom, who is closer to his own age and, like Steve, is Jewish, a loving husband and father, a decent man.

The thought of Bloom inevitably brings Nora Doyle into sharp focus, although in truth she has scarcely been out of his mind, and tomorrow night she will be coming to dinner. Thinking of Nora – his Nora, and Joyce's Nora, the model for Bloom's wife, Molly, whom Joyce met on the June day in 1904 that is commemorated in *Ulysses* – Steve wonders whether he can still claim for himself the decency that characterises Bloom and makes him a twentieth-century hero.

All of Steve's affairs until now – not that he has decided to have an affair with Nora, of course, and hopes that he won't almost as much as he hopes that he will – have been with women, not girls. Increasingly, as he has got older, with women younger than himself, but still, women in their thirties, with established lives and careers of their own, women who understand the rules of the game. Would it be possible to give in to his own impulses, and still behave well by Nora, and by Martha and his daughters? He thinks again of *Ulysses*, where Joyce creates two versions of himself – Stephen as a young man, the same age that Joyce was in 1904, and Bloom the middle-aged husband and father, like Joyce when he was writing *Ulysses*. Perhaps he can combine both, Steve thinks, before rejecting the notion as a piece of casuistry. If, as he tells his students, you can't look to fiction for a naïve and transparent reflection of reality, then you certainly can't impose on your life the shape and meaning of a novel.

And yet . . . and yet . . . the ability to impose meaning is in some sense the key to living successfully. With that thought, Steve's mind drifts from Joyce to Beckett, his disciple and fellow Irishman, whose work expresses his present mood in a way that Joyce's doesn't, for all the similarities in character and circumstance, real or imagined, between himself and Joyce's creations. No one in the near-dying twentieth century, he thinks, has had a greater sense of the futility of life than Beckett, or summoned up such enduring images of that futility as Beckett has given the world: tramps waiting by a road going nowhere for someone who will never come; Murphy's game of chess with a madman; Moran's obsessive insistence on the rituals of a bourgeois family life; Molloy's description of sexual congress as 'a mug's game', and the other game that he plays, with considerably more relish, of keeping sixteen stones in circulation between his pockets and his mouth, where each stone is lovingly sucked. Are these pathologies, or appropriate responses to the human condition?

Steve thinks back to the meeting he has just attended, and wonders whether sucking stones might not be a more pleasurable – even, more meaningful – way to pass the time. Except, of course, that the one activity confers some kind of status in the world, while the other marks you out as a marginal character. And status matters to Steve. Part of his dissatisfaction with the meeting, as he now forces himself to confront, is the niggling anxiety that his own status may be in the process of slipping away from him. The forthcoming Gender and Ethnicity Conference was discussed and, unable to delay a decision any longer, he made it clear that he would not be taking part.

He sees again the curious eyes of his colleagues trained on him, waiting for the announcement – for word unfortunately gets round, despite one's own best efforts – that his time would be limited, that he had received an offer from a television company that couldn't be refused – and remembers his own wholly uncharacteristic confusion. Instead there was only the lame excuse of his book on Joyce, the kind of commitment that all his colleagues can claim, in one way or another, and which, in the past, would never have prevented him taking on more work. The worst of it was that Rowe, who had seemed so cast down by his earlier equivocation, allowed himself a satisfied smirk, as if to say, it comes to all of us, the disappointments, the growing weariness, the inescapable knowing that one's career has peaked. Only the constraints imposed by the occasion prevented Steve shouting, 'It's not what you think! It's not that I'm not up to it, it's just that I'm so fucking bored by the whole thing.'

He thinks again of Beckett and wonders whether status meant much to him; whether the Nobel Prize and the almost idolatrous affection he inspired in so many mattered to him, and gave him solace in his existential isolation. Then Steve has another, rather cheering thought. Beckett was a late starter, only beginning to get into his stride and win recognition at the age that he, Steve, is now. Just because, unlike Beckett, he has enjoyed one moment of fame, doesn't mean he can't go on to a second that eclipses the first. It isn't over until it's over. Or, in the words that close *The Unnameable*, 'I can't go on, I'll go on.'

He feels encouraged by remembering something that applies so directly to his own situation and strides along with a new sense of purpose, glad now that he had the self-discipline to choose a penitential walk on such a rotten day, and that the walk is nearly over. If nothing else, he's achieved that today, and in the course of the walk pondered the central mystery of Beckett's work: that he is at once the most depressing and the most inspiring of writers. Nobody saw with greater clarity that life in a godless universe has no inherent meaning, but that the craving for meaning, which makes us human, must none the less be satisfied. So we invent goals and strategies to fill the void, structure our lives around routines, which acquire the status of significant rituals. Beckett was a cricketer and chess player, after all, and enjoyed the oldest of all rituals, the wooing and winning of women, throughout his life.

By the time Steve reaches his front door, he has, with the help of Beckett, completely reversed the mood in which he left the English department. Life has to be lived, and it might as well be lived in the most enjoyable and meaningful way that can be managed, even if meaning is largely invented and pleasure is fleeting. Nora will not threaten but enhance his family life by sharpening his awareness of its distinctive qualities. The risk element, he tells himself, is largely an acknowledgement of convention and, in its way, not unwelcome as part of the game. Working out how it can be made to work will restore his zest, give him a goal. And it seems to Steve, as he turns the key in the lock and prepares to greet his family, that Nora is not only a good in herself, and worthy of pursuit, but will help him to overcome the sense of dryness and sterility that is infecting his work.

*   *   *

That same evening finds Nora in Covent Garden, scouring the shops to find something to wear for dinner with Steve's family. This is for her an almost unprecedented indulgence. Her budget is so tight that spending even small sums of money on what isn't strictly necessary has been ruled out, but the extraordinary nature of the occasion seems to demand extraordinary behaviour. When she tries to imagine what it will be like, she recoils from the idea of turning up in something from a charity shop or in some of the surplus created by Phoebe's random shopping habits.

This little expedition, unremarkable as it would be for anyone else of her age, is also a deliberate attempt to break free from some of the constraints that have become habitual to her. She sees that it isn't just her secretiveness that inhibits her but the habit of keeping herself apart, which was established long before her arrival in London. For years, it seems, she'd been saving herself up for her real life to begin, only to find, when it was scheduled to start, that she didn't know how to live.

The friends she has made – Phoebe, Nick, Pete – have all grown up with a sense of freedom, of not having to test their behaviour against hostile judgements, of the world around them as theirs to enjoy. She, by contrast, since she's been in London, has had to be alert and on guard, not just to avoid exposure or financial disaster but to stop herself falling apart when there was nothing to support her. In the context of her own austerity, London has seemed to her a place of excess, dedicated to pleasures that she hasn't known how to enjoy. As she tentatively launches herself into a new phase of her life here, she tries out a word for the self she's trying to shed: 'puritanical'. With its associations of Protestantism and Oliver Cromwell, she wouldn't have used it at home.

Now, with a sense of exhilaration that's new to her, she picks over racks of clothes and enjoys her own reflection as she tries them on, treating the occasion as a rite of passage. For the first time, she's behaving like any other girl of her age, although she cannot abandon her habitual caution altogether. Despite the rain, this is just a preliminary search of all the likely shops; whatever she buys she must be able to wear again. And when she projects herself, in whatever new outfit, into the future, the figure of Nick, who has remained attentive but seems to be waiting for a sign from her, is always hovering, not doing anything in particular but just somehow there.

She is still frightened by the prospect of parting with money that has been accumulated with some effort, and while she considers what she's seen and what she will buy, she finds herself a table in the Seattle Coffee Company's space in the Neal Street Warehouse, where she settles down with a caffè latte.

Although she is alone, and all the surrounding tables are occupied by pairs, or noisy groups, of mostly young people, she feels at ease with herself and in her own company. This isn't so much the anonymity of the circumstances – something she welcomed when she first arrived in London – but because she is experiencing a new sensation of belonging. In some way that she can't immediately identify, this seems to be linked with Steve's invitation. Then she realises that what he has given her is a kind of recognition. This has nothing to do with his being impressed by her work, because there are other students – Nick, for example – who are at least as impressive but haven't been singled out in the same way. And by including her in a family occasion, he has dispelled those doubts (which she refused to share with Phoebe and the others) about his motives.

At the same time, it's a gesture that seems to go beyond simple liking, of a kind that he might feel for any of them. She feels that, with an empathy she didn't suspect in him before, he has responded to her situation as nobody else in London has: that he has sensed both her isolation and her desolation; her need, not for somebody to replace her father – she realises that that would be asking for too much – but for a concerned, older person in her life. She's not so foolish as to think, as Phoebe might in similar circumstances, that in some mystical way he knows her story without being told, but she cherishes the hope that he might understand enough to relieve her of some of the burden of telling, so that what she has feared as an ordeal might be easy and natural. And once that burden is gone, she will be released into a new spontaneity with her friends, especially Nick; will no longer bear an undeserved reputation for coldness and caution. And then she will no longer feel, as she has since coming to London, that she is going through the motions of a life that doesn't really belong to her.

This prospect has given her a new insight into this frightening city, where she has sometimes suspected that the inhabitants – even her friends – speak in a code she hasn't yet learned to interpret. Every conceivable ethnic background seems to be represented at the tables around her, and she wonders which of this noisy, animated crowd 'belongs' in London, in the sense that her father belongs in Ballypierce, the place where he was born and brought up and to which he returned after his studies. But is her father's example much of an argument for the virtues of belonging, when all that it seems to have done for him is harden his self-righteousness and bigotry? London is a city of outsiders, or incomers, and authenticity is measured and judged differently from the way it is in Ireland. It's up to her to make herself a Londoner. If she feels one, she is one. That's all it takes, but what an insurmountable hurdle it has seemed.

She finishes her coffee and buttons up her coat as she prepares to make her way back to Jigsaw and French Connection where, with a recklessness that now seems appropriate, she will buy the silky red skirt and the tight black top, the most glamorous, least serviceable, of the clothes she tried on. Part of being a Londoner is to be a consumer, a hedonist, a risk-taker and, with a steely resolve, she leaves the building to take her rightful and ordained place in the city.

'So he said, this boy' – Jessica lingers just perceptibly over 'boy' in ironic acknowledgement that, while she regards this unnamed person as her junior in opinions and powers of analysis, he is her equal in years – 'that he couldn't see the point of the play. And remember, this is *The Winter's Tale* he's talking about.'

Nora, who arrived at the Woolfs' house twenty minutes ago, is perched on the edge of an armchair, nervously clutching a wine glass, while Jessica describes a seminar she attended that afternoon for members of her A-level English group (at a girls' comprehensive) with boys from a nearby school. Jessica's thoughts on *The Winter's Tale* are well within the scope of a clever, well-taught A-level student, but the polish and accomplishment of her delivery are astonishing. She is a girl who is used to having her opinions taken seriously. Her sense of entitlement was clear from the beginning, when there was no question of her cutting short a performance that was already under way in deference to her parents' guest.

Far from being offended, Nora is pleased not to have

the spotlight turned on her. Since nothing is known about her, she was dreading a barrage of questions, but Jessica's monologue leaves her free to absorb the details of the room and its inhabitants. This first-floor sitting room is lit entirely by lamps – at home there were only bright, central lights – and Nora, having chosen by pure chance a seat in relative gloom, can observe without coming under too much scrutiny herself. She was expecting something outside her previous experience, but what she has found is beyond anything she could have imagined.

Initially she found herself unable to take her eyes off Steve, whose attention is entirely Jessica's. Steve at home, surrounded by his family, is a revelation, difficult to reconcile with his professional self. Even his face seems different, softer and gentler, as he responds with smiles, nods, at one moment an ironic upward turn of his eyes, to everything his daughter says. She has a feeling of acute loss as she thinks that she has never seen a father take more pleasure in his daughter. It isn't just his transparent love for her, but his willingness to allow her own sense of who she is, her own thoughts, her own place in the world. She feels that she is party to a special kind of intimacy and vows that never, under any circumstances, will she talk about this to any of her friends.

Jessica is sitting on a rug in front of the fire – a real fire, Nora notes, remembering her mother speak of the drudgery of life in her parents' home before central heating – a position that gives her command of the entire room although most of her comments seem directed at her father. Since she has no need to seek his attention, Nora speculates that this might be for her benefit, so that she will be left in no doubt that, however she stands as Steve's student, Jessica is the favoured daughter of the household.

She lets her eyes stray round the room, and although she has almost no basis of comparison – she rarely paid visits in Ireland, and in London has seen only Phoebe's house – she knows that this room is special and reflects a way of living that she's never directly encountered, although she's had intimations of it from novels.

There is no television. Instead, the activities for which the room seems designed are indicated in the many books, stored from floor to ceiling in shelved alcoves; in the positioning of chairs, sofas and lamps, for conversation; and at the other end of the room from the sitting area, in the piano, music stand and clarinet, resting on an open case. Half-remembered phrases from novels – Henry James's, perhaps? – about living beautifully, significantly, spring to mind.

The room is richly textured, with many pictures on walls and rugs on polished floors, photographs and pieces of china on tables, but it isn't opulent. Curtains and rugs are faded and even in the dim light it occurs to her that a family more concerned for appearances might consider reupholstering the chairs. But everything is beautiful. She realises that she wouldn't know where to buy anything she can see, so removed is it from the world of the department store or the boutique. She toys with the idea that there are places, known only to those with the gift of living well, where such things may be acquired.

Meanwhile, Jessica continues with the anecdote that is also an exposition of *The Winter's Tale*. 'He said that the play isn't about anything,' Jessica continues. 'That it has no overarching theme, that it's all about process – you're born, you enjoy your youth, but it passes, you have children, you make mistakes, you regret what you've done and then, if you're lucky, you get to live through your children.'

'Not a bad description, I should have thought,' Steve

says, amused by her outrage and not disinclined to goad her further. 'I don't think I'd be too hard on him, if he were one of my students. But what did you say, Jess? I sense that this narrative isn't yet complete, that a killer blow is about to be delivered.'

'You can bet on that,' says Emily, from the sofa, where she sits in a heap, leaning against her mother. 'We wouldn't be hearing this story at all if Jess didn't have the last word.' Because Emily and Martha are so placed that Nora hasn't been able to look at them unobserved, Emily's intervention allows her to satisfy her curiosity about them for the first time since she arrived.

Most evident is the contrast between the two girls. Jessica's poise is clear in the set of her head and neck, her rather stylised gestures and mannerisms, her clear, ringing voice, the ease with which she holds the floor. Although in some respects young for her age – she doesn't seem to Nora to have the adolescent need to distance herself from her parents but, then, with parents like these why would she? – her dress, of tailored black trousers and expensive sweater, gestures towards sophistication. Her sister, however, who is wearing a shapeless tracksuit and woolly slippers, looks as if she is trying to disappear into her mother. Nora judges her to be about fifteen, rather old to be so physically affectionate towards her mother, especially in company. She isn't as pretty as Jessica, but Nora finds her more appealing, and realises that her wide blue eyes and extraordinary openness of expression remind her of Felix.

It is Martha, however, a largely silent figure so far, who interests Nora most, as Steve's wife – like most of the Irish-literature class, she has found it difficult to picture him in a domestic setting until the revelation of this evening – and as the woman who presides over this enchanted place, beautiful both in person and character, respectful of each family member, and who inspires such open affection in her teenage daughter. Since she is doing nothing to draw attention to herself, however, Nora cannot observe her too closely without rudeness. As Jessica delivers her reply, Nora turns back to her.

'I said that that is precisely the point of the play, not a weakness but a glory. It isn't about personality, or action, or grand themes, but the lives of human beings within the natural cycle. Youth and age, loss of innocence, growing old, families.'

'Fathers and daughters.' This is the first time that Nora has spoken since introductions were made, the due civilities and pleasantries performed.

'Yes, of course, fathers and daughters,' says Jessica, rather sharply, as she turns to face Nora directly for the first time.

Nora is stung by the sharpness, not knowing that she is the first of Steve's students to enter the house and that speculation between the two sisters has been intense: Emily had suggested that at last their father has found a student cleverer than Jessica. She feels put in her place, as though she has claimed more than is due to her, and is embarrassed to feel tears spring to her eyes, as they so often have in the past when she's known she's done nothing to deserve a rebuke.

Steve steps in immediately to smooth things over, simultaneously flattering Jessica and rescuing Nora. 'As far as I'm concerned, the message of *The Winter's Tale* is that if you're a father your daughter will step in and redeem you in your old age. I have to say that I can't get over my luck in having two daughters on hand to perform this kindly office.'

There is a barely perceptible hesitation, as he turns briefly to Nora, wondering whether to bring her into the conversation by referring to her own status as daughter. Then, realising that he knows nothing at all about her family circumstances and might say something to cause embarrassment, he turns back to his older daughter. 'So, Jess, are you happy with the pattern of the human life-cycle, as laid bare for us in *The Winter's Tale*? That after a brief youth, life is downhill all the way until, as an aged parent, children step in and rescue you?'

'Oh, my feelings are beside the point. I was trying to establish what's there,' Jessica says airily. 'But since you ask, it doesn't seem real to me at the moment. I can see that that's the way it is but I hope I'll be exempt.'

'Don't we all?' says Steve. While the discussion of *The Winter's Tale* has continued, Martha and Emily have slipped out of the room. There is an awkward pause as the remaining three find themselves alone together, which Steve fills by topping up Nora's glass and his with white wine. Jessica is offered some, but refuses. Steve is barely settled back in his chair when Emily can be heard, calling from a lower floor that dinner is ready.

By the time they reach the basement, Nora has reasoned herself out of her sense of hurt. While it's unnecessary, it isn't surprising, she thinks, that Jessica should be so jealous of her father's attention. She has not so much a memory as a memory of a memory of a time when her father's pride in her was the most precious thing in her life. She must be careful not to take Jessica's snub too personally. What makes her resolve easier is the pleasant bustle in the kitchen as the final preparations for the meal are completed.

It is now clear to her that the Steve who teaches her, the public man, isn't the real Steve, even though he would reject the notion that any of the selves within a single identity is more real than another. Seeing him here, however, with his family – genial, teasing, attentive to the needs of everybody around him – she feels that the 'other' Steve is engaged in an elaborate, and perhaps necessary, professional game. Maybe it's just that some people are more at ease, more themselves in their families than in their professional lives. There was certainly some kind of split in her own father, but it was his family who saw the worst of him.

Not wishing to spoil the evening with thoughts of home, she applies herself to noticing everything, and thinks herself lucky to have been placed with her back to the window and a full view of the room. She is both inhabiting the moment, nervous but savouring her status as guest on this particular evening, and eager to take in the fullness of the Woolfs' family life, imagining other occasions, other times of day, groupings within and beyond the family.

The refectory table is enormous, and she sees it as the centre of their life together, the site of continuous conversation, both intimate and encompassing their many interests. The table is capable of seating more than twice the number there this evening. She wonders what it must be like when it's crammed with guests, drawn from the huge circle of family friends who often gather to enjoy the Woolfs' hospitality. In the candles, the highly polished wood and the jug of red tulips in the centre of the table she senses a distinct style, but one that's expressive of their collective personality with no reference to fashion. She regrets, with a kind of shame, the bunch of chrysanthemums she handed to Martha when she arrived. They have been placed in a tall vase on the dresser, but look stiff and awkward, neither dead nor alive, an affront to the taste and vitality of her hosts.

Although the style is informal, the process is ritualised, with each member of the family performing an allotted task. While Martha checks what's cooking in the oven, Jessica pours water from a bottle, Emily passes plates and Steve tosses a salad. They start with it, a mixture of mushrooms, different-coloured peppers and green leaves she doesn't recognise, but which certainly aren't lettuce. Emily, who is sitting opposite her on the other side of Steve, who has taken the father's traditional place at the head of the table, leans across and confides in her that this is one of Steve's specialities. 'The secret of success,' she says, in a tone that gently mocks her father, 'is for the mushrooms to be raw, the peppers roasted, the rocket absolutely fresh, and the dressing to be just the right proportions.'

Nora is touched by what she takes as a gesture of acceptance by Emily, admittance to some kind of inner circle. 'It's certainly delicious,' she says, feeling the words to be an inadequate measure of her feelings. And the food is delicious, quite unlike anything ever served in her family, or by the Metcalfes, who assemble their meals with rare items only obtainable in the latest delicatessen. It lacks the element of display that both the Metcalfes, and her parents, in that distant past, remembered or fantasised by her mother, when dinner parties were a feature of their lives, would consider appropriate for entertaining. The Woolfs, she thinks, don't need special ingredients or elaborate recipes; every meal here would be an occasion.

'Proportions of what?' she asks.

'You'll have to ask him yourself, to see if you can get any sense out of him. There's apparently some secret ingredient in the dressing, apart from the oil and vinegar.'

Steve smiles at them both, as if pleased to see them making friends. 'If I were to tell you everything, I'd have no standing at all in this family. I have to keep something up my sleeve.'

Emily is seated next to Martha, who faces Jessica on Nora's left. Now that they are regrouped, Nora takes every opportunity to observe Steve's wife. She says little during the first course, and Nora assumes that she's preoccupied with the mechanics of bringing the main course to the table because she is on her feet as soon as the salad is finished and busy in the central kitchen area, taking dishes and plates from the oven and checking vegetables. Nora admires her slenderness, the speed and efficiency of her movements, even the little frown of concentration as she prods the potatoes. Beyond what can be assumed from her appearance, however, and her professional status, which she has learned about in the course of the evening, Nora finds her elusive, as though something is being withheld. But, of course, it's Steve who invited her so it will take time for Martha to get to know her. She's surprised by how much she wants this woman, whose daughters are not much younger than she is, to like and accept her, but she's too inexperienced at this kind of social occasion to know how to win her over.

She scarcely notices when a plate of food is placed in front of her, with instructions to help herself to potatoes and beans. They begin eating, and Nora takes a mouthful of something both familiar and wonderfully exotic – chicken breast with little pieces of courgette baked into it, Parmesan and a spicy flavour she can't identify. As with everything else this evening, she knows at once that this is the way it should be, this is how chicken should taste, but that she had no way of knowing this until she was initiated into the Woolfs' way of life. While she savours the moment and waits for an opening to ask about the spice, she sees that Emily hasn't yet started to eat.

Emily turns to her mother and asks, 'These are cheerful chops, aren't they, Mum?'

The Woolfs explode with laughter, while Nora looks on, bemused.

'Of course they are, silly,' says Martha, as though Emily were much younger than her years. And Emily doesn't resent this, but seems to invite it, completely unperturbed that she still enjoys the sensation of being mothered. She isn't yet prepared to let adolescence claim her and force her to give up what she appears to value more than anything else.

'There, you've confused Nora, who can see perfectly well that she isn't eating a chop, cheerful or otherwise.' Martha looks at Nora as she speaks, bestowing on her a warm smile of acceptance, so that Nora thinks, It's all right, she was just waiting for an opportunity. 'Emily doesn't really like eating meat,' she goes on to explain, 'because she's concerned about animal welfare. But I insist that she has some because I don't want her getting anaemic. The deal is that it's always free-range or organic. And since she was quite young, we've called all meat that comes up to Emily's exacting standards "cheerful chops". It's family code, incomprehensible to anyone else.'

What Nora is thinking is how wonderful it must be to have a family code and shared family jokes to reinforce your sense of who you are and where you belong, but because she can't say this, and because some comment seems to be required of her, she says instead, 'You should sell it to an organic butcher as a slogan. It's so neat and memorable.' This seems unworthy of the occasion even as she says it, but her unthinking remark, rather than being swallowed up in the drift of conversation, is exposed in all its crassness when Jessica says loftily, 'We don't have a commercial mentality in this family.'

Just as Nora is thinking that the evening is in ruins, and that she will never get over the shame, at the same time disliking Jessica for bearing down so hard on a remark that was, if inappropriate, entirely harmless, Steve restores some kind of equilibrium by saying, 'We might have to acquire one when the estimates come in for the new roof.'

'I'm going to be a vet,' Emily says to Nora. Steve gives a deep, theatrical sigh. 'Daddy doesn't want me to. He says that veterinary medicine has no intellectual content, only loads of information that has to be learned. But I don't care, I'm going to do it anyway. If I never hear another idea again, I've already been exposed to enough to last a lifetime.'

Nora responds with a rare confidence of her own, for any mention of family or home is dangerous and risks questions that she may not wish to answer. But the temptation to establish some kind of bond with Emily is overwhelming.

'Really? Where I come from, vets are respected members of the community, because it's still so agricultural. They're like doctors or priests. Well, maybe not priests so much now.'

'Daddy doesn't reckon doctors either, for the same reasons. He says doing medicine is like doing twenty-five GCSEs. There's plenty of it, but anybody with a good memory can manage it.'

While Nora is considering this, Martha says, 'What do you parents do, Nora?'

Nora swallows before replying. 'My mother doesn't do anything and my father's a pharmacist.'

'A pharmacist.' Martha smiles at Steve as she repeats the words. There's nothing exotic, after all, in Nora's background – neither poetry nor poverty, but provincial respectability.

Nora sees and misinterprets the signal that is passed from Martha to Steve. In this family, bound by love and loyalty, anger and conflict have no place. Jessica's sharpness, after all, was directed at her, not at another family member. There are disagreements, though, as in any intelligent community, and one, part comic, part serious, is Emily's choice of career. On this issue the parents take different sides, and such are the dynamics of the evening that Nora finds herself on the side of Martha and Emily (whom she finds more lovable than Jessica) and welcomed by them. She is delighted by this turn of events, since it offers her a role not just as Steve's favoured student but within the family circle.

Jessica, of course, picks up on this and appears to resent it, for she remarks, with undisguised disdain for Nora's father's profession, 'How useful.'

'Yes, it is,' says Emily. 'I bet he wouldn't have minded you being a vet, would he, Nora?'

'No, I don't suppose he would, but I had no taste for science.'

'Do you have any brothers or sisters? Perhaps they'll be vets.'

'I've a younger brother, but he's unlikely to be a vet.' Then, careful not to give anybody the opportunity to continue this line of questioning, Nora turns to Martha and says, 'The chicken has a lovely flavour, but I don't know where it's coming from.'

'Well, it could be the cheese, Parmesan, or it could be the nutmeg.'

'Nutmeg, how interesting. I thought that was only used in cakes.' As the words come out, stiff and formal, she realises she has chosen something of a dead end.

A useful pause in the meal rescues her. All the Woolfs, except Jessica, are on their feet again as the plates are cleared, baked pears, biscuits and yoghurt are produced and glasses are refilled. Nora, having already drunk more than she is used to, takes a large gulp of wine and wonders how she will get through the rest of the evening. She wishes they would talk among themselves for a while, rather than bombard her with questions.

She is now encountering the same obstacle with the Woolfs that enters every relationship she's made since coming to London. She doesn't want to lie about her family but she isn't ready to talk about them. If she had been more candid in the recent exchange with Emily – if she had said, 'Yes, I do have a brother, but he can't be a vet, or anything else for that matter, because he has a severe mental handicap' – what then? There would doubtless have been murmurs of sympathy, and perhaps even Jessica would look on her more kindly, but her sense of shame would make their sympathy unwelcome. And it would be impossible to sustain that candour, for how could she tell them the story of her family after Felix's birth?

From the reactions of neighbours after Felix was born she knows that well-meaning people, with no direct experience, fall back on comforting platitudes about the mentally handicapped. There's nothing to say that the Woolfs, intelligent and informed though they are, would have a fuller repertoire of responses that would meet her own case. She has never been frank about her family circumstances but that's partly because she's refused the easy option of telling people what they want to hear. What she's never been able to do is find a substitute for the truth that her own sense of honour finds acceptable.

She hopes that one day, however, when she knows them better, she will be able to tell her story to Steve and Martha, who will imaginatively grasp the truth of her predicament, but this isn't the occasion. She feels tired from the effort of it all.

Once they are reassembled Steve, who has taken little

part in the conversation so far – as though, Nora thinks, his main concern is to see how they all get on – starts a new initiative. 'We've all been taking a lively interest in the peace process,' he says. 'What does your family think about the appointment of Peter Mandelson as Northern Ireland Secretary?'

Nora stares judiciously at her plate, knowing that if she looks up she will find three pairs of eyes turned earnestly on her. She can hardly say that she doesn't know, that she hasn't asked them. Nor does she want to tell them that she scarcely knows herself any more what's happening in Northern Ireland; that Northern Irish politics, because of her father's obsession with them, were so entangled in her own reasons for leaving that she hoped never to have to think about them again. 'Their views are pretty much those of the rest of the Catholic population, I should imagine,' she says finally, in an attempt to shift the ground from the particular to the general.

'And what does the Catholic population as a whole feel?'

She summons up in her mind images of the new cabinet minister, and one in particular, with his predecessor, Mo Mowlam, immediately after his appointment – she, fat and dishevelled, miserable in defeat, looking unnervingly like Nora's own mother; he, suave and toned to the peak of physical perfection. 'I think they may have difficulty in trusting him.'

'Ah, well,' says Martha, 'his reputation has preceded him. There are plenty in the Labour Party, including myself, who feel exactly the same.'

Nora is relieved to find the conversation drifting away from her, but Steve determinedly hauls it back again. 'I sense that that isn't quite what you meant, Nora.'

'No, it isn't only that,' says Nora, carefully feeling her

way. Mediating between these two particular cultures – Northern Ireland nationalism, and a secular urban liberalism determined to give the Catholic population the benefit of the doubt on any issue – is not a role she relishes. As she sees it, she has less reason than most to defend republican excesses. None the less, she is tied to this table by good manners and by the concerned attention of her listeners, who are unlikely to be deflected by further questions about cooking spices. And it isn't just that. She wants them to like her and she knows that affection can only be won by trust and openness. She would also like to disillusion them about the Irish without forfeiting their warmth towards her. 'If you see him with a group of Belfast politicians, he looks like an alien. You'd think he was just stepping out for cocktails at the Ritz.'

Steve is amused. 'He's certainly revived for us the idea of the lounge lizard. But is that enough to damn him?' Then, before Nora has mustered a response, 'He's actually got the right skills for the job, if he stays long enough to have a chance to use them.' He says this as one who knows the Secretary of State personally, not just as a name in the newspapers.

'Do you mean that he looks gay?' asks Martha, turning the focus back to Nora.

'Well, that would certainly be part of it,' Nora says. 'Political correctness hasn't yet reached Northern Ireland, on either side of the divide, come to that.'

Jessica and Emily look outraged.

'That's terrible,' says Emily, who is clearly as concerned for the welfare and treatment of gays as she is for her cheerful chops.

'It's a traditional society,' says Steve. 'Once there's a settlement, and they feel less beleaguered, those attitudes will wither away, as they largely have in the Republic.'

'So we can't judge the Northern Irish in the way that we would anybody else, particularly if they're Catholic,' says Jessica. 'Is that what you're saying?' Although this is addressed to Steve, she steals sideways glances at Nora as she speaks.

'People aren't always ennobled by suffering,' says Nora. 'We just like to think they are.'

'Quite right,' says Steve, approvingly. This is a line he has often taken himself, in discussions both of life and literature. 'That's the old liberal humanist fallacy, which in the end serves to maintain the status quo.'

Jessica, who is visibly displeased by Steve's praise of Nora, says, 'What about him being Jewish? Is that a problem too?'

There is an awkward pause, before Nora says, 'I suppose it might be – more for the nationalists than the Protestants, I would imagine.'

'You do know that we're Jewish,' says Jessica, accusingly. 'At least, Dad is, so we're not, technically, but we feel we are, or partly.'

Nora, who is already feeling the strain from the extreme caution with which she has negotiated her way through the barrage of questioning, now feels confused and close to tears. If she admits to 'hearing' that they are Jewish, then it might seem that this is a subject of gossip among the students. If, on the other hand, she claims not to know, she will leave the impression that she wouldn't have said what she has said. Suddenly the pleasing ritual of family dinner, which she has seen as conferring grace on the humdrum business of living, has become a torture chamber from which she longs to escape. Then Martha leans across the table and touches her hand, and when Nora looks up and catches her eye, the older woman's face is alight with kindness, allowing Nora to see that her special gift – beyond price in a mother – is her quick perception of other people's feelings.

'You mustn't mind us,' Martha says. 'We all talk far too much and ask too many questions, and now we've behaved just as we would by ourselves, forgetting that this is the first time you've been here.'

Nora is flooded with relief, a feeling that is associated in her imagination, though not in her experience, with a mother's intervention on a child's behalf as she assumes a burden that the child cannot carry. She smiles gratefully at Martha, who lightly withdraws her hand, then begins to clear the plates. There comes a sudden revelation of what life might have been like if Martha, or someone like her, had been her and Felix's mother. She feels certain that Martha's maternal love is all embracing and unconditional; and that while she would have grieved for a child like Felix, she would have loved him and done her best for him and made sure that Nora's life was not made wretched by her parents' disappointment.

'I'm not suggesting that I share these attitudes,' Nora says. 'If I did, I'd probably try to hide it. I'm just saying that they may well be there, and that maybe these prejudices will create difficulties for Mr Mandelson, though it'll never be talked about publicly, just among themselves.'

'We never thought for one minute that you shared them,' Emily says. 'You're much too nice and intelligent. But it must be horrible to live with. Is that why you left?'

Nora shrugs but says nothing. It seems inevitable that the price of any intimacy in London will be speculation about her background, her family and why she's here; and until she's ready to tell her story, she has to accept the distortions imposed on her. If this is to be her fate, then the identity proposed by Emily – as a champion of minorities and warrior against prejudice – is one she can live with, and preferable to Phoebe's version, of the wild Celtic heroine whose true nature has been crushed by religious and political forces. At least now it's established, and if she's ever here again, as she so much hopes she will be, tonight's interrogation will not have to be repeated.

As she leaves to catch her bus, having overcome Steve's offers to drive her home with an embarrassed insistence, they each, beginning with Martha, kiss her on both cheeks. And it is Martha's overture that she particularly cherishes as she makes her journey home.

'It's so lovely to have you share our Christmas, Nora, and particularly gratifying to find you looking so well. More than well, glowing, I'd say, wouldn't you, Phil?'

Janie Metcalfe turns to her husband, who gives a lazy smile of assent, and sketches a gesture with both arms outstretched that is broadly suggestive of superlatives beyond his power to articulate. They, with Nora, Phoebe and Phoebe's brother Zach, are sipping champagne in the Metcalfes' Chelsea drawing room, where the style of Oriental opulence that they favour in interior design – carved antique Indian cupboards, tables and sofa frames, brilliantly coloured silk cushions and curtains, intricately patterned rugs on walls and floor – is today overlaid by the clutter of a northern European Christmas. The tree, the tallest that the room can accommodate, is smothered in white lights, coloured glass globes, stars and a baroque museum-shop angel, and is already, so early in the season, sloping precariously to one side, while the floor is almost hidden under a litter of discarded wrapping-paper and opened presents.

Janie, who is in a semi-reclining position on one of the

sofas, where she looks seasonably picturesque, having favoured the occasion with a claret-coloured velvet dress, heavy with embroidery, from Liberty, is being particularly attentive to her young guest. While the presents stacked by Nora's chair are by no means as costly as those bestowed on the children of the family, care has been taken to ensure that they are the same in number, so that she hasn't had to look on admiringly while others opened their glossy and beribboned parcels.

And there is one present that has given her particular pleasure – a silver and garnet pendant necklace which she is already wearing because it's so well suited to the black top and red silk skirt that she bought for the Woolfs' dinner, and is wearing again today. It seems that Phoebe helped her mother to choose it, with the new outfit in mind. Phoebe has always been generous, in the random, careless way of someone who has never learned the value of money, but the choice of necklace suggests real attentiveness towards Nora and anticipation of her wishes. So the reservations that she has begun to entertain about the Metcalfes' giddy levels of self-indulgence, of which she has been an undoubted beneficiary, have melted in the warmth and gratitude of the moment.

'So, what's the secret?' Janie continues. 'Something must be responsible for the transformation.'

Nora feels uncomfortable under the glare of their attention, especially since they are all so much larger than she is, however well their flesh is concealed under the variously brocaded garments that they have all, including Phil and Zach – who could easily be playing two wise men in a school nativity play – felt appropriate to wear for Christmas. Yet it is true that since her dinner with the Woolfs she has felt different, as though she has miraculously come into her own;

and although she hasn't yet shed the anxiety that has been her companion for as long as she can remember, she can now entertain the possibility that life might be led one day simply, easily and openly, and that there need be no impediment between a desire and its realisation.

For the last two or three weeks in particular, she has had the sensation of floating. Her work is going well. For the Christmas holidays, she has found a job waitressing at lunchtimes in an Italian restaurant, which allows her time for study, and where the proprietor's wife treats her with maternal concern. The situation with Nick is still in a state of suspense, but full of promise. The last time she saw him, before he left to spend Christmas with his family in Bristol, they went out for the first time alone together, to see a film, and in an off-hand manner, as though he didn't want her to read too much into it, he gave her a present, not gift-wrapped, but still in the bag from the shop, a book of poems by Robert Lowell. She had never even heard of him until a few days before, when Nick admitted to an enthusiasm for his work that he was now inviting her to share. The tears had started to her eyes. Even so, she had been glad that he was going away for a few weeks because, for now, she is more comfortable with the thought of him than with his presence. At any moment the atmosphere between them could change and he might demand more of her than she is prepared, just yet, to give.

But best of all – a priority that she would not be able to confide in Nick, who couldn't be expected to understand – she was invited to a drinks party by the Woolfs. There, Martha took particular care to introduce her to all her guests as 'our new young friend and Steve's star pupil', and Emily dragged her off for a complicit giggle about her father's attitude to veterinary medicine.

'Oh, it's probably just the term coming to an end and being able to catch up on some sleep,' Nora says noncommittally, wishing that someone would introduce a topic that would occupy the whole group, especially since Phoebe and Zach are slumped in their chairs, eyes vacant and evidently bored now that there are no more presents under the tree.

'Well, I won't probe, but it's my belief that you're keeping something from us, and that you've waited until Phoebe came home for Christmas to embark on a little adventure.'

For the past week, Phoebe had been staying with her parents, helping with the preparations, taking part in their demanding social life and, doubtless, refreshing her bond with her mother in impromptu shopping expeditions and lunches out. During her absence Nora, far from embarking on the kind of amorous adventure that Janie is imagining for her, has been enjoying a life lived on her own terms, one that she is becoming confident will be hers in the future. Not for the first time Nora wonders whether Janie's attitude to her children's sexuality – and by extension hers, as Phoebe's friend – is typical of English parents of her generation. She appears to regard sex outside marriage as morally neutral, as long as 'nobody gets hurt', and as promoting physical and spiritual well-being, and is as concerned that her children are getting enough of it as she is for their vitamin intake and regular attendance at the dentist's.

In the pause that opens with Nora's refusal to satisfy Janie's curiosity, Zach lumbers to his feet and listlessly passes round a huge platter of bruschetta – olive and chicken liver pâtés, prawns, various roasted vegetables – which have been brought in to accompany the champagne.

As he reaches his mother, she strokes his hand and smiles to indicate how moved she is by his consideration and good manners.

When Nora arrived in the middle of the morning, in compliance with the Metcalfes' insistence that she should spend no portion of the day on her own, Janie pressed a glass of Buck's Fizz into her hand and explained that, although they are not a conventional family – Nora knows them well enough to have no doubts on that score – they take Christmas very seriously. 'It is, after all, a spiritual time, and although we're Buddhist, Phil and I were brought up as Anglicans so we recognise the significance of the festival, which we celebrate in our own way.' One of their family traditions, she went on to explain, was that every minute of the day should be filled with joy and spent together. 'So we try very hard to have no gaps, when nothing's happening.'

Nora's own family Christmases had been rather mournful occasions, the more so, perhaps, because the Doyles had felt required by convention to acknowledge the season. They always had a tree because Malachy McGready had continued to reserve for them the best specimen in his shop, as her father had demanded in the days before Felix; and an enormous turkey from Tom O'Neill, on the same principle. At some point in the day Gerald would declare that nobody could say that his children didn't have as good a Christmas as anybody in Ballypierce, despite the difficulties that beset them, and would discharge the obligation of present-giving by handing out banknotes to Bernie and Nora. Not to Felix, of course, whose presents would have been taken care of by Nora.

Then, in one of those long stretches of the day when Gerald found reason to absent himself – checking on the safety of the shop or having a drink with the boys in Liam's bar – her mother would weep over memories of past Christmases, while Felix stuffed himself with chocolate.

Nora's ideas of what a real Christmas might be like – by the time she left home, it was clear to her that nothing in their family life was 'real' in the sense that other people understood it – have largely been formed by television and the films that she used to take Felix to see. So, when she was invited by the Metcalfes to spend Christmas with them, she envisaged games, family carols, perhaps a walk in the park. What she is finding instead is that they have ritualised the business of eating, drinking and present-giving. Presents have been opened throughout the day, but only in certain designated slots: the 'amusing' ones with the Buck's Fizz, the 'useful' ones at tea and, once the suspense has been allowed to build, the 'big' presents with the pre-dinner champagne.

This has been punctuated by a series of eclectic meals, appropriate to their multiculturalism: an assortment of mezze at lunch, German cake for tea, as a kind of homage to Prince Albert, and now Italian bruschetta before they move on to a traditional English dinner. The only inter-ruption to this relentless ordeal of eating, drinking and present-giving, took place between tea and champagne, when the annual ritual weep over the video of *Casablanca* took place. They follow the day's programme with a kind of liturgical solemnity – even the fidgeting of Phoebe and Zach reminds Nora of church, where children protest but buckle under – and this serves the useful purpose of disguising the greed that underlies it all. If it were possible, Nora would return to the flat now and avoid dinner, but she is too extensively indebted to them not to surrender to their kindness.

Zach, finding no takers for the bruschetta, says, 'Come on, Mum, let's get on with it.'

'Get on with what?'

'All the rest of the stuff you've got lined up for us – goose, crackers, pudding, whatever. I'm scared that if I sit down again now, my arse will get welded to the chair.'

Janie sighs deeply. 'Zach, there's one day, only one day in the year that you're required to spend quietly with your family, being reminded of the precious bonds that knit us together and offering hospitality to a friend. Is that too much to ask?'

None the less, to a chorus of 'Yeah, yeah' from Phoebe and Zach, she gets slowly and heavily to her feet, wincing visibly with stiffness as her legs, which have been draped along the sofa, adjust to her weight. As she moves, there is a jangling from the numerous bangles and beads that bedeck her.

Half an hour later, they are seated at the oval table in the dining room. Despite the relatively late hour, and the number of meals that have already been consumed, this is the first time that any of them has entered the room in the course of the day. Lunch was eaten in the kitchen, to suggest its humbler role in the festivities, tea in the drawing room, allowing the day to climax with dinner in a room that none of them has yet been allowed to see. The table was set yesterday afternoon, and every piece of crystal and silver polished by the Filipina cleaner, who was paid double time for working on Christmas Eve afternoon (any earlier and the dust might have settled), then the room decorated by Janie with the choicest evergreens – garlands for table and fireplace – available in their local florist.

The effect on entering the room is of pure spectacle:

for the first time in her life, Nora has the sensation of seeing a fantasy fully realised. And that fantasy, it seems, is largely Janie's. There have been mutterings from Phoebe and Zach about what they are missing on television, which their mother has chosen to ignore, and now that they are gathered at the table there is an air of weariness as they toy with the mélange of smoked fish and salad leaves that precedes the goose. Zach seems particularly disaffected, Janie having refused his request for beer with the plea that 'just this once' he might bring himself to sample the white Graves his father has selected for the first course. Clearly there are disciplines and constraints even here, and Zach suffers them as gracelessly as any other teenager.

As Phil clears the plates, Janie does her best to whip them into a frenzy of excitement over the goose. 'Normally,' she confides to Nora, 'we're rather sparing with the amount of meat we eat. When you've spent as long as we have in India and seen how simply people live – and how happy they are because of this amazing spirituality that envelops you – then you do become just a little bit disgusted with Western culture and religion. I hope that you'll visit India yourself one day. Perhaps we'll find an opportunity for you to come with us. Who knows? I'd be very interested to have your perspective on it, as an Irish person.'

Nora, baffled for a response, tries throughout this speech to adjust her expression to the loops in Janie's thinking and her evident desire to involve Nora in them.

'Nonetheless,' Janie continues, 'I do think that from time to time – and Christmas is certainly one of those times – one has to give oneself permission to bend one's principles.'

While Janie and Phil are in the kitchen, putting the

finishing touches to the day's most theatrical event – they have refused Nora's offers of help – the three young people are left to their own devices. Zach removes the paper crown that has been perched on his dreadlocked hair.

'Mum won't like that,' says Phoebe. 'If you want to avoid a diatribe about how much work's gone into the day, blah, blah, blah, I'd put it straight back on.'

'It makes my scalp itch,' says Zach. 'I've been in agonies.'

'I'm not surprised. God knows what's nesting in that lot.'

Then the door is opened by Janie, who stands to one side, clapping, while Phil carries in the goose on its enormous silver platter. He is buckling under the weight and there is a grease stain on his brocade Nehru jacket where the fat from the bird splashed as it was transferred from the roasting tin to the platter.

'You should have been in training for this, Dad,' says Zach. 'A bit of weight-lifting to get you in shape for the big day.'

Phil is panting from the effort of what is possibly his only manual task in the whole year, and hasn't sufficient breath to reply to his son.

'You should get it airlifted in next year, if you want to avoid Dad having a heart-attack,' says Phoebe.

The platter hits the sideboard with a thud, and soon plates laden with goose, stuffing, cranberry sauce and a variety of vegetables face them all. Once the food has been exclaimed over, nobody appears to have the energy to introduce another topic of conversation. Nora, who is anxious to do her duty as a guest, turns to Zach, seated on the other side of her from Phil. 'What are you doing with yourself now, Zach? Have you applied to university yet, or will you wait until after your A-levels?'

Zach prepares to speak by adopting a position appropriate to his reply. He pushes his chair back from the table and sits sprawled, chest wide and legs open, the picture of young male confidence. 'I've decided not to bother. What's the point? The band's going pretty well, and I reckon that if we can give it some time, we'll really take off.'

Zach plays the drums in a group he formed with other boys from his public school. Nora has heard them play once or twice when his family have given them rehearsal room, and has been baffled by their persistence in pursuing an activity for which none of them seems suited. She is no judge of pop music, however, so she nods and makes encouraging noises.

'It's a great pity in some ways,' Janie says. 'All his teachers agree that, despite his dyslexia and problems with concentration, he has great academic potential. But what can you do? We've always maintained – haven't we, Phil? – that if your children have a talent, which is after all a gift from the gods, they have a duty not to squander it and we have a duty to support them.'

Phil looks up from his plate – he is the only one doing justice to the food – and seems about to challenge the view his wife claims they share. Then, as if the effort is too much for him, or perhaps from an unwillingness to destroy the Christmas spirit, he lifts his hand in a vague gesture of assent.

'We're encouraging him to do a course in composition at the Royal College of Music,' Janie continues.

'It's really hard to get on to,' says Phoebe. 'Especially for someone who doesn't read music.'

'I think you'll find that's a detail,' her mother rebukes her. 'Originality counts for far more, I'm sure. It's such a responsibility, Nora, to have gifted children. They're so eager to express themselves creatively, but that can be crushed so easily by a world that doesn't fully understand the nature of their talent. So, one finds that one's nurturing role continues but has to take a rather different form.'

Nora merely nods attentively. She is ill equipped to comment on the nature and extent of Zach's talents, and only too well equipped where Phoebe is concerned.

'Take Phoebe now,' Janie continues. 'Wouldn't you agree – and I'm sure nobody is in a better position than you to give an opinion – that she isn't appreciated by the academic staff? That she's almost too creative to conform to the requirements?'

Nora glances swiftly at Phoebe, expecting her to protest and turn the conversation in another direction. Phoebe isn't easily embarrassed, but even she must feel uneasy at her mother's gross – even grotesque – exaggeration of her abilities. Instead, Phoebe is doing her best to look unconcerned and avoids catching Nora's eye. At the same time, it becomes apparent that a certain stillness has settled over the party assembled at the table – even Phil has laid down his knife and fork – as a moment has arrived for which they have all been prepared.

'Well, yes, I suppose so,' Nora says at last.

'I'm so glad you agree. You can't think how much we all value your opinion. Phoebe thinks so highly of your work and intellect. Now, you do know that she wants to write? We're so thrilled by the prospect of having a writer and a musician in the family. Phil and I would both have liked to do something creative but our parents didn't give us the support – well, enough said. It's Phoebe we're concerned about just now, and her ambition to write.'

'Yes, of course, she's mentioned it,' says Nora, who has

imagined this to be not so much a settled ambition as one of those passing fads – like making jewellery or going to Morocco and living in a Berber village for six months – which take up residence in Phoebe's imagination until they are displaced by something else.

'Well, we've given it some thought over the last week while Phoebe has been here and, really, I find it quite heartbreaking because she's convinced that her best hope of embarking on this life is through the creative writing MA at UEA, or one of the journalism courses, but she says they won't take her because she's unlikely to do well enough in her degree.'

'Oh, I'm not sure that that's the case,' says Nora, although she thinks Phoebe is almost certainly right in her assessment of her chances. 'Surely the UEA MA is a bit like art school. I imagine that what they look at is a portfolio of creative work rather than academic grades.' To the best of her knowledge, Phoebe has never written anything but her essays, and those only with great difficulty, but she doesn't see it as her role to draw attention to this when Phoebe's family seem so determined to overlook it.

'You would think so, wouldn't you? But we're not sure, and at the moment Phoebe thinks journalism might suit her better. Couldn't you just see her with her own column? She has such an original mind.'

'Yes, yes, that's true.'

'So I'm asking you to help her, because she's much too shy to ask you herself. She says you have a knack of knowing what the teachers want.' Nora feels a surge of anger at this characterisation of herself as someone with a mere 'knack', by contrast to Phoebe, whose originality (presumably like Van Gogh's or Joyce's) is in danger of going unrecognised by an uncomprehending world. Politeness requires her to control it, though. 'If there's anything I can do, I'd be only too pleased but—'

'We can't do anything about the exams, except I'm sure you're only too happy to discuss likely topics and things with her, but Phoebe tells us that the assessed work – and, most especially, the dissertation in the third year – carries a lot of weight.'

'I don't know how much,' says Nora, cautiously.

'Well, whatever, that's a detail. We've got to know you terribly well over the past year, and feel about you almost as if you were one of the family.'

Nora mutters her thanks and, inadvertently, her hand reaches up to touch the silver and garnet necklace. Although she is careful not to meet anybody else's gaze, she can feel four pairs of eyes on her.

'We knew you would be only too happy to give her what help you can with her essays and dissertation, and since you're already living together, it's so much easier for both of you than it might be.'

Ballypierce

By the time that Nora took her eleven-plus, the atmosphere in the Doyle household had perceptibly lightened. Gerald's temper had improved since Margaret Thatcher's removal from office – an event he had followed with obsessive attention, and still replayed endlessly at home and at the shop, his relish for the drama apparently undiminished. It wasn't just the spectacle of the former prime minister's humiliation that had restored his zest for life, but the now undeniable proof that he had been right all along about the ruling Conservative Party. He would pace up and down, punching his right fist into his open left palm as he itemised the treachery, ruthlessness and naked self-interest that they had always displayed towards the Irish, and when the chips were down, it was now clear, they were prepared to turn on their own leader, a woman they had venerated as an idol when she was winning elections and bundled off unceremoniously at the first hint of approaching defeat. On this topic he was at his most morally splendid, his righteousness fuelled by an apparent indifference to worldly success and failure. As far as he was concerned, the rottenness at the heart of the English gentlemanly ideal had been exposed in all its reeking ugliness. And now he had the Gulf War to look forward to. He never tired of reminding whoever was prepared to listen to him that the Brits, when it suited them, had cosied up to Saddam Hussein, and now that their oil was threatened, they were prepared to bomb him to smithereens.

He was more cheerful than at any time since Felix's birth, and although Bernie and Nora didn't exactly share his interests, he was talking to them at any rate, soliciting their agreement as each assertion was hammered out. For her part, Bernie was finding life easier since Felix had started school, and was collected and brought home every day in a minibus provided by the local authority. She complained, of course, about the extra work and constraints imposed by the new routine. They had to be up and dressed in time for the minibus, although it was usually Nora who got Felix ready for school and escorted him outside if Bernie was still in her dressing-gown.

The effect of the changes on Felix's state of mind was more of a mystery. It was undeniable that he hated the uniform he was forced to wear. His school was nominally a convent, and while the nuns were mostly ageing and not being replaced by a younger generation so that his teachers were mostly lay, the convent ethos had been preserved. As Bernie had been told at the meeting she was required to attend – Gerald had of course absented himself – wearing a uniform fostered the children's self-respect and helped to integrate them into the wider community. And for much the same reasons, parents were encouraged to attend certain religious services.

'Self-respect,' Gerald had scoffed, when Bernie had given him an account of the evening. 'What the devil does a creature like that know about self-respect?'

It was certainly true that, try as she might, Nora couldn't

interest Felix in his grey flannel trousers, blue shirt, maroon pullover and maroon and black striped tie. Either his resistance to the uniform had become a way of asserting himself, of expressing his distaste for the discipline of school, or the top button of his shirt and the waist button of his trousers, which could barely contain the small bulge of his belly, the wool of his pullover and the knot in his tie – all hurdles to be overcome in the race to get him ready to leave on time – inflicted genuine discomfort. Once dressed, he looked lost and vacant, as though the identity imposed on him was as alien and uncomfortable as the uniform itself.

Nonetheless, he had become more docile since starting school and, once home and changed into his baggy track-suit bottoms and T-shirts, too tired for anything except to watch endless cartoon videos. Bernie now had the day to herself, and although she spent much of it watching daytime television, she managed, with the earlier start, to keep the house moderately clean and to do her shopping. Nora, who now had fewer demands on her own time, prepared for and sat her eleven-plus examination. Her parents' indifference to her education continued, but they mostly left her at liberty to pursue it.

Later, when she looked back on this period in their lives, Nora felt she should have realised that its relative normality couldn't last. Her mother in particular was going through the motions of her life, as though she were tranquillised, as indeed she might have been. It was in matters of religion, however, that Bernie was at her least characteristic, and it was only later, after her brief flirtation with religion had reached its predictably messy climax, that Nora gained some insight into its source.

Despite coming from a family that – while not noted for exceptional piety, as some families were – took religious practices and beliefs for granted, Bernie had taken little interest in the Church and its devotions. Catholicism had little to contribute to her internal drama. Because her imagination tended to dwell on the wrongs done to her rather than her own lapses from virtue, she wasn't much interested in the Church's cycle of sin and redemption; while her conviction that since Felix's birth her neighbours had gloated over her misfortune isolated her from its communal life. Nor was she susceptible to the devotional aspects of Catholicism, which she had always seen as the refuge of the old and the ugly.

As a girl, she had taken care to conceal her indifference to religion, but marriage to Gerald, who was both a prominent local figure and, as he described himself, a tribal Catholic but a principled unbeliever, had given her the confidence to adopt a bolder stance of semi-detachment. She never involved herself in arguments about religion, but considered herself at greater liberty to absent herself from religious practice.

Recently, however, there had been small but significant changes in Bernie's relations with the Church. It wasn't so much that she had felt the need to turn to the Church in her troubles, as might have been the case for other women who found themselves similarly distressed, as that the Church had turned to her. Like Gerald, who saw priests as interfering busybodies, licensed by their office to make interventions in people's lives that would not be tolerated by anybody else, she had always disliked having them in the house. Father McCaffrey, who had featured so prominently on the day of Felix's birth, had been just such a priest but his successor, Father Flynn, was younger and had an altogether different view of his priestly role.

Since taking over the parish, he had fallen into the habit

of dropping in on the occasional afternoon. Once he had overcome her initial reluctance – he never lectured her or reminded her of her duty or spoke of the glory awaiting Irish Catholic women who served God and their families with no thought for themselves – she began to welcome his visits. She had always mistrusted other women and was instinctively deferential towards men; and it seemed to her that, although Father Flynn was perfectly correct in his behaviour, she appealed to him as a woman rather than as a parishioner.

Gerald had always made the decisions, but had steadfastly refused to involve himself in anything concerning Felix, as though he wasn't prepared to admit that the boy was his son. So it was Father Flynn who advised her about schools and arranged for the minibus in the mornings and afternoons and interested himself in Felix's welfare. And although she ignored his delicately offered advice on managing her son's behaviour, she had the welcome sense of her burden being shared. In time, as he got to know her better, he encouraged her to transform herself from a mere victim to a noble victim, while carefully avoiding a religious, or even ethical, context for this nobility.

Bernie had always craved to be above the crowd, to be distinguished, and before Felix's birth she had relied for her sense of her own distinction on her looks, her marriage and the precociousness of her daughter, although her rivalry with Nora complicated her pleasure in her. Father Flynn recognised this need, and her hunger for flattery. The trick was to use Felix, who in Bernie's mind had demolished everything she valued, to fuel her sense of her own extraordinariness. His concern was not so much for Bernie's soul, about whose existence he had his doubts as he did of his own, but the welfare of the children, particularly Nora. If a way could be found to integrate them better into the community, then the community would be in a better position to keep an eye on them.

It was after Felix had started school, when Bernie's pain and humiliation were losing their initial rawness and intensity, that he began his assault. By the time of the Gulf War and Nora's eleven-plus, he had refined his technique and was ready to move on to the next stage in his master plan.

'You know, Bernie, there are people in this town who are jealous of you, and I think you ought to know that. You're always saying that they have their knives into you, but I think you should consider the reason.'

It was early afternoon, in the quiet time before the children arrived home from school, when they had settled down together with the bone china, the teapot and the plate of shortbread. Since Father Flynn had come into her life, Bernie had resumed some of the rituals (lapsed since Felix's birth) that had always given her a comforting sense of her social status. She had even got into the habit of putting on makeup and changing her clothes when the housework was finished, in preparation for a possible visit.

'God help us,' said Bernie. 'You'd have to be a very twisted creature to be jealous of me.'

'That may be, but people can be very funny. Look at the Kennedys now, the late president's family.'

'What on earth have I got to do with them?' Bernie's words were dismissive, but her interest had clearly been aroused.

'Well, on the one hand they have everything – looks, class, money, brains – just like your own family but on a different scale, of course. On the other hand, no family could be more unfortunate. But you see, in some people's minds, that singles them out still further. It's as though

171

they're special, and everything that happens to them is on a grand scale. So it is with Felix. He's not your average, under-achieving boy, which might lead some people to think that the Doyles aren't all they're cracked up to be after all. Instead he's a kind of aberration of nature, in one sense nothing to do with you at all, although you have been singled out to take responsibility for him. It's as though the gods themselves are jealous.'

'The gods?' Bernie had never taken much interest in Catholic doctrine but the importance of monotheism had impressed itself on her.

Father Flynn paused while he lit a cigarette – a liberty he wouldn't have taken if Gerald had been there. 'Well, now, that's a term I wouldn't have used with my less sophisticated parishioners, but I can be sure that you won't misunderstand me and report me to the bishop. You see now, Bernie, the ancient Greeks – who were pre-Christian, as I'm sure you'll know, so hadn't had the revelation of one God – felt that the gods could be jealous of men, and women, who were too special, too much like gods themselves. And so they felt the need to bring them down by visiting misfortunes on them. Except, of course, that the misfortunes only served to confirm their special status. Am I making myself clear?'

'I think so.'

'Now, with Christianity, of course, we've gone beyond the ancient Greek understanding of the world but we're still all of us subject to these primitive feelings that the Greeks understood only too well. And I'm telling you, as far as some of the people here in Ballypierce are concerned, your having been victimised in this way only serves to make you even more an object of jealousy.'

Bernie knitted her brows and nodded slowly as she

struggled to take in Father Flynn's argument. Some of the detail eluded her but she was enjoying the drift. She had reservations, though. 'That's all very well, Father, but I always thought that if you're jealous of somebody, it's because they have something you want. I can't believe you're telling me that there are people who are jealous of me because of Felix. Who could wish such a misfortune on themselves?'

Father Flynn stooped in concentration, brushing the fallen ash off his trouser leg as he marshalled his argument. In general his parishioners didn't require much in the way of debate from him. If they absented themselves from Mass he was inclined, unlike earlier generations of Irish clergy, to leave them alone. Observant Catholics felt honoured by his visits and plied him with refreshments ('Will you take something, Father?'). But he helped out with religious studies in the sixth form of the local grammar school, where the students frequently gave him a hard time, so the casuistic skills he had learned in the seminary were in good order.

'Of course, you're right, Bernie,' he said at last, 'but the situation's a bit more complicated than that. They may not wish Felix on themselves, but if you were to get about more with him, and they could see the dignity with which you bear your misfortune, they would feel diminished. And this would confirm them in their idea that you and your family were set apart in some way. Chosen, if you like, for the best and worst that can happen. Like the Kennedys who had a similarly disadvantaged child in the family.'

Bernie remained silent. She wasn't going to commit herself to anything until she knew what it entailed.

'So here's what I would suggest to be going on with,' Father Flynn continued. 'We're having a big Ash

Wednesday service for the local primary schools to which parents are invited. I'd like you to come with Felix and Nora, and sit as a family group. I'll arrange that with the schools, who'll be only too delighted. I tell you, you'll make a grand picture, the three of you – a fine woman like yourself, a lovely girl like Nora, and Felix who, for a Down's child, is remarkably good-looking. They do have the family genes as well as the extra chromosome, after all. You'll be an example to the parish. What do you say?'

Bernie found herself agreeing to attend, although when she looked back on their conversation later she had difficulty in remembering quite how Father Flynn had persuaded her into it. However, he had restored some kind of meaning to her life, and given her something . . . not exactly to look forward to (she had never enjoyed going to Mass) but to work towards, to relieve the monotony of her days. Now that she had the freedom to shop, she could buy herself some new clothes and, thanks to Gerald's generosity – he had always worked on the principle that a gift of money cancelled all other obligations – was in the position to plan an outfit beyond the reach of most Catholic women in Ballypierce.

When she told Gerald of her plans to go to Mass on Ash Wednesday, she didn't attempt to reproduce Father Flynn's argument. It wasn't only that she had been left with little more than a general impression: some of the more striking details – like the Greek gods and the comparison with the Kennedy family – seemed even to her rather far-fetched without Father Flynn there to carry her along with his own earnestness and conviction. She suspected that, if she exposed what the priest had said to her to Gerald's scrutiny, the feeling that had remained from that afternoon, of vague anticipation, as though her engagement with life were about to become more vivid and intense, would wither under her husband's mockery.

As it was, apart from handing over the clothes money in a tight wad of notes, Gerald showed no interest one way or the other. British forces were now launching air missiles on Iraq – he had always overlooked the involvement of Americans, French, Egyptians, Saudis and Syrians – and he had even less attention than usual to spare for his immediate family.

When Ash Wednesday dawned Felix, who was in many ways the point and centrepiece of the day's outing, proved as remote and locked in his own world as his father was in what was taking place in the Persian Gulf. Although more docile since starting school, as long as he was left to his own devices – allowed endlessly to play and replay favourite videos – he was also more inaccessible, often retreating to a point within himself that nobody could reach. He would tear off long strips of lavatory paper and as he sat, cross-legged on the floor, a few feet from the television screen, he would wave it like a banner; meanwhile, he would turn from the television to his free hand, which he positioned like a ventriloquist's dummy, and address it earnestly, apparently interpreting and explaining the events in the video. Since his speech was limited in the extreme, and his diction poor, these conversations with his *alter ego* were beyond the comprehension of observers, but his expression, variations in tone and occasional bursts of simulated anger, crying or laughter suggested that, for him, they were not meaningless.

Although his parents expressed irritation at these practices – Gerald, who was concerned for his own hygiene, was forced to bring bulk packs of lavatory paper home from the shop, concealed in the boot of his car, while

Bernie grumbled about the number of discarded banners that festooned the house – they found it easier to have him occupied than not, and were incurious about their growing importance to Felix. Nora, by contrast, was both concerned and interested. School now was where she felt most secure and most herself, but she remembered the difficulties she had had at the very beginning, the constant fear that she would be asked about her family and not know what to say, and the impossibility of sharing any of this with her parents. She often wondered what Felix made of school, whether he was being taught anything that had any meaning for him. Often she sat with him while he was absorbed in his floating world, trying to catch recognisable words from the flow of sound. It was clear that some kind of dialogue was taking place and that Felix was telling this ghostly presence what couldn't be told to anyone else.

On the morning of Ash Wednesday Nora was up and dressed, as usual, before her parents. Felix was in general a heavy and enthusiastic sleeper, but instead of having to wake him, she found him already installed on the edge of the sofa in the lounge, his banner flying. He refused even to look at her when she suggested breakfast, and when she tried to pull him off the sofa and into the kitchen, he wrapped his arm round the arm of the sofa and locked himself into position. This behaviour wasn't unusual if he was allowed to sink too far into his fantasy world, and on school mornings she did her best to distract him until he was safely installed on the minibus.

She brought his clothes from his bedroom, eager to press on with as much of the morning's routine as she could manage. With difficulty, she pulled his pyjama top over his head and, kneeling on his legs so that he couldn't run away, pushed and pulled him into his vest and shirt, moving quickly to do up the buttons before he slipped out of it. His pants and trousers proved impossible, however, since she couldn't dislodge him from the sofa.

By the time her parents appeared, she was crying with frustration. Felix, by contrast, was the picture of stern impassivity. He was sitting, ramrod straight, lips tight, eyes wide and staring, like a prisoner being interrogated and refusing to give any information under torture.

'You'd wonder who he thinks he is,' said Gerald. 'All he needs is a little moustache and a uniform, and he could be Saddam himself.'

'It's not funny,' Bernie wailed. 'Oh, what are we going to do? Can't you coax him, Nora? He minds what you say to him.'

'I've been trying for the last half-hour.'

Gerald wandered off into the kitchen, picking up the newspaper from the hall floor on the way. By the time his wife and daughter caught up with him, he was sitting reading at the table, waiting for someone to make the tea.

'Please, Gerald, you've got the strength,' pleaded Bernie. 'You could get his trousers on if you tried.'

'I don't see what you're so bothered about,' Gerald replied, eyes still fixed on his newspaper. 'You don't have to go to this Mass. If you want my opinion, you've been conned into it. Look at him – it's even more mumbo-jumbo to him than it is for the rest of us. Shall we ask him what Ash Wednesday means to him, what sins he's got to repent? Or maybe what he's thinking of giving up for Lent?' He paused for effect, then adopted a more conciliatory tone. 'Once it's over I'll run you into school with him. He'll have come round by then.' This was a small concession, made so that they could leave unspoken what they all recognised, but never acknowledged, that Gerald would go to any lengths to avoid physical contact with his son.

'What do you think, Nora?' Bernie asked.

'Maybe it's best if you stay with Felix. I really must go to the Mass but I can get there on my own,' said Nora, who hated to be guilty of any failure to meet the requirements of school.

'Then how will I get his trousers on? You're the only one that he'll let do anything with him.'

'You'll have to stay here and help your mother,' said Gerald, who was always alert to other people's duties. 'I'll run you in at the same time as the boy. That way, your mother won't even have to come.'

Nora knew it was useless to protest, but in the event it was Felix who saved the situation; he wandered into the kitchen carrying the rest of his school uniform, having apparently undergone one of his sudden and inexplicable changes of mood. She set to work at once, before Felix changed his mind again, and pretended she hadn't heard her father's request that, 'for decency's sake', she might choose somewhere other than the kitchen, where people were trying to eat their breakfast, to expose the boy's private parts. Then, having forced a few spoonfuls of cereal and some juice on her brother, with Gerald safely concealed behind his newspaper, she rushed through her own breakfast. By the time Bernie had finished washing and dressing, Felix had been washed and brushed and he and Nora were waiting in their outdoor clothes, ready to leave for church. They still had a little time in hand, but Nora knew that any appearance of haste on their part was likely to provoke another show of resistance from Felix.

Her parents were not to be hurried, however, so that a

last-minute rush, with its attendant irritations and mutual recriminations for lost time, began to seem inevitable. Bernie insisted in pacing up and down in front of her daughter, in her new Jaeger coat and Bally shoes and bag; when Nora declared that either of the two scarves her mother was considering wearing 'looked equally nice', she found herself on the receiving end of a sudden outburst of hostility.

'Could you not try and show an interest? Is it too much to ask of you, just this once?'

'I only meant—'

'Oh, I know what you meant,' said Bernie, darkly, but without specifying the hidden intentions she had discerned. Nobody knew better than she the value of sketching a sense of injury in vague outline, leaving the details to be filled in later, as required. This strategy had the added advantage of keeping Nora on her toes, doing her best to please her mother and to make up for a wound that she hadn't knowingly inflicted.

Bernie was now ready, but nothing could be done until Gerald was finished in the bathroom.

'It may be Ash Wednesday,' he said, 'but I'm not going through the day, like a penitent, with yesterday's grime still upon me.'

When the time came for them to leave the house, Bernie was already panicking, and expressing her turmoil in a number of unfinished sentences all beginning, 'If only . . .' Nora, sitting in the back of the car with Felix, aware of the silent, ominous bulk of her father in front of her, sensed another change of mood in her brother. Unused to the car, and already disturbed by the change of routine, he settled back into what Gerald had described as his Saddam Hussein mode. Nora knew, even before the car stopped, that they would have trouble shifting him. In the event, while her mother hovered on the pavement outside the church, and her father remained in the driver's seat, staring ahead, showing as much indifference and detachment from what was going on behind him as a train driver might, Nora manoeuvred Felix out of the car by dragging his feet on to the pavement, then pulling the rest of him out by his arms. As soon as Felix was clear of the car, her father called, 'Will you shut the door?' and drove off,

Bad though the outing had been so far, it was nothing to the humiliation ahead of them. Bernie, finding herself in a public place and open to observation, had to be seen to behave like an actively involved parent, but although she had reached the point where she could perform certain routine tasks for Felix, her only response to his stubbornness was to ask anyone who would listen what she had done to deserve it.

Nora and Bernie took an arm each and started to pull him into the church, but he wrenched his arm away from his mother and insisted that Nora alone should take responsibility for him. Bernie tolerated this until they were inside. Then, seeing the church already full, the massed, menacing backs of the congregation, ready to judge and whisper about her, she panicked and tried to take Felix's hand, despite Nora's reassurances that she could manage him.

A boy from Nora's class (which, in this primary-school congregation, had senior status), acting as usher, intercepted them as they were about to slip into a back row.

'Father Flynn says all the family groups are to sit in the front, if you'd like to follow me.'

He strode importantly ahead up the centre aisle, with Bernie, Nora and Felix following, until Felix broke away from his mother and sister and, disoriented by the situation, ran at full tilt up the aisle towards the altar. The

Mass hadn't yet begun, and Father Flynn's curate, who was overseeing front-of-house, spotted him and caught him before he'd managed to enter the sacred precinct. After a brief struggle to get away, Felix went limp, and by the time Bernie and Nora caught up with him, he was lying spreadeagled on the floor, refusing to move, with the young priest standing above him, pleading with him to get up.

Bernie was mortified, and her feelings weren't helped when her ankle gave way under the stress of wearing high heels. The young priest put out a hand to steady her, preventing a fall, but the interpretation that would be placed on the incident by the women in the congregation – mothers, grandmothers and teachers – was clear: that she was dressed to kill but couldn't manage her own son.

'Nora, you'll have to do something,' Bernie hissed.

The priest, immediately grasping the situation within the family, said to Nora, 'If I take his shoulders and you his feet, we can carry him round to the vestry. Can you manage that?'

Nora nodded, but Felix resisted all attempts by the priest, whose intention had been to take the heavier burden, to lift his shoulders from the floor. They were forced to swap ends before Felix was successfully raised and carried into the vestry, with his mother following. Father Flynn, meanwhile, who had been alerted by one of the ushers, delayed his entrance until the disturbance was under control.

The small family group sat on a row of straight-backed chairs in the vestry throughout the long Mass. The curate made Bernie some tea and offered her what he could in the way of consolation but, sensing that his presence was unwelcome, eventually left them.

Once they were alone as a family, Bernie wept and blamed everybody – Father Flynn for suggesting that they come, Nora for insisting that they stick to the plan, Gerald for making them late and Felix for making her life a misery – while Felix resumed his stern, intransigent Saddam Hussein pose, and Nora sat, locked in her own thoughts, dreading the show of sympathy that teachers and class-mates would feel compelled to make once they had all returned to school.

In other ways, however, their situation was a relief to Nora. They had placed themselves in the hands of the clergy so on this occasion her mother couldn't turn to her for a solution to their problems. It was almost soothing to sit passively, waiting blankly, knowing that there were adults on hand to take responsibility. When at last Father Flynn appeared, vestments removed and dressed for the street, he immediately took control. He pacified Bernie as far as she would allow for the ordeal she had undergone, but instead of apologising for his foolhardy scheme, suggested that she needed more help with Felix.

Bernie's face briefly lit up. 'I've been wondering whether he wouldn't do better in a boarding school somewhere.'

In the past she had broached this idea to Gerald, but prosperous though they were by local standards, they couldn't afford the high fees demanded by the kind of establishment that Felix would need; and Gerald had refused to approach the local authority, who would in cases of need fund a boarding-school place.

'That boy has humiliated me in every other way,' he had said. 'He's not going to make a beggar of me too, so that I'm forced to run cap in hand to the Unionists in the education department.'

If help were to be offered, though, without having to

be sought, he might take a different view of the matter. But Father Flynn immediately dashed that hope.

'Well now, Bernie, I think that the current view is that, at his age, the boy needs his family. I was thinking more of one of those experts in child management. I've seen them work wonders in children with behavioural difficulties.'

Bernie's face set, and Father Flynn, judging that there was no point in pursuing this line of argument, especially when feelings were still so raw, showed them out and bundled them all into his little car. He stopped first at Felix's school, where Felix, perhaps recognising the priest's authority and superior strength – he was a man of impressive build, a rugby player at school and university – meekly allowed himself to be led in by Nora. Her school was next, and on the way she heard Father Flynn telling her mother that he was tied up for the rest of the day so would drop her at the gate but would be back later. By the time Nora came in from school he hadn't yet called. She had expected that her mother would blame her for conspiring with Felix to humiliate her, but Bernie seemed to be holding back – Nora supposed in expectation of the priest's visit. With any luck, the delay would allow Bernie's active sense of grievance to find another outlet.

In the event, Father Flynn's visit coincided with the nine o'clock news, which gave Gerald his last fix from the Gulf before bedtime. Since he liked Bernie and Nora to watch it with him so that he could point out to them the BBC's pro-government bias and give them the benefit of his own interpretation of events, the family, with the exception of Felix who had retired, exhausted, to bed at an early hour, was assembled in the lounge when Father Flynn arrived. Gerald wasn't particularly pleased to see him in his capacity as priest, especially since he held him responsible for the day's débâcle, but that aside, he was not unwilling to extend his audience.

'So, what do you think?' he asked Father Flynn, indicating the television screen.

'It's a sad business, right enough, but the man has to be stopped.'

There was nothing Gerald liked better than an argument that he was sure of winning, so he immediately rose to the challenge of enlightening Father Flynn and exposing him as a dupe of British propaganda. He was interrupted in mid-flow: 'If it's all the same to you, Gerald, I didn't come here to talk about the Gulf War.'

Gerald soon recovered his poise. 'If you've come to talk to me about me going to Mass, there's nothing doing, though if you insist I'd be glad to give you my reasons.'

Bernie and Nora were both on their feet now, making for the door, but Gerald summoned them back.

'Whether you go to Mass or not is your own business. I think you'll find the Church has moved on a bit since you last had anything to do with it. You won't find many priests now who see the outward forms of piety as an indication of a man's worth.'

There was a pause while Gerald, pacing up and down, sought a way of taking the initiative. If he were to ask Father Flynn why he had come, he might find himself facing an assault for which he was unprepared.

'Maybe it would be better if Nora went to bed,' said Father Flynn, who was clearly in no mood to wait. 'I'd be sorry to be the cause of keeping her up when she has a full day at school tomorrow.'

'Don't you think I'm the best judge of when she does and doesn't go to bed? Sit down, Nora.'

'As you wish,' said Father Flynn, with a deep sigh. 'Gerald, I've come here not as a priest – I know you have no respect for the priesthood, and your beliefs are entirely your own affair – but as a concerned observer. You're not going to like what I have to say, but somebody has to do it and I don't see anybody else volunteering. Felix needs a father and I'm asking you to take a more active role, for his sake and for the welfare of the whole family.'

While Father Flynn was speaking the colour drained from Gerald's face. Whatever edge in argument the priest might have, Gerald had the advantage of being in his own house and on his feet. He took a few steps towards his guest, whom Bernie had seated in an armchair, and loomed over him as he spoke. 'What right do you think you have, a man without a family, to come and lecture me about my conduct as a father? You're a disgrace to the priesthood, spewing out all this social worker's crap – "concerned observer" and "active role". Did you go on some course where they taught you all this jargon?' He turned his back on the priest before he could answer, and took up position a few feet away, then faced him again. 'I feed and clothe the boy and keep a roof over his head, which is more than you'll ever do for any living creature.'

Bernie and Nora were observing the scene with appalled fascination. They were steeped in Gerald's conviction that he was right about everything, and that when he pronounced, his arguments were unanswerable, so it was inconceivable that Father Flynn might find anything further to say. Because Gerald had never struck any of them, and often expressed contempt for men who did, they were unaware that much of his power lay in the threat of barely contained violence.

Father Flynn watched Gerald closely while he was

speaking, then allowed time for the other man's anger to subside before he replied. When he did speak, he gave no sign of being overwhelmed. 'It's only natural that Felix's birth made you angry. You wouldn't be human otherwise. When something like that happens, everything you value, everything you've worked for, seems meaningless. But if you let yourself hang on to it, you suffer more. In the end, it's in your own interest to make the best of the situation.'

Gerald, who hadn't expected a reply, stared at him in disbelief, lost for words.

'He's a nice boy, Gerald, if you'd only let yourself see it, and more like you than you're prepared to admit. He's got the same stubborn streak, as we saw today, so you're probably in a better position than anyone to understand how his mind works.'

By the time Father Flynn had finished speaking, Gerald was at the door, holding it open. 'You've had your say. Now, don't ever presume to enter this house again and lecture me. You've caused enough trouble here already.'

Father Flynn got to his feet, but he took his time, even delaying his departure from the room while he felt in his pocket for his car keys and the glasses he wore for driving.

'Well, I'll say goodnight to you, Bernie, and Nora.' As he reached the door, he turned, looked at Nora and said, 'That was a grand job you did in the church today. There's not many could have risen to the challenge.'

After he had shown the priest to the front door Gerald returned to the lounge, where he paced up and down for a while before speaking. When at last he turned to his wife and daughter, he said, 'It's as well you were here to see for yourselves that idiot exposing his own folly. If it had been left to me to tell you, I doubt you'd have believed me, so he's done us all a service. So, Bernie, you won't be going back there in a hurry. I knew it would all come to no good, but you had to find out for yourselves.'

And that was the way that Ash Wednesday in 1991, at the time of the Gulf War, became a landmark in Doyle family history. In the event, Bernie was pleased to have been given such clear instructions by her husband. She had no wish to revisit the scene of her humiliation, but it was in every way preferable that she should withdraw under orders from Gerald. He had given her a way of blaming the Church, in the person of Father Flynn, for the débâcle, and she interpreted her husband's intervention as proof that, however indifferent he might appear, he still cared for her. For a brief period, she experienced a sense of solidarity and would often preface a statement or an order to Nora with 'Your father says . . .', much as Father Flynn, if he were so inclined, might invoke the Pope.

The effects were short-lived. By the end of the summer when Nora, having passed her eleven-plus, was preparing to go to grammar school, certain changes in her mother were not only apparent but settled. Bernie was again reluctant to leave the house, even though she was free of Felix during school hours, because her Ash Wednesday outing had exposed her to blame and ridicule, and it was her belief that whenever she was seen in public, gossip about her was revived. Most of the shopping was now done after school and at weekends by Nora, who was baffled and embarrassed by the increasing quantities of cake, biscuits and chocolate requested by her mother, especially since she was the one who had to endure the comments of the woman in the local grocery.

'Well, you must be growing, to be developing such a sweet tooth,' had become the inevitable refrain. 'Perhaps we'll see some weight on you soon.'

It was her mother and Felix who were growing, however. Bernie now spent her days in front of the television, consoling herself with food, and when Felix came home from school, he joined her. For the first time mother and son had achieved some kind of harmony as they sat, one at each end of the sofa, sharing packets of crisps and biscuits. When Bernie was forced to rouse herself, to cook Gerald's dinner, the effort needed for her to get to her feet was painful to watch. By the time Nora started at the grammar school, she was no longer urging her mother to go out more. Her fear was that, if she did, they would all be shamed by her shapeless garments and lumbering gait. As far as possible, when she wasn't required to help with Felix, she avoided the lounge, with its flickering screen, drawn curtains and discarded wrappers.

At the grammar school, she had found a place of discipline and order, where each moment of the day was filled with activity, and the judgements delivered by teachers were always rational. She soon found that she could re-create the atmosphere of school in her bedroom. For the first few years at school, when she settled down with her homework, she gained particular satisfaction from those subjects – French, Latin, mathematics – where the patient exercise of mind on code and symbol revealed meanings and answers that were clear, impersonal and resistant to the human desire to shape the world to its own purposes.

PART FOUR

Ecstasy and Longing

London

It is now some weeks into the spring term, traditionally the lowest point in the academic year. Whatever hopes accompanied them in September have faded for many students who, facing an accumulation of unfinished essays and reading, recognise that they are now unlikely to distinguish themselves in the time available. Some of those who are heavily in debt are wondering whether it's worth it. Many of the relationships begun in the autumn term, when they were new to each other, or after the refreshment of the summer break, as good as new, have petered out, and those that they embark on now, if they can be bothered, will be with diminished expectations. The summer examinations are looming, clouding their amusements and relaxation, but are too far away to have had any effect on their dedication and concentration. Most are relying on the Easter holidays to repair the damage, but meanwhile they are gripped by lethargy.

Nonetheless, on this particular Wednesday there is a heightened sense of anticipation in Steve Woolf's Irish-literature class as they start a new venture. This is the first of four meetings that will be presented, as a seminar, by one of the students. Nick Bailey will lead a discussion on

191

Joyce's *Portrait of the Artist as a Young Man*, a novel with which he is assumed to identify, some saying that he has become more sardonic and intellectually superior since he volunteered to take it on. Pete Davies, on the other hand, has chosen to work against type, and will be entertaining them on *The Importance of Being Earnest*, while Emma Leigh has promised a feminist critique of the entire Irish literary canon. That will be some time in the future, however, when she has had time to grapple with the monumental scope of the subject.

The most intriguing is likely to be today's opening seminar, which Nora Doyle will lead with a close reading of Yeats's 'Among School Children'. They think they can predict, within more or less generous limits, what Nick, Pete and Emma are likely to say, but in the case of Nora, of whom so little is still known, there is always the possibility that something will be revealed: a clue to interpreting her, as she interprets the poem for them. With the spotlight on her, she'll find it impossible to take flight or deflect attention from herself in the manner that they're only too familiar with when she thinks that her privacy is being invaded. And while it's true that they can hardly use the seminar as an opportunity to interrogate on personal matters, Pete, Nick and Annie in particular are hopeful that, in an undefended moment, her guard relaxed by the themes of Yeats's great poem, she will reveal something about her Irish childhood.

It's possible, of course, that she chose the poem for reasons other than its themes. There's been a new steeliness about her since Christmas, less inclination to disguise a sense of purpose that was probably always there. When a poem is as difficult as this, a close reading can be a virtuoso performance, where an opaque lump of text may be transformed into something radiant with meaning. But it will still be difficult for her to evade the emotional issues intrinsic to the poem; and her response to them might reveal something beyond her powers of analysis. For despite Steve's persistent attempts to nudge them in that direction, they are still resistant to the idea of literature as a field in which linguistic, political and cultural forces are in play. They cherish the idea that poetry in particular is dominated by emotional effect and, as Pete has been arguing, no other poet delivers such an emotional wallop as Yeats.

So will Nora respond to Yeats in the manner that he deserves? Or will she frame her discussion to suit Steve, who can never mention Yeats without drawing attention to his dangerous flirtation with Fascism? For everybody now is aware that some kind of special relationship exists between Steve and Nora. How could they not, when Phoebe is in possession of privileged information that she is only too willing to pass on? Despite evidence of a growing closeness between Nick and Nora – a sore point for their friends, who've been offered no confidences by either on the state of play – some would prefer to think of it as a sexual relationship. It makes better gossip and brings them down to the same level as everybody else.

It has to be admitted, however, that Steve's introduction of Nora into his family – a circumstance revealed to them not by Nora herself but by Phoebe – makes this unlikely. Pete's view, which prevails within his own particular circle (Phoebe excepted: she is keeping her options open), is that Steve is grooming Nora for stardom, for a Ph.D. under his supervision, after which a steady progress through the academic hierarchy, where she will be keeper of the flame, ensuring that Steve's views become attached to a whole school of criticism, will be guaranteed her. This, again, according to Pete, is exploitation of innocence of a different order. Nora, coming as she does from Ireland where education is reputedly venerated, might not be aware that Steve probably represents the last generation of academic stars in literature. Science is now the sexy area of research, and otherwise those with the brains now go where the money is, into the City or law, or the media, not into what Steve likes to call the academy. For all his apparent cool, he's irredeemably old-fashioned.

The room has filled and they are ready to begin. Steve has surrendered his place at the front of the class and is sitting apart from the group, towards the back of the room where it will be difficult to observe his reactions. Nora's friends have all taken places in the first two rows, but not together. Nick is seated at the end of the first row, a few seats away from Phoebe and Emma, who are increasingly in each other's company, with Pete and Annie behind them.

Before Nora begins, there is a moment of stillness in the room while she prepares herself for the ordeal ahead. The tension resonates with her own sense of occasion, for she does indeed see this as an opportunity for display, even as a turning-point in her life. She's become tired of keeping her head down, and realises that it was her willingness to accommodate other people's expectations (forced on her, she thinks, by the circumstances of her London life) that encouraged Janie Metcalfe's brazen assumption that she would place her 'knack' at the service of Phoebe's 'talent'.

Eclipsing even her anger with the Metcalfes, however, is the strong urge she now feels to be 'known'. And while she can't yet bring herself to the point of confession, she's chosen the poem because it does indeed express something of her life before London: the atmosphere of corrosive disappointment that ruined her family life after Felix was born; her own feelings for Felix, his often thwarted capacity for joy, their isolation from their parents, and the bond she had with him that both shackled and sustained her. These are woven into her reading of the poem, and she hopes that someone – Steve or Nick – will be moved to ask her the right question, the one that will unlock her heart and allow the words and emotions to flow.

Nora is in Steve's place, but will not, it seems, attempt to emulate his style. She is seated, rather than perched commandingly on the desk and, in addition to a copy of Yeats's poetry, has pulled out a sheaf of notes and placed them on the desk. She looks smaller behind the table, tense with nerves, and there are two bright spots of pink in her cheeks that draw attention to the pure, clean line of bone and give emphasis to the unusual colouring – the black hair, pale skin and blue eyes. Celtic colouring. She is wearing, with her black trousers, an emerald green sweater, fine-ribbed, narrow, V-necked, of the sort she favours, which accentuates her slenderness and, in the grown-up role that she is assuming today, makes her look particularly fragile; the choice of colour raises the possibility that some kind of nationalist statement will be included in her interpretation of the poem.

After glancing at Steve, who nods for her to begin, she says, 'We'll start by reading the poem, but rather than do it myself, I've asked Nick if he'll do it for us. I want as many people as possible to contribute, and that way we'll start with somebody's voice other than mine.'

This is unexpectedly theatrical, lending a sense of occasion to the proceedings, hinting at a taste for showmanship that Nora has never displayed before. At the same time, whatever she has to say about the poem, she seems to be openly encouraging speculation about her relationship with Nick. As he begins his reading, glances are exchanged between Phoebe and Emma, Pete and Annie, all of them wondering how often Nick and Nora have read the poem together, and whether its emotional content, released within the intellectual context that they both find so congenial, acted as a spur to extra-literary activity.

Whether or not Nora's choice of Nick as reader indicates a new level of partnership or complicity between them, it's certainly justified by the quality of his reading. His voice is sensitive to changes of mood and levels of intensity, and he effortlessly combines as easy conversational manner with an attention to rhyme and meter. And while many of those listening are unable to find a consistent thread or argument in the poem, they are all moved in one way or another by an arresting detail: by the ageing poet himself, tormented by loss and memory; by the little girls in the convent school, who are described in the poem's opening sequence; by the image of the flowering chestnut tree that closes the poem.

Nora's mood is noticeably heightened, and although she begins nervously, her mastery of the poem soon becomes clear. It's as though she's on home territory, confident of her bearings. Very often, when questioned about Ireland, she's been studiedly disengaged, resisting the categories that her friends have been eager to place her in. Now, however, as she explains that it was in his role as senator (the 'sixty-year-old, smiling public man') that Yeats visited the convent school, and that he was awarded the honour because the newly independent Ireland had chosen to define itself as a nation of poets and scholars, her pride and partisanship are evident.

'She thinks we're the real peasants,' Pete whispers to Annie, who silences him with a sharp stab in the ribs.

Steve, meanwhile, is barely attending to the discussion. In recent weeks it seems that thoughts of Nora have taken over his mind, driving out all his usual concerns, and now, for the first time ever, he can observe her without being observed himself. So potent is her physical presence and the sound of her voice that he finds it impossible to concentrate on what she's saying. Instead he finds himself identifying with Yeats, at the moment when he wrote the poem, meditating on his own past, on youth and age; and on the disappointments that life inevitably brings. And Steve, although not yet sixty, and probably, in the opinion of his students, not much given to smiling, is also a kind of public man. Three or four times a week, on undergraduate and postgraduate courses, he faces groups of staring students who have no idea of the turmoil he is experiencing. And while he has no women in his past to remember with passionate regret – no equivalent to Yeats's Maud Gonne – he still has a powerful sense of loss.

He regrets that he squandered his youth, though not, as that is conventionally understood, on idleness and hedonism: the sex, drugs and rock and roll that Pete saw as epitomising modern Ireland. Instead he squandered it on ambition, on a succession of goals that he set himself, from adolescence to middle age, which absorbed his time and energy. These now, since his recent failure to break into a more adventurous and creative world, are like dust in his mouth.

Even his marriage to Martha was governed more by reason than emotion: the recognition that she would never irritate him, never let him down, never restrict his freedom and would always offer him the solace of good humour and companionship. Of course he loves her, but not with the overwhelming passion he knows she has always felt for him. Meanwhile, his need for something else has been satisfied by risk-free little sexual adventures that now, in the light of the feelings that Nora has stirred, seem miserable and sordid. Perhaps if he had allowed himself some of the ecstatic longing and dreamy idealism of Yeats's youth – qualities that, in the past, he has been inclined to mock – his professional life might have been more creative and he might not be vulnerable now to a passion that, if he gives in to it, could wreck his life.

He returns to the poem when Nora is discussing a recalled incident from Yeats's youth, when the adult (though still young) Maud Gonne tells Yeats of events in her own childhood. So the operation of memory has a double action within the poem: the poet remembering his beloved remembering. This allows him to 'remember' a child that he never actually knew, or not as a child.

What Yeats has dramatised in the poem is a particular stage in the love relationship, the gratifying period of discovery as lovers tell their story to each other. The poet listens as Maud reveals incidents from her own childhood: 'a harsh reproof or trivial event' that seemed tragic at the time.

Steve knows nothing about events of this kind, traditionally used by lovers to strengthen the bond of sympathy between them, in Nora's life. Everybody has them, after all. He suspects that even his beloved daughters, reared by him and Martha with a watchful concern for every aspect of their welfare, will dredge up from their memories instances of painful neglect or misunderstanding to offer their own lovers. Nora is unlikely to be an exception.

Yet although he is drawn to enact with her just such an event as Yeats describes – sitting by the dying embers of a fire whose flickering light enhances an already unsurpassed beauty – he prefers her past to remain a mystery. Part of her initial attraction for him was indeed her

Northern Irish Catholic childhood, with its associations of heroic struggle and victimhood, ideas given poignancy by her physical fragility. The little he does know about her, however, has dulled his curiosity: the father with a chemist's shop, a small provincial town, the Catholic grammar school. No bombers, hunger-strikers or political activists in that quarter, he would guess.

He fears that, if he were to question her, he would uncover the predictable *ennui* of provincial life, and stories about the nuns that convent-educated women produce at dinner parties until well into middle age. Whatever childhood miseries lie hidden in her background, however, it's clear there's been nothing to inflict serious harm on her. She is too perfect to have been damaged in any way.

Steve surfaces to hear Nora quoting Auden's memorial poem for Yeats – 'He was silly like us' – though in what context? He'll have to concentrate.

'Precisely,' says Nick. 'Pete's already talked about the way he rages against old age. I'm sure a lot of people feel like that, but they think it would compromise their dignity to admit it. Instead they use clichés, like "the compensations of age".'

Steve, who has been surprised by his emotional volatility in a situation where he would expect his mind to take over and work with relentless efficiency, experiences an irrational surge of rage towards Nick. He supposes the younger man to be right, but feels that he has no right to be saying it. Only those like Steve who are indeed aware of the process of ageing may speak satirically of the clichés the old employ to preserve their dignity. Is it, he wonders, the fear of looking ridiculous that inhibits him from declaring his feelings to Nora? But surely he's ridiculous not in entertaining such feelings but in underestimating himself. Unless he's utterly self-deluded, he thinks he might still claim to have what Yeats calls 'pretty plumage'.

When his anger subsides and he is again able to concentrate on what is being said, he finds that Nick is holding forth again, this time on Yeats's description of Maud Gonne's 'image' in later life:

> Hollow of cheek as though it drank the wind
> And took a mess of shadows for its meat.

It seems to Steve unlikely that Nick's failed to notice the parallel here with Nora's own style of beauty. Does he envisage a life spent with her, watching her age with the same grace as Maud Gonne?

As though repudiating Nick's entitlement to be harbouring such thoughts, Steve drifts off into a reverie of his own, in which he and Nora disclose their mutual love, as a prelude to their first sexual union. He doesn't remember fantasising in this way since adolescence, perhaps because he's never had a problem in turning wish into reality. If the young people around him were party to his thoughts, they would find him preposterous, even repellent, but this only encourages him to see himself as engaged in an act of heroic defiance. Why shouldn't he?

He is roused by a change in atmosphere in the room. As far as he's been able to tell, the discussion, while occasionally heated (as you would expect of a successful seminar), has been good-humoured, but now seems to have soured. Doing his best to catch up, he realises that Emma has objected to Yeats's suggestion that women might be disappointed in their children. Her sense of outrage is not particularly remarkable, given her known opinions, but Nora's response is uncharacteristically sharp, as though she has more at stake in the issue than an objective reading of the poem: 'Don't you think you're allowing yourself to be sentimental, Emma? That you're ignoring the full range of human possibility in the service of your own theories? That you're not allowing yourself to respond to the nuances of the poem because you feel you have to defend women above all else?'

Steve is dismayed by Nora's reaction. Because it sounds like a personal attack, it falls short of the high standard she's otherwise maintained, but there's something more than he cannot quite grasp, something raw and unassimilated in Nora that's been briefly exposed, but not enough for any real understanding.

It's a relief when she recovers her poise and shifts the debate from the personal to the abstract.

'Rather than take what he says about mothers in isolation,' she says, 'we should see it a part of a more generalised argument against idealism. I don't mean against having ideals, in the sense that we normally understand the term, but against having ideas about the way things ought to be, rather than accepting the way they are. The poem says that, whether these ideas come from religion, or philosophy, or are simply the hopes that we have for our children, in the end they cause heartbreak. We suffer because they're unrealisable and because they prevent us from engaging fully in life, from rejoicing in imperfection as part of the human condition.'

What, Steve thinks, does this girl – who at the moment is for him the embodiment of human perfection – know about human reality, if by that she means disappointment, frustrated idealism, decay and the frailties of the flesh? Yet she seems to have an instinctive understanding of these things, to be old beyond her years, and this, paradoxically, completes her perfection: that she combines youthful beauty with mature knowledge. When he comes to reveal his feelings for her, she will respond with complete sympathy.

'The pursuit of what is unrealisable,' he hears Nora saying, 'distracts us from the life that is there to be lived. And from the kind of fulfilment and joy that are actually available to us.'

Steve can hardly bear to listen to this. Everything seems to have direct relevance to him. Nora herself is both an unrealisable ideal (if he allows himself to be swayed by caution and prudence) and a real person, whom he could reach out and touch . . . Not here, of course, but in the right circumstances, why not?

'And this brings us to the wonderful final stanza. Although Nick read it so beautifully, I'll read it again to remind you of it. Bear in mind that the chestnut tree brings the natural world into the poem. Until now human beings have been placed in relation to ideas, but here they're seen in terms of the life cycle, the process of nature. And dancing expresses a joy in being, as opposed to the despair that comes from striving for the unattainable. So the poem closes with an ecstatic celebration of the wholeness of being that can only be achieved in the moment, in the body, when "labour" is the body's joyful celebration of itself and its own vitality.

'Labour is blossoming or dancing where
The body is not bruised to pleasure soul,
Nor beauty born out of its own despair,
Nor blear-eyed wisdom out of midnight oil.
O chestnut tree, great rooted blossomer,
Are you the leaf, the blossom or the bole?
O body swayed to music, O brightening glance,
How can we know the dancer from the dance?'

While discussion continues, with Nick arguing that Yeats was in no position to champion natural man at the expense of cultured man, Steve is in a state of near ecstasy himself. No matter how irrational he might judge his feelings to be in other circumstances, he cannot shake off the conviction that Nora has been issuing him instructions and reassurance, through her reading of the poem. As student and teacher, after all, their relationship might be said to have begun in the study, where 'blear-eyed wisdom' is acquired through burning the midnight oil. But now Nora, whose voice has fused with that of the poet, is arguing for the primacy of the body over the mind, and for the joy available to us through the body. Then, with the force of a revelation, he remembers that it was under the college's chestnut tree that he first saw her.

While Steve is busy enumerating the striking parallels between Yeats's theme and the drift of his own feelings, he becomes uncomfortably aware that the room has gone quiet. He glances at the clock, sees that the session is almost over and realises that his students are waiting for his contribution: a summing-up, perhaps, certainly a comment on Nora's performance. His mind is blank and, to buy time, he takes off his glasses and massages the bridge of his nose, a gesture that often accompanies a pause for thought. What he doesn't realise is that, rather than looking reflective, his naked face seems vulnerable. One or two of the more attentive students, who have been aware of his self-absorption, are beginning to wonder whether he has taken a bad turn. His face is pale and slack, his body without the tension and energy that they associate with him.

As he struggles to find a suitable reply, he is rescued by Pete, who takes on the role that he would normally perform himself. 'I'd just like to say, Nora,' says Pete, opening his arms in an expansive gesture, 'that we knew you were good, but not that good.'

A short burst of applause follows, but Nora, who has been unusually animated, even elated, during the seminar, now looks anxious, the smile that she manages in response pinched and wary. Steve, meanwhile, who has mastered his resources in the breathing space given him by Pete, has made his way to the front of the room.

'That's been a salutary experience for me,' he says, glancing briefly at Nora before turning to the room at large. 'We – that is, my generation of academic critics – have all spent so much time attacking Yeats's views and exposing his links to every barmy movement of the time that we've forgotten how his poetry works and why we still want to read it. It's been an exemplary seminar in every way.'

He goes on to clarify the order of coming seminars, who's doing what when, and to talk about essay dead-lines. His manner is efficient, but he appears preoccupied, as though he has mentally moved on to the next item in his busy day. And indeed, rather than lingering as he some-times does, allowing students to approach him with queries in relative privacy, he gathers up his possessions immedi-ately and makes for the door, pausing only briefly for a few words with Nora. 'That was great. Really great. Well done. I've got a meeting now, but I'll be in touch. There are one or two points I'd like to discuss further with you.'

Nora slowly gathers up her own papers and packs them away, pausing from time to time to smile and thank those who stop to offer comments and congratulations on their way to the door. While the room empties, Nick remains seated, flipping through his edition of Yeats's poems, but keeping his eye on Nora, making sure that she isn't borne away by the others. His timing is impeccable, and the moment she is alone, he stands facing her at the desk, where she lingers uncertainly, as though she hasn't yet made up her mind what to do next.

'Suffering from anti-climax?' he asks her. He is smiling, looking into her eyes, willing her to engage with him. For months he's been biding his time with Nora, never pushing her further than she's prepared to go, proceeding step by cautious step. But now he feels they've reached the moment of decision. The afternoon has dispelled in him any lingering doubts about Nora's capacity for emotion – it's unlikely that poetry alone can rouse her to excitement – and he's tired of waiting, though less confident than he'd like to appear. If she were less preoccupied – she seems to be finding it difficult to shift her mental focus from the seminar to something else – she might notice that his knuckles, gripping the front of the desk as he stands over her, are white with tension.

'I suppose that's right,' she says, smiling up at him. 'It's like exams – you can't wait to get them over with but once they're finished you don't know what to do with yourself.'

'Well, if it was a kind of exam, there's no question that you've distinguished yourself, so the only thing to do is celebrate. Come and have a drink with me and we'll make an evening of it.'

'It's a lovely idea, Nick, but there are things I should be getting on with. Let's do it some other time.'

She looks doubtful, however, and Nick, who has decided she would like to come but is nervous of taking the final step, presses on: 'You just said you didn't know what to do with yourself, after all the recent excitement. I don't believe that even you are capable of going back now and writing an essay.'

'I know it must sound terribly rude, and maybe I haven't been entirely honest. The truth is that I feel restless and I don't think I'd be very good company.' She picks up her bag and jacket and, before Nick has time to protest that he'll allow her not to be very good company, says, 'Do you think Steve liked it? He said all the right things, but I don't think he was paying attention. Towards the end, I even thought he'd nodded off.'

She seems eager for his opinion, not just making conversation. The class gossip about Nora's relations with Steve, which Nick has always dismissed as unlikely, suddenly seems more plausible. There might be reasons for her secretiveness – that, for example, there are things in her life now, rather than in the past, that she would prefer to keep hidden – which he's never considered. It would make more sense of why she's kept him dangling, holding out the possibility of something she can never quite deliver.

'I think he liked it well enough,' he says drily. 'He probably didn't want to lay himself open to charges of favouritism.'

They are by the lift now and when it stops and Nora gets in, Nick says, 'I've got something to sort out in the library.'

Before the door closes on her, she says, 'Thanks for the marvellous reading, Nick, and for all the support,' but he's already turned away.

Nora leaves the building and begins aimlessly to wander the streets. After about half an hour, she realises that she has doubled back on herself and is again approaching the college buildings. One thing she's clear about is that she doesn't want to run into anyone who was at the seminar so she takes a sudden change of direction and cuts through to Russell Square, where she chooses a bench that's partly hidden by trees, away from the main paths and sits down.

She doesn't know quite what she was expecting from the seminar, but her expectations were all the more potent for being vague. She put so much into it – not just work but, as Steve might describe it, she had encoded herself into her reading of the poem – that she had envisaged some kind of climactic moment, a sign from Nick, or Steve particularly (although she now thinks bitterly that anybody would have done), that she was understood. Under the circumstances she thought she was creating, it would have been easy for her to say (later, not in the class-room), in response to the right question, that the flowering chestnut tree for her was Felix, whose 'labour' was simply to be and to communicate a joy in being; and that since she left him behind, her own capacity for life has atrophied. To say that they were both, she and Felix, victims of their parents' thwarted idealism, although that's too noble a phrase to apply to the resentment that gripped them after Felix's birth: they couldn't bear not being better in every way than the people around them.

'Among School Children' was the closest approach she could make to the life that she hasn't been able to leave behind, which she replays endlessly in her mind through remembered scenes and conversations. She realises now that it was foolish of her to expect a response to such an oblique act of soul-baring, but Steve didn't even seem to be listening. What he said at the end was adequate, perhaps more than adequate – rationally, she can see that – but it was professional, not the response of someone who has a vested interest in her. As for Nick, he was undoubtedly moved but in the wrong way.

It isn't that she doesn't want, at some ideal level, the kind of sexual relationship Nick surely has in mind, but she has a keen sense that her childhood is still unfinished.

She feels a yearning, not for what she left behind but for what she was missing even when she was there, which her immersion in the poem has revived. It's as though her own experience of family life, which she's come to see as an aberration, has allowed her to preserve intact an ideal version of how it might have been. She knows that she was right to leave home, but she has forfeited the place where she belongs. If she had taken up Nick's offer, surrendered to the moment, would that eventually have taken her to another such place, one where she might truly belong, only better, more sustaining?

It isn't what she wants at the moment, though. What she craves instead is unconditional love and approval, of the kind that only a parent can give. She wants not to have to make a constant effort to sustain the momentum of her life, not to have to live with the feeling that, if she slackens her effort, she will fall through a black hole into nothing. She wants a place to go where she can throw down her coat and bag and tell the achievements of the afternoon (for it was, within its own terms, a success) to someone who will hang on her every word, who will never charge her with conceit, because that is the only place where such things can be said, and where her feelings will be shared, not judged. She wants to be lapped around by warmth and approval.

Suddenly she thinks of Martha, sees her head inclined towards Jessica or Emily, a little smile – not a social smile, designed to disarm and charm, but the involuntary smile of pleasure – playing about her lips, lighting up her eyes, all thoughts of herself obliterated by her delight in another. She isn't, of course, Martha's daughter, and Martha could never feel for her as she does for them, but she has sensed Martha's warmth and goodwill towards her. If she were to take herself there, Martha would surely respond. There is no competition, after all, between herself and Jessica and Emily, so what Martha gave her could never compromise what is due to them.

Of course, she wouldn't be able to speak to Martha as though she were indeed her mother. Steve was present at the seminar today and might have a different story to tell; and a mother – a real mother, who fulfils all the requirements – would never see her daughter as boastful, where an outsider might, however well disposed. Nonetheless, it would be pleasant to sit in Martha's kitchen and participate in, however minor a role, the warmth of family life.

She gets up from the bench and, head bowed, walks round the square, arguing with herself over whether the terms of her relationship with Martha and her daughters license an unannounced and uninvited visit. She isn't even sure that Martha will be home from work, and if she were, how Jessica and Emily would react, though she assumes that Steve is still occupied with his meeting. If she doesn't do something, though, she feels she will explode, so urgent is her need for company. Her heart pounding, she makes her decision and walks to the bus stop.

Twenty minutes later, she is standing in Steve's road, not outside the door but behind a tree that gives her adequate concealment, and from where she can judge the mood of the house. Reluctant to impose herself where she may not be wanted, and without any real knowledge of these people and their ways, so different from what she grew up with, she is now crippled by doubt. She was last here before Christmas, for a drinks party, when the door was ajar for guests to make their way in without knocking, and the rooms were brightly lit so that groups of people, laughing, chatting, holding out their glasses for more wine, were visible from the street, caught in the act of enjoying the Woolfs' hospitality.

Although she was intimidated by the apparent sophistication and worldliness of the guests, enhanced as they were by the framing effect of the door and windows, the house was open and welcoming to those outside the tight inner circle of family. Today, however, it looks to Nora, searching for clues to the possible outcome of a knock on the door, self-contained and forbidding. The afternoon sun is shining on to the house, reflecting light off the windows. Small clumps of bulbs, placed strategically in the small front garden, and a dark camellia by the front gate that she failed to notice on earlier visits, seem designed to shield the front basement window from prying eyes, as though the family has closed in on itself.

She is about to turn away, having no right to proceed, when she feels a tugging at her sleeve. She turns with a start and sees Emily. 'Hi,' says Emily, her eyes shining with the pleasure of seeing her.

She is wearing her school uniform, in which she looks surprisingly comfortable, sporting none of the sexier adjustments that Nora has become used to on the London streets, and is slightly stooped from the schoolbag she is carrying on her back. Even stooping, however, she is taller than Nora, though in other respects appears younger than her years. Her hair is clean, but looks as though she hasn't bothered to brush it all day. Her skin is clear and her eyes without guile. 'Wholesome' is the word that springs immediately to Nora's mind. 'Oh, hi, Emily, how are you?'

'Oh, you know, all right, apart from a chemistry test tomorrow, and I'm late tonight because I've had Drama Club.'

'I'm sure your father wouldn't mind if you didn't put too much effort into your chemistry,' says Nora, remembering Steve's disdain about Emily's veterinary ambitions.

'Don't you believe it. He likes us to excel in everything, and then reject the options he disapproves of. If you've come to see him, I think you'll be unlucky. He's hardly ever in at this time.'

'No, I don't want to see him. I'm sorry, that sounds rude, but you know what I mean.'

'You haven't come here for him. That's all right, I'm not offended.' She waits expectantly for Nora to declare the purpose of her visit, since there is no other apparent reason for Nora to be where she is.

'I'm on my way home, but since it's a nice afternoon I decided to walk part of the way and I found myself here. I was wondering whether to drop in, but I'd just decided I wouldn't disturb you all.'

'Oh, do. Mum'll be glad to see you. She's going in to work and coming home early these days because of Jess's A levels.' The last words are delivered in a kind of awed stage whisper.

'Surely they're not until next term.'

'They're not, but Jess likes a drama and she's had us all running round after her since Christmas. The line is that if she doesn't get all As, she won't be able to go to Oxford and her life will be in ruins.'

'Oh dear, that sounds serious.'

'That's what she'd like us to think, but it would be nice to have some light relief. Mum doesn't seem herself at the moment, and Dad isn't quite there even when he is there, if you see what I mean. You wouldn't think one person doing one set of exams could have a devastating effect on so many people. And Jess is being really foul to me because I'm not taking her seriously enough, so if you come in she'll have to be polite and I'll have somebody on my side.

After all, you're living proof that all the best people don't go to Oxford.'

'You have a chemistry test, don't forget. No, I won't, Emily. It's very nice of you to ask, but I didn't realise when I thought of dropping in that . . .'

Emily, however, is tugging at her arm, pulling her across the road. Unless she's prepared to struggle with the girl, Nora cannot see a way of extricating herself. As soon as they're inside the house, Martha's voice calls from the basement: 'We're downstairs, Em, come and have some tea.'

Nora follows Emily down the stairs. Martha and Jessica are sitting at the table, where cups and saucers have been set out. A chocolate cake that looks as if it has come from one of the French pâtisseries that flourish in this part of London is waiting to be cut. Nora immediately feels that she shouldn't have come, that the preparations that have been made were not with her in mind. She draws back instinctively, but Emily pushes her forward, saying, 'Look who I found outside,' as though she has brought home some amazing trophy she is eager to show off and have admired.

Martha's smile, meant for Emily, undergoes an immediate but unreadable transformation when she sees Nora. She continues to smile in welcome, but there is something there besides pleasure, as though she is on her guard. Nora cannot think why she might have that effect on her. The change in Jessica is less marked. She was not about to greet her sister with any particular warmth, and Nora is just a further inconvenience, yet another person to siphon off some of her mother's attention.

Martha soon composes herself. 'This is an unexpected pleasure, Nora. Sit down and have some tea with us,' she says, but Nora caught her initial reaction and feels wretched, her hopes dashed and fears confirmed.

'I hope I'm going to get all this classy confectionery when I do my A levels,' says Emily. 'You've come at the right time, Nora. As you can see, it's Liberty Hall here, these days – chocolate on tap, anything you like if it makes you happy. That's one of my grandfather's expressions, 'Liberty Hall'. It's his way of saying that we all get far too much now, compared to when he was a boy. He doesn't really mean it, though, he's a real softie. I rather like the expression, don't you? I've sort of decided that when I have a house, that's what I'm going to call it.'

While Emily rattles on, apparently unaware of the tension in the room, Nora, when she can bear to raise her eyes from her teacup, observes the others. Jessica, who has barely acknowledged Nora's presence, is languidly eating tiny morsels of the cake, which Martha has now cut. Martha, she thinks, looks tired and drawn. This offers Nora some comfort. Whether Martha welcomes her visit or not, she can hardly be responsible for a change that would take days, if not weeks, of stress or worry to become apparent, so her response may have less to do with her personally than with other circumstances in her life. Jessica, both from what she has observed and from Emily's account of her recent behaviour, is likely to be a drain on any mother's energy, especially one with such a demanding job as Martha. She feels suddenly protective towards her. Somebody should give Jessica a good talking-to.

As if reinforcing this more comforting interpretation of her own behaviour, Martha turns to Nora, when Emily has been silenced with cake, and says, 'So what have you been up to, Nora, since we last saw you?'

'Oh, not a lot,' says Nora. 'Nothing very exciting, anyway. Work. The usual.'

'And will you be going back to Ireland for Easter?'

'No, not this time. I have a job lined up for the holidays. I need to earn some money.'

'You must spend Easter with us,' says Emily, eagerly. 'It's horrible to be on your own over the holidays, and we're going off to a cottage in Wales that has loads of room. Isn't that right, Mum?'

Nora moves quickly to squash Emily's suggestion, but not soon enough to forestall Martha's immediate expression of panic as she wonders how to cope with an invitation that she would not have issued herself. 'That's really kind of you, Emily, but I have to work over the Easter weekend. It's a restaurant, you see, and Easter's the start of the tourist season. Besides, the pay's better if you work over the holiday.'

Jessica, who seemed briefly curious about Nora's need for paid employment – an eventuality that she doesn't anticipate for her own university career – has just as suddenly lost interest. She begins to talk to Martha about *The Knight's Tale* – or, rather, to resume a conversation about an essay she is writing on *The Knight's Tale*. She takes care to exclude Nora as she addresses her mother.

'Why don't you talk to Nora about it?' Emily asks. 'Have you done *The Knight's Tale*, Nora? I bet you've got some really good ideas on it.'

For the first time on this particular visit Jessica gives Nora a direct look that communicates her certainty that nothing Nora might have to say could possibly be of any interest to her.

'I'm sure Jessica doesn't need any help from me,' says Nora, rising. 'I really must go. Thank you so much for the tea.'

Jessica barely acknowledges her imminent departure.

Martha makes a move to show her out, but Emily is already on her feet. At the front door she says to Nora, 'You see what I mean about Jess? I don't think exams are any excuse for being rude, but they seem to have taken her that way. If it's any consolation, she's like that with everyone.'

Nora doesn't believe that, but is grateful for Emily's kindness. She says, 'Your mother seems very tired.'

'Yes she does, doesn't she? You can hardly blame her, with Jess hanging on to her like a leech. I'd talk to Dad to see if he can sort it out, if I thought I could hold his attention for long enough. He's probably working too hard. That's usually the problem. It seems to be something of a family affliction. Sometimes I think I'll just go and work in Boots. Do you want me to give Dad a message?'

'No, no. Thank you. Goodbye, Emily. Thanks for everything.'

Emily stands at the door, waving vigorously, until Nora disappears at the top of the road.

Nora walks on, head down, hunched in on herself. She feels mortified, humiliated, and what makes it worse is the knowledge that she's brought it on herself. Her cheeks are burning with shame, but her anger isn't turned solely against herself. Even when all the excuses for them have been made, there was no reason for Martha and Jessica to treat her with such coldness, even hostility. She has done nothing to them, except maybe infringe some petty social law by calling uninvited. Since she's been in London, she's done her best to reject everything that the Irish say about the English, but it's hard to avoid thinking that there's some truth in what is commonly said – that English friendliness is only superficial, with no real warmth, that they're hypocrites who tell you to drop in at any time, then make sure you know you're not welcome when you do.

And now she has to face the prospect of returning to the flat. Since Christmas, when the Metcalfes' expectations of what she might do for Phoebe were starkly presented to her, relations between her and Phoebe have been strained. Phoebe has become openly proprietorial about her flat, reminding Nora, when she remembers, which are her grandmother's teacups; pointing out minor infringements of house rules (imagined overloading of the washing-machine was the most recent) that were never made in the first place. This has been most marked when Nora has been publicly praised for an essay, or a comment that she's made in a seminar has been greeted with enthusiasm. Meanwhile, complaints about the 'favouritism' that 'everybody knows' is rife in the English department have become more frequent.

It's been hard for her to contain her resentment, which sprang from the knowledge that the Metcalfes' apparent generosity comes with a price, and the suspicion that they always had it in mind to exploit her. Yet she feels under an obligation to them and knows that her situation in London is too precarious to allow her the luxury of a principled stand-off. So, in her own mind she's established that there's a business arrangement; that she gives Phoebe remedial teaching in return for lodging.

Short of actually cheating, she's done as much as she can to help Phoebe with her work. After lectures and seminars she takes time to discuss them with her, doing her best to clarify what Phoebe has failed to understand. So far, Phoebe has proved unresponsive to this approach, generally taking the view that the problem lies in the current theories deployed by the lecturers, which don't make sense and should be abandoned, rather than in her own inability or unwillingness to grasp them.

When it comes to her essays, Phoebe's stubbornness is even more intractable. She sits, staring into space, while Nora analyses the essay title and sketches a plan; then, at the point where the preliminary work is done and she is required to take over herself, she makes it clear that she is withholding her own labour. It is, Nora thinks, like trying to teach a child to tie his shoelaces. Phoebe refuses to engage in the process because she is confident that, in the end, somebody else will do it for her in a fraction of the time that it will take her. So far, Nora has managed to avoid writing Phoebe's essays for her, and Phoebe hasn't yet asked her to take that final step, but Phoebe's claim on her is implicit in all their dealings, and as essay dead-lines come and go, Nora wonders how long it will be before the situation reaches crisis.

As soon as she lets herself into the flat, Nora is bombarded by the sound of Phoebe's music, coming from the sitting room. Since she can hardly avoid Phoebe's pres-ence in her own flat, she puts her head round the sitting-room door. It is evidence, she has been told, of the more traditional style of parenting in Northern Ireland that she is always careful to observe the civilities. She finds Phoebe and Emma reclining on floor cushions and sharing a joint. Her heart sinks when she sees Emma. Her attack on her during the seminar, which she'd forgotten in the subsequent turmoil of events, now seems foolish, even shameful. She shouldn't have allowed her feelings to get the better of her. It seems now that she's spent the day making enemies.

'What happened to you, then?' asks Phoebe, without turning to look at Nora. 'Did you go for a drink with Nick?

'No, I chatted to him for a bit, but he had work to do in the library and I went for a walk to clear my head.'

Having asked the question, Phoebe shows no interest in the answer, as though she is clear in her own mind that it is unlikely to be truthful. She is browsing idly through CD cases, apparently engaged in selecting some more music. Emma, as if by prior arrangement, takes over.

'Why did you ask Nick to read the poem?'

Nora is so surprised to be interrogated on this point – if Emma had raised Nora's dismissal of her views as 'sentimental', she would have apologised unreservedly – that she has no time to prepare an answer. 'Didn't you think he read it well? I had a feeling that he would, and it was nice to have that instinct confirmed.'

'I just think,' Emma says, 'that since the group is dominated by men – apart from yourself, of course – it would have shown a bit of solidarity if you'd given it to one of the women to read.'

Nora pauses. 'Well, that's a consideration that didn't occur to me, perhaps because the speaker of the poem is a man. Would it not have been perverse, in a mixed group, to have it read by a girl?'

Emma shrugs dismissively, indicating that this is the kind of argument that has always been used to hold women back.

'Well, if you'll excuse me, I have work to do.'

Nora shuts herself in her room, but she doesn't work. She doesn't even want to work. What she wants is company, perhaps even the opportunity to unburden herself. Tonight, her feelings released by the events of the day, she feels she will burst with the weight of unspoken history unless she can find a sympathetic listener. She tries lying on the bed, but is too restless to settle so she paces the room. The last few hours have been dreadful. The euphoria she felt during the seminar has mutated from a sense of exclusion, of belonging nowhere, of being unjustly treated, into barely containable feelings of grief, loss and anger.

The final little episode, with Phoebe and Emma, would have been laughable, were it not for the suggestion of conspiracy and menace. For the first time since she came to London, Nora feels contempt for the people around her – for spoiled children of privilege like Jessica, Phoebe and Emma – with their pettiness and self-obsession and assumption that their whims should be gratified. For all its harshness, the Northern Ireland of her childhood (outside her own home) had a cold, clean, bracing quality, and she remembers with respect the seriousness of her contemporaries. Caught between the imperatives of religion and political conflict, it was harder for them to feel that they could impose their will on the world. All her efforts to adapt to London and its ways suddenly seem misdirected, because she doesn't want to be like the people here.

Then she thinks of Nick and wonders whether she should include him in all this. He certainly isn't silly, like Phoebe and Emma, but does his intelligence mask a deeper moral frivolity? She'll never know unless she tests it. Of all the people she might confide in, he's certainly the most likely candidate.

Now she bitterly regrets brushing him off. It's clear to her now that he would be the ideal confidant. She takes out of her bag the mobile telephone she bought with her Christmas earnings to give her some privacy, some defence against Phoebe's curiosity about her dealings with Steve, and wonders whether she should ring him now. Then she remembers Emma and Phoebe's insinuations, and Nick's coldness when they parted. She couldn't bear him to rebuff her. While she stares at the mobile, trying to convince herself that nothing will change in her life unless she's prepared to take a risk, it begins to ring.

'Hello?' Her voice is thick from crying.

'Is that Nora?'

'It is, yes.'

'It's Steve. I said I'd ring – do you remember? Are you all right? You sound different.'

'I'm fine, I was sleeping.'

'I'm so sorry.'

'No, it's OK, if I hadn't woken, I wouldn't have slept tonight. You've done me a service, really.'

'I'm not surprised you're tired, you put so much into your seminar. It was wonderful.'

'Thank you.' She tries to say more, to turn the conversation into another, less embarrassing, direction, but can't. The warmth and sympathy in his voice, coming as they do after rejection and hostility, have brought her again to the brink of tears.

'Would you like to see *The Playboy of the Western World*?'

'What?'

'Synge's play, there's a revival of it – only a small rep production, I'm afraid, but I thought you might want to see it.'

'Yes, I know what it is. I'd like that, thank you.'

Details of time and place are settled.

'Thank you for agreeing to come,' says Steve. 'I'll look forward to it. Very much.'

'Yes, yes, so will I.'

Ballypierce

During the summer holidays when the IRA declared a cease-fire, Nora was in a permanent state of contained excitement, as though her temperature was slightly elevated but with none of the disagreeable symptoms of infection. Her energy seemed boundless. At the beginning of the holidays, she had taken it upon herself to spring-clean the bungalow, a concept she had acquired not from life – vigorous domestic activity had never been part of Bernie's repertoire, and was now, at her present weight, altogether beyond her, even if the will had been there – but from books. For, while her contemporaries were reading late-twentieth-century fictions of divorced parents, playground bullying and teenage pregnancy, Nora had acquired a taste for nineteenth-century novels in which young women of extraordinary virtue, usually expressed in the domestic sphere, were, if they managed to escape an early death, rewarded with recognition and lifelong happiness.

It was at this point in her life that Nora lost interest in the certainties of mathematics and Latin, except as subjects that she needed to realise her ambitions, and decided to study literature, which fired her imagination with undreamed-of possibilities: that lives could change and individual effort be rewarded; that those who were good and lovable might be unjustly treated at the beginning of their lives but that was not the end of the story.

Windows were cleaned, curtains washed, floors and surfaces scrubbed, furniture polished and mounds of hidden rubbish – crisps and biscuit packets, chocolate wrappers, empty drink cans, cereal boxes – were unearthed and removed.

Felix, who was now ten and followed her everywhere, was refining his talent for mimicry. He would observe his father, studying his expression and manner, and then, brows knitted, voice deepened and shoulders slightly hunched, give a passable impression of Gerald's now chronic state of anger. Only the occasional word could be distinguished, but the cadences of Gerald's conversational style were accurately caught. Fortunately, Gerald took too little notice of his son to be aware that he was an object of fascination for him and that, in however perverse a way, he had indeed become his role model. Nora, however, who hadn't yet learned to distinguish between fear of her father and respect for him, found Felix's irreverence liberating. She would take him off to her room or the further reaches of the garden and encourage him in further feats of impersonation so that, in the course of the summer, Felix perfected not only a passable imitation of his father's habitual pacing but also of the stabbing movements with his fingers that were used to re-inforce his arguments. At the end of each 'turn' they would both collapse into helpless laughter.

If Felix mocked his father, he emulated Nora, and she turned this to good effect in occupying him over the long summer holiday. With his little rubbery face puckered in concentration, he assisted her in the feats of cleaning that took up the first few weeks. Then, because he had had so much of her company and was reluctant to leave her side, they spent long hours in the garden together as she taught him to play badminton. This was in many ways an unrewarding task, since Felix was apt to forget overnight what he had learned in the course of the day, but he was able to hit the shuttlecock, if not to return it, and his pleasure was intense.

When Felix was happy, as he was throughout that summer, he clung tenaciously to the immediate source of pleasure – badminton, mimicry, food and, above all, Nora's presence – never wearying of it, never wanting to move on, living entirely in and for the moment. Nora, by contrast, was able to tolerate Felix's unquenchable need for her not only because his love for her was entirely uncontaminated but because she felt herself to be marking time, living through a phase in her life for which she could now envisage an ending. Cramped though her immediate circumstances were, with only Felix for company, she saw that she had the capacity, ultimately, to transform her life, and this was the source of her new excitement and energy. Sometimes she felt she would burst with the sense of what her life might be, and didn't know how she would live through the time, and jump through the necessary hoops of school syllabuses and examinations until what was potential became reality.

The IRA ceasefire was on 13 August, when the holidays were already drawing to a close, but Nora's memories of that summer were illuminated by it. This was in part because the sense of a new beginning, of a threshold or boundary between one state of being and another, matched her own mood. Her first reaction, when the news broke, in what she was later to see as her political naïveté, was that her father would be deprived of his ruling obsession. For if peace broke out, there would no longer be the

223

pretext for a chronically besieged mentality. The immediate effect on Gerald, however, was precisely the opposite of her expectations.

'We'll be sold down the river again,' he declaimed, pacing up and down the kitchen and using his rolled newspaper to bash chairs and cupboards. Felix was mesmerised, his eyes darting about as he tracked the newspaper, storing every gesture for future use.

'Why should they trust John Major? This is the man who betrayed his own leader, betrayed the Kurds in Iraq . . .' His litany proceeded undisturbed but, with the exception of Felix, his audience was unmoved. When he had finished, after a rousing reprise of the IRA's commitment to 'No Surrender', there was silence.

'Well, do you females have nothing to say on the subject? This boy here, for all his brainlessness, is taking more interest than you are.'

Bernie, who usually endorsed all Gerald's political pronouncements, if only because politics was the one subject on which he ever addressed her, and if she disagreed with him on that he might stop speaking to her altogether, dared on this occasion to express dissent. 'Well, I think it's great,' she said. 'People will be able to lead normal lives again – get out and about without fear of a bomb going off.'

Gerald stared at her in disbelief, affecting to be stunned by the depth of her ignorance. 'This is what comes of years watching television all day. You start to believe the pap they feed you. Do you not realise that the only reason Catholics enjoy any measure of security is because the IRA protects us? Men have sacrificed their lives so that women like you can sleep soundly in their beds.' Then, turning to Nora, he said, 'I suppose you agree with your mother.'

Nora knew enough by now of life in Northern Ireland

beyond her immediate and circumscribed world to be dimly aware that it was the Catholic housing estates of Belfast and Derry that the IRA routinely policed, not the select bungalows of Ballypierce; but she also knew enough not to share this thought with her father. 'I think we should wait and see,' she said.

'Wait and see,' he mocked. 'We've been waiting since nineteen bloody twenty, and so far we've seen nothing.' Now well into his stride, he turned back to Bernie. 'Let's hear you tell me what difference you think this is going to make to you. When was the last time you left this house, except maybe to waddle down the road to the sweetie shop? Come on, I think I have the right to an answer. Can you honestly tell me that you're going to start hopping on and off buses to Belfast, or getting behind the wheel of a car again because of this? Well, are you?'

He stood glaring at her for a while, enjoying his triumph and her distress, then stamped out of the room. Bernie's lip was trembling and the tears ran down her fat cheeks.

'Don't be upset, Mummy,' said Nora. 'It'll blow over.' Within the family, only Felix was in the habit of showing affection, and over the years, having failed to elicit any response from Bernie or Gerald, he had come to restrict his attentions to his beloved sister. Nora wished that she could put her arms round her mother, behave with the ease, spontaneity and simplicity shown by members of her ideal, notional family, but reserve towards her mother was now too deeply entrenched, whatever her present predicament, and she felt paralysed, incapable of the healing gesture. Instead she whispered to Felix, who was responsive to sadness and had always comforted her in those sorrows that couldn't be taken to their parents, to go and comfort their mother. With the air of serious intent that he always displayed when bidden to something by Nora, he walked round the table and rested his arm on his mother's shoulders, giving a fair impression of a kind of manly protectiveness that, in this case, was not learned from observing his father.

'Doan cry,' he said. "Eer up.'

Bernie looked at him, briefly puzzled, and then her tears turned to sobs. Then, fighting to get the words out while the spasms of grief continued, constricting her breath, Bernie spoke for the first time since she had given her support to the peace process: 'I know it's not his fault, he couldn't help being born.'

These were sentiments that could hardly be addressed directly to Felix. She was anyway not in the habit of speaking to him, even in happier circumstances. As she had once confessed to Nora, in a moment of unusual candour, she had never been able to understand how people could talk to their pets and, as far as she was concerned, Felix fell into the same category.

'But nothing's ever been the same since, everything's changed. Since the day he was born, your father's hardly touched me.'

Nora shifted uneasily in her chair. This wasn't something she wanted to hear.

'It's as if he blamed me, though the midwife said it could just as easily be his fault. He didn't lose interest in me because I got so fat. I put on the weight because he could hardly bear to look at me, so it made no difference. Do you remember how proud he used to be of me when we went out? He used to say, "Bernie, you're a picture, you'll outshine them all." And I did. Would you believe it, that other women were jealous of me? It's hard to credit now, but there was a time when I could go anywhere and hold my head high.'

Felix, who was baffled and frightened by the outpouring of grief that his gesture of sympathy had provoked, had run back to Nora. With his hands over his ears to keep out the noise, he buried his head in his sister's lap.

'Do you remember the time he gave me that gold cock-tail watch, when we were going to the pharmacists' dinner-dance? In those days he took me to functions, he wanted to show me off. Nothing was too good for me. I didn't have a notion that he'd taken himself off to Belfast to buy it. Then, just before we left the house, he pulled it out of his pocket and, like, dangled it in front of me. "What do you suppose this is?" he said. Then he put it on me himself. I felt like a million dollars, and now he can hardly bear to look at me.'

Nora sat very still, doing her best to disguise her embarrassment, knowing that a wrong move would bring accusations of coldness and failure to sympathise with her mother's predicament. She had no wish to be her mother's confidante on the intimacies of her married life, but knew that there was no one else in whom Bernie could confide. Even if she had retained with her sisters the family bonds that had been weakened by her marriage and effectively broken with Felix's birth, she would never have compromised her pride by exposing these raw wounds, which were unlikely ever to heal.

There was the further difficulty for Nora that her memories of the time before Felix, scant and hazy though they were, did not entirely match those of her mother. Her father had indeed been proud of his wife's appearance, but he had often been neglectful and bored by her company. It seemed to Nora that Bernie, in choosing to see in the past an irrecoverable ideal, was experiencing the present as worse than it need be, and feeding her lethargy and despair.

'Do you remember the holidays we had?' Bernie continued. 'It's hard to believe now that we were the first Catholics in this town to go to Spain, not one of the cheap resort places that everybody goes to now, but a gorgeous hotel where you had to dress for dinner every night. I had so many outfits that I didn't wear anything more than twice. Now he doesn't even take us to the west coast, even though he's never done saying that people should stay at home for their holidays and Ireland beats anywhere in Europe. Not even a day trip. Wouldn't you like to go on holiday?'

This was the first of the questions in Bernie's monologue that seemed to require an answer. It wasn't that Bernie wanted Nora to lay claim to the same sense of desperation that she felt herself. Since Bernie was assured that her own plight was unmatched, any hint from Nora that she, too, had suffered because of Felix would not be welcome. What she wanted was confirmation of her own sense of outrage: to be told that she was right to feel hard done by, that she was being denied what the rest of the population took for granted.

As it happened, Nora had no wish to go away with her parents, even though, when school broke up, a number of the girls were vying with each other about their parents' choice of holiday destination. It wasn't that she never wanted to travel, but that was for the future, part of the life she had been envisaging for herself all summer, which would be lived fully and on her own terms. Indeed, it was impossible to picture them all on a family holiday. Both her parents still avoided being seen in public with Felix, and what could be more exposed than a beach? Even if that obstacle were overcome, would her mother be able to get into a deck-chair without humiliating them all? And what would her father do? She tried to picture him, adapting his customary pacing up and down to sand, as he held forth on his current obsession.

An answer was required, however, and on a sudden inspiration she evaded her mother's direct question in favour of her passing reference to day trips. 'Why don't we do something – you and me and Felix? Why don't we go to the sea – just for the day? It would do you good.'

Her form at school had had a day's outing at the coast, with a picnic lunch, ice-creams, races, games and splashing about in the ice-cold waves, while the teachers sat huddled in deck-chairs, gossiping and taking it in turns to peer out to sea and shout at any girl who had gone beyond acceptable limits. What she was remembering now, however, was a little café with a few tables outside – Ireland, in the cliché of the times, was becoming more continental – which was just above the beach, where her mother could sit (no need for a deck-chair) and look out to sea.

Bernie was stunned into silence. The purpose of sessions like these was not to find answers or solutions or temporary alleviation to chronic and painful problems, but confirmation from Nora that all effort was useless and her mother's life doomed to disappointment and grief.

'Why not?' Nora coaxed. What had begun as an attempt to distract Bernie from useless reminiscence, which would almost certainly end in observations about Nora's failure to sympathise, was becoming a challenge to her powers to persuade and control. The diffuse energy and optimism of that time, and the influence of her summer reading, which had encouraged her in the belief that individual acts of goodness, especially when performed by girls of her age, could transform the lives of those around them, made her unusually eloquent and insistent. She told her mother about the nice little café where she could sit undisturbed, the view of the sea and the easy walk from the bus stop. 'You won't have to do a thing. I'll see to everything.'

'What about Felix?'

'I'll look after him. He'll be good as gold, you'll see.' At the mention of Felix, she looked down at him, nestled against her, his head resting on her lap, and stroked his hair, which was still thick and silky but cut short now to meet the requirements of school and darkening as he left infancy behind. Since Felix had no effective voice of his own, it was impossible not to speak of and for him, but Nora always tried to do him the courtesy of acknowledging his presence. He rewarded her with a contented smile and burrowed further into her lap. Sometimes it seemed as though he were trying to melt into her.

Bernie, meanwhile, was still bewildered by the novelty of Nora's suggestion. In recent years she had become as lethargic mentally as physically, so that it was as difficult for her to entertain a new idea as to get up from the sofa. She remained unconvinced as Nora tried to anticipate and remove obstacles, and then, just as Nora was on the point of giving up, she said, 'What do you think your father would say?'

'I don't see that he could object. He'd certainly be surprised.'

'It would show that I meant what I said about the ceasefire, wouldn't it?'

'Well, yes, I suppose it would.'

For the rest of the day, Nora applied herself to sustaining her mother's mood. The episode had given her a sense of power, of being able to make things happen, which reinforced her newly awakened sense of life's possibilities. Felix, who had only ever been taken swimming from school and who had had the planned treat carefully explained to him by Nora, trailed her around with his trunks and towel in a plastic bag, until the rare delight of swimming in the sea with Nora might begin.

When Gerald came home, Bernie bided her time until she made her announcement. As soon as he had finished his supper, and before he had drifted away to his own pursuits, she said, 'You might have to wait for your dinner tomorrow night, though there's ham and salad in the fridge if you're hungry.'

Unused to being surprised by his wife, and preferring always to take the initiative in conversation, he sought refuge in sarcasm: 'Is that so? Don't tell me they've rescheduled your favourite television programme.'

'No, I'm taking Nora and Felix to the coast for the day – if it's fine, that is. I thought we could all do with a day out.'

He looked from one to the other as he tried to get a grip on this new turn of events. 'Is this one of your bright ideas?' he asked Nora.

'It was Mummy who said she'd like a day out, and I suggested somewhere we might go.'

He nodded slowly, displeased by what appeared to be a conspiracy. 'And what will you do if she has a heart-attack while she tries to get on to a bus? I don't suppose you've thought of that.'

Nora's first thought was that Bernie would withdraw from the scheme after this crude reminder of its possible dangers, but she had underestimated the fighting spirit she had kindled in her.

'At least I'd die happy, with something to look forward to,' Bernie said.

In the event, Bernie avoided a heart-attack, although Gerald had been right to identify the bus as a crucial strategic problem. As Bernie's emotional life, never wide in its range, had narrowed to the point where self-pity alone sustained her, Nora's sympathy for her mother had dwindled. On the morning of the outing, however, Bernie was remarkably uncomplaining. Nora watched her standing at the bus stop, tremulous but trying her best to pretend that there was nothing unusual about her being there, and felt a sudden, painful stab of love for her mother, a desperation that she shouldn't be humiliated. She had prepared Felix for the ordeal by telling him repeatedly that he must be a good boy and help her with their mother, and he, too, was assuming an appropriate demeanour. Head high, unsmiling, shoulders taut, he was imagining himself into the role of responsible son, right-hand man to his beloved Nora.

When the bus stopped, Felix jumped on first, at a signal from Nora, and with one hand on the bar, extended the other towards his mother, every muscle straining. Nora took up position behind her and pushed until Bernie made contact with Felix, then with the bar. For a while Bernie was so breathless that Nora feared Gerald would be proved right and the expedition would end with a medical emergency only yards from home; but in time she recovered and they settled into their seats, Bernie in a double seat to herself and Nora and Felix behind, with Felix by the window.

Although Felix was used to the school minibus, he had never travelled in this way with Nora. He stared out of the window, entranced, and asked repeatedly where the sea was, never relaxing his grip on Nora's hand. Bernie, too, took an interest in the surroundings, commenting on housing developments, shop closures and other changes since she had last travelled this route.

The unaccustomed exposure to the outside world set

off a train of reminiscences in Bernie of a more soothing and benign nature than the usual lament for a golden past that had been abruptly destroyed by Felix's birth. Over coffee and cake, and a can of Coca-Cola for Felix, at the café overlooking the sea, she talked about growing up in a large family: the bus trips to the coast or to Belfast to shop or see a film, the sessions with her sisters, trying out hairstyles and makeup. This was the first hint that Nora had had from her mother that she had ever enjoyed some kind of communal life, rather than standing always apart, attracting admiration and jealousy in equal measure.

Felix sat bolt upright during the coffee-and-cake interlude, his entire body apparently concentrated on the task in hand, as he raised his paper napkin to his mouth after every bite or swallow to brush away stray crumbs and smears. Every so often he looked at Nora for approval or guidance, but he was behaving so beautifully that all that was required of her was a nod of approval. Since he was never taken out to eat and didn't observe such rigorous standards at home, she wondered where he had learned his notions of appropriate behaviour, until she remembered the romantic comedies of the 1950s – often starring Rock Hudson and Doris Day – that her mother sometimes watched in the early afternoons. Cocktails and candlelit dinners were regular features of the genre, so it was at least possible that Felix, in his own mind, was occupying an unbelievably sophisticated urban milieu where eating and drinking were occasions of display, rather than a seat at a plastic table above a windy and almost empty northern beach. It would scarcely have been surprising if, when he had finished, he had produced a lipstick and mirror and touched up his lips, for he identified in fiction and in life with whoever touched his feelings and imagination, regardless of sex; he was more likely to emulate Nora than his father, the only man in his life.

Suddenly, from nowhere, it seemed, for Nora was enjoying Felix's enjoyment, she felt tears prick at her eyes. It was the thought of him living out lives in his imagination that he would never be able to live in reality. Did it matter, if he was happy? Perhaps not, but she had come to realise that it was her presence that secured his happiness, and her plans for the future, which had begun to clarify in the course of this summer, didn't include him: how could she take him with her to university, to work, and perhaps, one day, into a family of her own? She could at least make him as happy as possible now, and after settling her mother with a magazine, more coffee and cake, she took him down to the beach.

'Shall we swim now, Felix?'

Instead of replying, he laughed his funny, almost soundless laugh and, stooping slightly, rubbed his hands together vigorously. This was a new form of expression for Felix, which Nora had come to recognise as his way of anticipating the most intense moments of pleasure. Nora found a spot where they could leave their towels and clothes and, because Felix had insisted on bringing his bathing things in a bag, rather than wear his trunks under his trousers, set about undressing him. She wrapped the towel round him and pulled down his trousers and pants from within the towel. Then, as a sudden gust of wind blew the towel apart, taking his breath away, he hopped about from foot to foot with excitement, making it almost impossible to pull up his trunks.

She looked around the beach to see if they were being watched. There were one or two mothers with young children and a group of teenagers, perhaps a year or so older than herself, laughing, chatting and smoking with the awkward self-consciousness of novices. She had an acute dread of showing herself up with her contemporaries, particularly boys, but this was Felix's day, as much as their mother's. She struggled with Felix until he was decent, then pulled off her own jeans and sweatshirt to reveal the regulation black school costume. As the cold wind touched her thin arms and legs she felt the goosebumps rise, and before she could think better of it, she grabbed Felix's hand and ran with him into the cold sea. She saw Felix's lips turn blue and heard his teeth chatter, but the cold seemed, if anything, to give an extra edge to his pleasure. He splashed water over Nora, and when she squirmed with cold, he danced about laughing, exhilarated by his power: in the sea he was strong where Nora was weak. His laughter turned into a kind of wordless chant, like a Latin Mass sung not by a choir but by the priest and his servers – tuneless, continuous, with no apparent climax. As Felix sang his song, he turned in a circle at the edge of the sea, lifting his feet high to clear the waves.

Then Nora became aware that Felix was attracting attention. Nearby a boy a few years younger than Felix, seven or eight, perhaps, was standing and staring at him as at a previously unsuspected phenomenon. Catching Nora's eye, he said to her, 'Is that an Apache war dance he's doing? I seen something like that in a film once.'

'Yes, I expect that's it,' said Nora, although she felt sure that, at this moment, Felix was not imitating anything he had seen but was completely at ease in his own body; and that his weird song and wild dance directly expressed his response to the moment.

She wondered whether the group of teenagers, who were likely to be more mocking, less purely curious than the younger boy, had also noticed Felix – but a mixed group of boys and girls, passing round their illicit fags and cans of beer, were probably more absorbed in each other than attentive to what was going on around them. But if boredom were to set in, Felix might prove a welcome distraction, binding them in a sense of how cool they were. Nora knew this because she had often been a target for such groups – girls from school out with boys from the nearby grammar – and had been mocked for her studiousness, her drab clothes, her failure to engage with youth culture. There was no doubt that having Felix as an appendage placed her at a disadvantage. Her pleasure in the intensity of his ecstasy was suddenly clouded, and she had to remind herself that one day, having shed the distorting effect of family, she would be elsewhere, experiencing the bliss of being herself, and at the same time belonging to a community of people who saw in her what she truly was. For it seemed to her that her true self had a solitary, contained existence beyond the circumstances of family and Ballypierce, but was being held in reserve because it was not yet allowed to flourish.

Briefly, she wondered about protecting Felix from mockery, of scooping him up, taking him back to their mother and saying that the sea was too cold, they should go home, but it was clear that Felix felt none of her painful self-consciousness. And since this moment was for her merely part of the prelude to the glory that awaited her, she couldn't find it in herself to interrupt what was perhaps for Felix the purest happiness he would ever know. She forced herself not to look round, to pretend as much indifference to the notice of others as Felix himself. She plunged in with him, splashing and leaping, although she drew the line at singing, and in time was swept along by Felix's mood. Then she encouraged him to take her hands, lift his body and float, kicking out his legs while she pulled him along. The cold ceased to matter as she became more aware of the warmth of the sun on her back and arms, and the way it sparkled on the sea, than of the biting wind and icy water.

Apart from a break for lunch, when they sat with their mother and ate sandwiches and ice-cream, they stayed in the sea throughout the afternoon. Felix was tireless and each new activity that Nora introduced – throwing a beach ball, holding hands and ducking their heads under water, swimming side by side along the shore (for Felix, as his school report had claimed, could indeed swim, in an unco-ordinated, shambolic, but strangely effective and powerful manner) – he wanted to repeat. He would start yelling, 'Again,' before they had reached the end of what they were doing. He wanted the day to go on for ever, and Nora found that by surrendering herself to his mood she, too, could simply inhabit the moment, and her mind could be as weightless as her body.

Eventually, however, it began to cloud over, and she wondered whether they had left their mother for too long. She coaxed Felix out of the sea, wrapped him in a towel, and together they trudged along the beach to the steps leading up to the café. Suddenly Felix's engagement with the day was over. He clung to Nora with one hand, but the thumb of the other found its way into his mouth as his eyes became glazed and dead. When they reached Bernie, she was in conversation with a woman at the next table.

'Well, here they are,' said Bernie, to her new friend, as they approached. Her manner, Nora thought, was just like that of other mothers, except that she seemed nervous, more with Nora than with the other woman, as though she was frightened that whatever she had been saying might be contradicted.

'Well, would you look at that?' said the woman, whose name, they soon learned, was Rose. 'You won't believe what your mammy's been telling me about you both. So this is Felix. The Lord love him, but he's a credit to you, Bernie. Such a fine lad, aren't you, Felix?'

Felix, as so often with strangers, stared straight ahead, refusing to make eye-contact. Nora suspected him of discouraging all attempts at conversation that he knew he could not sustain.

'Oh, I see, I see,' said Rose. 'He's thinking, Who is this woman, when all I want is to be with my mammy and my sister?'

'He is very clinging,' said Bernie.

'Oh, I can see. He's no fool, he knows when he's well off.' Then, her voice lowered, 'I don't know how you've done it, all that sacrifice and hard work.'

She continued for a while in this vein, and Bernie appeared to take it all as her due, smiling bravely, with downcast eyes, as her new friend enumerated her virtues. Nora, while realising that it was unlikely, thought there might be something to be said in favour of her mother developing a friendship with this woman, who must be lonely to be sitting alone in cafés, striking up conversations with strangers. A steady stream of flattery, even if unearned, might give her some pleasure in life.

Tired from the sea, she sat back and let the soothing, uninterrupted flow of conversation wash over her, until she became aware that Rose, having exhausted Bernie as a topic, was now talking about her.

'She's a lovely girl. In a few years, when she fills out a bit, she'll be gorgeous, and you won't know what's hit you, with all the boys who'll come knocking at the door.'

Nora glanced at her mother to see how she was responding to this shift in attention from herself. She seemed puzzled, as though she were being forced to consider what would never have occurred to her unprompted.

'Now, who does she favour? You or your husband?' Rose glanced from mother to daughter, and then at Felix. 'I'd say the boy's more like you, with his colouring and all – the lovely blue eyes and fair hair – but Nora has quite an exotic look.'

'She has my husband's colouring.'

'It's often the way, isn't it, that the girls take after their fathers and the boys their mothers? Is your husband very slim, too, like Nora here – not that she couldn't do with a bit of extra flesh on her?'

Bernie's face seemed about to crumble. As much as anything, she was confused by the direction the conversation had taken: flattery had given way abruptly to what she felt as spite.

On the bus home Nora tried to reassure her – Rose hadn't meant anything by the remark, and her conversation anyway was an inconsequential babble as she said the first thing that came into her head – but Bernie stared blankly out of the window, refusing consolation. Nora had become the enemy because the implied insult to Bernie had arisen from an unfavourable comparison with her.

When they reached home Gerald was already there, rather earlier than usual, but his mere presence made the point that he had returned to an empty house and an unattended kitchen. He picked up on Bernie's mood before anything was said. 'So you enjoyed your day's joy-riding, I see. We're to expect more trips and outings before the holidays are over.'

'No, the once was enough,' said Bernie, sinking down on to a chair while Nora put the kettle on for tea.

'What happened? Did it tire you out? What did I tell you?'

'You were right. I shouldn't have thought of it.'

She did indeed look tired, and the habitual lines of misery had returned to her face, whereas for a while – on the bus in the morning and sitting at the little café with her magazine, coffee and snacks, and with Rose before their brief acquaintanceship had soured – she had been more animated, her cheeks flushed with air and sun and the pleasure of achievement. Nora knew that it was useless to encourage her mother to remember the real pleasures of the day, to defend the outing as something that might be repeated, just as it was to disrupt Bernie's established routines. Sooner or later something would always happen to make her lose her bearings away from home, and no defiance of Gerald's authority could ever be sustained. At home she felt miserable, but safe in her misery. Her allegiance to her husband was fixed, while any relationship that Nora tried to form with her would always be unstable, subject to her fluctuating moods.

'Well, I hope you've learned your lesson, young lady,' said Gerald. Since his keenest pleasure in life was to be right, he was enjoying his triumph. 'I'll not have you putting pressure on your mother to push herself beyond her strength again.'

Bernie smiled to herself. If this was the closest she would come to being cherished, she would settle for what she could get.

'I really don't understand it,' Gerald was continuing, in his most reasonable, I'm-trying-to-see-all-sides-of-the-picture voice. 'Aren't you a bit old now to be nagging your mother to take you off cavorting to the seaside? Can't you find something else to do, more suitable for the age you are?'

The sense of injustice that Nora had so far suppressed sparked into life. 'If you must know, I wasn't really thinking of myself. I thought it would do Mummy good, and Felix enjoyed every minute of it.'

Gerald could scarcely believe his luck at the turn the conversation was taking. 'So, this whole folly was a completely selfless act on your part. Who do you think you are – Little Nell or someone?' Then, turning to Felix who, tired from the sea, had retained his glazed, absent expression throughout the journey home, and was now sitting with his head resting on his arms, which were folded on the kitchen table, sucking his thumb, he said, 'If that's the way he looks after a good day out, I'd rather not think what a bad day might do for him.'

'He loved it at the time,' said Nora. 'He's tired now. That's just the way he is when he's tired.'

'Oh, did he love it at the time?' said Gerald, with a sudden, lunging swing of his body. 'You would know that, I suppose. Did he tell you, in words that none of the rest of us manage to catch? What exactly did he say? Come on, I'd really like to know.'

'There are other ways of telling what Felix is feeling.'

'And you're the expert, of course. Is there anything you don't know more about than anybody else?'

There were many things that Nora had a mind to say: that this was a rich taunt, coming from him, who started arguments all the time that he insisted on winning; that she did indeed know more about Felix than he did, since he had neglected his son from the day of his birth; that it wouldn't go amiss for him to thank her, just occasion- ally, for all the hours of care she devoted to Felix; that he should be proud of her, of her achievements at school, of her efforts to please, instead of using her as a butt for his anger. But the iron discipline and control that had become second nature kept her silent. No good would come of it, and she had her future to think about, when she would be surrounded by people who loved and respected her, and who would acknowledge the value of those qualities that provoked her parents to anger. The thought of that other life was consoling, but her hold on it was not yet secure. There was the danger that if she did answer back, and speak her mind, her father would feel justified in thwarting her ambitions – would insist on her leaving school without the necessary qualifications. Meanwhile, she had to bide her time in this house, but she wouldn't give him the apology to which he felt himself entitled.

'I'll go and bath Felix and put him to bed. As I said, he's tired.'

While she went through Felix's routine, bathing him, dressing him, reading to him, her parents stayed in the kitchen with the door closed. Their conversation, which – making allowances for the inevitable digressions to the ceasefire and related matters – was almost certainly about her and the dreadful ordeal to which she had subjected her mother, went on for hours. Her mother would be pleased. Her day, at any rate, after a bad patch, would end well, although her father would only give her the attention she craved for as long as it suited his purposes. For herself, she had years of good days to look forward to so it didn't matter that this one had ended badly. She stayed with Felix until he fell asleep, glad of the company. Would he, she wondered, remember this day, which he had spent at the sea with her, leaping in the waves, in a state of perfect happiness?

PART FIVE

The Slaying of the Father

London

It is the Easter vacation, and Steve is waiting for Nora in a pub in Kilburn, where they will have a drink before going on to see *The Playboy of the Western World*. The pub is crowded and noisy and he is already regretting his choice of meeting-place. There is enough awkwardness in their situation of professor and student, about to embark on a new and potentially perilous phase in their relationship, without the gratuitous and wholly avoidable (if he had only had enough foresight) difficulty of having to shout at each other and push their way through tight knots of burly drinkers. For the ambience, he realises with dismay, is largely and overbearingly male, so there is a risk that the wrong tone will be set at the very beginning of the evening. He doesn't want to clarify his feelings for her when her responses have been muddled – not to say muddied – by images of men expressing their maleness in ways that are likely to be offensive, even repugnant, to such a sensitive young woman.

Even in his own mind, he notices, he takes refuge in a phrase as dry as 'clarifying' his feelings. Why can't he have the courage of those feelings and name them for what they are? It must be that he is so used to telling students that romantic love is a social construct, a useful way of elevating and containing sensuality, that such notions have distorted and displaced his instinctive life. Yet he knows that the intense longing he feels for Nora, his constant preoccupation with her whatever else he is doing, is what the poets and songwriters would instantly recognise as romantic love, an insight he has carried with him since Nora's seminar on 'Among School Children'. And he knows that he has never felt this way for anyone else, not for Martha, for whom he has deep affection, admiration, respect, or for the other women who have punctuated the otherwise steady and even flow of his married life. Their attractions, both physical and as women of some standing in their professional lives, represented a challenge; and once the game was won, those attractions were soon exhausted. These liaisons, for the women as much as for him, were purely recreational, welcome distractions in their otherwise busy schedules, leaving behind no bitterness.

His history, varied though it has been, leaves him completely unprepared for this moment. It's as though Nora's transparent unworldliness has undermined his own sophistication and everything about him this evening suggests the nervousness of the undeclared lover. He has arrived far too early, leaving him with an unwelcome stretch of time that he fills by bobbing up and down to make sure he sees her as soon as she arrives. Compulsively, he keeps rehearsing the evening in his mind, trying out a number of opening conversational moves and speculating on which course the evening would then be set. Earlier that day he bought a new navy blue linen suit, which he is wearing tonight with a cream open-necked shirt, but ever since he arrived at the pub he has been distracted by the thought that it looks too new, and too light for a windy spring evening, and exposes him as having made too much effort.

He is nervous, but does he really feel in any doubt about the outcome? He tells himself that this is the way he felt waiting for exam results. Rationally, he always knew that he was in line for a string of As, a first, whatever, but until he had confirmation there was always the nagging doubt that something might have gone wrong. And although he has seen Nora since, he keeps returning in his mind to the night after her seminar, when he rang to suggest their date this evening. Nora, in her soft voice, her Irish accent exaggerated by the telephone, had so nearly echoed the end of Molly Bloom's soliloquy in *Ulysses*, 'Yes, I will yes.' He cannot believe that she wasn't aware of the reference.

So, although tonight he is suffering from a kind of stage fright – the anxiety to please, a sick feeling of dread that something could go wrong – his rational worries lie elsewhere. Will he (they) be able to limit the impact of this relationship, once it is under way? He wants to surrender himself to it, to allow it to dominate his every waking moment, to experience what Yeats felt for Maud Gonne, and Joyce for his Nora. This degree of abandonment, however, seductive though it is to his increasingly engaged imagination, is hardly compatible with his role as husband.

He values Martha too highly to be prepared to hurt or lose her. He utterly rejects in himself the patriarchal cliché of enshrining in his wife and marriage the traditional virtues while finding pleasure and fulfilment elsewhere. Such a figuration is as unjust to Martha as it would be to see Nora as a tasty bit on the side. Martha is sexy, clever, competent, funny, kind, a brilliant mother who has adapted to her daughters' needs through every stage of their lives, and the one person in the world to whom he has always been able to say anything and find relief from the burden of his own consciousness. Until now, that is. Oh, she knows about Nora, and almost certainly guesses more of his feelings than he has told her, but he cannot tell her everything. The force and extent of his feelings for Nora would be too painful for her, and for him in inflicting that pain.

Martha should be enough for any man, but he is not any man and he must have Nora – and not in the way that he has 'had' other women. He needs to spend real time with her, to be with her in a way that allows the relationship to transform him, to take away the dryness that has been destroying his engagement with life. The danger is that a relationship as life-affirming as he envisages will not recognise limits. Yet limits there must be. Despite his dreams of abandonment, he is confident of his own ultimate capacity for restraint. In addition to his maturity, and entrenched habits of discipline, he has too much to lose in relaxing his caution entirely. He has, after all, shown considerable restraint already, spent time preparing the ground, ensuring to his own satisfaction how he wants the situation to develop. More practically, if he continues to take things slowly, to woo Nora patiently and attentively, not pushing too hard, then the relationship shouldn't reach fruition – if that isn't too coy a term – until after the summer exams, when he is no longer teaching her and cannot be accused of favouritism. He has no fears of Nora herself, but if word of a sexual entanglement were to get round there is always the possibility of other students behaving vindictively towards them, the more especially since a girl as beautiful and gifted as Nora is bound to have aroused resentment.

Yet Nora is still his principal worry. She is so young, pretty much a quarter of a century younger than he is. That, of course, is part of the attraction, although he rejects the stereotype of himself as an ageing man ogling young flesh. It's never happened to him before, after all, and unlike a number of his colleagues, before the spectre of sexual harassment stalked universities and students became more assertive about their rights, he has avoided even mild flirtations with students. But when he thinks of her age, so close to his daughters', he feels slightly queasy.

The real danger, as he sees it, is that, young and inexperienced as she is – for she is free of the knowingness that many girls of her age possess – it may be difficult for her to accept any limit to the relationship. Then, almost as a warning against further speculation about his future with Nora, he remembers Nick Bailey – Nick, with his elfin good looks and curling hair, his effortless, crumpled chic (no need in his case for an expensive new linen suit) and appraising intelligence.

Is Nora really as inexperienced as she seems? Part of him would be relieved to discover that she wasn't – the part that shrinks from the thought of a man of his age deflowering a twenty-year-old virgin. It's a role that should be taken by somebody of her own age. No, it's her feelings, her imagination that he prefers to see as untouched, and Nick, he is almost sure, has made no progress there. So if some tentative relationship is under way between them, he need feel no guilt at seeing it off.

The potential for guilt, as the situation develops, lies elsewhere. He isn't fooled by Nora's reserve, self-possession and cool intelligence. On the contrary, the earnestness and intensity that she sometimes displays in argument suggest to him a capacity for passion that hasn't yet found an appropriate outlet. Her seminar on 'Among School Children' had an erotic edge that was all the more beguiling because she seemed unaware of it. Once she allows it free rein, the consequences, he thinks, are incalculable. The thought of Nora overwhelmed by passion is thrilling, but disconcerting too. How can he ask so much of her, when he cannot give her everything? What complicates the picture is that he can't yet see how he will manage the rest of his life when his equilibrium has been destroyed by the kind of relationship he must have.

So absorbed has he become in his own thoughts, and lost to the world around him, that he has forgotten to look out for Nora and is startled by a light tap on his arm.

'I'm sorry, I made you jump. You were miles away.'

Nora looks hesitant, vulnerable and not entirely well. For the first time her pallor seems unhealthy, her eyes dark from tiredness or strain. He has spent so long thinking about her, picturing her in his imagination, that he cannot immediately adjust to the reality of her physical presence. Then his recent thoughts come to his rescue, and he finds in her altered appearance evidence of the strength of her feelings for him, and the turmoil into which he has thrown her. He feels both flattered and painfully protective towards her. 'Miles away was the best place to be before you arrived. I don't know this area very well, I'm afraid, otherwise I might have chosen a better place to meet.'

There is a momentary awkwardness while Steve looks around, wondering how they might arrange themselves. He arrived early enough to find a seat, but all the others around him are now taken. If he gives his seat to Nora, he will have to stoop over her and they'll both have to shout to be heard. He can't believe that he has handled the mechanics of the evening so badly, spending more time in choosing a suit than in making sure they can feel comfortable together. He places his hand on her elbow and guides her to a quiet corner where she can at least lean against a wall, then fights his way to the bar to buy drinks.

When he returns he says, 'You look tired. I hope you don't have an exaggerated idea of the amount of work required for these exams. You know you'll sail through them.'

'I've been doing real work – waitressing,' she says flatly. 'I've done it before but I always forget how exhausting it can be.'

Steve doesn't know what to make of this. Many students work in the vacations, of course, often in term time too, but the idea that Nora is forced to work not only upsets him but doesn't fit the idea he's formed of her family circumstances – of the prosperous pharmacist and his stay-at-home wife, both of them, in the manner of the Irish middle classes, eager to further their daughter's education.

Then, with that thought, comes the realisation that she has stayed in London for the vacation, accompanied by the memory of an uncomfortable incident at home, of being told that Emily had found Nora wandering the streets – stalking him, as Jessica had half-humorously suggested – and had then invited her to Wales because she wasn't going home for the holiday; a memory he had suppressed not because of Nora, who had seemed much as usual when he had next seen her, but because of Martha's sad, reproachful look and his daughters' curiosity.

It has never occurred to him that Nora might not be available in London whenever he decided that the time was right to move things on, but her presence here throughout the vacation and her need to work raise possibilities about her circumstances that he should probably investigate. All his theoretical knowledge of Irish culture appears to have been of little use to him in 'placing' Nora. Before he has been able to think of a line of questioning that might be pursued against the raucous noise of the pub, Nora has come up with an unwelcome line of interrogation of her own.

'I thought maybe Martha, Jessica and Emily would be here tonight. Don't they like the theatre?'

'Oh, yes, of course they do. Well, Emily pretends she doesn't – or maybe she really doesn't. But the theatre is part of the package of culture she claims to see as rather effete by comparison with the world-improving realities of science.'

'Emily's a very sweet girl,' Nora says, with a little smile. 'And transparently honest. I'm sure she wouldn't pretend to something she didn't actually think.'

The last thing Steve wants is to share warm, loving thoughts about his daughter with the girl he's hoping to sleep with. To avoid this, he blunders down an equally unrewarding path. 'Anyway, they're not in London at the moment. Martha's taken them to Wales for part of the school holidays.'

'Will you be joining them?'

'I'll be going for Easter, but there are a few bits of work I want to get out of the way first.'

The evening has not begun well for Steve. The conversation is unutterably banal, and, in view of the underlying situation between them, full of uncomfortable implications. There is the contrast between Nora's vacation, spent far from home, overworked and exploited by unscrupulous employers (for so, from the look of her, he imagines them to be), and that of his daughters, enjoying the fresh sea breezes and their mother's tender, loving care. It's like the plot of a Victorian novel, with himself in the role of philandering husband, seizing the opportunity of his family's absence to make an assault on the virtue of an unprotected young woman. Except, of course, it isn't really like that: the moral issues are nowhere near as stark, and this particular narrative will have a much happier outcome for everybody.

It doesn't help that he is finding it difficult to pick up on Nora's mood. This is the first time he has seen her outside a classroom or family setting, and he assumed that her manner towards him would be different, more in tune with his own, as yet undeclared, feelings: not exactly flirtatious, but more intimate, suggesting that she, too, is ready for a different kind of relationship. But she seems, if anything, more remote and less attentive to him than usual. She keeps looking round this terrible pub – why on earth didn't he put some effort into finding somewhere more suitable? – as if she isn't sure what she's doing there. Perhaps she really did expect this to be a family occasion, with Martha and the girls. Certainly, the only real interest she has shown since arriving has been in Emily, as if she felt the need to defend her against his own blinkered views and determination to squash her laudable ambitions.

'Have you seen *The Playboy* before?' he asks, forced to resort to conversational short change to fill the vacuum.

'I've hardly seen anything, apart from one or two plays with Phoebe's parents, and nothing recently, so I'm looking forward to it.'

She is beginning to seem brighter, so he is pleased to be offering her a treat.

'I have read it, of course,' she goes on.

'Of course. Just as I would have expected.' He smiles warmly, gazing meaningfully into her eyes and holding them for longer than is appropriate in this kind of social interchange. Most women, in his experience, find the combination of warmth, flattery, attention and hints of unspoken meaning irresistible, but Nora is evidently bewildered: her brows knit ominously and he draws back. 'You'd be surprised how many students think they can do an English course without reading the texts. You're obviously not one of them.'

He finishes his drink quickly and suggests that, when she's ready, they move on to the theatre: the seats are unnumbered and they should get there early. There's a chance, he thinks, that if they get away from the noise he may be able to regain the initiative and move them on to a better footing.

The theatre is one of those converted spaces that have been opening all over London, giving young actors and directors the chance to flex their muscles before audiences composed largely of friends and family. In general, because he can't bear to be in situations where it's almost obligatory to celebrate mediocrity, he avoids them. When he was still beside himself after Nora's seminar, however, he picked up a flyer for this production from his desk, which he had presumably been sent because of his association with Irish literature. Normally he would have binned it but, in his exalted, optimistic mood, it seemed like a gift: an Irish play, so connected with the course, but with the bonus of some of the most lyrical writing about love in the language. His thinking had been, that if the evening didn't turn out as planned he could always fall back on his role as professor, encouraging one of his most able students and forging a comradely bond at the same time. Then he had thought Nora would be comfortable with the relative informality of the event, where she was likely to be surrounded by people of her own age, and where he, too, entering into the spirit of it, might feel the years drop away.

Now, as they settle themselves on dusty benches, so cramped that it will take a miracle to prevent his joints seizing up by the interval, he regrets his choice, sound though it seemed at the time. And while he complains about the National Theatre – the middle-aged, middle-class audiences, the unadventurous repertoire, the corporate sponsors – he would have been more comfortable there and wouldn't have had to wince at the lack of professionalism. And maybe it would have lifted Nora's spirits to be in a bright, cheerful place, with a little tub of ice-cream and a glossy programme to fill the awkward moments and, instead of the scruffy crowd around them, who make him look even more over-dressed, a sprinkling of established actors in the audience, supporting their friends and adding tone. He should have tried to see it from her point of view, and flinches at the possibility that Nora may think he's economising on the evening.

They are sitting so close together – unnervingly close, without an armrest to separate them – that it's difficult to look at her. She gives away so little of herself that he has no idea of her tastes, of how, apart from work, she fills her time. Her composure is one of the qualities that initially distinguished her from her fellow students, for the young, in general, haven't learned how to disguise their egotism and keep themselves in check. Now that same composure, in circumstances that he hoped would create a greater degree of intimacy, is unsettling. It occurs to him that, wherever she is or wherever he has seen her, she

looks . . . not out of place, because that suggests awkwardness, but not of the company in which she finds herself.
In this particular audience it is her neatness – her ironed
clothes and polished shoes – that sets her apart. In some
contexts she looks elegant, though he is sure that that isn't
an effect she works at, but that, too, is unusual for a girl
of her age. He wonders whether she would like to be one of
the crowd – her friendship with Phoebe, whose range
of acquaintance seems to be as amorphous and eclectic as
her opinions – would suggest that she might; or whether
she relishes, has even cultivated, her apartness.

The play begins, but it takes him a while to settle into
it. It isn't just the discomfort. There is no consistency in
the Irish accents, most of the cast opting for what they
are familiar with from their television screens – light-
entertainment Dublin, or the Ulster accent of news reports
and political drama. The particular cadences of the west
of Ireland, which Synge heightened and poeticised, are
wholly absent. The entire cast is of an age, he would guess
between twenty and twenty-five, and since this is a play
in which conflict between the generations is crucial – the
hero, Christy, acquiring heroic status with his tale of killing
his father, and Pegeen, the girl with whom he falls in love,
chafing at a life spent pulling pints in her father's bar –
this seems a serious weakness.

The exuberance of the cast, however, and their relish
for the language soon win over the audience, and Steve
finds himself, if not transported, sufficiently engaged to
put aside his other concerns, although he's always had
reservations about the play's politics. Synge, like Yeats and
other writers of the Protestant Ascendancy in the decades
leading up to independence, invents a wild, amoral Irish
peasantry, preferring it to the reality of conventional

Catholic Ireland. At gut level he shares their prejudices, but takes pride in laying them to one side in favour of a more enlightened and refined political analysis that sees those conventions as a response to colonial repression.

Even so, he can acknowledge the risk Synge took in dramatising the possibility of another Ireland, and loves the subversiveness and intoxication of the language. When one of the regulars in Michael's bar suggests that they leave Pegeen in Christy's care overnight while they all go off to a wake – 'Now, by the grace of God, herself will be safe this night, with a man killed his father holding danger from the door' – he laughs aloud for the first time, and forces himself not to notice that Nora seems unmoved. Anti-authoritarian himself, he applauds the sentiment that fathers and all they represent should be slain (at least metaphorically) so that the young might live according to their desires.

What really moves him, though, is the idea of escape from the limits of the self, through the power of the imagination to transform. He is a father, and middle-aged, and has no right, most people would say, to be harbouring designs on a girl who is scarcely older than his daughters. Christy, through the power of language, through telling his own story, transforms himself from 'a poor fellow would get drunk on the smell of a pint' to 'a daring fellow and the jewel of the world' – one who, having convinced others that he's the author of a deed he didn't commit, goes on to win the races and become the authentic playboy of the western world.

Will he, Steve, be able to find the words to move Nora, and through her love redeem the rest of his life, achieve what is still unfulfilled in his early promise? For although he is middle-aged, a professor, a husband and father, he still sees himself as in a state of becoming, with his real life, his most glittering achievements, still ahead of him. He just needs to be revitalised and renewed.

At the interval he and Nora make their way with the rest of the audience to a draughty passageway, doors open on to the street to let in some air, where drinks are being sold. The choice, as Steve sees it, is between leaving Nora with nowhere to sit and nothing to look at while he fights his way through the crowd for a drink, and suggesting that they wait and have a decent bottle of wine with dinner. Since she doesn't seem to be much of a drinker, he decides to make up some lost ground and begin a conversation that might lead somewhere.

Nora, who looks tired enough to welcome the support, leans against a wall with Steve facing her, isolating her from the rest of the crowd with his body as he asks how she enjoyed the play.

'It seems to give a very English view of the Irish.'

Even though he has similar reservations about the play, Steve feels the need to defend the playwright. 'But Synge wasn't English. Surely we have to allow the Protestant Irish their own identity.'

'I know that, but he was an outsider to this particular world. He went to the western isles with a notebook, like an anthropologist studying a tribe and, surprise, surprise, he found what was missing in his own life, a kind of primitive joy.'

He is on the point of reminding her of her seminar on 'Among School Children' when she argued – with a fervour that has had the power since to lift his spirits – that the continuing vitality of the poem is in its expression of this same primitive joy, but he is chilled by a cynicism that he has never seen in her before. Besides, he is aware that he could be described, by the unsympathetic, in the same terms that Nora has used for Synge – as an outsider, even a voyeur, in relation to the Irish. Instead he says, 'Are you suggesting it wasn't there?'

Nora shrugs. 'I don't know the western isles, so I couldn't say. Maybe it's seeing it in London. When I read it at home I thought it was wonderful. Here it strikes me as Oirish rather than Irish.'

'Isn't that a bit unfair? I'm not sure he could be said to romanticise this community when he has them all, even Pegeen, turning against Christy in the end. The conventions reassert themselves.'

'They only turn against him when they find out that he didn't murder his da.'

They seem to have reached an impasse. If this were a class or a seminar, he would point out to her that the play maintains a balance between cruelty and romance, desire and convention, and offers a critique and a celebration of the society it mediates. What disconcerts him is that, in a pedagogical setting, Nora would very likely point these things out for herself but, in the manner of a weaker student, she appears to have become fixated by something in the play that touches her own experience at the expense of the cooler appraisal he has come to expect of her. He has the sense of something buried and inaccessible to him that he is reluctant to disturb, not knowing what he will uncover. And he, too, after all, was carried away by what they have already seen, though in a different direction: he has allowed himself to be transported by a poetic idiom that she, perhaps more accurately, finds strained and unnatural.

They return to the hard, cramped benches for the rest of the play and watch as Christy's newly won position as epic hero unravels. He wins the races, but with the appearance of his father, who survived the blow to his head, the community that made of him an idol becomes a hostile mob. 'There's a great gap between a gallous story and a dirty deed,' says Pegeen, who leads the cry for Christy's branding and lynching. But the final word is Christy's. Although it's at his father's intervention that he's released, the old man recognises that Christy has won the Oedipal struggle that the play has enacted. And although Christy has lost Pegeen, he has been transformed, through the experience of adulation, into 'a likely gaffer in the end of all', who'll 'go romancing through a romping lifetime from this hour to the dawning of the Judgement Day'. So, while desire is defeated, so is the father, and the play closes with a partial triumph over patriarchal Ireland.

Steve finds the end of the play unexpectedly chilling, and as they reach the street, where he finds his new linen suit inadequate for the cold spring night, a shiver passes through him. They walk more or less in silence from the theatre to the Italian restaurant where he has booked a table. He is feeling awkward and self-conscious, painfully aware of Nora's physical presence, but because they are still locked in their roles as professor and student, he is as careful not to brush accidentally against her as he would be in a professional setting. As they enter the restaurant and wait to be shown to their table, he places a hand on Nora's arm, but feels it stiffen and quickly withdraws.

Later, as they face each other over the breadsticks, candle and wine bottle, Steve leans towards her and asks, 'So, what was your final verdict on the play?' They are seated in a dark corner at the back of the restaurant – the waiter, it seems, has them down as a couple who would prefer not to be observed – and have completed the business of consulting the menu and ordering.

Nora smiles, for the first time, he thinks, since the evening began, and there are two spots of colour in her cheeks. Attributing this to the Valpolicella, Steve quickly tops up her glass.

'I'm sorry,' she says, 'I started off the evening in a jaundiced mood. It just seems at the moment that wherever I go people make assumptions about me because I'm Irish, and it affected my reaction to the play. Sometimes I feel I'd like to be seen just as myself, and not as someone who's carrying the burden of the whole race.'

'Now, come on, Nora, you know that who you are is to a degree determined by history, upbringing, culture. I'm not saying that people are right to stereotype you . . .' He trails off lamely, catching a look he has never noticed in her before but which he associates with her generation: raised eyebrows, pursed lips, head cocked slightly to one side – what he's come to classify as the here-we-go-again look. He's mortified to realise how pompous he must sound. Pomposity, like censoriousness, is a failing of the old, and her response is exactly that of an impatient young person towards an older person who's lost the plot.

Part of her allure has always been a kind of refinement, or fastidiousness, rarely found in her age group, and which he's sought to preserve in his own daughters: the impression she gives of being untouched by the common currency of youth culture. This evening, however, for all the vulnerability of her dark-ringed eyes and unhealthy pallor, he has sensed a new hardness in her, a capacity for sarcasm that's incompatible with innocence. This is disconcerting, forcing him to question his judgement, but also sexy, suggesting that she might be more accessible than he had imagined. He must be on his guard against these lapses into a professional manner and allow Nora to set the tone and pace.

Rightly interpreting his sudden silence as humility, Nora takes it upon herself to kindle the conversation into life. 'You asked what my final verdict was on the play. I found the second half more interesting because it faces up to things about Ireland that are uncomfortable and that liberal opinion in this country is inclined to ignore.'

'Like what? Do you mean things you've experienced yourself? I know so little about your life before you came here.'

'There's not much to know,' she says, freezing slightly, then warms again to her theme. 'There's romance in the idea of violence among people who would never themselves engage in it.'

'Surely that—'

'I know, I know, or I think I know what you're going to say. It's a kind of morally indignant *Daily Mail* position to see violence as an absolute evil when sometimes it's the only resource people have. And it's a comfort position. If you hold to these absolutes, you don't have to consider the reality of people's lives. And, of course, independence would never have been achieved without violence. I'm aware of that argument, of course I am, and I wouldn't disagree with it.'

She is flushed and animated and Steve has to suppress the instinct to lean across and touch her, to connect with her experience in a more intimate way than as a mere listener. The time for touching will come, but first she must be allowed to open her heart to him.

'But however justified the struggle may have been, the idealisation of violence has seeped into people's souls and damaged them.' She pauses to gather her thoughts. 'You're always talking about the personal being political, but there's an aspect to that that's never considered. It can encourage people – people not actively engaged in the struggle but with a sectarian interest in it – not to get on with their own lives, or to think that the anger they might feel for quite different reasons – family, domestic, whatever, in the end not everything in the lives of people in the North is dictated by politics – is justified so they never need take responsibility for it. Every day you can find something, if you're looking for it – the latest action of the Brits, or the intransigence of the IRA, depending on which side you happen to be on – that will feed and fuel a sense of grievance, and in some people that becomes the whole purpose of their lives.'

She stops and sinks back into her chair, as though exhausted from the effort to organise her thoughts. It's clear to Steve that she has been telling him something of great significance to herself, something that could provide him with a key to what is mysterious about her, but she is telling it in code. Is this because she wants him to uncover her secret – rather as if she has set him a quest that he must complete before winning her – or because this is the only way she can approach what is so deeply personal that she hasn't yet found a way of talking about it?

He senses that he must tread very carefully, and while the waiter settles them with the main course, he tries to work out a strategy. 'Is this something you've come across yourself – the appropriation of the political as an escape from the personal? What you've described is a kind of displacement activity—'

'Yes, I know what it is,' says Nora sharply. 'I wouldn't have brought it up if I hadn't experienced it.' The shutters appear to fall as she applies herself to her plate of risotto.

This is indeed unnervingly reminiscent of the medieval quest, which, as it happens, belongs to a species of literature – aristocratic, romantic, religious – in which Steve takes little interest. It seems that Nora wants him to uncover something about her, as a prelude to winning her, but the crucial test is to ask the right question. His evident interest and concern count for nothing in relation to some pre-ordained structure in Nora's mind that will determine the outcome of their relationship.

'What's your view of decommissioning?' he asks finally. 'Do you think that Peter Mandelson was right to suspend the Northern Irish Assembly?'

The Secretary of State has recently suspended this new body, composed of a fragile coalition brought into being by the combined efforts of the British, American and Irish governments, because the IRA has so far refused to place its armoury beyond use.

'Ah, decommissioning,' says Nora. For the first time in his acquaintance with her, she looks impish and mischievous, and Steve has the uncomfortable feeling that she is laughing at him. 'Now, there's a word. I wonder what Synge would have made of it.'

'It's not very poetic, certainly,' says Steve uneasily, wondering where this is leading.

'It seems as though it were coined by a committee,' Nora replies. 'As it happens, I think they should be made to decommission. Peter Mandelson is right to take that line.'

'Really? Surely for the IRA it's tantamount to surrender, to saying that the struggle wasn't justified.'

'Only because they choose to see it that way. You could say that it's about being responsible and having the courage to let go of all the anger and the Catholics' status as victims.'

She falls silent and Steve, rather than rushing in with another question (which would almost certainly, he thinks, be the wrong one), reflects on the importance of anger in her observations about her home. Instead he sits still and expectant, encouraging her to say more.

'If people have suffered a lot,' she goes on, 'they feel angry and resentful. It's only natural. But then they reach a stage where they think that if they stop feeling angry and resentful it will lower the value of their suffering. The rest of the world will think that they haven't really suffered if they let it go. So they hang on to it all, but in the end the ones they hurt are themselves, or whoever they have in their power. So it's in their own interests to let go, though it's often difficult for them to see it in that way.'

Her eyes are wide and her cheeks burning and she looks like a child – a precocious child, admittedly, not just because of her intelligence but because, for the first time since he's known her, Steve senses that she has experienced more than she should, certainly more than he would like his own daughters to experience, in order to arrive at this insight into adult suffering. He aches with desire for her. Choosing his words carefully, he says, 'I've never asked you before because – well, because one observes a certain reserve, one doesn't want to appear voyeuristic – but have you ever been the victim of terrorism in any way?'

To his surprise, the suggestion seems to amuse her. 'Well, now, that would depend on how you define terrorism.' Her manner is almost flirtatious.

With a sudden urgency, he reaches across and takes her hand. 'Don't play with me, Nora, please. You know how I feel about you, and I'm sorry if I've been insensitive but I've been trying to reach you, to break down some of your reserve. Please try and be more open with me.'

Nora becomes very still, but doesn't withdraw her hand. 'How do you feel about me? You say I know, but I don't have a clue what all this is in aid of.' With her free hand, she gestures at the table – the wine bottle, the candle, the plates of food – and then out into the restaurant.

'I . . . I . . .' He swallows before proceeding. 'I think I'm in love with you. No, that's wrong. I know I'm in love with you. You must have realised. And I'd like us to be together in some way.'

She looks aghast. The colour has drained from her cheeks and she pulls away her hand. 'What about Martha, and Jessica and Emily?'

'It's all right, if that's what's bothering you. Martha knows and she's fine about it. Well, maybe not fine, but she understands.'

She sits back in her chair, stunned, as if she's received a blow. 'Is that the way you do things in London?' Then her tone and expression become angrier, as another thought occurs to her. 'Is that why you invited me to your house, so she could look me over? Did you have to get her approval?'

'It's not like that. You're making it sound much worse than it is.' Steve hears the note of desperation in his voice, and pauses to get it under control. 'When I invited you home, I wanted you to be part of my life, not some clan-destine—'

'Bit on the side?'

'That's not the way I would put it myself. I wanted to make it clear that this is different from other – well, from the way these things are usually portrayed.'

'Other what? Other affairs? You mean you make a habit of this kind of thing?'

'No, not this kind of thing, because I've never felt like

this before. But, yes, there have been other women. I've been married for more than twenty years, for God's sake.'

'Oh, well, that's all right, then.' She makes as if to get up, then drops down into her chair again. 'And Martha knows about them, these women?'

'Yes, she does. I don't like deceit, and being open with her has never compromised our marriage. But you have to understand that with you it's different. I knew from the beginning that you had that power – the power seriously to unsettle things – which is another reason why I invited you home. I didn't want her to feel excluded.'

Nora nods slowly, as though taking it all in. Heartened, Steve says, 'And it could work, really it could. Nobody need get hurt.'

'Yes, that's the refrain here, isn't it? You can do what you like as long as nobody gets hurt. You know, when I came here, from a place where people hurt each other all the time, I found that rather appealing. I couldn't quite throw myself into it, but I thought, It must be better than all the pain and self-righteousness and hypocrisy and repression. But it's so self-deceiving. Can't you see that?'

Steve remains silent, his head slumped forward over the table, supported by his hands.

'You say Martha knows about your propensities—'

'You make it sound like a perversion,' says Steve, stung into speech by the need to defend himself.

'You must be about the same age as my father. But what about Jessica and Emily? Do they know?'

Steve looks up, alarmed. 'No, no, of course they don't.'

'Doesn't that suggest that this is something you shouldn't be doing?'

'I would say it's something that's inappropriate for them to know, like a lot of other things about their parents, which are not bad in themselves and like a lot of things that young people do without forcing knowledge of them on their parents.'

'I see. All personal behaviour is morally relative, but you're a bad person if you don't take the PC line on IRA violence, say. Let's choose to forget that it takes effort to restrain your instincts but it's quite easy to uphold "correct" views on political issues where you're not actually required to do anything and you never suffer any consequences.'

'All right, Nora, you've made your point, and I'm sorry, really sorry, and I admit to being sufficiently egotistical and vain to have misread the signals.' Having avoided her glance, he now seeks it out and looks pleadingly at her. 'But let's be clear. I haven't forced myself on you, I haven't jumped on you, I haven't abused my professional position for sexual favours.'

Nora raises her eyebrows.

'Nora, please, you're a brilliant student and I admire your work. You don't need any special treatment from me and I haven't demanded any favours in return. The professional side of our relationship hasn't come into any of this. However wrong and mistaken I've been. Surely you can be generous enough to see that.'

She lets him wait for an answer, then says, 'Yes, I suppose that's true. There hasn't been any manipulation.'

Relieved, he lets her words settle between them, gathering the authority of an implied commitment. Eventually he says, 'I can't let you go this evening before asking you something. I'm taking a risk, I know, but I need to understand why I've been so mistaken. You've given me no encouragement, you've never flirted with me, none of those things, I can see now that it's all been in my own head, and the only excuse I would offer is that, like other men of my age who are perhaps susceptible for one reason or another, I've been knocked off balance by meeting someone so special and unusual—' He stops abruptly in response to a warning glance. 'But I need to know – without implying that it suggests acquiescence or anything else on your part – where I've gone wrong, why you agreed to meet me this evening.'

She is silent for so long that he thinks she is refusing to answer. Finally she says, 'Because I was feeling particularly lonely and vulnerable when you telephoned me. Because I need friends – not the usual sort of friends that you have as a student, but family friends. I wanted you and Martha, as a couple, to befriend me so that I could feel I had something solid and secure in London. Does that satisfy you?'

Awkwardly she gathers up her possessions. Her jacket has slipped and got caught up by the leg of the chair; her bag has fallen on to its side and some of the contents have spilled out. When she is on her feet and ready to leave, he says, 'At least let me give you the taxi fare home.'

'I can manage, I'm earning good money.'

Left alone, Steve becomes aware that he is trembling. He looks at the bowl of congealing pasta in front of him and feels a sudden spasm of nausea, but he's forced, for the moment, to sit there. He hasn't paid the bill and feels that, if he were to stand up, his legs would give way. He pours himself some more wine, hoping it will settle or, at least, numb him.

The desire for Nora that has been building, reaching its climax this evening, has drained away, driven out by fear. How could he have got it all so wrong? With extreme reluctance, as though he's forcing himself to bite on an infected tooth, he tries to remember what she said about wanting 'family friends'. The pathos of this is unbearable. He can't believe his own egotism in failing to recognise her loneliness. But how was he to know, when she persistently refused to tell him anything about herself, even with the opportunities he offered her this evening? Then, with a terrible feeling of dread, he wonders whether hers is a pathological neediness, the source of which would never be disclosed, a flaw in her personality that drove her to manipulate him to the point where she could then humiliate him.

For the second time this evening – how long ago the first now seems, since when the world has changed utterly – he remembers Jessica's suggestion that she was stalking him. Perhaps he wasn't the one targeting her, but she who was targeting him. Jessica's closer to her in age, and more likely to be able to see her clearly; but Emily, when the suggestion was made, said that Nora was 'just perfect', which had filled him with a warm, secret pleasure.

The thought of Jessica and Emily makes his agitation worse and brings him no nearer to clarity on Nora and her motives. In a sudden moment of illumination, he makes the painful decision that the blame is his own. He's compromised his integrity (a quality on which he's always prided himself) enough, without trying to shift the responsibility on to a twenty-year-old girl. He should have tried to find out more about her, not by quizzing her on her political views (he winces at the thought of 'decommissioning'), as though the right opinions would confirm her suitability as soul mate, but by using the details he had to draw her out.

It was his own snobbery that had made him obliterate the provincial pharmacist in his chemist's shop. He had thought Nora's father, or stories about him, couldn't be other than boring, and if there's one thing he avoids whenever he can, it's being bored. Instead he'd preferred her to remain exotic, an essence of Ireland distilled from poetry and history.

It seems that, with Nora, he's violated every principle he holds, allowed himself to see in her what he wanted to find rather than try to uncover what was actually there. The fantasies that he was constructing now stand exposed in all their folly and absurdity. What did he think was going to happen? That with Nora as inspiration, and sexually renewed, he would become another James Joyce? Confound those who thought his career had peaked by writing the great end-of-millennium novel? And all this with the compliance of his family? Nothing can justify the risks he's taken with their happiness – and with his own, for the one thing that is absolutely clear to him is that they, Martha, Jessica and Emily, are the greatest good in his life.

For the first time since Nora left the restaurant he feels a kind of relief. What he has to reproach himself with was all in his head; nothing actually happened. But this is only the prelude to a renewed onset of dread. Is this how Nora will see it? He can't remember what she said clearly enough to be sure that any undertaking was given that this would go no further. She was hurt, in the kind of state when behaviour is unpredictable. He sees that his hands are trembling again, but he can't bear to stay here a moment longer.

He summons the waiter for the bill and, as the transaction is completed, thinks he detects a hint of mockery beneath the elaborate politeness. Is this the shape of things to come? Is this not so much the end of something as the beginning of something worse?

Ballypierce

'Decommissioning,' said Gerald, expressing his contempt in the exaggerated prolonging of each syllable. He switched off the television and turned to face his audience. 'What kind of a word is that? Did anybody hear of it before that eedjut Major needed an excuse to abandon the peace process to satisfy the hard men of Ulster who are keeping him in power?'

Bernie would have liked the television kept on so that she could put in an extra hour or two's viewing before bedtime, but Gerald hadn't yet exhausted the topic currently dominating his thoughts. He had been at it all day in the shop, but his indignation and the need to express it were undiminished.

His questions were directed at no one in particular, but Bernie's habitual response was one of silent acquiescence – since her unfortunate championing of the IRA ceasefire, she had thought it prudent to assume Gerald's views on everything that mattered to him – and Felix was excluded as a participant; so the burden of response, if one were required, fell on Nora. Rather than rise to the bait, she got up and walked towards the door, closely followed by Felix.

'So do you not even have the grace to answer me?' Gerald boomed at her.

'I'm sorry,' said Nora. She turned to face him, but retained her hold on the door handle. 'I thought they were rhetorical questions.'

Gerald was ominously silent and still for a few seconds. Then, in obedience to a routine he had long perfected, he nodded slowly and deliberately, as if giving serious consideration to what Nora had said. 'Rhetorical questions. Rhetorical questions. Is that the kind of thing you're learning on your fancy A-level course?'

Nora was now in the first year of the sixth form, and her choice of A-level subjects – English, French, History and History of Art – had been settled only after fierce opposition from Gerald who had wanted her, if she insisted on staying on at school, to follow him into science; in consequence he had refused to sign the consent form. Only after he had received a stern letter from Nora's headmistress, reminding him that there were regular parents' evenings where he might, were he able to find time to attend, receive the benefit of the teachers' advice, and predicting a distinguished academic career for Nora if she were allowed to follow her instincts, did he yield, but he had refused to talk to his daughter for a month afterwards.

Rather than this closing the matter, however, he had embarked on a fresh course of hostilities once her A-level course started. It was at his insistence that she interrupted her work every night to watch the news with him, and when he was sufficiently fired up he would do his best to provoke her into argument. The more desperate he was that she should agree with him, however, the more he drove her into a position of defiance.

'I didn't think they were real questions,' said Nora, wearily. 'I thought they were observations.'

'I know what a rhetorical question is. Do you think I'm ignorant?'

'No, of course not.'

'Then sit down while we have a discussion.'

'Daddy, please, we've been through all this before and I've such a lot of work to do.'

They had indeed been through it before. It was now November, and the Mitchell commission had proposed IRA decommissioning, in parallel with talks, in January. Since then there had been an end to the IRA ceasefire, with the blame placed on British intransigence – a moment that Gerald had relished – followed by Sinn Féin's acceptance of the Mitchell proposals in May. Then, throughout the summer, there had been a wave of sectarian violence on both sides. The IRA had attacked a barracks in Lisburn and now, with John Major's government hanging on by a thread until certain electoral defeat, the IRA's continued failure to decommission had become, in the view of the British and of the Ulster Unionists, the main barrier to progress.

'This is more important than your work. A man could be forgiven for thinking, from the time and energy you give to it, that the nation's welfare depended on what you personally think about *Hamlet*.'

So Nora came back into the room and sat on the sofa, newly entangling herself on the way with Felix, who kept as close to her as he could without being physically joined. He was holding a long chiffon scarf, now very ragged, which Nora had long since persuaded him to substitute for the banners of lavatory paper, and which he was flapping about, muttering to himself meanwhile, as though enacting a drama that ran parallel to the one taking place around him.

'Now, just you tell me,' said Gerald, in his most reasonable tone, his voice at a normal conversational level, 'whether you agree that decommissioning, the word and the idea, has been made up by or for John Major to give him the excuse not to negotiate with Sinn Féin. Because the only way he can stay in power is with the help of Trimble, Paisley and the rest.'

'I don't think there's any dispute about John Major's motives,' said Nora.

Gerald smirked with triumph at his daughter's admission, before proceeding. 'Well, you and I might agree – and I'm glad that in this instance we do because it shows you're learning something – but to read the British press you'd think he was a man of the highest bloody principle. So what does that tell you about the difference between them and us?'

'I think that's only true of some of the British press,' said Nora. 'If you were to read the *Guardian* or the *Independent* instead of the *Mail* you might have the satisfaction of finding that some of the British are of the same mind as you.'

'And you do read the *Guardian* and the *Independent*, I suppose?'

'At school, yes.'

Gerald nodded. Nora had learned that these apparent gestures of agreement were always a bad sign; and indeed, when he did speak, after a suitably lengthened pause that allowed theatrical suspense to mount, it was to deliver what he clearly considered to be a crushing blow to this particular line of argument.

'And how many Brits do you suppose read your precious *Guardian* and *Independent*?'

'Not many, by comparison with the number who read the *Mail*.'

'That's right. Too bloody right. I read the *Mail* not for pleasure or information but to find out what the average Brit thinks, and it's sickening.'

'If you say so,' said Nora, rising. 'Can I go now?'

Gerald looked briefly uncertain. His daughter's manner belied her nominal acquiescence, and he was reluctant to let her go without a more unequivocal surrender to his point of view.

'If you're forced to admit that you're wrong in argument, then you should do it with a better grace. Do you or do you not agree that the average Brit agrees with the *Mail* on this issue?'

He stood over her, rather too close for comfort, willing her absolute submission. Felix made low, growling sounds and adjusted his position to cover Nora's body with his own. He stared up at his father, his head just beneath his sister's chin. Since he had gained considerable bulk over the last few years, he provided Nora with an effective shield. Gerald ignored him, and kept his gaze firmly fixed on Nora.

'I don't know what the average Brit thinks,' said Nora, pushing Felix to one side so that she could sit up. 'They may buy the *Mail*, but so do you, so I'm not sure how much that means. And if John Major is widely seen by the English as a man of principle, why does he have to rely on the Ulster Unionists to prop him up? He's lost every by-election since the last general election so, as far as I can see, they can't wait to get rid of him over there. Maybe we have to wait for the next government to see what the British really are thinking at the moment.'

Gerald looked at her with an exaggerated show of disbelief while he tried and failed to muster an argument that would smash hers on its own terms. Failing in his search, he shouted, 'Whose side are you on?'

'I didn't think this was about sides,' said Nora, in a cold, level voice. 'I thought you wanted to demonstrate to me how a rational argument is conducted.'

'Oh, no, you wouldn't,' said Gerald. 'We all know you're above all that. But if we could just ignore your elevated position for a moment, what do you think this whole bloody conflict is about if there are no sides?'

Suddenly roused, Felix shot to his feet and faced his father, growling and gesturing his defiance.

'Would you stop shouting, Gerald?' said Bernie. 'We won't get the boy to sleep tonight if he gets too excited. And as for you, Nora, I don't know why you don't just agree with your daddy, especially when he knows so much more about this than you do.'

'Oh, no, she couldn't do anything as simple as that,' said Gerald. He had lowered his voice in response to Bernie's plea, but he took no direct notice of Felix. Felix, meanwhile, seeing that he had made his point, raised his arms, palms outward towards his father to indicate that he was backing off.

'If I was to say that the earth was round, she'd do her damnedest to prove that it's flat. So,' turning back to Nora, 'you haven't answered my question yet.'

'Of course it's all about sides,' she said, 'but I didn't think that was what this argument was about.'

'You're the one turning it into an argument.'

'I thought we were talking about the *Daily Mail* and John Major and his level of support in England. If, as you seem to think, it's about whether the conflict here is caused by sectarian division, then of course there is no argument. It's self-evident.'

Nora had a way of agreeing with her father that, because of her manner and the language she used – he visibly winced at 'sectarian division' and 'self-evident' – maddened him more than disagreement.

'You're beginning to talk like a BBC newscaster,' he said. 'You don't even sound like one of us any more.'

'I'm sorry. Please can I go now? I've got an essay to finish.'

'Let her go, Gerald,' said Bernie. 'Until she's finished, we won't get the boy to bed.'

This was indeed the night-time ritual. Felix had always made sure that, where possible, only Nora would take him through his bedtime routine – a persistent stubbornness to which Bernie adopted a stance of hurt, but resigned disapproval, though it was an arrangement that suited her – but recently, as Nora kept to her room as often and for as long as she was allowed, Felix had begun to insist that he go to bed at the same time as Nora. Indeed, his preference was that once they were both ready for bed, he should tuck her in, smooth her pillow and settle her with her bedtime reading, then take himself off to his own room. Just as he had always relied on her for mothering, so he was beginning to assume some kind of parental role in her life. There were nights when Nora played out this ritual with Felix and then, when he appeared to have settled, got up and finished the task in hand. Tonight, however, after her enforced compliance with Gerald's demands, which he seemed to be interpreting as outright rebellion, she had no wish to bend further to somebody else's will, even Felix's. Taking her cue from her mother, she stood up and turned again towards the door.

'Hold your horses,' said Gerald. 'We haven't finished yet. As you said yourself, what have I been trying to teach you over the years if not the proper way to conduct an argument? And one thing that you don't appear to have learned is that you do your opponent the courtesy of not walking out on it until it's finished, when some concessions have been made.'

The more the direction of Nora's education took her away from Gerald's professional sphere of expertise, at the same time equipping her with debating skills to challenge his own, the more he was inclined to claim for himself the role of principal influence on her intellectual development. 'This is more quibbling than discussion,' she said. 'I can't really see it getting anywhere.'

Gerald turned, with his arms outspread, to address an imaginary audience. 'So who's doing the quibbling and getting sidetracked by the readership of the *Daily Mail* because she doesn't want to confront the real issues? I'll go back to where we started. Do you or do you not think that decommissioning is a word made up by John Major, because it has the kind of bureaucratic sound that the Brits respect, to give him the excuse to delay the peace process?'

Nora's small, white face was now as set as Gerald's large, florid one. 'Do you really want to know what I think, as opposed to what you think I ought to think?'

'Be my guest,' said Gerald. They were all uncomfortably aware of his physical presence, throbbing with barely concealed menace, which communicated his mood more effectively than his words.

'I don't know the origins of 'decommissioning' as a word, though if you're really interested I could look it up for you. As far as I know, it was first used for the IRA by George Mitchell in his report. I agree with you completely, as I've already said, that it gives John Major a parliamentary reprieve because the Unionists wouldn't support him without it. If you want my opinion on whether they should decommission, since I assume that that's what all this is about, I think they should. That way, they'll be seen to have left the past behind them. I don't think we'll move on until all the interested parties have the courage to draw a line under history, as Nelson Mandela has in South Africa. That's my opinion, and I'm sorry if you don't like it but I think I'm entitled to it.'

With that she walked calmly to the door, though the dignity of her exit was compromised when she became tangled up with Felix and his scarf. This time she ignored Gerald's calls for her return. She knew that there would be repercussions – her father would sulk and there would be endless scenes of recrimination with her mother, who would claim that she was destroying the peace of the household with her stubbornness – but she felt strong enough to weather them.

When Gerald didn't get his own way, his tactic was to ignore whoever had offended him, as though, she had sometimes thought, his attention was a grand and sought-after gift, and his withholding it painful to the offender. When she was younger, his angry withdrawal had indeed frightened her and filled her with the desolation of solitude, but now she felt that to be ignored might be restful and allow her more time to herself. She would be inconvenienced by her mother's pleas that she should apologise, and Felix would cling even more closely to her as a refuge from the atmosphere that would settle on the house, but she calculated that the benefits of defiance would outweigh the penalties. If there had still been anything she wanted from her father that she had a reasonable chance of being given, it would have been different, but she had given up all hope of any return to the relationship that they had once had.

Felix was still inches away from her when she reached her bedroom door. She placed a hand on each of his shoulders and gazed steadily and intently into his eyes. 'I have to work now, Felix, and I really mustn't be disturbed. Now, you be a good boy and get yourself ready for bed, and when I'm finished working I'll come along to your room and make sure you're fine and kiss you goodnight. You're a big boy now and I want you to show me that you can do what I ask you.'

He refused to budge, and Nora was forced to close the door on him. He made no attempt to come in, but neither did he move. As she settled herself at her desk, and glanced through what she had already written, she could hear him muttering quietly to himself outside, but it was a sound to which she was accustomed and she had by now schooled herself not to give in to guilt every time she was forced to ignore his appeals.

Within a few minutes she had achieved a sufficient level of concentration to pick up her pen and write.

When we read The Playboy of the Western World *now it is tempting to find in it a poetical, mythic, rural Ireland of the kind that has continued to haunt the Irish imagination and, perhaps even more insistently, the perceptions of those who have never actually lived there. This is partly an effect of the western dialect, which has been heightened and poeticised by Synge in ways that I have already discussed; and also of the play's central dramatic device, the willingness of this particular community to embrace the outlaw, Christy Mahon. There is also the global, even cosmic scale that the characters lay claim to for the events of their lives. Christy woos Pegeen with references to the heavens, the moon and the stars. He is himself described as the 'jewel' of the world and the 'playboy of the western world', and his account of the slaying of his father draws liberally on all the points of the compass, as though they were two titans engaged in an epic struggle at the dawn of the world.*

To an extent, this suggests that the characters in The Playboy *occupy a world that was threatened even at the time Synge wrote – one that is more primitive and elemental and, for all its squalor, grander than the commonplace, increasingly commercial reality of Dublin, where the play was first staged. Its separation from the larger world is not total, however, though it is easy, in the rush of events, to overlook references to the Boer War, the 'peelers' and other forces in society that impinge even here. Indeed, it is possible to read it more ironically, as a play about people who see themselves as at the centre of the universe in part because they are so far from the centre; whose egotism is a bombastic retort to their unimportance in the larger scheme of things; and whose apparent independence of authority is exposed as empty bravado as soon as they see themselves to be actually threatened by the law.*

At the end of the play, the fearfulness, smallmindedness and cruelty of the community are in the ascendant. And it is arguable that the Pegeen of the play's opening, before the appearance of Christy, the Pegeen who is prepared to take as her husband Sean Keogh, the young farmer whose conscience is in the keeping of the parish priest and, beyond him, the papacy, is more fully representative of the Ireland of the time.

Yet something of the epic still clings to the play at the end, and is the more compelling because it reflects the circumstances of contemporary Ireland. Christy's father has bullied and humiliated him to a degree that is perhaps only possible in a poor, rural society where possession of the land bestows on the older generation a power that is reinforced by all the sanctions of a traditional, patriarchal society. Christy's 'slaying' of his father is a botched job that is transformed into a heroic deed only in the act of telling, and through the power of language, but it is nonetheless effective. When his father reappears, Christy has the upper hand, and at a metaphoric level an epic struggle may be said to have occurred. The final irony of the play is old Mahon's pleasure in his son's transformation. A patriarchal society values manliness, and Christy has now shown himself to be a man.

Nora managed to finish only by ignoring the increasing activity outside her room. In time Felix was joined by Bernie, whose apparent attempts to handle him and get him to bed were ineffectual and half-hearted. The real purpose of her intervention, it seemed, was to be heard by Nora.

'Come on now, Felix, it's useless making all this fuss. Nora doesn't want to be bothered with you tonight. You come with me and we'll get you ready for bed. Will I bring your daddy? You wouldn't want him to be cross with you now, would you?' Then, finding Felix unmoved by exhortation, she fell back on a familiar refrain directed more at Nora than at Felix. 'You've been completely ruined, so you have. There's nobody can do anything with you except Nora, and she's always too busy, these days. I can't stand here all night, my legs are aching already. What are we going to do with you?'

Nora held her ground through all this, and eventually heard her mother's slippered feet shuffling back to the lounge. Shortly afterwards she returned with Gerald. It was almost unknown for him to intervene directly with Felix. He had continued, as far as possible, to behave as though his son wasn't there, and when difficulties arose, to disappear with a newspaper rather than become involved. However, he assumed his fatherly role on this occasion with a relish that had little to do with his sense of responsibility towards Felix.

'Has she left you out here, then?' he boomed, as though his son were deaf in addition to his other disabilities. 'It's a hard lesson but you're better learning it now, that your own family can desert you sooner than they would strangers. Family loyalty means absolutely nothing to some people.'

As far as Nora could tell, Felix ignored this piece of wisdom, just as she was doing her best to ignore it.

'Come on, your mother's tired of looking after you all day and needs to go to bed. None of us will be able to sleep with the racket you're making.'

In general Felix was a good deal quieter than most boys of his age. Not only did he have very little speech, but he was also free of the tendency, which Nora had observed in other children at his school, to loud, incoherent wailing. He muttered to himself most of the time but, as on this occasion, it was only just audible. She gathered up the pages of her essay and secured them with a paper clip. Then, bracing herself for battle, she joined the rest of her family where they were gathered in the corridor outside her bedroom. Felix was sitting on the floor leaning against the wall, but as soon as he saw her he got to his feet.

'Time for bed, now, Felix,' said Nora, directing all of her attention to him. She linked her arm through his and together they moved in the direction of the bathroom.

Enraged, Gerald yelled at her, 'What game do you think you're playing at, young lady? If you think that this family is going to dance to your tune, and you can hold us all to ransom, you'd better think again because I will not tolerate it. Do you hear me? Do you?'

His two children turned to face him. Nora, for all her resolve, was white and trembling, but her brother was fearless. He placed a restraining arm on her, then stepped protectively in front of her. 'Top it, 'top shouting at 'Ora. You go 'way,' he yelled at his father. Gerald was so taken by surprise that he was lost for words, the more especially since he had never acquired a way of speaking to his son. Then Felix faced Nora. He placed his arms on her shoulders and looked intently at her, in imitation of the way she communicated matters of importance to him. 'Doan worry your head about Dad,' he said. 'I'll 'ook after you.'

Usually, on the rare occasions when Felix spoke in the presence of his parents, Nora was forced to take the role of interpreter because they had never become used to his manner of speaking, but this time what he said was unmistakable.

'Well, I'll be damned,' said Gerald. He couldn't have been more astonished if he had witnessed a dog breaking into speech. His anger briefly forgotten, he stared at his son and, for the first time ever, graced him with a little half-smile as he continued to stare at him in amazement.

'Leave it now, Gerald,' said Bernie. 'We're all exhausted already with the rowing and hollering there's been here tonight.'

So Gerald, again breaking new ground in his behaviour towards his family, retired from the battle, shaking his head and muttering, 'I'll be damned,' as he retreated to the lounge.

PART SIX

Understanding Women

London

It is the first week of the summer term and second-year examinations are looming for the members of Steve Woolf's Irish-literature class. As they gather, waiting for the session to begin, they compare notes on how much work they managed during the Easter break and arrange revision sessions with each other, when they will work through past exam papers and discuss strategy.

Steve has set aside the few working weeks of this term for the discussion of general themes and ideas. This will help prepare them for a paper that will concentrate not so much on individual authors as on wider issues: the contexts – historical, social, religious, political – in which the writers worked; the continuities and discontinuities in the Irish literary tradition and its links to other literatures and movements.

Having announced this, towards the end of last term, he found himself outmanoeuvred by Emma. Since this was his plan, she had piped up, why didn't they delay her seminar – the eagerly awaited feminist critique of the entire Irish literary tradition – until the beginning of the summer term? She would, after all, be presenting some kind of overview and would attempt to demonstrate that attitudes to women in Irish writing were not 'down to' individual men but products of the wider society. Moreover, if he didn't mind her saying so, as a man he had – unconsciously, she was sure – colluded with the male authors on the syllabus in relegating women to the margins of discussion, except in the case of those women who figured in the work of some writers as inspiration and muse.

Steve had been too taken aback, or perhaps too stung by Emma's implicit criticism of his teaching practice to protest. He had anyway, as they had noticed at the close of last term, been rather mellower in mood, less abrasive in manner, readier to laugh – as he had when Emma had finished presenting her case. He raised both arms in a gesture of defeat and, when the general laughter had died down, said, 'Okay, you win, Emma. As long as it won't interfere with your revision if we delay the seminar, go ahead.'

Today, however, on the first occasion that they have seen him since the Easter break, he looks far from mellow. 'Haggard' was the word used by Pete to Annie when they were waiting for the rest of the group to assemble and they had time to observe Steve, who had arrived rather earlier than was his custom. His eye sockets are dark, as though he has been losing sleep, and his manner is agitated. He glances nervously at the door as each student or group arrives, and when the time comes for him to give Emma the signal to start, there is one notable absentee – Nora, the model student, usually as punctual in her timekeeping as in delivering her essays. No one has failed to notice that she isn't there, or that Steve, who usually asks after latecomers and absentees has chosen to ignore it.

So, with everybody's mind distracted by the missing Nora, Emma begins: 'When we look for women in Irish literature, we find them notable for their absence, but it is, of course, precisely those gaps that post-structuralist criticism, including feminist, has encouraged us to investigate.'

In the present context, her assertion seems deliberately taunting, though it can only be coincidence – surely? – that Emma's statement of her thesis comes just at the point when Nora's absence is beginning to cause comment. Steve, who has placed himself by the window, is seen to turn his head sharply towards Emma, but she carefully avoids his side of the room as she looks from one to another of the group. Does this increase, or lessen, the potentially confrontational aspect of what she has to say? On the one hand, she isn't as yet taking up a blatantly combative stance towards Steve but her strategy may be to unite the group against him. But for what? Many of them are meeting for the first time in weeks so they don't know what part, if any, Steve has played in Nora's failure to show. Phoebe, who has taken up position in the front row, is looking particularly knowing, but whether this is because she knows something or is basking in the importance of being Emma's right-hand woman isn't clear. There is certainly an atmosphere of heightened tension in the room.

The apparent collusion between Emma and Phoebe, who arrived together, and Steve's wholly uncharacteristic look of distress encourage a backlash in his favour. This is particularly marked among the young men, who usually think it politic to keep their heads down and say nothing when feminist issues are raised.

'Do you mean women as authors, or women as characters in novels and plays or as they occur in poems?' asks Pete, before drawing attention to some of the women in the literature. A number of others join in and supply names: Maud Gonne, Pegeen, Gwendolen and Cicely in *The Importance of Being Earnest.*

'It's not a question of the number of female figures,' says Emma, dismissively. 'I'm not interested in doing a head count. It's more how they're treated by male authors, how much subjectivity they're allowed, how they're judged for "deviant" behaviour. So, for example, Yeats gives a lot of space in his work to Maud Gonne, but regards her political allegiances and activity as a form of madness. When he writes about how he wants his daughter to grow up, he makes it clear that he wants her merely to exist beautifully and not to entertain any of those opinions that disfigure women in the eyes of men.'

Nick, on the other hand, wants to talk about women as authors, about whether, given its volume, Irish literature compares badly with the literatures of other European nations, before any generalisations are made about Ireland. He mentions Maria Edgeworth, Somerville and Ross, Lady Gregory, Elizabeth Bowen, Molly Keane . . .

Steve, meanwhile, has detached himself from the proceedings, leaving his students to slug it out among themselves. Even if the quality of the debate were better – Emma's approach, for all the angry verve of her delivery, has been established orthodoxy since the early eighties, and encourages even strong students like Nick and Pete to lapse into list-making – he wouldn't be able to concentrate. He hasn't been able to concentrate on anything much since he last saw Nora. All the qualities that he's taken for granted – discipline, rationality, the ability to master a subject or situation – seem to have deserted him, leaving only a keen sense of his own misery. This must be a foretaste of dying, he thinks, when the external world recedes as pain takes over. And since that night, for the first time in his married life, there is no solace to be had at home.

When he joined Martha and the girls in Wales, Martha knew, with that sure instinct she has always had for everything concerning him, that something was wrong, but he couldn't bring himself to tell her what had happened. It would have been hard enough to admit how totally he had misjudged Nora's feelings, but to acknowledge that he'd placed himself at risk of public exposure – a danger of which she'd been aware since the beginning – was too much for him. Cravenly, he had tried to carry on as though nothing had happened and Martha hadn't questioned him, either because she refused to make it easier for him or because she knew that she wouldn't be able to bear what he had to say.

But where his instinct – against all his earlier habits of honesty – was to pretend that everything was as usual, she had steadily refused to collude with him. Instead, while maintaining a show of normality in the presence of Jessica and Emily, she has effectively withdrawn from him so that now, when he is most in need of her, she is inaccessible to him.

Worst of all is her mute sadness. It's as though she lacks the energy for any speech beyond what the immediate circumstances require, and for the first time since he's known her, she spends hours sitting listlessly in front of the television. Now that he's lost it, it seems to him that the continuous conversation of married life has been central to his happiness, the greatest of his achievements and a treasure that he has wilfully squandered. He surfaces to hear Emma take a brisk swipe at Swift's misogyny and, with less justification, Beckett's, and thinks, How little she knows: it's not misogynists that women should fear, it's the men who love women but don't know how to value them.

Then he hears James Joyce mentioned and forces himself to concentrate. His professional involvement with Joyce's work is, of course, known, although the scope of the course has allowed no more than a brief canter through *Portrait of the Artist as a Young Man*, ably chaired by Nick. *Ulysses*, the principal object of any true Joycean, had to be ruled out because its length and complexity would seriously have unbalanced the course. None the less it is *Ulysses* that Emma appears to have singled out for 'deeper' analysis, after a statutory and predictable swipe at Stephen's (aka Joyce's) use of prostitutes in *Portrait*.

'*Ulysses* concludes,' Emma is saying, 'with Molly Bloom's soliloquy, which takes place in the marital bedroom while her husband is sleeping and she is using the chamber pot.' There is tittering around the room, some of it expectant, some nervous. These students are from a generation with few inhibitions about sex, but many are still squeamish about a public discussion that might include details of excretion, and since few have read *Ulysses*, they don't know what to expect. Steve, however, is resigned to a session of combined boredom and anxiety, rather like a visit to the dentist. He steals a glance at his watch. Still twenty minutes to go. Emma's voice, like the dentist's drill, drones relentlessly on. Let me just get through this, he thinks, and I can ring Nora to find out why she isn't here; smooth things over, try to make peace and, above all, make sure that she isn't harbouring a grudge. She's probably ill, he thinks, and nobody's thought to tell me because they assume I know already.

'Now, Joyce has been widely praised by male critics for the "Penelope" chapter, as Molly's soliloquy is known.'

Which male critics? Steve asks himself. None these days would dare but, more importantly, he's spent the last two terms trying to drum into them the importance of avoiding unsubstantiated assertions with vague phrases like 'most male critics'. 'He bravely courted charges of indecency, or so we are supposed to think, making it difficult for him to find a publisher. What they don't tell you is that this lone male warrior couldn't have done anything without the help of women. It was Sylvia Beach, an American woman with a bookshop in Paris, where he was living when he wrote his masterpiece, who arranged the publication for him, much of it at her own expense, and Harriet Weaver, a well-to-do English woman, who supported him financially while he was writing it.

'So we have here that all too familiar story of the great man who is supposed to have struck a blow for women, first by ending his great work with Molly – who, incidentally, scarcely appears anywhere else in the book – and then by his masterly presentation of female sexuality, when all the time it was the kindness and support of women, often acting against their own interests, who made it possible. Now, you might think, as people have felt throughout the ages, women as well as men, Fair enough, the man was a genius, and geniuses – have you ever, by the way, heard the word 'genius' applied to a woman? – always have to be treated as special cases and have always relied on women to create the conditions in which they can work.

'But this exploitation of women goes further than that and involves the content of the book as well. For it was his common-law wife Nora Barnacle – whom he refused to marry because he didn't believe in social convention – who supplied him with the information he needed about women's inner lives. Nora Barnacle, the wild and beautiful Irish girl whom he met just before he left Dublin for Europe, and who, bravely in my view, agreed to go with him.'

She pauses for the group to take this in. There is an embarrassed silence. Suddenly, everybody appears to be looking down at their desks, at their notebooks, at their feet. It seems that everybody has made a connection between Joyce's Nora and Nora Doyle; between Steve and Joyce. Steve feels that the consensus in the room would hardly be clearer if they all got to their feet, turned to face him and pointed their fingers accusingly at him. The only one who doesn't appear to be embarrassed by what Emma has forced on them is Phoebe, who catches Steve's eye, a smug smile fixed on her fat, vacant face. Steve is in agony, for he is no longer in any doubt that the whole exercise has been designed to expose him. But what is there to expose? Did Nora tell Phoebe and Emma what had happened, or did she embroider her narrative, exaggerating a pathetic tale of unrequited middle-aged love, misunderstanding and apology into an epic saga of unbridled male sexuality and violence?

'But here's the real joke,' Emma continues. 'Richard Ellmann, in his biography of Joyce, quotes a letter that the psychoanalyst Jung sent him after he'd read *Ulysses*: "The 40 pages of non stop run in the end is a string of veritable psychological peaches. I suppose the devil's grandmother knows so much about the real psychology of a woman, I didn't." Then, having quoted the letter, Ellmann writes, "Joyce proudly displayed this tribute to his psychological penetration, but Nora said of her husband, 'He knows nothing at all about women'." Isn't that the best joke of all? He asked Nora how women thought and felt, but then he didn't listen.'

Steve is frightened on his own account, but he is also experiencing a rising tide of anger that matches the anger and contempt Emma is expressing – anger with what she is saying and with the confident righteousness of her tone and demeanour. He knows that most of this is directed against him, that the whole drift of her argument is to collapse him into Joyce. But when has he ever used the word 'genius'? Doesn't she know that, among his generation of critical theorists and their successors, that kind of mystification has been outlawed? None the less, Joyce was a very great writer and it's ludicrous to imply that his work, which is among the greatest produced anywhere in the world in the twentieth century, rested on the unacknowledged contribution of the barely literate Nora.

What would Nora, a chambermaid from Galway, have been without him? The life he gave her, among the Bohemian intelligentsia of Europe, was beyond anything she might have imagined for herself, and his love for her was unswerving until the day he died. If Emma has taken the trouble to read the whole of Ellmann's biography, which he doubts, she has chosen to ignore all evidence of Joyce's devotion to his wife (for he did, of course, eventually marry her): his constant attendance at her hospital bedside when she was ill, his eagerness to meet her demands for fine clothes and expensive restaurants.

Suddenly there is silence – or, at any rate, the absence of Emma's hectoring, hammering voice – broken by uneasy shuffling, and he realises that she has finished. Unlike the earlier student seminars, and with the exception of the brief attempts to challenge some of her statements, there has been remarkably little in the way of contribution from others. Steve knows this to be the mark of a bad seminar but he can hardly say so. Her manner has been over-bearing and dismissive of any alternative point of view, the content a medley of anecdote and assertion, discour-aging critical debate. But that isn't all. These young people, many of whom he has grown to like, have been conned by her – the girls into thinking that if they dare to disagree with her they are violating the principle of solidarity, while anything that the boys might offer in the way of dissent would be seen as tainted and without value: proof, indeed, of the male conspiracy to silence women.

But he, too, has been silenced – by the fear that this young woman has poisoned the minds of her colleagues against him. For the first time in a life of successive triumphs, punctuated by the most trivial (as they now seem) setbacks, when he has always taken for granted his own control over events and never had to consider what other people think of him, he senses a creeping paranoia. As he gets to his feet to comment on Emma's perform-ance, his legs feel stiff and unsteady, those of a man much older, threatening loss of balance and collapse. His hand goes out and clutches the back of a chair for support. He has been so tense throughout the session that his muscles have gone into spasm. He clears his throat.

'That was a very spirited performance, Emma, which has illuminated the texts we've been reading – and others that some of us have yet to read, I suspect – in unexpected ways.' He looks at Emma as he speaks, but she avoids looking at him, in a show not of modesty but of contemp-tuous indifference to whatever he might have to say. She gathers up her notes, clips the sheets together and stuffs them into her bag, along with Ellman's biography of Joyce. She is, to use the vocabulary of her generation, 'blanking' him. He is filled with a rage that cannot be allowed an outlet. 'You might consider next time including more detailed textual analysis, but you did cover a good deal of ground. Does anybody else want to make a comment?'

Nobody does, but a number, prompted by the direct appeal, raise their eyes to look directly at him. Is it real hostility, or imagined, that he sees on the faces of some? Certainly there is a considerable air of unease in the room. Then he catches Pete's eye. The boy gives him a rueful smile, then rolls his eyes, as if to say, 'What a pile of crap.' Or so Steve interprets it, and feels heartened. Then, after a few words about the programme over the coming weeks and some encouragement about revision, he brings the class to an end. After shifting his weight speculatively from one foot to the other, to test that he can use his legs without them buckling, he makes a hasty retreat.

Twenty minutes later, Pete, Annie, Nick, Phoebe and Emma are gathered in Marco and Gianna's café. Pete waylaid Phoebe and Emma at the end of the class with the suggestion that they have coffee together. Emma was indifferent but allowed herself to be swayed by Phoebe's eagerness. As Pete will say afterwards to Nick, 'You have to have a grudging respect for Emma's integrity. She has no taste for conspiracy, mystery, popularity or even attention, except for her point of view, and she'd already made that clear. Whether she's right or not is another matter.'

Since this is the quietest time of day in the Italian café, they have the smoking area at the back to themselves. This is approached through an arch and down some steps so it's almost a separate room. The five are huddled round the small, Formica-topped table and are already shrouded in a thick pall of smoke, which heightens the air of crisis.

Pete, with his arm loosely slung round Annie's shoulders,

sits facing Emma and Phoebe. He has assumed the role of interrogator.

'So, you haven't seen Nora since before Easter,' he says.

'You got it,' says Phoebe, who appears to have undergone something of a metamorphosis. While always subject to moods, and often careless of other people's feelings, she had still exuded a certain boisterous friendliness. She had wanted to be liked, to be one of the group, to be an insider. Now, in partnership with Emma, for whom the BA course has always been more important than the transient allegiances of student life and who has never compromised her views to court popularity, she has an air of truculent authority. The change in her isn't total, however. She has always enjoyed being in possession of a secret, but where she would once have used it to strengthen and extend her network of acquaintance, the power of privileged information now seems to have become an end in itself.

'And do you have a telephone number? Can we get in touch with her?' Since they are taking different options, and not everybody turned up for the first meetings of the term, they have only now established that Nora seems to have absented herself from all her courses.

'She hasn't told me where she is. She said if I needed to contact her to do it through her email address.'

'So you don't know where she is?'

Phoebe shakes her head.

'What about a mobile?' asks Annie. 'I know she's never seemed part of the modern world, but doesn't she even have that?'

Phoebe glances briefly at Emma, who nods. 'She bought one recently but it doesn't seem to be working.'

'Do you at least know whether she's all right?' asks

Nick. 'Hasn't she contacted you about anything? Presumably you know why she's gone.'

Phoebe and Emma look at each other, but say nothing.

'I take it that we're none of us wrong in thinking it's something to do with Steve?'

Emma shrugs and Phoebe looks down at her lap.

'Now wait a minute,' says Pete. 'You seem to want us to think – though you won't actually say – that Steve's guilty of some unspeakable act towards Nora. Is that right?'

'After all,' says Nick, 'there's no question of him trying to trade a leg-up for a leg-over. Nora isn't in need of that kind of preferential treatment, even if there were any likelihood of her being tempted by such a deal.'

Phoebe tosses her head angrily.

'Nick's right,' says Pete. 'So really you're suggesting physical force, like some old-fashioned melodrama. I don't buy it.' He looks round the group, excluding Phoebe and Emma, for support, and they nod.

'This is just the kind of show of male solidarity I would have expected,' says Emma. 'You reduce the situation to an either-or logic, and in so doing you think you've demonstrated the absurdity of the great Steve being in the wrong. There are many ways in which a man like that can abuse his power.'

'I see,' says Pete. 'So the poor sod's damned if he did and damned if he didn't. You're going to get him either way.'

'You're making it sound like a personal vendetta, rather than an act of injustice for which there are procedures,' says Emma.

There is an uncomfortable silence. It is as though they are at some kind of tribunal – an impression that's assisted by Emma's habitual austerity of dress and manner, a style that Phoebe, who loves dressing up, appears to have adopted too – and are intimidated by the unfamiliarity of the occasion and its procedures.

Pete rouses himself to say, 'Let's leave Nora on one side for the moment. I know that's difficult because this seems to be about her, but she isn't here to speak for herself. But tell us, Emma, what exactly do you have against Steve? You're not convincing me that your interest in this is strictly impersonal.'

After a brief hesitation, Emma says, 'I would turn that another way. You're trying to make out that because I dislike him, anything I say in this particular instance has to be disqualified. But since you ask, I think he's arrogant, up his own arse, a hypocrite. He claims to believe in open debate and thinks he encourages scepticism about received opinion, but wants everybody to come round to his point of view. He pretends to have all these left-wing values and to be on the side of the dispossessed, but in his own life he's an old-fashioned élitist. If you're not beautiful or clever in the particular way he admires, he takes no interest.'

Pete nods slowly. 'I think all that's true, more or less, although you're being a bit hard on him. I'd say he's the most conscientious of my teachers, but I suppose you'd say that's neither here nor there. But none of that makes him a rapist.'

The word casts a chill, even though the deed itself seems already to have been eliminated. Nora's disappearance, however, suggests the most exceptional of circumstances, charging the atmosphere with innuendo and suspicion.

'Hang on a minute,' says Nick. 'You should be careful, Pete. I know that what you're trying to do is make the whole thing seem ridiculous, but you don't want things to be said here that could then be spread and twisted. This man's whole life could be on the line.' Then, turning back to Emma and Phoebe, 'Since you're the ones who've made these insinuations, I think you should tell us exactly what happened.'

The two girls look at each other but say nothing.

'You should at least confirm that there's been no violence or physical force.' He looks at Phoebe, as the one more likely to crack.

'Well, no, not exactly, but she was very upset, and it has to do with Steve.'

'I see,' he says, sitting back in his chair. 'She was very upset and it has to do with Steve. What were the circumstances? Were they alone together in his house, or at your flat?'

'No, he'd taken her to a play, and then to dinner.'

'Right, so they were in public places when whatever happened, happened. How did she get home? Did he drive her?'

'She came home in a taxi.' Phoebe is staring at her lap.

'With Steve?'

Phoebe shakes her head.

'Well, not many opportunities for anything suspicious on an evening like that, I would have thought.'

'Perhaps he made her pay for her own dinner,' says Annie, now that the tension has lifted. There is relieved laughter.

'It's all very well for you to laugh,' says Phoebe, 'but she was really upset. I've never seen her like that. I've never known her to cry before.'

They are all somewhat chastened.

'I'm really sorry about that,' says Nick. 'I like Nora

and she's a long way from home. But a lot of things could have upset her. What did she say had happened?'

'Whatever she said was in confidence,' Emma says. 'Isn't that right, Phoebe?'

'That's right,' says Phoebe, relieved.

'Okay,' says Nick. 'Fair enough. But I think we've ruled out the worst scenario. There's still something that's really bothering me about all this, though.' He leans back in his chair and plays idly with the discarded wrapper from a cigarette packet. A number of those present will say later that Nick should be a barrister and, indeed, his own decision to pursue law as a career can, more or less, be dated from this point, but only partly because he will be pleased with his own performance. Having toyed with the idea of the academic life, he loses all enthusiasm when he considers Steve's predicament. 'If Nora has indeed confided in you two, and has, so to speak, entrusted you with the burden of her cause, why is it that she's no longer living with you and you don't even know where she is?'

There is the sound of a chair scraping as Emma gets to her feet. 'I don't see why we have to put up with this. You're trying to protect Steve by putting us in the wrong. I've told you already what I think, that there's more than one way for Steve to abuse his position. You're behaving as though, if you rule out the worst, he's in the clear.' She glances down at Phoebe, who is hesitating. For all her apparent enslavement to Emma, she hasn't yet given up her aspiration to be liked and admired, to be one of the cool crowd. Since Emma has made clear her refusal to wait while Phoebe dithers, Phoebe, too, has to make a choice. She remains seated while Emma walks off without her.

'So, what is the situation, Phoebe?' asks Nick, more gently.

'Nora doesn't want Steve hounded, does she? She may have been upset, but she knew that what actually happened didn't justify ruining Steve's career. Isn't that right?'

The rest of the group, who are enthralled by Nick's performance, wait until he pauses before swinging their heads back to Phoebe, like members of a jury who must assess the witness's response.

Her head is down and there is a faint sniffling sound from behind the curtains of hair. This appears to be the moment of truth when, under Nick's close forensic examination, the false, self-protecting version is discarded and the truth is revealed.

'Emma thought that Nora should report Steve, but Nora didn't want to.'

'Did she leave that night?' Nick asks.

'No, the next day. I stopped her going then – I thought it was too late and she had nowhere to go.'

'She could have telephoned any one of us,' says Nick, wishing that she had thought to telephone him but knowing why she didn't: after he had felt himself rebuffed he had avoided being alone with her and, in a group, treated her as the most casual of friends, with just enough calculated warmth to protect himself from being questioned by the others. He saw that she was hurt, but thought it was no more than she deserved. He finds it hard to believe now that he harboured so much resentment; that he allowed himself to interpret Nora's situation solely through the prism of his own wounded pride.

'Well, you know what she's like – she's never found it easy to open up. Anyway, it was the holidays so a lot of people had gone home.'

'So then Emma persuaded you that you both ought to confront him or take it further,' says Pete.

Phoebe gives the briefest of nods.

'Hang on a minute. I take it that Emma was actually there?' Pete continues.

'Well, no, not really.' Phoebe cannot meet Pete's eyes as she says this.

'"Not really"? What's that supposed to mean?'

'I think Phoebe's told us all we need to know,' says Nick, sensing in Phoebe a shame that matches his own.

'Is it possible that she went home and hasn't come back yet?' asks Annie.

'I don't think so,' says Phoebe. 'As far as I could see, she wasn't in touch with her parents. In all the time she lived in my flat they never rang or wrote to her and she always changed the subject when I asked her about them. I used to think it was rather mysterious and romantic.'

They all feel ashamed of their failure, as individuals and collectively, to break through Nora's reserve and learn what she had been at such pains to hide. And while they all try to imagine what possible circumstances Nora finds herself in now, with no friends, as far as they know, beyond themselves and maybe not even a home to retreat to, Nick remembers that Phoebe, to whom they've all shown very little mercy, did offer Nora protection of a sort. In her own rather careless way, which was not entirely free from self-interest, she provided Nora with somewhere to live and was there when Nora returned from her ordeal to offer whatever support was within the scope of her limited understanding.

'I don't know about anybody else,' he says, 'but I've had enough of sitting here. I've got something to finish off in the library but is anybody on for a drink later?' Pete and Annie nod, but Phoebe says nothing, assuming that she has been excluded from the general invitation.

'You too, Phoebe, if you haven't got something else to do,' he says, as he squeezes through the gap between two tables. To emphasise that the invitation is genuine, he pauses to place a hand on her shoulder. 'I should think you could do with a drink, after all that.'

Phoebe looks up at him, her face shining. 'Yes, thanks, I'd like to come.'

Her relief at being welcomed back into the group is obvious, and she feels the lightness that comes from confession. She almost believes that her last meeting with Nora was as she implied, and in time will have forgotten other circumstances that she doesn't care to reveal.

That Nora was upset is undeniably true – upset in a way that Phoebe had never seen her. Nora is usually so composed and reluctant to demonstrate feelings that, for Phoebe, are in constant play – irritation, pleasure in a success or an indulgence, passing sexual attraction, jealousy or greed. Over time, it had inspired Phoebe to see her as a kind of holy monster, provoking her to awe, repugnance and an uneasy sense of her own lower status but greater humanity. But Nora, on that last occasion when Phoebe saw her, was in a paroxysm of grief: her face was red and puffy from earlier tears, and although in one sense she appeared to have cried herself out, she was unable to control the dry sobs that shook her frame and took her breath away.

Phoebe had heard her key in the lock and her footsteps in the corridor, but had stayed where she was, watching television. She thought that Nora had been working in the restaurant and, since relations between them had been steadily deteriorating since Christmas, expected no more than the usual, 'Hello, how are you? I'll be off to my bed then.' So, with her attention still on the television, she scarcely glanced up, but that was enough to take in Nora's condition.

She leaped up, drew her into the room and sat her on the sofa. It was a while before she thought to turn off the television, so the gestures that came to mind as appropriate – slipping off Nora's coat, stroking her hands, murmuring soothing baby noises – were accompanied by a late-night comedy show. She did indeed assume that Nora had been assaulted, since it seemed unlikely that anything short of cataclysm could have produced such a reaction in someone so reluctant to display emotion. What Phoebe was most proud of in her own behaviour – she had never before been called upon to play an attendant part in somebody else's crisis, and noticed with interest her own ready sympathy – was her patience. For, in addition to the emotions evoked by the evident suffering of another person, she felt the most overwhelming curiosity. What could Nora have experienced to rouse her to such a state, and if she had been raped or robbed, what did it feel like?

When Nora was calmer, but no more disposed to offer information, Phoebe began to question her. Had she been working in the restaurant? Nora shook her head. Where, then, had she been? Nora opened her mouth as if to speak, then sank back on to the sofa, defeated by the effort required. After some more stroking and an adjustment to the cushions to make Nora more comfortable, Phoebe asked, 'Did you go out by yourself or were you with someone?'

Nora appeared to consider for a moment, then whispered, 'Steve.'

'Steve?' Phoebe was stunned. She knew, of course, that

Steve had formed a special relationship with Nora, that he had admitted her into his life, but she had always seen him as too composed and calculating for an act as impulsive and devastating as Nora's condition suggested.

'Where did it happen?' she asked, hoping to form some kind of picture.

'In an Italian restaurant, somewhere in Kilburn. We'd been to see *The Playboy of the Western World*.' As she spoke, Nora became calmer but no more inclined to volunteer information.

The picture, instead of clarifying, was becoming more confused. It was unlikely that Steve, or indeed any man, had launched an attack in an Italian restaurant in Kilburn so something must have started there that got out of hand later. Phoebe, who was usually inclined to speak before she thought, took some care to phrase her next remarks.

'So it happened later – back at his house or on the way home. Is that what you're saying?'

Nora looked at her in incomprehension. 'I took a taxi home from the restaurant. For all I know he's still sitting there.'

At this point Phoebe's patience snapped. 'So what exactly did happen? You're not telling me that he – you know, had a go at you in a restaurant? What did he do?'

'I don't know what you mean by having a go,' Nora retorted angrily. 'I'm not a ride.' And as she used the word, its connotation at home in Ireland, where adolescent boys speculated on who was a 'good ride', hung in the air. 'He told me he loved me. He set this evening up – and me thinking his wife and daughters might be there – and then, bold as brass, told me I must know how he felt about me.'

Phoebe's sympathy evaporated in an instant, giving way

to bewilderment – the best-looking lecturers were regarded by some girls as prizes to be won – and a kind of contempt for Nora's prissy naïveté. 'Don't you fancy him?' she asked. 'I would have thought he was just your type.'

'Are you being serious?' Nora was now fully roused from the stunned state of grief in which she had returned. 'He's married and he's got two daughters not much younger than we are.'

Phoebe, who, with the easing of tension, was leaning back in the sofa now next to Nora, shrugged and said, 'These things happen. It's no big deal. A lot of my parents' friends – sensitive and artistic types, real revolutionaries in their day – have open marriages.' There was a note of pride in her voice that her parents moved in such unconventional circles.

'It happens because nobody here cares about anything,' screamed Nora. 'You want something, you just have it. People behave like that when they don't believe in anything.'

'That's not fair. I believe in all sorts of things, and so do my family – more than you do. It's not as if you go to church or anything that you have any right to act so superior.'

'Oh, right,' said Nora, with a sneering arrogance that Phoebe had never seen in her before. 'You believe in tarot cards and horoscopes and alternative therapists who'll pamper your every whim, and in giving yourself permission to do whatever you fancy – as though anything could ever hold you back. You believe in whatever sanctions your own selfishness and nothing that might make life a bit harder for you because it involves restraint or sacrifice or putting other people's needs first. Your own mother believes there's no harm in cheating since you won't get into journalism school any other way.'

As soon as she said this, Nora's anger subsided and she looked frightened. 'I'm sorry, I didn't mean to bring that up.'

Since Christmas, Phoebe had chosen to forget her mother's incautious request, at the same time nursing resentment against Nora for having it in reserve to hold against her and for failing to comply with it. 'Maybe my mother assumes that other people are as generous as she is. You said that nobody here cares about anything, meaning me, I suppose. So let's look at some of the things I don't care about, like not getting rent from a so-called lodger, and lending or giving you what you don't have. I suppose your parents are great, leaving you here without so much as a telephone call, let alone money to support yourself with. You're all fine examples of the proper way to do things.'

Nora heard her out, then rose to her feet. 'It's too late to go anywhere tonight so, if you'll allow me a last indulgence, I'll stay for one more night. But I'll be gone before you get up in the morning.'

And she was, with all her meagre possessions, but not those that had come from Phoebe, who found on the kitchen table the following morning the leather coat she had passed on to Nora in the first year and the skirt she had discarded for one that fitted better, with a few other garments and some books. Sitting on top of the pile was a note, thanking Phoebe and her parents for letting her live there rent-free over the last year, and suggesting that if Phoebe needed to contact her, she do so through her email address.

Ballypierce

In the heady weeks following the Good Friday Agreement, when former IRA men were seen to relish their new political status and respectability, and long-established Catholic and Protestant politicians proudly displayed their new, harmonious relations by appearing on stage together at pop concerts, Nora's own most pressing concerns – work and Felix – moved into a new and more intense phase. While Gerald talked of nothing but surrender and betrayal – 'Does John Hume not know how daft he looks, holding hands with David Trimble, for all the world like a young courting couple?' – Nora was concentrating on her A levels, now only weeks away. The work itself wasn't a problem, but she was constantly distracted by Felix. Or, rather, by her nagging, persistent awareness of Felix and the changes she had noticed in him; and by the impossibility of reconciling what she wanted for herself with what he might wish for himself, if he had the means to express it.

If Felix were still as he used to be – playful with her, distant with their parents, eager for her attention but prepared to wait until she could give it, entirely absorbed meanwhile in waving his scarf – she might have been able to maintain the precarious equilibrium she had established. She had grown used, after all, to accommodate her responsibility to Felix with her schoolwork, and had learned ways to pacify him and contain his need for her. Recently, however, they had moved into new and uncharted territory, which was all the harder to negotiate because her parents refused to acknowledge any change but in his size.

He was now rather taller than she was and threateningly broad and heavy. When he hugged her, she could feel the breath being squeezed from her lungs, not from any malice on his part, but because he appeared to have no awareness of his new bulk and strength. He had the physical awkwardness of a teenager after a period of rapid growth, but tried to force himself into clothes he had long since outgrown; he would still try to sit on her knee, as though the little pairs of shorts and T-shirts he favoured represented his real and essential self. When she looked at the stranger he had become, the only trace she could find of the earlier Felix, her little brother, was his eyes, which had retained their blue, limpid beauty, while the rest of him had coarsened and thickened. The expression in those eyes, however, was not only lost, but suffering.

She had begun to think he might be ill. His skin was the colour of the sludgy, inauthentic porridge paste he ate for breakfast, and he had developed a strange puffiness under the eyes. She had begun to wonder whether he had difficulty tolerating light. It had become almost impossible to persuade him out of the house, but since he went almost nowhere except to school, which he had never regarded with any enthusiasm, there were difficulties for her in presenting this as a symptom. His tenacity in trying to avoid the school bus was becoming unmanageable, especially since Gerald, who was the only one with the strength to dislodge him, was now leaving for work before the bus was due. Even Bernie, faced with the alternative of Felix hanging around the house all day, had accepted that Nora could no longer remove him from the house unassisted, and pitched in to help, though increasingly the bus driver was enlisted to throw his weight into the struggle. This was beyond the scope of his duties, and his insurance cover, but Nora looked frailer than ever beside her brother and strangers often took pity on her.

This could easily be dismissed as naughtiness rather than illness, however, especially since his behaviour relied on extreme physical strength. More troubling – and the reason for her theory of light intolerance – was his reluctance to go into the garden, even with Nora. When she did persuade him out, he retreated into the shed, where he had made a little nest for himself with an old picnic rug and a deck-chair; inside the house he now favoured the coat cupboard, where he sat in the corner under a pile of old coats, unless Nora let him into her room. On these occasions, he wrapped himself in Nora's quilt and lay where he could look at her.

It was useless expressing her anxiety to Bernie who, apart from the problem of getting him off to school, found life rather more peaceful now: at least she had uninterrupted use of the television and video player, in which he seemed to have lost all interest. So, Nora was forced back on Gerald. Although no longer in the habit of approaching her father, except when strictly necessary, she thought it might be possible to flatter him into taking a professional interest in Felix's predicament.

On the first Friday evening of the summer term, she found him at the kitchen table where, with a mug of tea at his elbow, he had a selection of the day's newspapers laid out in front of him. 'Could I talk to you about something, Daddy?'

Gerald took off his reading glasses before he looked up. When he spoke, it was with the heavy sarcasm that had become habitual in his dealings with his daughter. 'Well, I am honoured. What's it to be tonight? Will our theme be that nationalists are now showing the sense of responsibility that you've long found wanting in them? Have they heeded the call of sixth-formers to lay down their arms?'

'It's not about politics,' said Nora, keeping her voice quiet and calm. Any hint of excitement in her speech he now routinely dismissed as hysterical, and with it, whatever she might have to say. 'I want to talk to you about something more immediate.'

'More immediate?' He considered the word as he used it. 'Well, how could I refuse somebody with such a choice turn of phrase? So, what is this immediate matter?'

'Have you noticed that Felix is looking a bit odd these days?'

Gerald leaned back against his chair and sent his eyes upwards to a heaven and a god he didn't believe in. 'Are you telling me you've only just noticed? How old is the boy? Fourteen? Fifteen? Is fifteen years your idea of "immediate"?'

'About the eyes – and I don't mean the Down's characteristics. And his skin's a funny colour. This is something new, otherwise I wouldn't have raised it.'

'Ah, well, then, now you've lost me. The last time I looked, he still had two eyes in his head, which is as much as you can say for any of us.'

'They're very heavy and puffy underneath, and I've been wondering whether he's ill. He doesn't seem right to me, and I thought that, since you see a lot of sick people, you might have some idea of what the problem might be. I've heard it said that you're as good as a doctor at diagnosing things.'

Gerald raised his eyebrows at this tribute to his expertise. Whether or not her flattery had indeed disarmed him, he seemed sufficiently engaged to pursue the conversation. 'Well, now, I'll give you my opinion. There's a difference between being right and being well, and while I'd say he's far from right, he's certainly not ill. Look at all that good beef on him. The boy's an ox. I'm thinking of putting him forward to challenge the idea that we don't have mad cow disease in Ireland. It could be an explanation for the collective madness that has the country in its grip.'

Forcing herself not to be discouraged, Nora battled on: 'I've been thinking he may be developing allergies. It's the hay-fever season, after all. Maybe he's sensitive to some airborne substance.'

Gerald snorted his contempt. 'You know your trouble?' This had become a recurring refrain in conversation with his daughter. The answers to his question differed, according to context and occasion, but its regular repetition suggested his untiring quest to discover quite how she had gone so badly wrong. 'They teach you all the words at that school of yours and what they mean, after a fashion, but they've left you quite clueless as to what, in the real world, they might be used for.'

Gerald's sneering remarks on the value of her education had become more marked as her school years were drawing to a close and the need to make a decision about her future was becoming imminent. Her parents had not mentioned university, but Nora was sure that, were the issue to be raised, the flaws in the education she had already received would be used as an argument to keep her at home, maybe working but otherwise minding Felix.

'That boy's as sensitive as my arse,' Gerald concluded. 'And his skin's about as thick.'

Just on cue, Felix entered the kitchen, having changed from his school uniform into a pair of shorts that barely covered his buttocks, and a T-shirt bearing a print of Disney's doe-eyed, raven-haired and improbably slim Pocahontas, which ended well short of his waist. He stood bolt upright in front of Nora, waiting for her approval.

'Look at him,' said his father. 'I swear the boy's had his head turned by this nonsense about him being so sensitive, and now he thinks he's that wee squaw he's so proud to have blazoned across his chest.'

'Come on, Felix,' said Nora, moving to place an arm round his shoulders and propel him out of the room. 'We'll see if we can find something that fits a bit better.'

'Not so fast,' said Gerald, who was usually eager to have Felix removed from his presence. 'The boy will disgrace us all if he's seen like that. I can barely bring myself to look at him. Instead of diagnosing imaginary illnesses, if you really want to do something useful you might take him off tomorrow and buy him some clothes that fit properly.'

He felt in the back pocket of his trousers, drew out his wallet and removed a wad of notes. Then, after wetting his thumb and forefinger, he peeled off two hundred pounds in tens and laid them on the kitchen table. In the absence of other responsibilities assumed by him within the family, he particularly relished the role of provider, which he seemed to feel required periodic public display.

'You might get yourself something while you're about

it,' he said. The clear implication was that, while Nora left much to be desired as a daughter, he would never be found wanting as a father.

It was useless pointing out to him that, since he had never taken Felix shopping, he could have no idea of the impossibility of her trying to buy anything for herself with Felix in tow. Nora gave a show of gratitude nonetheless, knowing that anything less would be taken as an insult. Besides, since her father wouldn't notice whether she bought new clothes for herself or not, his own interest being fully satisfied in the act of giving, she would be able to add her share of the money to the small store she had been accumulating.

Gerald had given no thought, of course, to the ways and means of buying Felix clothes. There was nothing suitable locally, just a few men's outfitters whose windows were enough to discourage anybody under fifty from entering. Nora shrank from the thought of Belfast, both for the time it would take, so close to her A levels, and because of the unpredictability of Felix's recent behaviour. She could see no alternative, however. It had been a long time since anybody had tried to take Felix anywhere, apart from school, so the prospect of a day out with Nora, riding on buses and having pizza in a café for lunch, might lift his spirits and make him more amenable.

The day began promisingly. Having been prepared by her the evening before, Felix showed none of the reluctance to get up that he did on school mornings, and she managed to find a pair of trousers that met round the middle. Although he struggled for a while when she produced a shirt – hated by him above all other garments, ties excepted, because of the associations with school – he gave in with moderately good grace and allowed her to do up the buttons while she again explained to him their plans for the day.

'Well, aren't you the lucky ones?' said Bernie, when they were both ready to leave. 'I could do with a day in Belfast myself.' She was alert to any opportunity to express resentment even when, as on the present occasion, she would do anything to avoid the task that had been laid on Nora. 'I don't know how I'm going to get my shopping done, with you gallivanting off all day.'

'You'll be all right,' said Nora. 'Daddy's got your list so the shopping will be done.' Though not by Gerald, it was safe to assume. He would almost certainly send the girl from the shop, but that wouldn't stop him taking the credit for it and making them feel the inconvenience he had suffered.

The bus journey passed without incident, and Nora felt herself relax. Felix no longer seemed capable of the ecstasy that such a treat had induced in the past, but he was passive and obedient. They had a brief walk round the shopping centre, as Nora assessed the shops from the outside – there was no point in testing his tolerance by going in to any before she was sure they would find what they wanted – but then, noticing that he was flagging, she suggested a pizza before they move on to the serious business of the day.

It was in the pizzeria, however, that the first signs of trouble came. Felix wasn't unused to eating out. Over the last few years, during the school holidays, when Bernie could no longer bear to have him around, Nora would sometimes be given money to get him out of the house for a few hours, so the cinema and modest cafés of Ballypierce had become familiar to him. But this was the first time that Nora had taken him out to eat since his behaviour had taken its recent, mystifying turn.

He sat happily enough, straight-backed and proud to be in a public place with his sister, until the menus arrived. Felix was handed his own, which he accepted, like one long familiar with the routine. Almost immediately, however, he showed signs of panic. After pretending to read it, he became uncomfortable and self-conscious.

'What about tuna, with cheese and tomato?' Nora asked. 'You like that – you had it the other day from the shop.'

He shook his head, distressed. Then, rallying briefly, he began stabbing his finger at every pizza listed, insisting that Nora read out to him each list of ingredients. This pacified him for a while, but the choice bewildered him so she was forced to go back and repeat what she had already told him. He lowered his head and shook it violently, suddenly finding himself unable to cope with the procedure.

'Would you like a salad, then? Tomato and cheese, maybe?'

He shook his head even more violently.

'You don't like salad, do you? So you'd better have pizza. Why don't you let me choose the very best one, the pizza I know you like most of all? Will you let me do that?'

After a short pause, he nodded, but miserably, as though he suspected Nora of tricking him. He sat sunk in gloom until the pizza arrived, when he appeared to cheer up. He rubbed his hands together in anticipation of pleasure, a gesture once so characteristic of him but not seen for some time. Nora took it as a good omen.

'Now, why don't I cut it up for you? I don't have anything to cut for myself because I'm only having a salad so I'd like to cut yours.'

'No, I'll do it,' said Felix, decisively. He picked up his knife and fork, held them poised for a moment above his plate, then dropped them.

'Don't worry, leave it to me,' said Nora, but before she could help, he pushed away his plate, with a clatter of china and cutlery, then slid off his chair and under the table.

Nora froze to her chair, and then looked around to see what the other customers were making of his behaviour. As she did so, heads turned away from her and the surrounding groups launched into animated conversation. She tried to reason with Felix, as quietly and patiently as her own discomfort would permit, knowing that it would be a mistake to allow him to see her own mounting panic. He ignored her pleas. Instead, he pulled his own chair in from behind to wedge himself more firmly under the table.

She surveyed her options and decided that she had none, other than to wait for a change in Felix's mood. Her waiter appeared with an older man, whom she took to be the manager, and offered to help, but she shrank from the prospect of strangers getting involved, of Felix eventually being hoisted aloft by however many men it took and carried from the restaurant, to be dumped on the pavement outside. She remembered the Ash Wednesday fiasco. Felix must then have been a fraction of his current weight, and even then it had been a major operation to shift him. She thanked them, and assured them that, if they were all patient, Felix would eventually move of his own accord. But she didn't really feel the confidence her words conveyed.

Once they had gone, tears started to course silently down her cheeks. To hide her shame, she got down again to Felix's level.

'Felix.'

He shook his head violently and buried it still further in his chest.

'Felix, I'm really, really sad, really upset, and you've always been the one person in the world who can make me feel better. Why is that, do you think?'

There was a pause, when the outcome was uncertain. Either Felix would relent, or he would become more entrenched in the position he had adopted. Finally he said, 'You my 'ister.'

'That's right, I'm your sister, and you've always made me feel better. Will you do that now? Will we both get up and finish our lunch? I'm going to have mine because I'm hungry, and I expect you are too.'

Nora slid out from under the table and sat down, followed shortly by Felix. Instead of joining her at the table, however, he stood at her side. Then, after looking round to make sure he had witnesses, now that he had a chance to repair his public image, he locked his arm round Nora's neck and planted a noisy kiss on her head. 'Dere, dere,' he said. 'You're better now.'

A woman at the next table, who was treating her two teenage daughters to lunch and had covertly watched the whole procedure, said, 'Look at that, will you? What a fine young man that is, to look after his sister so well. And isn't he lucky to have such a sister?'

Felix stood up very straight, and Nora, who looked round to smile her thanks, saw that there were tears standing in the woman's eyes. All her experience until this point had encouraged her to see tears as the product of self-pity. She began to understand that there might be perspectives on herself, on Felix, and on the relationship she had established with him that their parents were prevented by their huge sense of grievance from grasping.

As they finished their meal, which included a large slab of chocolate cake for Felix as a reward for good behaviour, Nora became confident that the worst was over. Felix had asserted his independence, she had helped him out of the hole he had dug for himself, and now it seemed that his pride was engaged and he was anxious to put on a display of solid citizenship.

When they left the restaurant, they strolled arm in arm to Marks & Spencer, where Nora selected an armful of garments from the men's department. Felix showed little interest in the clothes she presented for his approval, but since he was indifferent rather than hostile, it seemed that they would get through the rest of the afternoon without further drama. She took him off to a quiet corner of the store to check the fit before she bought them. The shirts and pullovers were easy enough, but the trousers were more of a problem without trying them on. If she came home with trousers that failed to meet round the waist, there would almost certainly be jibes about the inadequacy of an education that failed to equip her for life's 'immediate' concerns. While she hesitated, Felix became restless and started tugging at her arm to leave. Just as she was beginning to think that she might abandon the project, even at the risk of her father's mockery, a smart young man with a tape measure bore down on them and offered to help.

She kept her brother at her side by holding his arm at the wrist and elbow, and said, 'I'm not sure about the fit of the trousers.'

'No problem,' said the young man, as he unfurled his tape measure and stepped towards Felix.

As he passed it round Felix's waist, Felix slipped through

the loop and, breaking into a run, headed for the door, pushing aside racks of clothes and stray trolleys that stood in his way. Nora dropped the clothes she was carrying and ran after him, wondering what she would do if he had disappeared into the crowd of Saturday-afternoon shoppers by the time she reached the street. As it happened, however, she nearly tripped over him where he was lying, sprawled on his back outside the central door, with a group of curious onlookers already gathered around him.

Once her relationship with him was established, some people drifted away, others stayed to offer advice and help. Although much of it was the useless kind that is wise after the event – 'A wee girl like you shouldn't be in charge of him at all. What can your mummy and daddy be thinking of?' – four men faced up to the challenge and at least managed to drag Felix away from the doors so that he was no longer at risk of being trampled on or of causing an accident to someone else. Felix, with all the apparent aplomb of a demonstrator, secure in the justice of his cause and committed to civil disobedience, submitted passively to being moved by the men, two clutching a shoulder and arm and the others a leg apiece, but refused to get back on his feet.

At this point most of the remaining crowd dispersed, now that they could get into the store, but the men who had intervened seemed to feel that their responsibility hadn't yet come to an end, especially since Felix was unresponsive to Nora's attempts to get him to his feet.

'Are you his carer?' one of the men asked. He was in his late twenties and had a girlfriend in attendance. Both stood out from the crowd of Saturday shoppers by the formality of their dress.

'I'm his sister.'

'But also his carer, for today at any rate,' he persisted.

'He's a social worker,' said his girlfriend in explanation. 'You're never quite who you think you are because he always has another word for it.'

'I'm just wondering why you have charge of him when you obviously can't handle him – not through any fault of your own, he must be twice your weight – and he's putting both of you in danger. Do you have parents?'

'Yes, but . . .' Nora paused as she tried to find a way to explain the situation that would satisfy his curiosity. Her mouth dried up with fear before she could say anything.

'It's all right, I'm on your side,' he said. His expression of concern was more than she could bear, and she began to cry. Nora was so used to hiding her feelings, at home and at school, that this public betrayal of herself, far from bringing relief, was almost painful.

'You stay with her,' he said to his girlfriend. 'I'll be right back.' After a word to the men who had helped him with Felix to stay at their posts in case he made a bolt for freedom, he broke into a run and disappeared into the crowd.

'I'm sure you have other things to do,' Nora said to the young woman, now that she had composed herself.

'We're meant to be going to a wedding, but I'm used to this. Dave thinks he can solve the problems of the world. For better or worse, isn't that what they say?'

Soon a police car pulled up beside them and Dave got out, followed by two RUC men.

'Look, we can't stay because we're due at a wedding – Michele's probably told you – but you need help to get the lad home. I think you'll find that these boys will do what's necessary.' He touched her arm lightly, and Michele put her arm round Nora's shoulders and gave her a squeeze. Then they were gone.

Nora knew at once that Dave and Michele were Protestants, though she might have guessed it before. No Catholic, even in the new world order that they were supposed to be living in since the Good Friday Agreement, would share their trust in the RUC, but then few Catholics would have the confidence that they had shown today in taking charge of complete strangers and assuming that they could solve their problems. Catholics, she thought bitterly, like to sit behind closed doors, blaming everybody else for their problems and seeking ulterior motives for apparent acts of kindness. She knew exactly how her father would judge her for accepting help from the RUC, but she felt suddenly weightless, relieved that somebody else was taking responsibility, and allowed herself to be carried along by the tide of events. Soon, she told herself, she would be out of all this, and would find a place where she could be herself, free from the hidden bonds that constrained everybody here.

Soon the men still securing Felix were relieved of their duties, and the rest of the crowd was dispersed. The two policemen stood over Felix who, even before the older one had finished saying, 'So what's all this about?' had sprung to his feet, awed by their uniforms and effortless air of authority.

'We'll get you and the little fellow down to the station,' said the younger one to Nora, 'and we'll have you right in no time.'

Nora and Felix were given tea and biscuits, and while Nora explained that her brother – who was usually so good – had taken a turn when she was trying to buy him some clothes, Felix played with a set of handcuffs he had been given to keep him amused. Then, when she had given them the details, they rang Gerald at the shop and suggested that he come and collect his children. To Nora's surprise, they asked her what schools they attended, and when she told them, a note was made in the logbook.

In less than an hour Gerald was there. Nora detected a degree of nervousness in his manner that she had never seen before, and wondered whether it was apparent to the RUC men, but whatever unease he felt, he had come prepared.

'Look at you both,' he said to Nora and Felix. He was the indulgent father, called upon to extricate his children from a scrape of their own making. 'Didn't I tell you, Nora, that it was a mistake to take the lad into Belfast on a Saturday afternoon?' Then, turning to the policemen, 'You know how headstrong they are at this age, I'm sure. She's a good girl, works hard at school, doesn't go gallivanting at night, but where her wee brother's concerned, she's always felt she knows best. And I have to tell you, officers, most times she does, but this will be a lesson to her to take advice sometimes from wiser heads.'

The policemen looked reassured. Gerald was, after all, a prosperous professional man, in his tweed jacket and polished brogues, not a feckless nationalist from a council estate. They weren't going to let him off the hook quite yet, however.

'He's a big boy for such a slip of a girl to manage,' said the older of the two who had picked them up. 'Did you not have any worries on that score?'

'Well, yes and no,' said Gerald. 'The lad's grown so fast recently that I don't think any of us has adjusted, least of all Nora. And, to be fair, he's always been like putty in her hands. He'd do things for her that he wouldn't do for his mother or me. And, as I say, she was quite insistent. You know how these young girls have their fathers wrapped round their little fingers.'

No wonder the RUC doesn't trust Catholics, Nora was thinking, when they can lie as effortlessly as this.

'So, have you learned your lesson, Nora?' asked the policemen. 'You'll listen to your daddy in future and not bite off more than you can chew? And you, Mr Doyle, you'll make sure the boy has a responsible adult with him in future when he's in a public place. It's a miracle he didn't cause a nasty accident.'

Once they were settled in the car, and on their way home, Nora waited for Gerald's outburst of rage. Instead he asked her, with carefully studied nonchalance, what she had told the RUC.

'Nothing. What was there to tell?'

'Did they not ask you what you were doing with the boy in Belfast?'

'I said I was trying to buy him some clothes.'

'Did they not ask whether it was your idea, or whether your parents had put you up to it?'

'They didn't ask and I didn't elaborate. It wasn't like that.'

'Then what was it like?'

Nora thought for a moment. 'It was a relief, to be honest with you. It was a horrible day and I was relieved that somebody else was looking after us. They were very nice to us. Felix rather enjoyed himself.'

Gerald, who under other circumstances would interpret a complimentary reference to the constabulary as treachery and a call for an instant history lesson, let this pass. Instead he asked another question: 'I suppose they didn't ask you how things are at home? With the boy, and all?'

Unseen by her father, for she was sitting in the back with Felix, Nora allowed herself a smile. I have him on the run, she thought. It seemed that the apparently impregnable self-righteousness he displayed at home could be dented. Was there somewhere in that great, bullying bulk a seed of self-doubt about his treatment of his children? She couldn't remember the last time he had asked her a question to which her answer might actually matter. Usually his questions were opening sallies to contests in which she would be routed by his superior skill and wisdom. For the first time since Felix was born, when she had ceased to have him wrapped round her little finger in the way he had presented their relationship to the policemen, she had some power over him.

'No, nothing like that.' Then, sensing an easing of the atmosphere as he began to relax, she said, 'They did ask me what schools we both went to.'

'And did you tell them?'

'It would have looked strange if I hadn't, surely.'

There was another pause, while Gerald digested this unpleasant information. 'And why do you think they asked you that?' he asked finally.

'I've no idea. They didn't say. Perhaps it's routine police procedure. I expect it's as you've always said, one of the ways of telling whether you're Protestant or Catholic. Maybe if they'd asked that at the beginning and found out we were Catholics, they would have left Felix lying on the pavement.'

Gerald didn't question this argument, which was, after all, his own; neither did he demand to know whether she was being sarcastic with him, an issue he would almost certainly have raised on another occasion. He was clearly not himself, for all his apparent calm.

'I didn't spend any of your money, except on lunch and the bus fare. I'll give it back to you when we get home.'

'Keep it,' he said. 'Buy yourself something another time.'

He seemed consoled by his own largesse, and by the time they were back at the bungalow had recovered some of his usual bluster. As they entered the lounge, where Bernie was in her usual place in front of the television, a carton of Quality Street close to hand, Gerald spoke to her without any preliminary greeting. 'The boy's filthy from rolling around on the pavement. Will you get up, woman, strip him off and bath him before you get stuck to that sofa?'

Bernie looked from Gerald to Nora to see if she was in on this too. The balance of power seemed to have shifted while they were absent, and she was evidently frightened. If Gerald had come in ranting at Nora's incompetence, or treachery in having him dragged to an RUC station, as seemed likely from the telephone call he had made from the shop before he left for Belfast, her role now would be one of passive acquiescence. Realising that a change had occurred, however, she adopted a conciliatory tone towards Nora. 'I've a nice piece of steak for your tea,' she said. 'I expect you need it.'

Nora, who had already decided that in her new life she would be a vegetarian, hated steak more than anything, but on this occasion took Bernie's offer in the spirit in which it was intended. 'Thanks, Mum. I'm not hungry at the moment, but I'll have it later.' Then, as Bernie struggled to stay on her feet, she said, 'It's all right, I'll bath Felix. You stay where you are.'

Bernie watched Gerald for his reaction and, since he merely shook his head and shrugged his shoulders in despair before leaving them for the study that he had recently fitted out for himself in what had once been the dining room, decided it was safe to accept Nora's offer.

Nora ran the bath while Felix undressed. His mood had changed with the appearance of the RUC men outside Marks & Spencer. In the back of the car on the way home he had shown his contrition by snuggling up to her and stroking her hand; he was now demonstrating his eagerness to please by faithfully following the routine she had been trying to establish – putting his shoes together where they wouldn't get wet and throwing his dirty laundry into the basket. He climbed into the bath and lay back, luxuriating in the warm water, while Nora sat on the lavatory lid and drifted off into one of her familiar daydreams. He should have been old enough to leave while he soaked and soaped himself, but once or twice recently, realising that it alarmed her, he had taken to submerging his head under water. As always with Felix, it wasn't clear whether he was aware of the danger and was testing his own limits, or was amused by her fear without understanding the reason for it.

She was roused from her thoughts when she heard Felix say her name, then repeat it.

'What is it? Are you ready to come out now?'

'Come over here, 'Ora.'

'What is it? Are you ready to come out now?' Nora stood up and stretched out the towel she was holding, but instead of getting out of the bath, Felix reached out and took her hand.

'You my 'ister,' he said.

'That's right, I'm your sister, and you'd oblige me by getting out now.'

Felix ignored what she was saying, and instead of getting out pulled her hand down towards his genitals. Nora saw

Felix's erect penis floating in the water, framed by a luxuriant growth of blond pubic hair. It was the first male erection she had ever seen, but she knew instantly what it was, just as she knew that Felix's reliance on her was now total. Over the years, she had come to satisfy all Felix's emotional and physical needs, and now that this new need had arisen, it seemed natural to him that she should satisfy it too. That was Felix's understanding of what he might expect of his sister: no less than everything. Still holding his hand, but at a more conventional distance, she took a step or two back and said, 'No, Felix, I can't do that.'

'Please,' he said. His eyes, with the lids lowered, were dreamy and unfocused and Nora pulled away abruptly, pulse racing. She stood outside the bathroom against the wall, breathing hard, and tried to bring her emotions under control. As regards Felix, she felt both pity and disgust, but overwhelming both was a fierce anger. Although sexually innocent, she looked forward to it happening one day, in the ideal life she imagined for herself, but what she had imagined was now tainted by Felix's crude and mechanical male need for satisfaction.

Most of all, however, she felt angry with her parents. Nora had long since realised that they might have responded to Felix differently, that they expected too much of her, that she was often blamed for what wasn't her fault when they might have done better to address their own inadequacies. But because she had inherited her father's pride, she had never confided in anyone of her own age group, and had paid the price for that reserve in being thought queer and stuck-up, not like other people. So she had come to see herself as different. That difference had fed her ambitions but, more damagingly, had fed a niggling doubt: maybe her father, who had once loved her so much, treated her as he did because she had genuinely disappointed him, because she deserved it.

For some time, she had held both views of her situation simultaneously, without being able to resolve the contradictions. In the course of this day, however, her sense of herself as victim had clarified. Having denied herself the solace of telling her story, and perhaps using it as a way to gain the confidence of her contemporaries, she had had to wait until today, when she saw the tears of the woman in the pizzeria, the barely suppressed anger of the social worker, Dave, on her behalf, the unspoken understanding of the policemen and, most tellingly of all, her father's fear and shiftiness for confirmation of what she had known all along. And from today, it looked as though she would be subject to further outrages from Felix, for which she blamed not Felix but her parents. And underlying it all was a great sadness, that the innocence of her relationship with Felix, which, for all its inconveniences, had given them both solace and comfort, had been destroyed.

After glancing into the bathroom to make sure that Felix still had his head above water, and hadn't drowned in the course of an ecstasy induced by masturbation, she threw open the door of the lounge, where her mother sat peering into the darkness at the television screen, the remote control in her lap and a praline chocolate in her mouth. Nora walked deliberately across the room, stood in front of the television and said, 'You're going to have to get Felix out of the bath. I can't do it myself any more.'

Bernie looked startled as she adjusted her focus to her daughter's presence, and then frightened. 'Why? What's happened? Will he not get out?'

'He doesn't want to get out, but that's not the issue. He tried to get me to touch his penis, and I think you or Daddy should deal with it. I can't dress or change him any more, either.'

Language such as this was never used in the Doyle household. Bernie had abandoned the practice of religion but retained all the prurience of her Catholic upbringing, which avoided frankness about bodily function as the mark of a dirty mind. She recoiled in horror, as Nora had known she would. 'What a terrible thing to say.'

'I'm only saying it because it happened,' said Nora. 'The fact that it happened doesn't give me any more pleasure than it does you.'

'Would you ask your father to come in and see what he has to say?'

When Nora returned with Gerald, the television had been switched off to mark the solemnity of the occasion. Bernie's initial shock had been replaced by indignation.

'Will you tell your father what you've just told me? I can't bring myself to say it.'

Nora repeated what she had said to Gerald, who stood silent for a while, absorbing the information. She decided to add to the already lengthy list of his misdemeanours his habit of never reacting spontaneously to anything that was said to him, always preferring a calculated response that would give him the advantage.

'So is this what you told those RUC bastards this afternoon – that you're being sexually abused by your handicapped brother while your parents turn a blind eye?' Since his brush with the law, he had been fretting about the ground he had lost to his daughter, and now he could scarcely conceal his joy at being handed such an opportunity to reclaim his natural ascendancy. 'You want to watch yourself, young woman. Those boys will know, even if you don't, that mongols don't have any sexual feelings to speak of.'

Nora stood her ground. 'I didn't say anything to the police because it hadn't happened, and it's not something I would have told them if it had. I'm telling you.'

Gerald was walking up and down, nodding to himself. 'I see, I see,' he said. 'This is why you said you'd bath him, when I asked your mother to. You got a taste for being a victim back there in the station, so you thought you'd try your luck with something else. Well, well, who'd have thought it?'

Nora was enraged by Gerald, but not confused and frightened, as she had often been in the past when confronted by his sense of his own rectitude and readiness to blame others. Her clarity of mind enabled her to keep her anger under control so that she didn't burst into tears. 'I'm not claiming abuse because Felix isn't capable of such a thing. You're distorting what I say so that you don't have to take it seriously. I would have thought that, under the circumstances, you might be concerned about what I'm feeling. You haven't enquired, but I'll tell you anyway. I feel shocked and upset, but not really outraged, not now I've thought about it, because Felix doesn't understand what he tried to do, and I feel as sorry for him as I do for myself. I also feel sad, because the relationship we have can never be the same.' She paused for breath, and allowed herself to take in her parents' astonishment. 'I don't recognise myself in what you've just said, but if you want to think like that, there's nothing I can do about it. What you need to know is that I shan't dress or bath Felix again because I think it's bad for both of us.'

Without waiting for an answer, she left them to digest

what she had said. She went to her room and stayed there for the rest of the weekend, leaving only to make the occasional snack when her father wasn't about. She didn't bother to avoid Bernie. Her mother was sitting in the kitchen when she made herself some toast on Sunday afternoon.

'Your father's out for a bit.'

'Yes, I heard the door as he left.'

'I don't think he'll talk to you until you apologise.'

'That could well be something of a relief for all of us. Where's Felix?'

'In the coat cupboard. Sure, he can't get up to any harm in there.'

'Not to anybody else, no, but you should speak to somebody about it. The doctor, maybe.'

Bernie said nothing, but sat looking at her daughter, confused by the change in her, by the distance she was marking out for herself from the rest of the family. Her eyes were wide and staring and her head restless, as though she was waiting for something to happen but lacked the will or energy to act. It occurred to Nora that she might be deliberately playing up the appearance of helplessness, in order to appeal to her better nature.

'Well, I'll be off,' said Nora, as she washed up her plate. 'I have an essay waiting for me.'

The following morning she left the house before her father, so that he would have to struggle to get Felix on to the school bus. She tried not to think about Felix: he would wrench her heart and weaken her resolve. When she arrived home that afternoon, Bernie was sitting in the same place at the kitchen table, for all the world as though she hadn't stirred since Nora had last seen her the previous afternoon. She was even more agitated, and this time Nora had no doubt that her distress was genuine.

'Will you read this while I make you a cup of tea?' Bernie's voice was pleading as she handed over an official-looking letter. It was from Felix's school, but unlike the usual communications to parents, it ran to three sides and was from the headmistress.

'I thought we should inform you of our mounting concern for Felix,' the letter began, before itemising aspects of Felix's behaviour that were rapidly placing him beyond their control: an almost total unwillingness to cooperate with teachers, sudden bursts of anger, which he appeared to find as distressing as they did, and 'inappropriate behaviour towards younger female members of staff'. They had tolerated this behaviour for some time, it seemed, because they recognised that these children had particular difficulties and, by and large, the staff were willing to deal with them. Recently, however, matters had taken what Mother Philomena described as 'a new and rather alarming turn'. He had become disruptive to the point of disturbing children who were already quite vulnerable. There had been a number of instances when he had offered violence, to both members of staff and other students. And that very morning he had disappeared from school, and by the time he was found, 'was cavorting around on the street in full public view, completely naked, his clothes strewn around him'.

The letter appeared to be leading to a demand for Felix's immediate withdrawal from school, until the last two paragraphs. It seemed – and this was news to Nora – that Mother Philomena had telephoned Bernie once or twice and had received her assurance that she and her husband would be especially alert to Felix's behaviour at home, and would do everything they could to cooperate with the school.

'You didn't tell me that Mother Philomena had been in touch with you,' Nora said.

Bernie, who had been watching Nora's reactions, now turned away as she fiddled with the teapot and kettle. 'Well, you know my opinion of nuns,' she said. 'They like to throw their weight around and let you know what martyrs they are.'

Returning to the letter, Nora read, 'We assume, since matters have deteriorated further, that you have had no greater success with Felix than we have, and might be in need of further help in managing him.' If the Doyles were willing to accept professional help, Mother Philomena and her staff were prepared to persevere further with Felix. Then she made a suggestion that seemed such perfect sense to Nora that she wondered why she hadn't she hadn't thought of it herself – that Felix might be clinically depressed. 'In our experience it isn't unknown for adolescence to trigger depression in young people with Down's syndrome. Felix would, of course, need to be carefully assessed, but he might benefit from treatment by a properly trained psychotherapist.' Mother Philomena was careful to stress that such a diagnosis would not ease the Doyles of their parental responsibility: any prescribed form of treatment would require their active participation.

While Nora was still absorbing the contents of this letter, Bernie said, 'What are we going to do?' As events had conspired to force her out of her torpor, which had come to seem her natural condition, her helplessness was increasingly exposed. And her reliance on Nora, which had been unspoken, unquestioned and unacknowledged, as though that, too, were natural, had in the course of the last few days become a favour to be sought.

'I think you should do what Mother Philomena suggests

and cooperate with the school in some psychotherapy for Felix. At least now somebody seems to have an inkling of what's going on so there's some chance of helping him.'

Nora had chosen her words carefully and, watching her mother, could see that she had noticed the significant omission: she hadn't offered to take control herself, or even to participate in the treatment, although it seemed likely that that would be required of her. She had already decided that she would do what was specifically required of her by the professions likely to be involved, but that she wouldn't assume any part of her parents' responsibilities.

'But your father would never agree.'

'I don't see that he has a choice. If he refuses to co-operate, the school might well suspend Felix and then where will you be?'

Nora thought it likely that, in such circumstances, her parents might be better off. Felix might be taken into care, or sent to a special boarding school, but while the latter might be welcome, her father would never be able to stand the shame. To reach that point, he would first have to be humbled by the social services and admit his own inadequacies. And while he had never participated in the care of Felix, he liked to present himself publicly as a man who had shouldered a burden that none would willingly seek. There were still enough sycophants among his fellow traders to allow him that satisfaction.

Forcing herself not to acknowledge her mother's fear and confusion, Nora pleaded pressure of work, but on her way to her room she looked in on Felix in the coat cupboard. He was sitting in the corner, an old coat wrapped over him, as though the cupboard alone were not sufficient to conceal him.

'How are you, Felix?'

He looked up as she spoke, and his face suddenly lightened, as though her presence alone relieved him of the burden of misery. She felt a clenching in her chest.

'I'm awight, 'Ora.'

'I have work to do now, but I'll see you later.'

'Fine, fine,' he said. Then, as she was turning to go, she heard the clearing in his throat that always preceded his more ambitious attempts at conversation. 'If you need me, I'll be in the cupboard.'

She wanted to gather him up and hug him, as she always had, but she controlled the impulse and said, 'That's good to know, Felix. I'll remember that. See you later.'

''Ee you later,' he said.

She worked at some history revision until she decided that the moment might be right to return to the kitchen. She had avoided her father since Saturday night, but was curious now to hear his reaction to the letter, especially since parts of it confirmed her own observations and experience of Felix. He was indeed ill, if not in the way she had supposed; and even Gerald might find it difficult to sustain his contempt for her in the face of Mother Philomena's claims of 'inappropriate behaviour' towards young women.

Her parents were seated in their usual places at the kitchen table. Gerald, who had long preferred to eat alone, had finsihed, and his plate was pushed to one side. Instead of his usual newspaper, however, Mother Philomena's letter lay on the table in front of him. Another departure from routine was the glass of whiskey he was sipping, which he usually reserved for a later hour when he was installed in his study.

Bernie said to her, 'There's a chicken casserole and some potatoes in the oven, if you want to dish some up for you and Felix.'

Gerald had avoided her eye as she came in, but now that her back was safely turned, he said, 'So, isn't the world turned upside-down, Nora? It's getting to the point where you'd wonder, getting up in the morning, whether the sun will still be there in the sky.'

'I'm sorry,' said Nora, turning. 'I don't catch your drift.'

'Well, you can be forgiven for that. Does any of us know where we are these days? First we have these IRA boys showing an indecent haste to get into suits and be ministers when the job's only half done. And this state of affairs brought about by a minister of the Crown who sends her officials out for Tampax.'

Bernie winced at this, but said nothing, realising that a certain latitude had to be allowed a man who owned a chemist's shop.

'And now we have a nun recommending psychotherapy for a boy who can neither speak nor think, as if he were some Jew-boy from New York. What's the fellow's name – the one who ran off with his step-daughter and says nobody understands him?'

'Woody Allen?'

'That's the one, though they're all the same, thinking they've been marked out for suffering because their grand-mother's third cousin died in one of the camps.' Gerald's tone of bitter hilarity was strained, and probably owed something to the whiskey, but Nora couldn't help admiring, even as she deplored, the ease with which her father had deflected attention from Felix's condition, and his earlier contempt at her accurate assessment of it, and from his own persistent neglect of his son, which had been carefully coded into Mother Philomena's letter, towards matters where he could feel comfortably superior.

'You know, in the old days, when your mother and I

were young, and nuns still behaved like nuns, it was a sharp rap across the knuckles and five Hail Marys. Is it your impression that the world's improved?'

'I can't see that the rap across the knuckles and the Hail Marys would do Felix much good, if that's what you're asking. I'll go and get him for his supper.'

When she returned with Felix, after a short struggle in the coat cupboard, her father was still there.

'That's all the boy cares about,' he said, as Nora settled Felix in his chair and brought him his supper. 'The day he goes off his food, we'll know that something's seriously wrong.'

As if on cue, Felix stared at his plate before pushing it away. His chin dropped on to his chest, and although they couldn't see him crying, they heard his sobs.

Gerald made a quick recovery from his initial surprise. 'Would you look at that? He's trying to show the old man up. It's all right, lad, I'll be off to my room and you can get on with it.' At the door, he turned to Nora and said, 'I suppose we must go along with this daft idea. I've told your mother I'll drive the three of you to Belfast, or wherever it is they send him. You'll know what to say to them – you seem to speak the same language, these days.'

He left before she had the opportunity to remind him that it was his presence that was being requested, not hers, or to suggest that her examination timetable might limit her involvement. She would have liked to say that she had no intention of going at all, but knew that, while she was in the house, she would continue to do what she could for Felix, within the boundaries she had set.

Felix didn't return to his supper but to the coat cupboard. Back in her bedroom, Nora opened her drawer and looked at the provisional offers of university places she had received. Her English teacher had wanted her to go to Oxford, but that would have meant an interview and she had made it clear that the business had to be managed without her parents' knowledge. Although she had never confided in her own contemporaries, her teachers had arrived at some understanding of her situation. It had been agreed that only those universities that didn't require interviews might be approached and that all correspondence should be addressed to school. She had been accepted everywhere she had applied, but in the last few days had decided on London. It was, of all the places in the world, the one that would most displease her father. The available loans wouldn't be enough to keep her, but she hoped that holiday employment would be easy to find there. Her English teacher had promised to help her arrange hotel work on the coast somewhere for the summer months, after her A levels, so that she would have a little money put by to start her off, in addition to what she had saved over the last year or so.

She loved Felix, and knew he would never love anyone as he loved her. If she allowed that to rule her, though, she would be destroyed. Even more than her father's breezy assumption that she would continue to fill the great void for Felix that he and her mother had created, his depression had decided her. She felt that she had done everything in her power for him, but it hadn't been enough to keep him from this. Nothing would ever be enough, so she must make the best life that she could for herself elsewhere.

PART SEVEN

Exile

London

It is the middle of May and the climax of the academic year is approaching. The trees have put forth tender green leaves, and tulips, wisteria and those shrubs – azalea, viburnum – that are valued for their fragrance and delicacy have brought an air of gaiety to the gardens of the wealthier suburbs. Last year Nora delighted in the scents and colours of her first London spring, and in the behaviour of Londoners, who spilled out into the squares and parks and on to pavements, where little tables and chairs had appeared overnight outside cafés and pubs at the first sign of seasonal change. London was like a southern city, scarcely part of the same continent as Belfast, and her spirits had been lifted. If she had had any doubts about moving to London they had been dispelled by that first spring, which held the promise that life might be taken more easily and that, in the traditional season of renewal, she might be reborn as her true and imagined self.

This year, however, Nora is indifferent to seasonal change. Not that she is much aware of it, in the house where she is now living in Brixton. When she left Phoebe's flat, her first requirement was to find somewhere before nightfall, but she was also anxious to be as far as possible from those areas north of Bloomsbury where chance encounters with former associates were most likely to occur. The room she now occupies meets both needs, though precious little otherwise. It's small, dark and appears to have been furnished from skips. She keeps it as clean as decades of ingrained dirt will allow, but outside the confines of her own room the house is unbelievably squalid.

Its other inhabitants, two men and a woman in their mid-twenties, claim to be involved in creative work, tenuously connected with the media or music, but the only activity that they pursue with any dedication is smoking dope. It isn't clear what they do for money. Nora assumes they are supported by the state, or by dealing in their own favoured substance, but whatever their source of income, it is sufficient to keep them supplied with enough cannabis for their own use and for the takeaway meals that form the bulk of their diet. The sitting room, which is shrouded in perpetual gloom because the curtains are never pulled back from the windows – Jake, the self-styled performance poet, has told Nora that the intended effect is of Aladdin's cave – has, next to each dusty armchair and sofa, a deep pile of polystyrene cartons, many still containing the remains of rotten food, which bizarrely remind Nora of her mother's nest of tables. In the far-off days when the Doyles still had visitors, the tables, varying in size, would be placed next to each seated person to hold plates, cups and glasses.

Nora fears that the cartons may harbour rats and enters the room only when she needs to speak to Jake, Rick or Saffron on matters of household business. Generally she keeps to her room, except for brief excursions to a local café for cups of tea and toast, or the public baths, where she occasionally swims, but mostly showers and washes her hair: the kitchen, although rarely used for cooking, is always densely covered with an unidentifiable layer of greasy slime while the bathroom appears to have remained innocent of any cleaning agent since the day it was installed.

She works incessantly. All the essays that will contribute to this year's marks have now been submitted and her examination revision is well under way. With the assistance of the university health centre, and of the student counselling service, who agree that she is suffering from acute anxiety, she has permission to sit her exams in a room apart, with her own supervisor, and exemption from the few remaining classes, tutorials and lectures. She has received concerned emails from Steve, Professor Rowe and the other lecturers whose courses she has taken this last year, and from Phoebe, Nick, Pete and Annie, but so far she has replied to none.

After weeks of isolation and invisibility, however, Nora is about to make an excursion, and to make her presence felt, though her whereabouts will continue to be secret. With an *A–Z* of London and a map of bus routes in her bag, she leaves her room at around lunchtime and, after a cup of tea and a slice of toast at the café where she is already known, makes her way north across the city. When she alights from the second bus, she consults her *A–Z*, glances up and down the street to get her bearings, then walks for about ten minutes until she reaches the gate of a large school.

She looks at the board to confirm that she is indeed at her destination, a girls' comprehensive which, by means of a rigorous selection policy, is widely regarded as one of London's best. She has arrived early, given herself time to identify all the gates from which the girls might leave. This is important because, while she is hoping to meet Jessica Woolf, she would rather avoid her sister Emily. If they both appear, and seem likely to go home together, she will make her way back without approaching them, but she is gambling on separate timetables and after-school activities. There is an element of risk, but she has chosen her day with care. When she last met Emily by chance, it was also a Wednesday, the day of her drama club.

A small group of mothers forms along the pavement, just as the girls begin to emerge, some in school uniforms, the older ones in their own clothes. Jessica will be in the latter group. It isn't long before Nora spots her coming out of a side door with two others. Jessica is in the middle and appears to be holding forth to her companions, who keep their heads down and laugh from time to time, very much as Nora has seen her dominate proceedings in her parents' house. Jessica holds her head erect and her hair streams out behind her, showing to advantage her clear skin and chiselled bone structure. Her extraordinary poise stiffens Nora's resolve, which seemed to be weakening when she saw that Jessica was not alone. Nora weaves her way through the small crowd on the pavement so that she can reach the gate before Jessica, who spares Nora the ordeal of having to attract her attention by immediately spotting her and coming to an abrupt halt.

'What are you doing here?' she asks. It isn't clear whether she is actively hostile or merely surprised.

'I was hoping to see you.'

Jessica just stands there, her eyes narrowed, appraising the situation, while her friends remain in place, just behind her, as though they're guarding her or are reluctant to leave before they're dismissed. The pause appears to Nora to be deliberate. Jessica wants to make it clear that she is in control, that whatever happens next happens because she has willed it. Nora judges that only someone who has never been gravely disappointed or outraged by events would handle the unexpected with quite such aplomb. She says nothing, merely holds her ground, while she watches Jessica yield to curiosity.

'You'd better go,' she says, over her shoulder to her friends, and then to Nora, 'I can't spare much time. As you probably know, I've got A levels in a few weeks. Balliol are demanding three As so there's no room to screw up.'

'I have exams too,' says Nora dryly, 'so we share that particular predicament, although I'm sure not so much is hanging on mine. Is there somewhere I can buy you a coffee?'

'I can buy my own, thank you,' says Jessica, with a toss of her head, but for the first time she appears uneasy. They walk in silence to the local shopping area, where Jessica turns into the first café they reach. Nora had expected her to choose one of the fashionable chains, but once inside, she can understand Jessica's thinking. It's quiet, mercifully free of loitering teenagers, and the table they select by the wall places them out of earshot of other customers.

'I thought you weren't going to do your exams,' Jessica says, once they are settled. 'I thought you'd dropped out.'

'I've dropped out of classes, but I have permission to do my exams.'

Jessica asks no further questions and they lapse into silence. Nora knows exactly what she wants to say but is reluctant to utter a bald statement without preamble or provocation. It will be impossible to hold Jessica for long, however. The younger girl isn't exactly fidgeting – she is too conscious of effect for that, and sufficiently disciplined to restrain those feelings that might betray her into an ugly or awkward gesture – but her attention is straying. She is glancing round at other tables, in the manner of teenagers who worry that they might be missing something more interesting that is happening elsewhere. Nora thinks that this is almost certainly an act, calculated to suggest that, if this is an overture of friendship from Nora, of the kind that has been so successful with Emily, then Jessica is having none of it.

'What made you think I wouldn't do my exams?' Nora finally asks her.

'Oh, just something Dad said. I can't remember exactly.' Her manner is careless. She avoids Nora's eye as she speaks, as though the matter were of the utmost indifference to her.

'Could you try to remember?' Nora asks. 'I'm sure it's of no importance to you but it matters to me.'

Jessica turns back to her, and it's clear to Nora that Jessica's curiosity is engaged and the hostility she has sensed in her very close to the surface.

'If you really want to know, he said he was very disappointed in you. Emily asked about you one time, whether you'd be coming round again, and he said he thought not. He said it sometimes happens that students who show promise, particularly girls, lose their nerve at the last minute. He said it should be a warning to us, that we shouldn't let it happen to us. Sorry, but you did ask.'

'Was that all?'

'I think it was all he said about you. Once he got on to the subject of how we'd do – me and Emily – he naturally became more interested in that. Mum said later that you were a bit of a troublemaker, so I assumed Dad was just being kind. He hates gossip and always says there's too much of it in universities. I thought from what Mum said that you'd blotted your copybook in some way and weren't being allowed to do your exams.'

Nora nods slowly. 'Do you want to know what really happened?'

The question takes Jessica by surprise. For the first time since Nora has known her, she is confused, but soon recovers her poise.

'If it's different from what Dad said, or Mum, why would I believe you?'

'You could always tell your dad the version I'd given you and see what he says. I don't believe he'd lie.'

'Of course he wouldn't. He hates lying.' She is angry at the very possibility that her father might be susceptible to human frailty.

'Well, then, you have nothing to lose.'

'I don't know what you're up to, but Mum is certainly right about you being a troublemaker. But go ahead, tell me. It isn't of the slightest interest to me, but since you're determined to do it, we might as well get it over with. Then I can go.'

If anything, Nora's dislike of Jessica is heightened by this, the only occasion when they have been alone together, and she decides to spare her none of the details.

'When you, your mother and Emily were in Wales, during the Easter holidays, he took me out for the evening – to the theatre and then for dinner. I thought, when he invited me, that it would be a family occasion, and that you would all be there, but it turned out he'd taken the opportunity of being alone in London. He told me he was in love with me. That's all, nothing happened, because I left him there in the restaurant. But that's why I dropped out of my classes.'

Even before Nora has finished, Jessica has scraped back her chair and is on her feet – but she can't bring herself to leave before she has heard Nora through to the end, when she will be able to have the last word.

'That's a really vicious thing to say, and I don't believe a word of it. I always wondered what you were up to, but I never thought you were as horrible as this. I thought you were a creep, but you're worse than that. You're manipulative, cruel and—' Before she can think of any more words adequate to describe Nora she has burst into tears.

Suddenly she looks like a child rather than a young woman, a very small child who hasn't yet learned that life is full of setbacks and disappointments, and that there might be occasions of grief that can't be instantly removed by her parents. She moves to go, then thinks better of it. She sits down again but behaves as though Nora isn't there. She takes out a packet of Kleenex, dries her cheeks and blows her nose, then smoothes her hair and generally repairs the damage to her appearance, before risking being seen by someone she knows.

'I'm sorry,' Nora says.

'No, you're not, and that just shows you're a hypocrite as well as a liar.'

'You're right, I'm not sorry. It's a reflex response to the sight of someone in tears. But I'm not a liar, or a hypocrite. I would have had a much easier life if I had been.'

'Right, now you're going to try and make me feel sorry for you, I suppose,' says Jessica, turning fierce, bloodshot eyes on Nora. 'Are you going to tell me stories of your disadvantaged Irish past? Well, it won't wash with me. Some of Dad's family were burned in the camps, but he never mentions it because he says you should never trade on a victim status you haven't earned for yourself.'

Nora is impressed in spite of herself, and begins to wish that Steve had tried a different means of breaking through the barrier between professor and student, and that they had got to know each other better, on a different footing from the one he wanted. 'I didn't know that,' she says.

'It doesn't surprise me. I'm sure you don't know the first thing about him, or any of us. I've never liked you, and I'm sure I've made that clear, but my mother and Emily were kind to you. Doesn't that make you ashamed?'

Nora says nothing.

'Before I go, I want you to tell me why you've done this. Is it just that you like making trouble? Or did your jealousy get the better of you?'

This is a question that Nora has been dreading – and one, furthermore, that Jessica has a right to ask and she an obligation to answer. She knows that on the night when she last saw Steve, the control she'd managed to exercise over her feelings since she first came to London finally gave way, leaving her in a chaos of grief and rage; and that in this turmoil, which has shown no sign of easing as the weeks have lengthened, the thought of telling Jessica was the only likely means of consolation to emerge. She has gone to bed night after night in a flat full of unspeakable horrors, and all that she has had to soothe her to sleep is the knowledge of this power that she has only today used. To say these things, however, would undermine the righteousness to which she lays claim, and she's convinced herself that the punishment she's devised is consoling precisely because it's deserved.

'I felt you should know, so that you weren't living in a fool's paradise any more.'

'Oh, I see, it's a dirty job but somebody's got to do it.' Jessica looks very nearly herself again, and having gained the initiative will not go until she delivers a blow that strikes home. 'I suppose you'd like me to tell Emily now, so that she doesn't live any more of her life in a state of dangerous illusion.'

Nora says nothing for a while. She has dreaded this even more than Jessica's first question, but she does have an answer of a sort prepared. 'Emily's very young, and still genuinely innocent. I'm not sure that you're innocent in quite that way so that older people have a duty to protect you. If you want me to be as honest with you as you've been with me, I would have to say that you're arrogant, and that the sense you have of your family's – particularly your father's – perfection feeds that arrogance.' She looks across at Jessica, who is angry but still listening intently. 'Emily is just purely innocent and I would prefer her to be left that way. Whatever advantages she has had from her family haven't given her a sense of superiority to the rest of the world. But, of course, I have no control over what you do. You must make up your own mind.'

'You're deceiving yourself. You know Emily's got a crush on you and you don't want to destroy it.'

Nora is touched by this revelation of Emily's feelings, but is careful not to show her pleasure. 'I don't think it's that. I'll never see her again, after all, so it can hardly make a difference to me whether she likes me or not. I think she's a special person, and I wish I'd had a sister like that. I hope you're generous enough towards her, and protective enough, not to let your dislike of me sway what you do next. The kind of person you are will show in the decision you make. It could matter for the rest of your life. If you do the right thing, you have a chance to prove that I've been wrong about you.'

Jessica is on her feet again, pulling on her jacket and

adjusting her schoolbag. 'You have a very exaggerated idea of your own importance. I don't ever want to see you again, and if you try to see me I'll tell the police I'm being harassed.'

Nora shrugs and says nothing. If Jessica wants her last words to Nora to take the form of a threat that she knows she will never need to enact, she should be allowed that satisfaction. Once Jessica has left the café, Nora realises that she is shaking. She buys herself another cup of tea to calm herself before she begins her journey back to Brixton.

It's another two days before Nora visits her local Internet café and sends an email to Steve, saying she would like to see him, and suggesting that, since she has no claim on her other than endless revision, he state a time that suits him in the course of the following week. When she returns to the café on Saturday to check for a reply, she finds a terse communication from Steve, informing her that he will be in his office from four to six-thirty on Monday afternoon. It's the soonest that she could reasonably expect, but she would have preferred not to have the rest of the weekend and most of Monday to think about the meeting. She drags herself through the days, mostly working, apart from a few hours on Sunday afternoon when she walks in Battersea Park. There is a moment when she sits on a bench in the park, trying to eat a sandwich, and realises that she has never felt so isolated in her life. She has been in London for nearly two years, and every relationship that began with promise has come to an end. She wonders whether she will ever find sufficient optimism and energy to embark on the process again.

When she presents herself at Steve's office at five o'clock on Monday afternoon she is braced for an angry outburst, but what she faces is altogether more alarming. Although

Steve is standing when she enters the room – he is behind his desk, with his chair pushed back and his hands clutching the edge – he seems altogether diminished. She is reminded of what fellow students have sometimes said, that when they first went home from university, their parents seemed to have shrunk, as though the loss of parental responsibility had accelerated the ageing process.

The changes she sees in Steve, however, go beyond those inevitable alterations in perspective that take place as the power balance shifts between generations. His face, which she remembers principally for the clean, chiselled quality that Jessica has inherited, has lost all definition. It seems that successive waves of emotion have eroded the distinctness of his features. Eyes, nose and mouth are suddenly too large, or too slack, and he looks vulnerable and exposed, with too much of himself showing. Nora is unprepared for the shock, and realises that the compulsion that drove her to seek out Jessica wouldn't allow her to consider the effect on Steve of what she was doing. It was her own father whom she wanted to see in this condition. Steve is a poor substitute and her father is as impregnable as he ever was.

'I assume you've come to gloat,' he says.

'No, not to gloat. I'm really sorry for the pain I've caused you.'

'Then why did you do it?' His bewilderment and incomprehension are genuine. Indeed, he seems incapable of masking anything. He nods in the direction of a chair, for Nora to sit down, then takes his seat behind his desk.

When she says nothing, merely sits there, hands folded, staring at her lap, he takes another approach.

'All right, we'll take it as read that you required some kind of revenge. You were undeniably upset when you left the restaurant, you were disappointed, disillusioned, your feelings were sufficiently outraged for you to feel you couldn't leave it there. Wouldn't it have been enough to make a mockery of me to your friends, as a vain, middle-aged man prepared to make a fool of himself over a young girl? And if that wasn't enough, why did you go for my family rather than my job? Unless, of course, that's to come. Stage one's finished, and now you're about to move on to stage two.'

'There's no more,' says Nora. 'There's no stage two.' She sits quietly for a moment while she decides what else to say. 'I'm afraid I'm incapable of what you suggest – making a mockery of you to my friends – though I can see that, for some people, that might have done the trick. I don't have the knack of taking life as lightly as that.'

Steve looks puzzled, disarmed by her candour.

'And if I'd gone for you professionally, it would have got back to your family anyway, so this way the damage is limited. Besides, you're really good at what you do. I don't just mean that you know your stuff, that you're a genuine academic star, but you're conscientious, you take your role seriously, which can't be said for all of your colleagues. Sure, you were abusing your position with me, but there was no coercion involved, no trading of favours.'

'Then why do anything at all? Why hurt my family?'

Nora knows why, but because the rage has left her, her response can only be cold and mechanical: 'Because I think you're a bad husband and father.'

'Bad husband maybe, but within the limits of my own selfishness I always tried to do what was right.' He stops abruptly, and when he continues, it's with difficulty: 'Looking at what Martha is going through now, I suppose I would have to own up to that. But bad father? You've seen me with my daughters. Can you honestly say that?'

She turns away and remembers Steve with Jessica and Emily – his fond looks, his pride in them, his concern, and her own gnawing, unappeasable need to have some of that for herself, rather than the gift of his passing desire, which was all that he eventually had to offer her.

'I saw that your daughters adored you and Martha, and that they thought you both perfect. As a matter of fact, Martha may be perfect.' She sees him wince at the distinction. 'But they thought you were perfect because they didn't know you. You were pretending to be something you're not. You kept hidden everything about you that might make them understand that you're an ordinary, flawed human being. I thought it gave them a false picture of the world.'

'But was it your duty to set them right? I didn't realise you were such a moral crusader. Couldn't you have hurt me without involving them, since it was, after all, my deceit?'

'I thought about that but I couldn't find a way.' Then she hesitates before asking the question that has already been answered: 'I asked Jessica not to tell Emily. Did she?'

'What do you think?' Steve tenses himself against the edge of the desk and pushes himself back, like someone in pain who hopes that a change in position will relieve his discomfort. 'She was so hurt that her first instinct was to hurt someone else. It wasn't enough to hurt me.' He falls silent for a moment, then says, 'Like you, I suppose. Except that I'm still baffled by why you were so hurt. I've gone over it and over it and I still don't understand. I'm not saying I was right to do what I did but I honestly find your response excessive.'

'Like the terrorist who blows up a pub and kills a dozen people for something that goes back a few generations?

360

It was my understanding you defended that kind of activity.'

'Is that the answer – a kind of English-Irish thing?'

Nora shrugs. 'To understand, you'd probably need me to tell you everything about me. And you know something? You never asked, not really. But I shouldn't blame you because there's too much to tell and I haven't yet found a way of telling it. And it may be one of those situations where even everything isn't sufficient explanation.'

'And it's too late to try to tell me now?'

She is moved that some vestige of concern for her has survived not only the end of desire but everything that she has done to hurt him, and briefly wonders whether this isn't finally the moment to tell him her story. She lets the moment pass, however. She doesn't doubt that he would be a sympathetic listener – unbelievable though it is, he really seems to want to understand – but she recoils from an appeal to his pity, from claiming the status of victim for herself when she's done so much to inflict harm on him.

'I think so,' is all she says.

Steve sighs deeply. 'You still haven't told me why you came today, if it wasn't to gloat.'

'I'm going back to Ireland, once I've done my exams. I'd like to transfer to Queen's and I expect they'd want you to write a report, or at any rate to contribute to something that one of my other tutors writes. I thought it was only courteous to warn you.'

Unexpectedly, Steve laughs. 'Do I take it you're checking that I'll write a good report – the kind of report your abilities warrant? I must say, your timing is . . .' he pauses while he searches for the right word '. . . unusual.'

'My timing is deliberate,' says Nora coolly. 'It would

have been unscrupulous to delay seeing Jessica until after the report was sent off.'

'But you have come to tell me what to write?'

'Not at all. As I said, professionally I don't have a quarrel with you. I have no doubt that you'll do what you think is right. And if on this occasion that works to my disadvantage – you may well feel justified in warning them that I'm a troublemaker – I probably had it coming.'

She gets up and moves towards the door. Before she leaves, Steve says, 'You're right. I should have tried to get to know you better rather than project my own fantasies on to you. Now the time that you've passed in exile is coming to an end and I shan't have the opportunity.'

'Exile?'

'Isn't that the Irish thing? Wilde, Joyce, Yeats, Beckett – they all left Ireland, some of them for a lifetime, but they carried Ireland around in their heads.'

'It isn't always the most pleasant thing to have in your head.'

She has reached the door and is about to leave, when Steve delays her again. 'You may find that you don't want to be there either. That's also part of the Irish experience, isn't it? But good luck, I hope you manage to settle somewhere.'

'Thank you. I suppose I'll just have to risk it.'

Ballypierce

On the day that Nora returned home from Wexford to collect her belongings, the first sign of change was the sight of her father digging along the border that ran beside the front wall of the property. The garden, once his pride and joy, the outward and visible sign of his status as a prosperous householder, stocked by him with the choicest plants from the garden centre, had been sadly neglected after Felix's birth. Many of the best specimens had died, the roses he had bought from specialist growers in England had grown spindly and weak, and the carefully nurtured grass had coarsened as his interest had dwindled to the minimum requirement of respectability – mowing the lawn and keeping the weeds under control. On that bright early-September morning, however, when Nora came home for what she expected to be the last time, and saw Gerald apparently absorbed in his task, she felt suddenly disoriented, as though her memory had played her false.

She sat in the tiny Fiat for a few moments, watching him.

'Will you be all right?' asked Claire, who had driven her there from the hotel where they had both been working for the summer season. 'Shall I come with you for, like, moral support?' As she spoke, she looked down at Nora's hands, trembling in her lap. Claire knew something of Nora's story because Nora had found in her a listener who was both sympathetic and transient, a friend for that strange period of her life whom she would never need to see again.

'It's better if I go in alone and get it over with. If I need help with my stuff, I'll come and get you. Thanks for offering, though.' She gave a tight little smile before bracing herself to open the car door.

She walked along the pavement and into the garden with her head down, not wishing to catch her father's eye until she had reached him. If she looked at him he would, she was certain, stare, unsmiling, at her as she made her awkward progress. As it was, when she took up her position a few feet away from him, he kept her waiting while he turned over the earth for bits of weed, which he then threw into a wheelbarrow. When he finally pulled himself upright, he wedged the shovel into the newly turned earth and swung round to give her a long, cold look. The memory of their last conversation, full of rage and bitterness, hung in the air between them. It was clear that he had no intention of greeting her or of opening the conversation. He was leaving it to her to say something, which would give him the pretext to attack.

'I'll go and say hello to Mummy,' Nora said.

She was, if anything, dreading the meeting with her mother even more. In the last weeks that she spent in this house, there had been a flurry of activity over Felix's condition, which had been, as expected, diagnosed as acute clinical depression. In this crisis, Bernie had relied as always on Nora's continuing help and support – albeit that her daughter had enforced a new authority in setting her own terms and limits to that help – but for the first time had been pathetically grateful. As she was forced to expose family circumstances to concerned professionals, and to reveal the scale of Nora's involvement with Felix while continuing to distinguish herself in her studies, Bernie had displayed an unexpected capacity for humility.

In that short time, while Gerald continued to find excuses not to interest himself in his son, her resentment towards her daughter seemed to have vanished. And when Nora had announced her intention of leaving – and not just intention, for her preparations were complete and her departure imminent – Bernie's helplessness had been painful. When it came to it, it had been easier to leave Felix, since he had no understanding of the blow he was about to sustain. By now, of course, he had had time to realise the extent of his altered situation so she had delayed her visit until after the start of the school term.

'You won't find her in,' Gerald said. 'She's gone out for the day.'

'Out? Where?' The reality of her mother going out for the day was as much of an affront to her memories of her family's habits as Gerald digging the garden.

'I'd say that was none of your business, wouldn't you? Somebody had to be here, so I said I'd stay at home myself. It didn't surprise me that you've shown no regard for anybody else's convenience.'

'Shall I go in, then, and pack up my things?' She had taken some of her clothes with her to Wexford, but now that she was about to go to London, she needed the rest, along with books, papers and other belongings. 'I've been lent some suitcases, and I've brought a few boxes. I'll go and get them from the car.'

'There's no need for that,' said Gerald, who had resumed

his digging, as though her presence were an inconvenience that he would, as far as possible, ignore. 'We threw everything of yours into some bin bags. You'll find them by the back door.'

Nora made her way up the path and round the side of the house and there, as Gerald had indicated, was a heap of tied black bin bags that looked as though they had been left out for the dustmen. She untied one or two to check the contents and found that her things had been thrown in at random, with no regard to the condition in which she would find them. Some of the books had been bent back, their spines possibly broken. Her clothes, which she always kept neatly folded, were bundled into balls. The files containing her A-level work were leaking papers, some of which were torn. She couldn't see whether the photographs of Felix, which she had taken over the years with a camera she had been given for her eleventh birthday, were among the chaos but she didn't dare ask. She tried the door, thinking she might go to her room and check whether anything had been left out, but found it locked. The message, that she wasn't wanted inside the house and had forfeited her right to be there, was clear.

She picked up two of the bags and dragged them out to the car. By the time she reached it, Claire was standing by the driver's door. 'Will I come and help you now?'

'Better not,' said Nora. She found herself avoiding her new friend's eye from a kind of shame. Whatever friends she made in the future would never have to witness such a scene, or to know that it had taken place.

As she lifted the bags to wedge them into the car, she noticed that one was split, so before she could move on to the others she had to retrace her steps and gather up the odds and ends that had fallen out. As she picked up a shoe, she felt tears stinging her eyes. The traces of eighteen years, her whole life to date, were strewn like rubbish around the only home she had known. She willed herself not to cry. She told herself again, as she had been telling herself throughout the drive from Wexford and during the stopover at Claire's house in Derry, that this wasn't just an end but a beginning, and that better times were ahead of her than she had yet known. She had enjoyed the camaraderie, if not the work, at the hotel, had shown herself capable of making friends, and nothing in the future could ever be as bad as this.

When the job was finished, and everything stuffed into the little car, she steeled herself for a final conversation with her father. She couldn't leave without at least trying to find out how Felix was. Gerald had finished his digging by now and had turned his attention to a row of plants that were still in their pots from the garden centre. When she walked back to the garden for the last time, he was levering one out of its pot into a hole he had prepared for it.

'Will you tell me how Felix is?' she asked.

After patting the shrub carefully into place, he straightened and turned to her. His eyes narrowed appraisingly as they met hers. 'Well, now, what do you want me to tell you? That he's been heartbroken since you left because you were the only person, after all, who mattered in his life? Or that he's settled down nicely, so you can run off with a clear conscience?'

She didn't answer because there was no answer. This was one of Gerald's familiar performances, designed to create as much discomfort as possible and to display his own ability to keep ahead of the game.

'Well, I have no intention of giving you satisfaction either way,' he concluded.

Without a word, Nora turned and walked towards the gate.

'So you're going to London,' Gerald called after her, when it was clear that she was going to leave without saying anything further. With her hand on the gate, she turned to face him and nodded.

'I wanted you to go to Oxford. I'd been putting money by for you for years.'

Nora was dumbfounded, and struggled for an answer. Finally she said, 'In that case you disguised your intentions very well. It looked to me as though I was to leave school and stay at home, doing your bidding.'

'In that case you're a foolish girl,' said Gerald. 'Did you ever think of asking me what I had in mind for you?'

'No, but I never found that you were reticent about telling me what was on your mind when it suited you.'

'Maybe in this particular instance I wanted to be asked my opinion, rather than have you behave, as you always did, as though you knew it all already.'

'This is just a game you're playing, to try to make me doubt my own memory and judgement,' said Nora, but her face betrayed more uncertainty than her words. If Gerald was indeed playing a game, so that she should leave doubting the decision she had made, then he was playing it skilfully, pretending to a candour and transparency that she would have thought quite alien to him.

'And do you think they won't play games with you in London?'

'In London? I don't know what you're talking about.' She was taken aback by the sudden change in tactic.

'Don't you know the way they treat the Irish in London?'

'No, but I don't think you do either. What recent

experience have you had?' She had asked the question, but was desperate to leave now. Once her father was launched on one of his tirades, there was no stopping him.

'They treat the Irish like slaves or pets, never as equals. Oh, I don't doubt that you'll find people who are charming enough to you, but with the English you always have to ask what they want out of you.'

'I don't know that they're any different from the Irish, in that case. I should be well prepared to deal with it.'

She was out of the gate and walking towards the car when he delivered his parting shot. Leaning over, with his hands on the garden wall, he said, 'I'll never have the satisfaction of you telling me I was right all along because I don't expect to see you again. But I'll tell you anyway, for my own peace of mind. The kind of people you'll meet – not the ones everybody ignores, those who sit on pavements drugged out of their minds, with their wee dogs beside them – but the others, the educated ones, live in a kind of bubble where they think they have a right to everything they want out of life. You've always said you love your brother, though frankly I have my doubts about that now, but I dare say you meant it at the time. Well, in London he would have been flushed down the toilet because people there think they can choose the kind of life they want. They have no notion of endurance, of putting up with what they can't help. You'll see. I expect you'll like it to begin with, but somebody always pays for those who like to get their own way. As far as the English are concerned, the Irish have always been convenient scapegoats. You can leave Ireland, but you'll always carry with you where you came from.'

Nora stood on the pavement and heard her father out, but she didn't look at him. When he'd finished she walked on and got into the car, where Claire was listening to the car radio.

'What was all that about?' Claire asked.

'You don't want to know. Anyway, it wouldn't make any sense, unless you knew him.'

As the car pulled away from the pavement, she glanced back at the spot where Gerald had been standing, but he was gone.

EPILOGUE

High above the sea, in a garden laid out in the manner of convent gardens everywhere – with paths for walks through banks of shrubs, little enclosed spaces for solitary meditation with benches for reading during the warmer weather, everything perfectly tended to honour God's creation – Felix Doyle sits waiting. He is on his favourite bench, close to the point where the headland drops down to the sea. From there he can hear the waves and see the lighthouse and ships in the distance. Throughout the summer there are trips twice a week to a bathing beach, where it's generally agreed that Felix, an enthusiastic and fearless swimmer, comes into his own; when he can't be in the sea, he likes to be in sight of it.

It's a warm Sunday afternoon in July but Felix is dressed, at his own insistence, in his grey flannel trousers, shirt and tie, with his school blazer on the bench next to him, and on the ground, by his feet, a small suitcase.

Watching him from another bench a short distance away, with an open but unread book on her knee as pretext for her apparent idleness, is Sister Catherine. It's recognised in the community that she has a special relationship with him; that wherever Felix is, Sister Catherine is sure to be close by. There was a time, still lingering in the memories of the older nuns, when particular friendships between themselves, or with the pupils, were discouraged, but Sister Catherine is young, the first new recruit to seek them out for some years, and they are so afraid of losing her that they indulge her, just as she indulges Felix.

She had only been with them a few months when Felix arrived, two years ago, for the start of the autumn term. He was in a sorry state, and she was the only member of the community who could make any headway with him. It wasn't that he was particularly disruptive or violent – problems that they have from time to time with some of their young people – as that he had sunk into a state of almost total passivity, like someone stricken with grief. They thought of him as a lost soul, though not, of course, in a religious sense. All the nuns believe that people like Felix are special to God, with places in Heaven assured them. But he was certainly more lost in the world than most of their charges, until Sister Catherine found clever ways to coax him out of his misery.

The first real breakthrough came when she persuaded Felix on to the swings, where the movement – comparable, she always thinks, to the rocking of a cradle – lulled him into a state of contentment. She still likes to watch him as, always facing the sea and suspended against the blue of the sky, he takes on a grace and lightness he otherwise lacks. Then she began to draw him into the little bits of conversation he could manage until, gradually, he began to adapt to his new surroundings, though he is still at his most comfortable when she is around. He even helps a bit now with the chores, and when he'd rather not, charms or jokes his way out of them. This is the side of Felix she values most.

He came with a statement from his education authority. He was suffering from clinical depression, and the authority had agreed to fund him because this school has a proud history of managing mentally handicapped children who have additional, complicating problems. His parents – the mother flustered, as though she didn't know what was required of her in this situation, the father making sure everyone understood his social standing in Ballypierce – claimed to be at their wits' end, having tried everything but to no avail. They were of the view that what had, in his father's phrase, 'tipped him over the edge' (as a pharmacist, he had considerable experience of people suffering from depression) was the departure of his sister, to whom he was particularly devoted, to university in London.

Sister Catherine thought it odd at the time that a boy suffering from an acute sense of loss should have another inflicted on him in hope of a cure. Except that it didn't seem that much of a loss on either side. They remind themselves in the convent that they shouldn't judge parents, that people don't always have the strength to face the ordeal God has imposed on them, but even so . . . The wad of notes that Mr Doyle handed over as pocket money was not the most effective form of solace for a boy who, it turned out, had no interest in spending it, while Mrs Doyle's hurried farewell kiss, and the slap on the shoulder bestowed by Mr Doyle seemed to take Felix by surprise. He didn't reciprocate in any way or show any emotion when they left, but there is no doubt, now that they know him, of his affectionate nature. A little too affectionate, sometimes, but Sister Catherine has learned to cope with that too, and Felix now has a better sense of boundaries.

They took him home for the first Christmas holidays,

but when Easter arrived, pleaded illness on the part of Mrs Doyle. Could they possibly keep him at the convent this one time? And so the situation has been allowed to drift, but while Felix's contact with his parents has almost ceased, regular sums of money have arrived from Mr Doyle. The fiction of pocket money has been maintained, but they use it to replace Felix's clothes as he grows out of them, and to pay for his accommodation in the holidays. When the school empties of young people and lay teachers – as it has now for the summer – the nuns remain. The convent is, after all, their home, and Felix now must regard it as his.

The situation is highly irregular, of course, and Mother Superior sometimes talks about informing Felix's local authority. Sister Catherine has her argument prepared: what good would be served by forcing him back into a home where he isn't wanted? He would be bound to end up in care, and what are they doing, if not caring for him? They only have to wait for a few years, and then they can suggest to the Doyles that they find an adult community for him, a landmark that all their charges reach at the end of their time here.

Sister Catherine has already started to dread the day that he leaves them, but is now faced with the possibility that it might come sooner than they expected. A few days ago, completely out of the blue, Mother Superior received a telephone call from Felix's sister, Nora, asking if she could visit him this afternoon. Sister Catherine was charged with preparing Felix for the visit, and his reaction has unsettled everything. Instead of having to remind him of who Nora is, as she expected, his face lit up immediately.

"Ora? My 'ister? 'Ora?" he kept saying, over and over, desperate for confirmation.

Since then he seems to have been preparing himself for departure, avoiding all his usual activities, and even Sister Catherine. Of course she minds, but more because he is likely to be disappointed than because she has had to acknowledge that she isn't quite as important to him as she thought. She has told him repeatedly that Nora is just visiting, that she'll have to go away again, but he shakes his head vigorously, certain he knows better. Then this morning, when she went to wake him up, as she always does, she found him already dressed in his school uniform, although he has worn holiday clothes since the end of term, and hates a shirt and tie. Most disturbing of all, there was an open case on his bed that he was waiting for her to close.

The contents were quite random – anything that came to hand, really – but the intention was clear. She told him he wouldn't need the case, that this was only a visit, that he would be staying here with her, but again he shook his head.

'You don't need to wear your uniform, Felix,' she said. 'It's Sunday and, besides, it's far too warm.'

'Have to,' he said. "S my fault.'

He came to Mass in the convent chapel, but refused lunch afterwards. Sister Catherine has tried to occupy him, but he won't even sit with her. So she's keeping her distance, watching him as he waits. His certainty is such that she's beginning to question her own judgement, and to wonder whether Nora might not have it in mind to take him with her, unlikely though that seems. Meanwhile they both sit, waiting for Nora to come and decide their fate.

Acknowledgements

Thank you to Lucy Ellmann for permission to quote from Richard Ellmann's magnificent *James Joyce*; and to A.P. Watt Ltd for permission to quote from W.B. Yeats's great poem, 'Among School Children'.

My earliest readers were my husband, James, and daughter, Rachel, who were the first to suggest that my own obsession with Irish literature needed to be tempered in the interests of the narrative. If there are still readers who feel that the tempering hasn't gone far enough, then the fault lies in my own obstinacy. My other daughters, Chloe and Hannah, and Chloe's partner, Tom, took care of my numerous problems with the computer, without making me feel too stupid. My thanks to all of you.

Flicky Mead read the novel within weeks of her death, when she was in considerable pain. Her generosity, enthusiasm and astute commentary would always have been valuable, but were made particularly precious by the circumstances.

I have been extraordinarily lucky in the professionals who brought this book to the point of publication. I thank my agent, David Grossman, who was undismayed by my being such a latecomer to fiction, gave me confidence and persuaded me that more work, unwelcome though it was, would result in a better novel. Clare Reihill, my editor at Fourth Estate, has been unfailingly enthusiastic, attentive and encouraging. She and Catherine Heaney have, with their courtesy, good humour and kindness, made the whole experience much more fun than I would have thought possible. I thank you both.

My son Tom provided the inspiration for the character of Felix in the novel. He will never understand the scale of his contribution, but my love and thanks to him nonetheless.